Enduring Fear

JESSICA WILBERFORCE

Jessica Wilberforce x

Cover design by BespokeBookCovers.com

ISBN: 978-1-69854-184-6

For the Boy, whom I love more than I ever thought possible - you are clever and kind, and you make me laugh every day. I'm a very lucky mum.

ACKNOWLEDGMENTS

Enormous thanks to:

Mark, for tolerating the clicking of laptop keys well into the early hours of every morning, and for letting me be my two favourite things — a mum and a writer.

Louise P, for being my amazing friend and alpha reader — your support and encouragement kept me going, so if anyone's to blame it's you.

My adopted family — Lianne, Pat and Tim, for your love and support. I'm so glad I talk to strangers in parks.

My wonderful friend and neighbour, Angela, for your unwavering enthusiasm and encouragement, not to mention all the cups of tea and lactose-free treats!

Rachel M, as much for your kindness, support, care and understanding as for your practical help and astounding subject knowledge, which all helped me to find myself.

Lynn Curtis, my editor and muse. Thank you for your sterling work and for somehow being able to deliver constructive criticism without making me angry or upset. That's a *gift*.

CHAPTER 1

WHEN I WAS SEVENTEEN, I LIED to my psychiatrist. "I used to be normal, before all this," I told him.

Starting my first appointment with a lie was probably not terribly conducive to successful therapy, but those were the first words that came to mind at the time. I'd wanted him to understand that I was not a hopeless case: with the right medication and a referral for talking therapy, I could be rescued from the bleak state I was in. Terrible things had happened to me, yes, but I was not a terrible person. Not as far as I knew, anyway.

I didn't know I was lying at the time, because when I was seventeen I thought I *was* normal. Well, almost. I suppose I'd always known I was a bit odd. However hard I tried, I never quite fitted in with all the other girls at school — the ones who always wore the right clothes, never had scabby knees, and knew what to laugh at, what to talk about and how to respond to each other without seeming weird. I tried copying them, but I always stood out — and not in a good way.

Fortunately, though, one of the main things that made me feel different was actually something that helped me immensely when navigating conversations and social situations. It meant that even if my responses might not exactly be on point, I could at least have a good guess at why other people acted in the way they did.

When I look at people, I see colours around them. According to my extensive research on Wikipedia, what I'm seeing are auras — souls. The shade of a person's aura will tell me if that person is basically good (in which case their base colour is a shade of Blue; the paler the better) or bad (with a base colour of Red; the darker the worse). Most people are a shade of Purple: neither all good nor all bad. I have the answer to the nature/nurture debate, by the way, should anyone ever ask: babies are always Blue; no one is born bad. They start to become Purple or even Red by the age of about nine. When I was younger, it was rare to see anyone under the age of about fourteen with even a hint of Purple or Red, so all I can assume is that old people are right to moan about the youth of today getting worse because I reckon they actually are.

On top of their Blue/Red/Purple, everyone has mood colours, which are helpful because I can judge at a glance whether it's a good day to ask someone for a favour. There are also some colours that are the same for everyone: mustard yellow is illness, bottle green is pain, black is grief or impending death, white is anger and pale yellow is fear. There are loads of others, but quite often I don't know what they mean because it's not as though anyone has produced

2

a definitive guide on the subject and people are either politely vague or surprisingly defensive when asked (for the purpose of research) how they are feeling at any given time. As long as I'm face to face with someone, their colours are the main things I see, and I would therefore have great difficulty in describing the physical appearance of friends or even family members because I don't really notice things like eye colour or nose size or whatever.

I don't tell people I see auras. I used to, when I was little and didn't know it was weird. Six years old is apparently the cut-off age for telling people things like that: before you're six, it's "cute"; after you're six it's "of concern" and people write things on forms about you and come to observe you in lessons at school.

So, growing up, I knew I was *quirky* with the whole auras thing and my inability to speak fluent 'girl', but underneath I assumed I was basically normal, hence my remark to my psychiatrist.

Then, when I was twenty-four, I was told that I had never been even remotely normal. I was told that I am unique, a one-off — and not *at all* in a good way. My very existence is actually illegal and I am some sort of abomination, apparently, though that seems a tad harsh.

I don't *feel* like an abomination. The man I love doesn't think I'm an abomination either, even though he's the one who first told me that — technically — that's what I am. When someone who loves you that much tells you you're a freak of nature, you've sort of got to accept it. To be fair, he's not entirely normal, either, and within three months of meeting him my world had changed beyond all recognition.

CHAPTER 2

August

ON THE LAST DAY I FELT (mostly) normal, my car was stolen. This was rather annoying, more than a bit saddening and ultimately it was very expensive, but that theft turned out to be a pivotal moment in my life — one that led me to discover who and what I really am. I suppose it was a small sacrifice in the grand scheme of things.

That night, at around midnight, I finished my waitressing shift at a little restaurant in the middle of Leeds and walked on sore feet to the multi-storey carpark near the swimming baths. Once there, I stared at the space my car had previously occupied, not quite registering the truth of what must have happened. My car had gone, without a doubt, but I searched for ages anyway, hoping that I'd simply parked it somewhere else and forgotten where. I admit I was a bit bereft when I finally accepted that someone must have taken it: I'd grown to love that car, even with its little dents and scratches (all of which I could explain, unfortunately); I worried about who had taken him and what they were doing to him; I felt a particular pang for the teddy bear on the parcel shelf ...

I'd worked blooming hard for that car, too. I'd started taking lessons as soon as I hit seventeen, but I was twenty by the time I passed my test. Initially I'd tried learning with a formal driving instructor but that ended ... well, let's just leave it at 'badly and abruptly'. My best friend, Matt, had stepped in and taught me himself. True, the lessons were a bit of an ordeal for both of us, but things improved when we swapped over to an automatic car (after an incident involving a bus I'd rather not dwell on) and eventually I'd got my full licence. In celebration, I'd bought my little run-around in order to build up some no-claims bonus. Well, *try*.

The idea of telling Matt that the car had been stolen after all the effort we'd put in to buy the blasted thing was not appealing. He's a policeman, a Detective Sergeant no less, so I doubted he'd be surprised that it had been nicked but it was still going to be a headache to sort out and I didn't want to bother him with it when he was at work that night.

So I decided I'd tell him the following morning when he got back to the house we shared, and turned my thoughts to how I was going to get home. I had enough money from my tips for a taxi, but I was reluctant to call for one because Matt had warned me repeatedly about taxi drivers. When someone applies for a licence to run a taxi, the council checks to see if the applicant has a criminal record, but having a criminal record is not actually a bar to getting a licence. You can knife someone or sexually assault someone or mug an old lady, but as long as you tell the council that you have done so, they will let you drive folk around in a taxi. Only a conviction for murder or rape is an absolute bar to becoming a taxi driver. This is true.

With the burden of this knowledge resting heavily on my shoulders, I walked round to the railway station in a foul mood, fretting about my car and not looking forward to running the gauntlet of public transport.

On arrival, I paid an extortionate amount of money to pass through the barriers. Standing on the platform, I hunched my shoulders against the cold draught of air that whistled past me, wishing not for the first time that evening that I had thought to wear a coat. A cursory glance at those nearby (a habit formed from years of being mindful to watch out for Reds) revealed that there were about fifteen people scattered along the platform, some standing silently, others in small groups laughing loudly together, insulated from the cool night air by alcohol. They were all varying shades of Blue and Purple except for one man, right at the far end of the platform, who was urinating unashamedly onto the tracks. His Red glow, visible as he turned his head slightly in my direction, made the hairs on the back of my neck rise as I registered the potential threat.

Perhaps he could sense my attention because, when he had finished relieving himself, he turned around and locked eyes with me. He started slowly stalking towards me. This did not surprise me. If I were ever in a room with a thousand other people and it were announced that something bad was going to happen to just one of us, everyone else could relax.

Even if I hadn't been able to see his colours, I would have been able to tell something was awry from his unusual wardrobe selection. Any grown man wearing a tight, pink Hello Kitty t-shirt, short shorts and a dapper pair of red wellies would have set a few alarm bells off. The nice thing about being able to see auras is that I can be fairly sure of recognising a threat accurately and being sufficiently confident to act early and avoid confrontation. On this occasion, by knowing that he was not merely some benign stray from a stag night or student outing, I immediately broke eye contact and looked round for my best route of escape.

Before I could move, though, the man suddenly darted towards me with surprising speed and grace and came to a halt about five feet in front of me, between me and the track, a slow smile spreading across his face. It was not a smile that warmed my heart. It was a bad smile, a smile that said, '*Perhaps the Chianti with this one ...*'

Alas, even with fair warning, my adrenal system kicked in at his sudden movement and I am not blessed with the 'fight' or 'flight' reactions that normally flow from a shot of adrenaline: I have the lesser-known 'freeze' response, which is not terribly helpful. Whichever long-dead ancestors passed that particular response down to me did very well to survive long enough to procreate, I've always thought.

Unable to move, I stood stock still, avoiding further eye contact with him, hoping he'd lose interest and go away. I sensed that even if I were *able* to try to run away I would merely trigger a chase and I knew that I could not outrun this man, so my eyes darted around in search of aid or easy egress.

Innate reserve prevented me from calling out for help — no one likes to shout when they're sober. Nevertheless, a few yards away stood a man I assessed to be in his sixties, who appeared to have noticed my predicament and seemed to be considering coming over to intervene. I toyed for a moment with the idea of mouthing 'help' at him, which I felt sure would be all the push he needed to come over and assist, but the welcome sight of his reassuringly Blue aura was marred considerably by the pall of blackness swirling all over it. Assuming the man wasn't recently bereaved, it was entirely feasible that the imminent death foretold by his aura could actually be brought about by the Red in front of me.

I decided against getting him involved.

Instead, I forced myself to start walking slowly away from my potential saviour, thinking vaguely of getting closer to the railway staff at the barrier. My gait was rather awkward because my legs were shaking and I was trying not to turn my back on the Red whilst also trying to protect myself from being barged onto the other track behind me. I must have looked like a very nervous crab.

The Red kept pace with me, mirroring me. Several people we passed were trying very hard not to notice us in our strange crab ballet and did not seek to intervene. The Red still hadn't said a word and although I steadfastly averted my gaze I could feel his eyes burning a hole in my face.

As we sidestepped closer to the barrier, he sped up and moved ahead so that he was between me and my intended place of safety, halting me in my tracks.

He grinned even more widely and looked for all the world as though he were going to tell me a particularly juicy bit of gossip.

"I know what you are," he stage whispered.

I had no idea what he was talking about and dismissed his words as merely those befitting a guy in a Hello Kitty t-shirt and wellies. Out of the corner of my eye, I saw the Blue man from further up the platform break his indecision and begin hurrying towards me. Before he could get much closer, though, another man appeared between me and the Red so suddenly that I flinched. I hadn't noticed him on the platform before, and I certainly hadn't seen anyone who had been near enough to have stepped in so quickly. But there he was, standing so close that I could feel the heat radiating from his back.

Whilst he remained facing away from me I couldn't see his colours, but judging by what I could see of his broad back and shoulders he looked like he spent a *lot* of time at the gym, which held my attention for a moment despite the circumstances. His well-defined arms were tightly wrapped in a crisp, white shirt and were spread wide to prevent the Red from darting around him. Undeterred, the Red made his move, baring his teeth and striding aggressively forwards, but the man between us put one hand out in front of him and said, simply, "Stop."

Amazingly, the Red *did* stop. In fact, he stopped so suddenly that his momentum made him fall on his knees.

My hero then said clearly, "Do what I say, or I shall report you to the high council. Do not tell anyone of this and do not report it yourself; you and I were never here. Leave. Now."

Again the Red obeyed, picking himself up off the floor and scrambling along the platform towards the barrier as fast as his red boots would carry him.

After the initial surprise, relief flooded through me as I watched him scamper away. I turned my attention back to the man who had intervened and gabbled, "Oh gosh, thank you so much, I thought I was a goner! Honestly, what a day...!" I sighed heavily and then, as I processed his words, added, "What the heck's the high council?"

My hero turned to look at me at last and I registered that his colours were flooded with utter terror. I marvelled that he had stepped in despite his obvious fear. But then, as our eyes met and I could see the aura that lay beneath his fear, the rest of the world fell away and there was only me and this man.

Physically, he was undeniably attractive, with blond-brown hair and closely trimmed beard, arrestingly blue eyes and the whole chiselled features thing going on; his body was just as distracting from the front as it had been from behind.

These were things I thought about later, though, because what I was initially so drawn to were his colours, which were stunning — easily the most beautiful shades I had ever seen. They were so appealing that without any conscious thought of doing so, and without regard to his deer-in-the-headlights expression, I reached out to touch them. I ran my fingers an inch above his arm, brushing the colours I could see radiating from him, although I couldn't feel anything other than the cold air of the train station. He glanced down at his arm and he appeared to be holding his breath as he watched my hand hover slightly above it, looking for all the world as though he thought I might be about to place a large tarantula on him. He was probably thinking he'd saved the wrong weirdo.

I became aware of my actions and, remembering that people generally don't like to be touched or have their personal space breached, quickly withdrew my hand. Before I could speak, though, a look of surprise crossed his features as his gaze moved from my hand to my face and a new colour appeared, one I had never seen on anybody before and the meaning of which I couldn't begin to guess. It was sort of a dusky pink but with a hint of gold. I didn't have a name for it, but it was breathtakingly beautiful and my eyes widened as though to absorb as much of it as I could.

With the appearance of the new colour his eyes suddenly softened; the angst that had flowed from him in stark waves abated. He spoke to me for the first time — just one, soft syllable: "Oh."

He took my breath away and for a moment I could only stare dumbly at him. A small crash to my right distracted me, though, as the Red gave up trying to work the ticket barrier and jumped over it, knocking over a sandwich board and losing a red welly before disappearing from view. Satisfied that he wouldn't return, I turned back to my Blue but he was no longer there.

I looked up and down the platform, I even stooped to look under the nearby benches, but he'd totally vanished.

CHAPTER 3

BY THE TIME I HAD SATISFIED myself that my rather gorgeous hero had definitely disappeared, the older man on the platform (the one who had looked as though he might have intervened) had seemingly 'stood down' since the threat had obviously passed. Gratifyingly, the blackness had disappeared and his aura was now his natural Blue with nary a threat of death in sight. I took a shuddering breath at the thought that I might have been instrumental in his death if I had called to him for help, and I wondered if my own colours had been swirling with blackness before the beautiful Blue had successfully intervened. Would that Red have killed me, too?

No one else on the platform seemed to have noticed that anything was amiss. Their eyes did not peer in the direction in which the Red had run; they did not give me sideways glances and did not show any signs of having borne witness to what had passed — evidence, if ever it were needed, of the famous British reserve.

My hands trembled as I fought to keep them still in my pockets and my teeth chattered as the impotent adrenaline made its way out of my system. Although I was distinctly relieved to be safe, it wasn't the Red's actions that had left me shaking: it was those of the other, the Blue who had appeared from nowhere (and my immediate, visceral reaction towards him) that made me have to sit down on the nearest bench. I could still feel my heart hammering in my chest when the train arrived, and every time I pictured the Blue who had stood so close to me my stomach gave an uncomfortable-but-lovely flip.

Arriving home nearly two hours after finishing work, I slept fitfully, thinking about him, my thoughts spilling into dreams. This was most unlike me; it had been a defining feature of my adolescence that at a time when my friends were all obsessed with finding a boyfriend I hadn't had the slightest inclination to join them in the hunt. I wasn't interested in finding a girlfriend, either, and had resigned myself to the idea of being completely asexual: this Blue, whoever he was, had somehow caused a seismic change within me and by the time morning arrived I had come to understand with an aching, physical yearning, that I really, *really* wanted to be with him. This became incredibly frustrating, incredibly quickly as I realised that I had no way of knowing who he was and had no way of finding him again.

When Matt arrived home at eight o'clock that morning, I told him about my car and listened to him berate me for not calling him or walking down to the police station where he worked so he could have arranged for me to get a lift home. He was grudgingly pleased that I hadn't taken a taxi, at least.

We researched how much I'd be likely to get from the insurance after my unfeasibly large excess was deducted, and discussed the impact that making yet another claim would have on next year's quote. After a heavy pause, we talked about where we'd find the money to buy a new car rather than bothering with the insurance. Ultimately, we agreed that he would report the car as stolen for me, and we'd shop around for a new one as soon as we had time, dipping into our rather meagre savings to do so.

I loved Matt for that: *I* never had a problem and neither did *he*: if one of us had a problem, *we* had a problem and *we* would sort it out. I'd known Matt my whole life — he's five years older than me, but we grew up living next door to each other. People sometimes assumed we were a couple, presumably because we were of a similar age and were obviously close, but to me Matt was just the boy from next door who made me laugh and kept me safe.

I didn't tell him about the Red or my Blue because I wasn't sure he'd be happy about my involvement with either one of them. The Red had scared me, but the Blue ... the Blue seemed to occupy my every waking thought. Matt would be sure to pick up on my obvious interest in the man if I mentioned him, and the thought of him asking me questions or teasing me about having a crush on a random stranger was just unbearable. So I kept quiet, though I was distracted and decidedly irritable throughout the day due to tiredness and a pervading feeling of unfulfillment.

Little did I know it then, but that feeling would stay with me for some considerable time to come.

CHAPTER 4

AFTER A FEW DAYS OF BAD-TEMPERED sniping and a general feeling of despondency that I knew was out of all proportion (given that it was born out of a very brief, largely non-verbal interaction with a complete stranger), Matt had given up trying to find out what was wrong with me. Instead, he must have decided that I was frustrated at not having a proper job, or perhaps that I was bored and restless without a busy routine, so he suggested that I should refresh my efforts at progressing my actual career.

I'd taken the waitressing job to make ends meet but I had in fact recently qualified as a solicitor. Of course, one might think that an ability to see colours that represent pain, illness and impending death might have led me into a career in medicine. It didn't, though, because knowing that someone isn't very well by virtue of being able to see black, bottle green or mustard yellow floating about in their aura isn't a terribly effective diagnostic tool; it's no more accurate than seeing that someone's complexion is a bit pale or peaky, and a headache would look the same to me as a brain tumour. Also, I doubted that I could work in a job that involves bodily fluids — not without upsetting my patients by gagging all the time, anyway.

With medicine out of the picture, and with excellent marks in English and Law, staggeringly good episodic memory plus a natural propensity to argue, becoming a solicitor had been a no-brainer.

Before relocating, I'd trained in the Family Law department of a small firm in Nottingham and I had loved every minute of it: the client contact, the thrill of courtroom advocacy and being paid money to tell people what to do. This last part was particularly attractive because I'd never been listened to at home for *free*.

Since arriving in Leeds three months earlier, though, my efforts to secure a position as a newly qualified solicitor had been more difficult than I'd anticipated. Most newly-qualifieds were retained by the firms that trained them, since they felt they were owed some serious fee-earning after investing two years in training up the newbie. I'd needed to get away from Nottingham, though, so staying with the firm that had trained me simply hadn't been an option.

Matt was quite right, though: I had to get myself sorted, especially if we were going to replenish our soon-to-be-depleted savings. So I sat yet again in front of my laptop and opened the document headed '*Curriculum Vitae*' with a heavy heart. I was saved a moment later by my ringing phone.

"Seph," said Matt.

My name's Persephone (pronounced 'Per—seff—oh—nee') and I think it's a testament to my strength of character that I survived a childhood on a council estate in Nottingham with a name like that. For obvious reasons, I prefer 'Sephy'. Matt had always called me 'Seph', not Sephy, but he'd done it for so long that I barely even noticed.

He sounded as though he was in a hurry and didn't bother with any further preamble. "Can you get to the Bridewell this afternoon? There's a PC Lockheart there who's selling his car."

I glanced at the computer and narrowed my eyes. "I should really sort out this CV …"

"Can you do that tonight? The car's a good 'un, and I've said you'd be interested and he's due back at the station about one o'clock. He's asking for a couple of grand but knock him down a bit. You know where you're goin'?"

"Is it the one by the Magistrates' court? On that side street, with the broken windows?"

"Yeah, that's the one. Probably best if you don't wear anyth— er, *owt* you want to keep nice."

I grimaced a little, wondering what I was letting myself in for. "Alright, thanks matey. Your Yorkshire's coming along nicely by the way," I added, slightly amused by the change of accent that had manifested itself so quickly.

"Ta."

He said he'd be home at around eight and would bring a takeaway; we said our goodbyes and I went upstairs to find something to wear. I decided on a summery dress with short-sleeved cardigan, some tan tights to take the glare off my pale legs, and some black pumps, since heels and I did not get on well.

Looking forlornly at the space outside my house where my car would normally be, I walked to the main road and caught a bus down into town. I enjoyed a hot chocolate and bagel and people-watched for a bit, with about an hour to spare before I was expected at the station.

After twenty minutes or so of sipping my drink and staring intently at passers-by, I realised that I'd been searching for my Blue from the railway station and made myself stop, since I was in danger of losing my grip on reality.

***

A trip to the Bridewell police station gave me a nice tight grip on reality again as I sidestepped a man yelling and spitting at the policeman who was dragging him unceremoniously into the station via a door marked 'Private'. The two disappeared from view behind the tinted glass.

Wishing I had a tissue or something I could use to shield my fingers, I opened the door to the public entrance, unhappy about touching the sticky handle. I stepped into what appeared to be a public toilet: a room perhaps eight feet by ten, tiled on every wall from floor to ceiling and all across the floor. The purpose of the tiles seemed to be to allow substances of uncertain origin to be wiped or hosed down. The ceiling looked like it could have done with some tiles too. There was a strong smell of bleach.

Along the wall to my right were four chairs bolted to the floor; one of the chairs was occupied by a slumped man who smelt strongly of alcohol and who burped loudly as he stared at me. I processed all this in about two seconds and was turning around to make a hasty retreat when the door closed behind me. I pushed, then pulled the door to no avail. I was locked in.

"They 'ave to let you out. Push t'bell, love," the man on the chair slurred, pointing vaguely around the room. With obvious effort, he used his other hand to hold his arm steady and managed to point more specifically towards the door area.

On closer inspection I saw a small buzzer to the right of the door about a foot above where a doorbell would normally be placed (I reasoned that it must have been installed by someone tall) and murmured a thanks to the man.

I pressed the bell whilst trying not to seem like I was starting to panic. I was afraid that I'd somehow walked into a cell rather than a reception area.

I pushed it again when nothing had happened after two seconds.

It took twenty evermore frantic buzzer-pushes before a disembodied voice said, "Can you *stop* ringing the bell, love?"

I didn't know where to direct my reply, so I called out: "Hello?"

"Can I help you?" spoke the disembodied male voice.

"Erm, yes, I think I'm in the wrong place. Can you let me out please?"

I heard an impatient sigh. "Can you talk into the intercom, love, I can hardly hear you."

I stood back from the door and stared round for anything remotely like an intercom, which shouldn't have been difficult in such austere surroundings but was. I spotted a box with a grille on the wall, which

I had previously taken to be some kind of air vent. I spoke into it, hoping I wasn't speaking into an air vent, and repeated my question.

"Where do you think you *should* be?" the voice barked.

"Erm, my friend DS Bishop sent me to see PC Lockheart?"

The vent replied in a slightly more friendly tone, "Oh, yes, hang on love, you are in the right place. I'll just get him for yer," and then fell silent.

I perched on the chair closest to the door and furthest from the room's other occupant, who had fallen asleep. Other than the grunting snores, all was quiet for another ten minutes or so, while I gradually began to feel lightheaded on the fumes coming from the drunk.

Making me jump slightly, a door opened beside me (I hadn't even noticed it was there since it, too, was tiled), and the policeman I'd seen coming in earlier popped his head round the door, smiling brightly. He was in his mid-twenties and had dark red hair and freckles that had probably been the bane of his life in school but were not unattractive now. He was wearing a short-sleeved shirt under his standard-issue stab vest and his walkie-talkie chuntered on his shoulder.

"Seph?"

"Um, Sephy," I corrected, emphasising the 'ee' sound at the end.

"Sephy, sorry, how are you? Come on, it's out the back," he said, nodding towards the door he'd just opened.

I smiled politely and walked over to him. He gave me a shy half smile in return and introduced himself: his first name was also Matt, which was going to get confusing; I decided I'd just call him Lockheart.

"You're quite a legend down in Nottingham, I hear," he said.

I surmised that he must be referring to something that had happened when I was sixteen: I'd been in the town centre one evening, after I'd been to the cinema with some friends. We'd parted ways at the bus station as I'd been intending to travel home by train, and en route to the railway station I had happened upon four men kicking the living daylights out of another, who lay sprawled on the ground in front of them. Although it was dark, there were plenty of people around but apparently no one else had wanted to get involved. I'm pretty stupid like that and so I'd yelled "Stop!" at the top of my voice.

The four men (all Reds) had paused and looked up at me, evidently stunned that some mad teenager had dared to scream at them. Although rather surprised by my own ridiculously misplaced derring-do, I was too angry to be scared. Seeing that poor man prone and vulnerable at their feet, I had shouted at them to leave him alone; I had fumbled in my bag for my phone to call the police and yelled at them to go away (or words to that effect). This had broken the weird standoff and the men had turned and fled.

I'd gone over to the man on the ground — who later turned out to be a plainclothes police detective called DC Cam — and held his head together until help arrived. After that, I'd never needed to worry about getting pulled over for speeding or anything. And when I'd really needed the police, about a year after all that happened, there had been no shortage of volunteers, DC Cam first among them. Clearly, Matt had made sure that word of my former heroics had reached the police in Leeds during the short time since he'd transferred here from Nottingham.

I nodded a bit to acknowledge Lockheart's statement and murmured something noncommittal. Smiling more broadly, he held the door open for me but I managed somehow to misjudge my aim (I blame the booze fumes), and instead of walking through the doorway I walked into the edge of the door instead. Pain shot through my face, radiating from my eye socket, which had taken the brunt of the collision. Rather embarrassed, I tried to pretend it hadn't happened and readjusted my trajectory to get through the door properly.

Lockheart was momentarily taken aback before saying, "Wow. You alright?"

I mumbled that I was fine but even I couldn't ignore the blood running into my eye.

"Let's have a look at it, then," I heard him say quietly as he gently pulled my hand away from my stricken eye to inspect the damage. It must have looked quite bad because he recoiled ever so slightly, and when a policeman or a doctor does that it's bad news because they're used to a much worse level of gross than the average person.

"Um, okay, I think we'd better get you round to the LGI," he said, and I wondered how bad it must be that he didn't just get me a paper towel and a pack of frozen peas.

"No, no, I'm sure it's fine, I'll just nip to the loo and get cleaned up," I protested to no avail.

He casually told not to be daft. I heard someone enter through the door from the street but had barely a chance to glance that way before Lockheart had ushered me through into the large, open plan office. He passed me a wad of blue paper towels (which I pressed firmly to my cut), gathered up his keys and wallet from one of the desks, and led me through another door that ultimately led to an underground car park. I climbed into the passenger seat of one of the marked police cars and Lockheart drove steadily out of the car park, having the presence of mind to pause and show me the car that he was hoping to sell to me. After I had made sufficiently appreciative noises, he floored the accelerator and drove at breakneck speed the very short distance round to Leeds General Infirmary.

En route, I remembered something important. "Can you phone Matt? *My* Matt — DS Bishop, I mean. He'll need to dismiss the security protocol when I get booked in at the hospital."

Lockheart glanced at me quizzically but when I didn't offer any more details, he clicked the radio on his shoulder and gave a brief message to be passed along to Matt at work.

We parked in the ambulance bay and he came around to open my door for me, holding my arm to help me out of the car and into A&E without further incident. Feeling self-conscious anyway at the attention that had been drawn to me already by the screech of tyres as we'd hared into the no-parking area in a marked police car before being led like an invalid into the busy waiting room, I cringed as Lockheart announced loudly (and slightly hysterically) to the woman behind the reception desk, "She's *bleeding*! Get a doctor!"

The receptionist looked as though she knew as

well as I did that all I needed was a couple of steri-strips or stitches at worst — hardly a life-or-death situation. I smiled apologetically at her and at the queue of people waiting in front of us, who had turned around to stare. The receptionist raised an eyebrow and nodded us through beyond the chairs in the waiting room to the triage desk where a nurse was finishing triaging a toddler with something stuck up his nose. The nurse took my name and address, got rid of the blue paper towels and gave me a wad of fresh gauze to hold to my still-dripping eye socket. He sent us to wait in a cubicle, warning us that it would be quite some time before I would be seen by a doctor.

I perched on the trolley bed and Lockheart sat on a chair he'd dragged into the cubicle. He made some jokes and told me some stories about other people he knew who'd walked into doors and walls and I listened and laughed in the right parts and we were getting on fine but he was very firm about the need for me to keep the gauze pad on my eye. I began to realise that my eye probably wasn't all that bad; Lockheart just wasn't very good with blood.

We'd been waiting there for about ten minutes and had pretty much run out of things to say to each other when the curtain swished open.

Lockheart looked up from reading an information leaflet he'd found on febrile convulsions, of all things, and I looked up from one on wound care, both of us expecting to see a doctor. Instead, there stood my Blue from the railway station.

CHAPTER 5

WEARING DARK GREY TROUSERS, A PALE blue shirt, dark blue waistcoat and matching tie, he held his suit jacket over the crook of one arm. He was slightly out of breath. It appeared that he had been looking for me, because on seeing me his eyes widened slightly in recognition and apparent relief — he wore the same expression, in fact, that I have whenever I'm late for work and finally find my keys.

There was a brief moment when we just stared at each other, then my Blue frowned slightly and cleared his throat. Evidently he didn't quite know what to say, because his eyes just flicked from me to Lockheart and back again and then he glanced behind him as though thinking of leaving. His hand still held the curtain open, as if he were unsure of which side of that curtain he wanted to be on.

Beside me, Lockheart stood up, alert.

A very loud, insistent voice in my head was yelling at me to not let my Blue leave, so I said the first thing that came into my head, which was a slightly desperate, "Wait! *Please* stay!"

He turned back to face me, a tentative smile beginning to blossom as he replied, "Of course," with a courteous nod.

He was *here* — the man who had probably saved my life, and towards whom I had felt an overwhelmingly strong attraction … and I was sitting on a hospital bed, face covered with dried blood, hair probably all over the place and not enough wit about me to say anything cool. I felt flustered and mildly annoyed that in all the imagined conversations I'd had with him since the railway station, I had clearly not managed to come up with anything I could actually use in the (albeit unlikely) event that I did happen to bump into him.

I racked my brain for something to say, but the best I could come up with was, "I'm Sephy."

Out of the corner of my eye I noticed that Lockheart's aura had changed colour: it was now predominantly puce and as that wasn't a colour I knew how to interpret, it caught my attention for a moment.

Lockheart wasn't looking at me, though; he was frowning at my Blue, and said "Are you a doctor, then?"

Joseph looked at him steadily and simply replied, "No."

When he didn't elaborate, Lockheart glanced at me and said, "Um," as if he wasn't sure if a random stranger was allowed into the cubicle.

"It's fine, Lockheart, he's … he's a friend," I hastened to reassure him.

Lockheart raised an eyebrow slightly and muttered, "Oh, of course he is. I should have guessed, from how he didn't know your name."

I chose to ignore him: my entire focus was upon my Blue, willing him to stay. To my relief, with another glance behind him he took a step further into the cubicle, placing his jacket over the rail at the end of the bed.

"Sephy," he said softly, his eyes warm, then added, "I'm Joseph."

Hearing him say my name did funny things to my tummy. His voice suited him: warm and deep, with cultured tones that made me suspect that he, at least, had not grown up on a council estate.

His smile faltered as he stood awkwardly in the narrow space between the end of my bed and the corridor and looked with some concern at my injured eye.

"Are you badly hurt?" he asked as he walked round to the side of the bed furthest from Lockheart.

He stood beside me, within easy touching distance. I could smell his lovely clean, soapy, washing-powder scent and the glow of the beautiful colours around him was breath-taking — it was taking a lot of concentration not to lean forwards and touch him. Thankfully, the bit of my brain that controls hand movements remembered that this was completely inappropriate and so I kept one hand on the gauze covering my eye and sat firmly on the other hand to prevent myself from inadvertently reaching over.

By way of reply I murmured, "No, I'm … lovely," which was a rather unfortunate combination of what I'd meant to say ("I'm fine,") and what I was thinking ("You're lovely,") and I blushed deeply.

His smile broadened. "Quite," he said softly,

halting my attempted clarification in its tracks. "What happened?"

"She walked into a door," Lockheart cut across me.

I looked at him sharply, annoyed that he'd been so blunt. Puce was still dominant in his colours, and I wondered what on earth it represented. My curiosity was fleeting, though, and my eyes were drawn back to Joseph almost immediately.

"It wasn't as open as I'd assumed," I mumbled.

A smile twitched at the corner of Joseph's mouth as if he were unsure of whether it was okay to laugh. Keen to distract him from my mishap, I focussed on why he might have turned up, rather than just on the fact that by some miracle he simply had.

"What are you doing here?" I asked him, trying to sound politely interested rather than interrogatory.

A slightly panicky shade darted across Joseph's colours and his eyes searched the room as though there might be a good explanation written on the walls. He quickly composed himself and if I hadn't been so adept at spotting Technicolor moods I might have missed his uncertainty.

"Oh … My mother works here and I called in to see her, and then I thought I saw you coming in; I recognised you from the railway station the other evening. I saw that you were injured and I was concerned, so I came to ask if you're okay."

The casual tone of his voice didn't quite fit with the colours I could see — he was nervous and on edge and was not being entirely honest with me.

I knew I should have been concerned that a complete stranger had coincidentally been in the same place as me twice in the space of less than a week, and that he had lied about why exactly he'd come to find me: if it had been anyone else, I might have been thinking, '*Stalker!*' (which, I suppose, might have been what was causing Lockheart's apparent discomfort). In Joseph's colours, though, I could see no malice, and the predominant Blue told me that I had no reason to fear him.

Lockheart interrupted my thoughts as he addressed Joseph. His tone was brisk as he said, "Look, I'm not sure what's going on here, but would you do us a favour and go find a doctor to stitch up her eye so I can get her out of here? I don't want to leave her in here on her own."

"Oh my god, don't say that, you make it sound like I'm under *arrest!*" I hissed, vexed. "I'm not under arrest," I added hurriedly to Joseph, who nodded, his eyes crinkled slightly with suppressed amusement.

I was about to suggest that Lockheart could leave me and get back to work, but I was distracted when the gauze dressing finally reached saturation point and blood ran into my eye. Joseph swiftly reached across me to get some fresh gauze from a box on the shelf beside Lockheart, his muscular arm passing dangerously close to my lips. I fought the almost overwhelming urge to kiss it.

Jerking me back to my senses (thankfully), Lockheart paled and said faintly, "Never mind, I'll go get someone," and he hurried out of the cubicle.

With a nod towards the still-flapping curtain, Joseph asked lightly, "Do you know him well?"

"No, no, we met just before the problem with the door," I replied, gesturing vaguely at my face. Feeling that Lockheart hadn't been very polite to

Joseph, I added, "He seemed quite nice, but now he's gone a bit … grumpy, for some reason. Sorry about that."

He scoffed to dismiss my apology. "Envy tends to make people grumpy, I've found."

He handed me the fresh gauze, which I took distractedly to replace the sodden pad on my eye.

"Envy? What's he envious of?" I asked. I wondered if that was what the puce meant, and I resolved to keep an eye out for that colour in future in case further context could help me confirm that it equated to envy.

"Me; because I have your attention, I'm pleased to say," Joseph replied with a contented smile.

I blushed again. My entire attention *was* fixed on Joseph; in fact, I found it difficult not to stare at him. That must have been apparent to Lockheart, though it hadn't occurred to me that that would have bothered him. As quickly as he had entered my thoughts, Lockheart was instantly dismissed from them as I smiled shyly at Joseph as we waited together for the doctor to arrive.

I had it in mind to ask him several pertinent questions, such as how he had appeared and then disappeared so completely at the railway station, or whether it had really been just a coincidence that he happened to be at the hospital when I arrived. But I didn't dare open my mouth to ask any of them in case less appropriate questions like, "Can I kiss you?" came out instead.

Instead, I said, "I never got a chance to thank you — for helping me, at the railway station. It was very brave of you to get involved."

Joseph waved away my thanks and, with a warm smile, said, "I was glad to be able to help. And I'm very glad we met."

A warm glow settled in my chest at his words.

The curtain swished opened and a harried-looking nurse appeared, Lockheart standing behind her.

Without preamble, she took one look at me from the far end of the bed and said, "There's no point me doing anything with that. It's next to your eye; you'll need a plastic doctor to look at you."

An image of a little Lego man with a stethoscope popped into my head. "A *plastic* doctor?"

"Yes, or you'll end up with a scar."

Academically bright as I was, my brain was far too literal at times and it took me a moment to process what she meant. "Oh, like a *plastic surgeon*. A job, not a ... not a thing, a toy ..."

My voice tailed off, taking in the slightly concerned expression she wore. She looked askance at me and asked if I felt sick or if I had a headache. I muttered that I just had a weird sense of humour, probably not concussion-related, and heard a soft chuckle from Joseph.

Looking over her shoulder at Lockheart, the nurse said brusquely, "Feel free to go and find a plastic doctor to harass."

He stood aside and let her pass. Shrugging, he said, "Be right back," and set off again on a mission to find a plastic doctor.

Joseph offered, "My mum's actually one of the plastic surgeons here, would you like me to find her? It might mean that you are seen more quickly?"

And risk him not coming back? "No! I mean, please stay. If you don't mind. I'm sure Lockheart will find someone."

Thankfully, Joseph seemed as reluctant to leave as I was to see him go. He nodded and sat in the chair beside my trolley. We looked at each other and then away again with a little laugh — it was rather odd to be alone with a relative stranger in such close quarters, especially one who was quite so glorious. I was relieved when he found something to say, sparing me any more time spent desperately trying to think of something myself.

"So, you've taken to employing a police escort since your encounter with the, uh, man at the railway station?"

I gave a strangled little laugh that sounded nothing like my own. I cleared my throat and started again. "I need a new car and Lockheart's selling one."

Joseph smiled broadly, his shoulders relaxing a fraction. "Oh. I thought he might be keen to be with you on his own in here for some other reason."

"Oh, no, we're not … he's not really my type," I said awkwardly.

"Ah … so what is your type, would you say?" he asked playfully, and my blush deepened.

I could not respond; I could only stare stupidly at him, at a complete loss for words other than 'You, Joseph'. Although (*thankfully*) those words stayed inside my head, my silence and inability to tear my eyes away from him meant that I couldn't have been more transparent if I'd thrown myself on top of him.

Sensing my discomfiture he merely chuckled and said, "Do you have someone — I mean, is there anyone at home who can watch you tonight, just to keep an eye on you for signs of concussion? Parents, friends ... boyfriend?"

His tone was light, but his colours told me that he was nervous and I tamped down a flutter of excitement at the idea that he was really just asking if I was single, telling myself most firmly that I was being far too optimistic and was therefore likely to suffer a huge let-down at any moment.

"Well, my friend Matt lives with me, I'll get him to check on me."

"Friend?"

It was my turn to smile now, fairly certain that he was asking me this because he was interested in me, too. "Just a friend, yes. I don't have a boyfriend."

His colours positively bloomed, which in turn made my smile widen.

"Maybe ..." Joseph paused for a moment; the frown was back, and his happy colours were now competing with anxious swirls. He glanced at the drawn curtains and then down at his shoes. As if coming to a decision, he looked up again at me. "Maybe I could give you a ring some time. To see how you are, I mean ... and because I don't want this to be the last time I see you."

He seemed to be holding his breath and his colours were flitting all over, revealing anxiety, relief, hope, guilt: I couldn't understand exactly what he was thinking.

I grinned happily, hoping he'd ring me sooner rather than later. "Sure."

He pulled out his phone and set up a new contact before handing it to me to tap in my details; his colours had become brighter, paler, suggesting his mood was much improved as I returned the handset.

Just then, Lockheart re-entered the cubicle looking distinctly out of sorts and sounding rather exasperated. "I can't find a plastic doctor anywhere; I don't even know what one looks like. No one can give me a straight answer on when you'll be seen. You'd think being asked by a copper would make people more compliant …"

"Don't worry," I told him, keen to be alone again with Joseph. "You should get back; I don't want to keep you. Thank you for bringing me — I'll get Matt to sort out another time for me to see the car if you don't mind?"

A blush began at his collar and began to spread slowly upwards. Avoiding looking at Joseph, he stammered, "Oh, okay. But actually I was thinking I could give you my number. Might be easier than involving the DS. We can sort out a time for you to come and give it a test drive, if you like. Maybe go for a drink afterwards."

He handed me a card with his details, a shy smile on his face. From the corner of my eye, I saw Joseph stand straighter and cross his arms across his chest, puce prominent amongst *his* colours. Interesting.

There was an awkward pause while I took the card, my cheeks burning, and tucked it into my handbag.

Lockheart then handed me an advice leaflet about head injuries and said more easily, "Right. Well, I'll be off. Give me a call, though, yeah?"

I said I would, carefully clarifying that I would call him about the *car*, and thanking him for all his help. With a brief nod and a smile, █████ cubicle and we listened for a moment ██ squeak of his shoes as he walked away do███ corridor.

"Bold," Joseph commented lightly.

I raised my eyebrows briefly in acknowledgement. "I might send Matt to have a look at his car. I do need one, after all. But I won't be taking him up on the drink," I said carefully, keen to impress upon him that the only man I was interested in was sitting in front of me.

My words made his eyes crinkle and his smile warmed, making his whole visage light up. The puce had faded from his colours, I was pleased to note, and I added it to my mental list of colours and their meaning.

"So, does that mean you might be free one evening soon for me to take you out somewhere?" he asked.

I had been finding it increasingly unpleasant to think that I would never see him again if we parted without arranging to do so, and was about to snap up his offer with both hands, when a woman in green scrubs came into the cubicle, wielding a tray of scary-looking surgical instruments.

She saw Joseph first, and exclaimed, "Oh! What are you doing here? Are you alright?"

Before he could answer, though, her eyes fell on me.

Though she had been smiling warmly at Joseph, her face became utterly immobile when she saw me. She looked back at her son, alarm clear in her tense features and fear reflected in her colours.

"Oh my days …" she breathed.

CHAPTER 6

SHE WAS A PALE BLUE WITH very pretty trait colours: I could see in an instant that she was loving, patient and kind. On closer inspection, I saw that she bore a physical similarity to Joseph: both of them had dark blond hair and pale skin, and both had the same beautiful blue eyes. I could only imagine that Joseph had inherited his height from his father though, because his mother was ridiculously petite: I'm five foot ten and whilst I'd had to peer upwards at quite a steep angle to meet Joseph's gaze, even sitting down I had a height advantage over this little pixie of a woman — I felt like Gulliver.

I watched as a flush of guilt and anxiety washed over Joseph's aura as he swallowed hard and dropped his gaze to the floor.

"It's … it's not as bad as it looks, Mum. I don't think it can be. Trust me," he said quietly, drawing her out of her state of apparent shock.

I touched the pad over my cut, wondering what could have made her look so shocked and hoping my head wasn't about to drop off.

She looked at me warily for a moment before taking a steadying breath and nodding at her son. "I really hope you know what you're doing," she said quietly.

"Is everything alright?" I asked, nonplussed by the reaction I'd witnessed.

At the sound of my voice, she quickly recovered herself and, acting as though nothing had happened, asked what I'd done. Wishing I'd been hurt doing something noble or brave instead, I told her about the door.

She looked at me, momentarily bemused. She asked how long it had been since it had happened and, after checking my watch, I said it had been about two hours.

She rolled her eyes slightly and said, "Well, you'll probably have a scar then, I'm sorry."

"That's okay," I said with a shrug.

A scar wasn't something I was truly pleased about, but I had never been terribly concerned about my appearance; I tended to avoid mirrors whenever possible. Men seemed to find me attractive, but it had been a long time since I could look at myself and like what I saw, despite the rather intensive therapy I'd endured over the preceding seven years. A scar near my eye would make no difference to how I perceived myself.

Working quietly whilst Joseph stood beside me, she stuck my cut together with some glue (which stung horribly) and slapped an adhesive pad over the top. As she gathered her equipment together, she told me not to get the wound wet or to pick at it. The words 'pick at it' lodged in my mind and it took a lot of effort to stop my fingers rising to the wound and doing just that.

"Joseph, may I have a word?" she asked crisply.

He nodded, his face set. Turning to me, he said, "I will not be long, if you would be so kind as to wait for me?"

I nodded agreeably, and they had just left the cubicle when Matt pushed his way in. His face was creased with concern and worry for the brief time it took for him to see that I was conscious and in roughly one piece; then he returned to his usual form.

"Great clot," he tutted. He leant down and gave me a one-armed hug before stepping back to study my injured eye. Sitting beside me on the bed he said in an exasperated tone, "I nearly had a heart attack when the Bridewell called and said you'd been taken to hospital. You'd only been there five minutes!"

"I know. PC Lockheart's not great with blood; I think he panicked. So here I am," I said with a shrug.

"And where's Lockheart now?"

"He had to go. He did well not to faint."

Matt tutted again, shaking his head slightly. He ran a hand through his mop of dark brown hair before shrugging his suit jacket off and dumping it on the bed next to me. "I'd have been here sooner, but I got a call to deal with something in Beeston. Bridewell said you'd live, so I went and dealt with the corpse, hope you don't mind."

"I've been alright," I smiled, still thinking of Joseph.

He nodded at my patched-up eye and said, "You've been seen by someone, I take it, so when can you go home?"

I shrugged again. "Now, I suppose. I'm just waiting for—"

That was when Joseph pulled open the cubicle curtain and began, "Sephy—" but stopped when he saw I wasn't alone.

He and Matt looked at each other for a brief moment in surprise. Then they said their names at each other by way of introduction and shook hands briefly. I pushed myself off the bed and picked up my bag from the floor, trying not to look like I was staring at Joseph.

Something in his manner had changed. His colours were obscured by what looked like anger, hurt. "I just came back to hand you a prescription for some painkillers, in case you need them," he said, passing me the piece of paper in his hand, before he added, "and to say goodbye." He said this with such sadness that I was nearly moved to tears — if he could do that on screen, he would receive every acting award going.

"Why?" I managed, conscious of Matt's questioning stare.

"I've spoken to my—" he caught himself, presumably about to say, 'my mum', and corrected, "—the plastic surgeon, and there's no need for you to come back. Just check for signs of concussion and obviously come back or speak to your GP if you experience any problems. Take better care of yourself." Then he added a single word, laced with a quiet desperation I couldn't really understand. "*Please.*"

Before I could reply he nodded a farewell to us both and swished back out of the cubicle.

Matt looked at me, bemused. "Bit weird for a doctor," he commented.

I didn't correct his assumption, not wanting to get into a discussion about who Joseph really was or how I knew him.

He stood aside so that I could leave the cubicle ahead of him and we walked to the exit together, where Matt's car was parked in the space in the ambulance bay that Lockheart's car had previously occupied. Matt's car wasn't a marked police car, though, and in the short time he'd been inside, he'd acquired a big yellow parking ticket, which he plucked casually from the windscreen and dropped in the passenger footwell as he slid behind the driver's seat. He reached over and unlocked my door so I could get in.

"You get chance to see Lockheart's car after all that?"

I made a sound like "pffft" and closed my door. "I saw it in passing from inside the police car, but there was a lot of blood in my eyes. Lockheart gave me his number, told me to give him a ring about arranging a test drive."

"And a drink, I bet," Matt muttered under his breath as he reversed the car before pulling out of the car park.

I looked over Matt's shoulder at the Accident and Emergency department and thought I saw Joseph looking back at me from a window, but the light wasn't good so I couldn't be certain it was him. Somehow I doubted he'd be calling my number after all.

CHAPTER 7

WAKING GROGGILY THE NEXT MORNING, I lay staring at the ceiling considering my future, which looked decidedly bleak given my lack of success in securing meaningful employment and without the prospect of seeing Joseph again. I didn't even know his surname, so there was no way I could find him, and I hated the fact that I was clinging to the hope that he would ring me, utterly powerless to do anything more constructive.

I realised that I had been thinking about him far more than was healthy in the days since I'd met him at the station — and giving him far more headspace than the arguably more pressing matter of finding a job deserved. I gave myself a mental shake to refocus on things that were within my control and that would actually do me some good, starting with my career.

After breakfast, I called Lockheart and made an excuse not to see his car after all — I said something about finances being a bit restricted and that I was looking for something a bit cheaper. The truth was I just didn't want to give him the wrong idea and let him think I was interested in him when I really wasn't. There was only one man I was interested in … and there I was again, thinking about Joseph when I should have been focussing on getting a job!

Seated once again at my computer, I turned to trusty Google, typing, 'newly qualified solicitor jobs, Family Law, Leeds'.

A few sites came up at the top of the list mysteriously trying to *sell* me 'newly qualified solicitor jobs, Family Law, Leeds' and I scrolled further down to see if anything matched what I actually wanted. All I found, though, were lots of sites for local firms of solicitors that specialised in Family Law and were based in Leeds. It looked as though I'd have to approach some of these speculatively and ask if they were thinking of looking for a newly qualified solicitor at any point soon. I sighed, went and made a cup of tea, and sat back down at my computer.

For those firms that had a contact form, I wrote an initial enquiry letter and attached my (good enough) C.V. and a copy of my reference from the firm that had trained me; for the others, I took a note of their number and — after steeling myself (since I was always inexplicably nervous when speaking over the phone) — called them to make the same initial enquiry.

The fourth firm I phoned was called Democritus; they were a large high street firm that had a range of departments including a thriving Family Law section headed by someone called Russ Democritus. Further investigation had revealed that the senior partner was called Thomas Democritus and other heads of various departments shared the same surname, suggesting either that the Democritus family happened to have bred a number of especially able lawyers or that their firm's recruitment policies rather favoured nepotism. Suspecting the latter, I was doubtful that I'd even get a foot in the door with the wrong surname, but I had nothing to lose by calling so did so.

I was put through to Thomas Democritus's secretary. She sounded pleasant but busy, so I cut to the chase and explained briefly that I'd recently completed my Training Contract and was looking for work in a Family Law team.

I could hear her typing as she spoke and was mildly impressed that she could multitask so effectively. "I'm afraid we usually seek to retain our trainees and our latest batch are qualifying later this month; all have accepted positions here this year and we have no further vacancies available. However, if you'd like to give me your details I will certainly put them on file in case a position becomes available?"

Understanding that this was polite code for, "Not blooming likely," I nevertheless agreed to email her my CV and she took my name.

"How am I spelling Sephy, please?" she asked, and I spelled it out for her. "Unusual name," she commented lightly as she typed.

"It's short for Persephone," I explained.

She repeated my name as though she liked the sound of it; then she exclaimed, "Oh!" and there was the sound of a small kerfuffle and of her phone being transferred between hands.

A moment later a man's voice came on the line.

"Persephone?" he asked, his voice more insistent than inquiring.

I frowned — his voice was really, really familiar, though I was at a loss to think where I'd heard it before.

"Y— Yes?" I managed, rather distracted by the abrupt switch in speakers.

He sounded slightly out of breath and spoke hurriedly. "My name is Thomas Democritus. I'm sorry to intrude on your conversation — my secretary shares my office and I overheard your enquiry. May I invite you to come for an interview with us tomorrow? We, erm, we have unexpectedly had a vacancy arise. Yes, that's it. Can you come in?"

I knew his name from the website, of course, but otherwise it meant nothing to me. I quickly clicked onto the page that showed photos of key staff members; his was at the top of the page, yet I didn't recognise his face. Still, his voice was so disconcertingly familiar that it was hard to focus on what was actually being said whilst I struggled to place it, so I paused slightly before replying. "Oh — oh, yes please, that would be great! I'll email my C.V. and a reference over if you'd like?"

"What? Oh, oh yes, certainly. Good idea. I'll hand you back for now. See you in the morning, nine o'clock."

Without further ado I was handed back to the secretary, whose voice sounded less assured and efficient than it had been previously. Apparently the vacancy was news to her. She recovered herself well, though, and ensured that I was familiar with how to find the office so that I could attend promptly at nine o'clock.

Arrangements duly made, I hung up, feeling giddy and excited about having secured an interview then terribly nervous for the same reason.

I spent the afternoon researching Democritus's as though my life depended on it. I really, really wanted the job — the more I read about the firm, the more I wanted to work there. I learnt that Democritus's had been founded in the early 1800s by an ancestor of Thomas Democritus. Quick calls to the local county and magistrates' courts and a chat with a couple of willing clerks revealed that the firm was well respected locally and highly successful. Pleased that they wanted to interview me and satisfied that I knew enough about the firm to sound credible if asked why I wanted to work for them, I only had a few hours left in which to feel sick with nerves.

Fortunately, when Matt got home from work, he proved his worth yet again by keeping me calm and helping me to prepare for my interview. He quizzed me with standard interview questions concerning who I was and why I wanted to work for Democritus's, and what I knew about the firm, and which five adjectives I would use to describe myself, and so on. He then got me to give mini presentations on things like what I'd done on my last holiday, to test my ability to deliver precise, time-constrained speeches. I thought he'd started running out of ideas on that front when he asked me to describe what an alien would make of a football match, but he swore that was something he'd been asked to do at his interview for Detective Sergeant.

The best advice he gave me was not to think of it as a job interview, but as a televised interview for

TV, as though I were a celebrity with thousands of fans who wanted to know more about my every waking thought.

I took on board all of his advice and tried hard to keep on top of my nerves, yet I struggled to get to sleep that night. At the back of my mind, I was replaying Thomas's voice and trying to place where I knew it from and that, more than the looming interview, was enough to keep me awake.

It wasn't until much later that night, when I'd finally fallen asleep only to wake shortly thereafter from my old, recurring dream, that I realised who Thomas Democritus reminded me of. I dismissed it as an odd coincidence and my memory playing tricks on me: with hindsight, though, I probably shouldn't have been so quick to disbelieve my own ears.

CHAPTER 8

With a combination of Matt's interview advice and thoughts about my recurring dream occupying my mind, I made my way to Leeds after breakfast on the oh-so-slow bus down the main road from Headingley. My interview was to be at nine o'clock and I thought I'd given myself loads of time by setting off at eight, but I hadn't factored in the rush hour. The blasted bus seemed to stop every few feet to let more people on or off and I cursed each and every person who stood up and pressed the bell a second after the bus had started from the last stop, knowing it was only another 200 yards or so to the next.

A blisteringly stressful forty-five minutes later, I arrived at Leeds on the Headrow, the main road that runs through the middle of the town from the courts at one end to the bus station at the other. I walked swiftly in the direction of the courts and turned right onto the road before the Bridewell police station. Democritus's turned out to be an immense structure of glass and steel, stretching up six floors and consuming the entire length of the street in front of me.

Pleased to have made it on time and in one piece, I entered the reception area. I informed the receptionist of my name and why I was there, and was directed to a waiting room that was otherwise deserted. "Celebrity, celebrity, celebrity," I thought to myself, to try to calm down.

In every exam I had ever sat I had spent the first five minutes thinking, "I just don't know. I don't know any of this. I should just leave. Yes, I'll just get up and leave," until gradually the panic faded and I was finally able to read the questions instead of having them leap round the page, forming nonsense sentences. I felt a similar sensation while sitting in the waiting room of Democritus's, wondering if I should just save myself the hassle and go home.

But before I could decide whether or not I should actually get up and leave, a tall, mature, besuited man practically bounced into the room, looking nervous and excited and full of an apprehension that almost mirrored my own. At the sight of him, the breath caught in my throat.

His hair was golden blond; his eyes hazel and almond-shaped; his features angular and pointed but pleasantly so; his complexion pale. I had never seen him before (other than on his firm's website), yet I had been right in thinking that his voice was familiar on the phone because I knew him very, very well.

He stood stock still for a moment, staring at me as though he knew me too; his colours reflected pure joy.

With a broad smile, he said, "Hello,

Persephone. I am Thomas Democritus and I am *very* pleased to see you."

***

I'm in a forest and I'm moving as fast as I can, which isn't very fast because I'm heavily pregnant; my hands clutch beneath my swollen belly in a vain effort to support it as I half run, half stumble through the scrub beneath my feet. I can smell foist and hear swift rustles as I disturb all the years of rotten leaves that have built up on the floor as I flee. The trees have silver trunks and their branches are far above me and I am in a tearing hurry; my life depends on escaping whomever is chasing me.

I break through the forest onto a sandy path that runs alongside the sea; the tide is in and waves crash over the path here and there. I turn to my right and although I can now run a little faster on the smoother ground, the brief moment I spent changing direction has cost me dearly: I am hit. I see a confused jumble of images as I tumble and then, before I can draw breath to cry out, I am falling, thrown into the water. I submerge in the icy, choppy sea and then there are hands holding me underneath the waves and everything is black and I clutch my stomach as a contraction tears through me, making me expel what little air is left in my lungs. I can no longer overcome my instinct to try to draw breath and inhale what seems like gallons of water ...

Then the pain is gone and I am lying on my back in cold, wet sand, and I know I'm dead because I can see everything from a new perspective, from just above my body. I know in my dream that it's me I'm looking at, even though I don't look like I do in real life: whereas in reality I am tall, with pale skin,

49

blue eyes and mid-brown hair, my 'dream me' has black hair and olive skin and seems petite and vulnerable, her brown eyes staring lifelessly into the sky. My body has been torn open and my baby is being lifted from my body. At first, I'm terrified because she has no aura, no colours at all and I feel sure she must have died with me. But then I hear her cry and feel overwhelming relief and joy, coupled with truly desperate sadness: I know I'm not going to see her grow up and that my baby won't have a mother. I try my hardest to get back to her but I can't move any closer.

Then I look at the people surrounding my desecrated body. There are four of them and they are looking at my baby very closely, turning her this way and that. I want them to get off her, not to touch her — what right have they to handle her? I feel boiling anger at the thought that they might hurt her. They all look similar in that they are tall and lean and aesthetically beautiful but three of them are Red and scare me. The fourth person — a Blue — is the last to take the baby and I sense that there is tension between him and the rest of the group; he speaks just once and even though it's not a language I recognise I understand him: "Leave the vessel with me, I will dispose of it in accordance with our laws," and then the three Reds leave.

The Blue man who remains behind is holding the baby and no matter how many times I see him in my dream I'm always taken aback by just how beautiful he is. He could be any age — his skin is perfect yet his eyes have depth and experience behind them: he could be twenty, he could be forty or even sixty. He has dark brown skin, hazel eyes and short, black hair; he is tall and lean with broad shoulders and strong arms. He has the most amazingly beautiful colours; his aura is so Blue he's almost silver and he has gorgeous pinks and pale greys and lilacs floating above that. But that's hard to see beneath the black that is his grief ripping out of his very core at this moment. He is crouched over my still body, cradling my bloody baby and crying like his soul is being torn apart; I've never heard anything so achingly sad.

I try to tell him that he will be alright, that I trust him to take care of my child — that I forgive him, though I do not know for what. He looks up and for a second I think he's looking at me, but he doesn't see me and that's when I know I'm really not coming back. So I spend my last moments staring at him and my baby girl.

Then I hear him murmur my name: "Persephone." I realise that he is naming my child for me. Then, instead of the blackness I am expecting, I am suddenly looking at the Blue man from another perspective — I am cradled in his arms, staring up into his eyes, which are filled with tears of grief and love in equal measure.

***

I have had this dream — this *exact same dream* — every single damned night for as long as I can remember. And there, in front of me, in the office of Democritus Solicitors, stood the Blue man from my dream. I had *never* seen two people with the same colours before: not family members, not even identical twins. Thomas Democritus may have looked *physically* different to the Blue in my recurrent dream, but his soul had exactly the same

51

colours: impossible though it should have been, I knew that he *was* the man in my dream.

For a moment he was all I could see; the rest of the room had become a blur. I managed to find my voice at last and said, "I'm pleased to see you too."

He snapped out of his own contemplations and strode over to me, arms outstretched and for a second I thought he was going to hug me. This was already turning out to be the weirdest interview I had ever had in my life: it beat Matt's alien-at-a-football-match question hands down.

At the last moment, he dropped one of his arms and settled for a handshake instead. I reciprocated, though I would happily have hugged him; I felt as though I'd known him for years.

"I am so glad you're here," he said warmly.

My face was frozen, eyes wide as if trying to make sure they were really seeing what should have been impossible; my hands trembled uncontrollably and my legs felt like they were made of water.

Ignoring my lack of verbal response, he continued, "When can you start?"

Seeing my startled expression, he shook his head slightly, apparently amused by something, and said, "Actually, no, first things first." He rolled his eyes and tutted, "Paperwork. And we'll have a chat in my office, if you've got time?"

I smiled, still bewildered.

"Lead the way," I replied.

That wasn't really what I wanted to say to him, though. No, the words that kept forcing themselves to the front of my mind (though, thankfully, remained unspoken) were, '*I've missed you*'.

CHAPTER 9

WE TOOK THE LIFT UP TO the top floor. It opened straight into a large office that was furnished with several large bookcases and an enormous polished wooden table, which was topped with a large blotter and numerous stacks of files. In the far corner stood a second, smaller desk with a computer; I surmised that this must be where his secretary worked (there was a silver frame holding a picture of two small children in school uniforms who bore not the slightest resemblance to Thomas), though the desk was currently vacant.

He wheeled her empty chair over to his desk and offered it to me before he walked around to his large, leather seat to sit facing me; for a moment we just sat and looked at each other. It was the strangest feeling — it was like being in the company of a relative remembered fondly from childhood.

He cleared his throat and pulled some papers towards him, leafing through them with a slight frown until he happened upon the one he needed.

"Ah, now, paperwork — where would we lawyers be without forms to fill in? I'll just ask you some of the questions on here, make some notes and then it's all done, okay?"

I shrugged happily, surprised by this rather surreal turn of events but pleased that I appeared to have landed a job without having to do a presentation. He proceeded to ask me some of the questions that Matt and I had anticipated, including why I wanted to work for Democritus's and why I had not been retained by the firm that had trained me in Nottingham, especially in view of their glowing reference. Throughout this part of my interview, Thomas's tone was hurried, the questions a formality that he was clearly keen to conclude as quickly as possible.

By way of reply, I explained about my interest in joining a large firm that did not deal solely with commercial law, and told him about my investigations with the clerks. I brushed over my reasons for leaving Nottingham, not wishing to go into detail, and instead intimated that I had moved to Leeds for family reasons. As to my academic qualifications, Thomas merely queried whether I had been happy with my A-Level grades, considering that they didn't reflect the promise I'd shown in my GCSEs. There was only so much I could go into about that in an interview situation, and I did not care to voluntarily relive the most traumatic event of my life thus far, so I stretched the truth quite a bit.

"I was mugged during my second year of Sixth Form. I was injured and ended up missing quite a lot of lessons. I was okay by the time I took my exams, and my marks were enough to get me into my chosen university, but I could have done better."

He seemed politely troubled by my answer, but did not comment; instead, he picked up the paper with his notes on it and placed it neatly on the side of his desk. There was a pause while he gathered his thoughts. When he began again, I judged that he was now seeking the answers that he was really interested in — and as I had a rather pertinent question of my own that I was keen for him to answer, I hoped that this new sense of intimacy meant that I would get the chance to ask it.

"So," he smiled. "Persephone is an unusual name for a girl born and raised in Nottingham. Was it your mother's choice, or your father's?"

"Oh, well, I don't know who my dad is, and I don't think he even knows I exist, so I assume it was my mum's."

Thomas frowned slightly and thought for a moment. "Is she Greek?"

"No, no, she's British. I imagine she just chose the name because it's got something to do with hell," I said with a casual shrug. In response to his quizzical expression, I added, "She really wasn't very thrilled about having a second child."

That was a huge understatement, but I hoped it would be sufficient to convey the idea that whilst my relationship with my mother was not good, it did not warrant further discussion. Much of the therapy I'd undergone following my attack had focussed on my troubled childhood, my mother's rejection of me and how neither of those things was a reflection on me. Nevertheless, it had left its scars and I always had an underlying certainty that I was undeserving of anyone's affection or kindness; when meeting new people, I felt it was only a matter of time before they would realise what I was like underneath and distance themselves. Part of me had felt that I'd deserved what had happened to me. Emotional neglect could be even more harmful than physical abuse, my therapist had told me, and with her support I had worked through the anger, sadness, disappointment and grief related to having a mum who just didn't love me — but hurt like that lingers.

He seemed concerned, and spoke with a measure of compassion when he replied, "Well, whether she knows this or not, I hope that you are aware that your namesake was the goddess of spring. She was forced to marry Hades, god of the underworld, against her wishes — she was *not* inherently evil."

I didn't know how to reply to this. Thankfully, though, he did not seem intent on pursuing more information about my spectacularly disinterested mother.

"You are your mother's second child, you mentioned?" he said, inviting more information.

I wondered if all his questions were going to be about my family. Perhaps this was his way of trying to work out where he recognised me from? The more time we spent together, the more certain I became that, on some level, he knew me as well as I knew him.

"Yeah, I have a sister called Zoe. Well, she's a half-sister: same mum, different dad. My mum's first husband, Daniel, was her dad, but he left when she cheated on him with whoever my dad was. Zoe's older than me, about the same age as Matt."

I realised without surprise that I hadn't heard

from my sister since we'd moved.

"And who is Matt?" Thomas enquired, distracting me from that brief sting of rejection.

I smiled more freely, happy to be onto a less emotive subject. "My best friend. He lived next door when I was born, so I've always known him. He was my family growing up, really — well, him and Nana. I had to leave home when I was seventeen, so I moved in with him and we've lived together ever since; we get on really well."

"Your Nana?" he asked intently, leaning forward in his seat slightly.

I felt a keen pang of grief. It had only been three months, and part of me had still not processed her loss. "Oh, she isn't really—" I broke off, hating that I had to correct my tense. "I mean, she *wasn't* really related to me. She's— she was my godmother, but she was Nana-aged, you know? She looked after me sometimes and I loved her like family. She … she died, not long ago, just after I came to Leeds."

No, she wasn't really family, biologically, but she was estranged from her grown-up son and had sort of taken me under her wing, filling a need both of us felt. I relished the attention and affection she gave me; I suspect she was not blind to the way I was treated at home and through her unfailing kindness she had given me some respite from feeling unwanted. She didn't like or trust my mother any more than I did and above everything else she did for me, that act of loyalty was what warmed me the most: the feeling that someone was on my side was invaluable.

"I'm sorry for your loss," Thomas said gravely. "It sounds as though you were very close."

I swallowed hard, a lump having manifested in my throat. "She was like a mum," I managed.

Thinking about her now, I could almost smell her Lily of the Valley perfume and feel the velvet of her easy chair by the fireplace. She used to give me biscuits when I went to her house as a little girl, and let me sit and watch her TV as a teenager. She'd give me presents at Christmas knowing that I didn't get any at home. She'd listen to me prattle on about seeing colours and would often play a game with me where I would try to guess how she was feeling — I was nearly always right, of course, and she never made me feel weird or silly, merely corrected me if I was wrong.

After a respectful pause, Thomas said, "I'm sorry that your relationship with your actual mother is not a strong one." He frowned. "Seventeen was very young for you to have left home."

I shook my head dismissively. "It was my mum's decision, but I was happier after I left."

He seemed perturbed by this but merely commented, "Hmm, well, I suppose we can't choose our parents ... Still, no father and a no-good mother. I am sorry. You deserved better."

For someone who had just met me, he certainly seemed to have taken my troubled past to heart.

Perhaps he realised that he had been too intense because he sat up a little straighter and made an effort to seem more business-like. "Speaking of families though, I must introduce you to my son, since you'll be working in his department — in fact, you'll be working in his office for a few weeks until you find your feet. Please excuse me for a moment," he said as he picked up the phone. Speaking to someone on the other end of the line, he instructed briskly, "Yes, can you ask Russ to join us, please? In fact, you might as well ask all three of them to come up."

He hung up and took a deep breath that he let out with a sigh before saying more brightly, "So, you've got the job, obviously. If you would like it, I mean?"

I smiled happily, "Of course! Thank you so much, it's — it's —" I wanted to say 'unexpected' but wasn't sure how that would sound so opted for, "— really exciting!"

He returned my smile and then frowned slightly as he said, "My children won't be a moment. There are three of them, and they each head their own department. I — well, please don't be offended if they are a little less than warm towards you. I will speak to them later, but this will come as a surprise to them and people don't always deal with surprises with the greatest of grace. I assure you that they are good people and will soon adapt."

I didn't quite know how to respond to that slightly ominous warning and began to feel nervous once more. Aware, though, that I would not have much more time on my own with him, I plucked up the courage to ask a question of my own. I chose my words carefully.

"Erm, this feels like it isn't the first time we've met. *Have* we met before?"

This was the only explanation I'd been able to come up with as to why his soul was so familiar. Perhaps I'd seen him as a very young child and incorporated his soul into my recurrent dream without consciously doing so?

Thomas went very still, one hand suspended

above the pile of papers he had been in the process of moving to clear his desk a little. He blinked a couple of times and looked at me, distractedly placing the papers on the floor beside him. "I don't believe so, no," he said hesitantly. "At least, not in this lifetime," he added with a small smile.

Under different circumstances, I might have dismissed his words as a turn of phrase used to disguise awkwardness at not remembering me as I remembered him. But there was a ring of truth to them that vocalised my own, private thoughts about my dream — it had always felt like more of a memory than a dream. He held my gaze for a moment longer.

"Yes, that's what I thought," I replied quietly. Looking at him closely to spot any tell-tale change in his colours, I asked, "Do you believe in things like that?"

He regarded me steadily. "Oh, yes," he replied seriously.

CHAPTER 10

I TRIED TO THINK OF A WAY to get him to expand upon his reply, but just then a glass door to the side of the lift was opened by a powerfully built man who was slightly out of breath from having chosen to climb the stairs.

"Ah," said Thomas, rising to his feet. "This is my eldest son, Russ. He is head of Family Law here. Russ, this is Sephy — she will be working with you as our newest solicitor."

Russ was a Blue and had trait colours that were very easy on the eye — at a glance I could see that he was kind, fair-minded and patient. On closer inspection, I saw that his features were pleasantly symmetrical, his skin was like alabaster and his dark hair was carefully styled to look like he'd just fallen out of bed.

He moved his attention from his father to me and I smiled, anticipating a greeting; instead, shock and fear flashed across his face and aura and I tensed in response. He gripped the door behind him as though to steady himself and his mouth fell open; I quickly turned to look behind me, assuming that there must be a giant spider on the wall or something, but there was nothing untoward there. He was looking directly at me.

With an effort, he moved his hand from the doorway to grasp more tightly the file of papers in his arms, and I noticed that he left a rather sweaty palm mark on the glass as he did so. There was no other way to interpret his physical symptoms and the flash of pale yellow that had permeated his colours — I had scared him.

Before he had a chance to speak, though, the lift doors opened with a 'ping' and two more people entered the room. The first was a woman who was a rather dark Blue; her trait colours were less pleasant than Russ's. Physically, she was blonde and very pretty, with large blue eyes and enviably clear skin. She looked either like a very short catwalk model or a really tall fairy: she was noticeably more petite in stature than anyone else in the room and, just like when I had met Joseph's mum at the hospital, I felt instantly over-sized and clumsy in her presence. The next thing I noticed about her was that she was staring at me and looked like she was going to faint.

I quickly looked to the man who had exited the lift behind her, hoping that he had noticed how unwell she seemed and could catch her if she passed out.

With a happy jolt, I realised that the other man was my Blue — Joseph — though he looked rather more tired and careworn than when I had last seen him only two days before.

"Oh, hey, it's you!" I said with a big grin.

My smile faded slightly as I remembered his abrupt change of attitude towards me at the hospital, compounded by the distinct lack of a phone call that I might have expected in the meantime if he'd been as keen as he'd seemed initially.

Recognition flitted across his features and a smile of his own appeared, but it was fleeting and quickly replaced by a look of horror as he turned his attention to his siblings and father. He pushed past his sister and practically ran towards me, which I'll admit was a little startling, and placed himself directly in front of me, facing the others in the room. His hands held out placatingly, he said quickly, "Please, please, wait — *don't*. Dad, just listen—"

Thomas did not seem remotely fazed by this rather odd behaviour, though I was utterly dumbfounded. Joseph was acting as though his dad and siblings were about to attack me, rather than offer me a job. Glancing at the face of the woman, who had gone from looking afraid to looking very angry indeed (presumably at being shoved out of the way), I wondered if he might be right.

Interrupting whatever it was that Joseph was about to tell him, Thomas raised his own hands in a reassuring manner and said, "Joseph, it's alright, I know how you feel about these things; you and I are on the same side here — we always have been. Relax." He glanced at the other two and stressed, "*Everybody* relax. This is Persephone. Sephy, I mean. She will be working here and she is going to be line-managed by Russ but ultimately she is *my* responsibility. She is part of the Democritus team now and, as such, she will receive the same respect and support as anybody else here. Is that understood?"

Nobody moved or replied.

Thomas was about to speak again when he glanced at Joseph and did a small double take as he looked between us. Joseph was still standing in front of me, though his arms had dropped to his sides now, apparently satisfied that I was not about to be set upon for whatever reason he had initially feared. His close proximity was very distracting and it was taking some effort on my part not to reach out and stroke his back; I told myself that there could be all sorts of reasons why he hadn't called, and anyway did it really matter? I was absorbed by his scent, the warmth radiating from his body and thoughts of what it would be like to be in his arms ...

"Joseph? Am I to assume that this is the reason you have been quite so *distracted* lately?" asked his father, a shrewd expression on his face.

I jumped slightly, having momentarily completely forgotten where we were and who else was in the room; all I'd been aware of was Joseph, who had occupied every ounce of my attention until Thomas had brought me out of my reverie. Now, I saw a blush creep up the side of Joseph's neck. He nodded by way of reply and folded his arms across his chest defensively, glancing at his siblings as he did so.

"Ah. Well, that complicates matters slightly, but there is nothing that cannot be overcome. We shall speak more of it later," Thomas said quietly.

Russ finally spoke, addressing Joseph in an accusatory tone. "You've met before?" he asked, his voice dangerously low.

Joseph nodded once.

"And you did not mention this?" Russ went on, gesturing vaguely in my direction. "Her name is *Persephone* for heaven's sake!" He practically shouted my name, making me jump again and causing Joseph to tense as though ready to ward off an attack.

"We can talk about everything tonight," Thomas said loudly, seeking to forestall whatever it was that Russ had on his mind to say. "For now, Russ, perhaps you could show *Sephy* round your department. Did we agree on a date for you to start?" he asked me.

Not having expected any of what had gone before, I said faintly, "Um, no, but whenever you'd like."

"Monday, then. Good to have you on the team." He smiled broadly.

Russ and the woman did not look pleased, but Joseph turned towards me and his colours told me everything I needed to know — he was really, really happy. "I'm glad you're here," he said softly.

I gave him a shy smile in reply — still somewhat perturbed by his rather dramatic entrance — and found it difficult to look away.

Russ coughed pointedly, drawing my attention. Rubbing the back of his head in a gesture of agitation, he stepped to one side to peer past Joseph, apparently forcing himself to look at me. Through gritted teeth, he said, "Very well. I am Russ Democritus, and I am head of Family Law." He nodded towards the now positively incandescent woman, who was standing as far away from me as she possibly could, her back pressed against one of the bookshelves. "This is our sister, Erica

Democritus, head of Civil Litigation." Glaring at Joseph, he added a final, "And you appear to have *met* our brother, Joseph Democritus, who is head of Intellectual Property. Come."

He turned his back on me and exited the way he had entered, allowing the door to fall shut behind him; moving swiftly past Joseph so as not to inadvertently stroke his face or squeeze his bicep, I hurried after Russ, and pulled the door back open.

I could hear Erica's rather shrill voice behind me as we descended the stairs: I caught the shouted words, "Does *mum* know?", but everything else became muted as the door to Thomas's office closed properly.

Russ moved so swiftly down the stairs it was difficult to keep up. I caught up with him as he pushed open a door on what I judged to be the third or fourth floor. We entered a large, open office filled with natural light from a wall of windows; the central area was occupied by four secretarial desks and was surrounded on the other three walls by four private offices.

As we walked past the secretaries, Russ barked out my name by way of introduction and I gave a shy wave as everyone turned to smile and say hello. I had rarely seen so many people with such lovely Blue auras in one place.

"I won't bother telling you all their names now, you won't remember them and you'll learn them all soon enough anyway. Assuming you stay, that is. My secretary is Lu — she's the one sitting closest to my door. She's good and fast and keeps me organised, and I do not want anything to annoy her into leaving, is that understood?" Walking briskly to the second office on our right, which displayed a doorplate naming it as his, Russ pushed the door open with a bang, held it open for me to see inside and said gruffly, "This is my office. *Our* office now, apparently."

It was a large, if unremarkable, office with one wall made up of windows that looked out over the city from three storeys up. Leeds is nothing to look at from street level — just a load of same-old, same-old high street shops, but up at roof height there is some pretty beautiful architecture. My favourite so far was the Bank of Ireland building, which had tiles coloured emerald green, and though I couldn't see that one from Russ's office I could certainly see a great deal of the city's fascinating skyline.

Within the office itself, I noticed that some attempt had been made to make the modern room look more homely: there was a slightly neglected potted plant, and some photos of a woman so aesthetically perfect that she could have been the model whose pictures had come with the frames. Seeing me looking at them, Russ muttered, "My wife." There was a hint of pride and affection in his colours that the surly tone of his voice could not disguise, which I found a little endearing even under the circumstances.

Russ turned and marched back the way we had entered and continued down the stairs as I scurried after him once again. At the foot of the stairs, in the entrance hall, the receptionist smiled warmly at me and said, "Did it go okay, then?"

I nodded and (slightly out of breath) told her I'd got the job and would be starting on Monday. She began to congratulate me but then took in Russ's thunderous expression and turned quickly back to her computer.

"Monday. Nine o'clock," he said shortly, and I automatically reached out to shake his hand. He looked at my outstretched arm with something approaching disgust and turned away, heading up the stairs at a pace.

I was deeply conflicted. I wanted the job, of course I did, and I liked and wanted to spend time with Thomas — I wanted to discover how I knew him and how he seemed to know me. But if I had to work with the grumpy Russ, who was apparently determined to treat me as though I was some kind of dangerous criminal unless and until I proved that I wasn't — well, that wasn't going to be easy.

I headed out of the building and walked towards my bus stop, half set on never going back to that law firm if I was going to be treated that way — no job was worth that.

But *Joseph* worked at Democritus's: if I worked there then I would see him all the time ...

Nine o'clock Monday it was, then.

CHAPTER 11

"MATT?" I YELLED UP THE STAIRS when I got home.

"Yeah?" I heard him reply from the bathroom. "I got it!"

There was a pause as I listened to bathwater being displaced, a plug pulled and water cascading down the pipes somewhere in the walls. The bathroom door lock was pulled back and Matt appeared at the top of the stairs with a towel wrapped around his waist.

"What, really?" he asked, then saw my scowl and quickly added, "Well, of course you did. They'd be insane not to hire you. That's great news, well done mate, when do you start?"

I didn't immediately reply. I didn't often see Matt without a top on and although I could appreciate that he was toned and decidedly buff (even though I did so in a purely platonic way), my eyes were drawn not to his abs but to the jagged silvery scar that ran across them. A familiar sadness stirred deep within me, a profound sorrow at the harm I had once caused my best friend. That feeling never seemed to lessen. Correctly interpreting my silence, Matt held up his hand in a silent request for patience before disappearing briefly and reappearing wearing joggers and pulling on a t-shirt.

He padded down the stairs towards me and I remembered that he'd asked me a question; as much to distract myself from all thoughts of scars and dark times as actually to make conversation, I answered, "I start on Monday," and then fell silent again. I had thought that I would launch straight away into the tale about my bizarre interview, but somehow I didn't know how to do that without explaining about Joseph. And I didn't want to tell him about Joseph because I was embarrassed by the strength of my own feelings — I felt like a schoolgirl with a crush.

So instead, as I made us both a cup of tea in the kitchen, I told him about the building, Thomas and the questions he had asked (omitting the whole recurrent-dream-man thing and talk of past lives, again for reasons I wasn't sure about). Of Russ I said nothing, not wanting Matt to worry that I'd be going to work for a psychopath.

Matt smiled broadly, pleased for me. "Great. So the big bucks are gonna start rolling in then?" he smiled. "You can keep me in the manner to which I'd like to become accustomed."

I smiled but it struck me that I hadn't asked how much I'd be paid: I hoped it would be enough to cover the rent, at least. Sitting beside Matt, I rested my head against his strong shoulder; in response, he tipped his head so that it rested against the top of mine and he gave my hand a brief squeeze.

"You sure your old surname won't show up anywhere when you start work? With the Law Society or whatever it is?" he asked quietly.

"There's no reason it should. It'll be fine," I replied, injecting my voice with as much confidence as I could.

"And you'll tell them about Makris so he can't just turn up pretending to be a client?" he asked, his tone more demanding than enquiring.

I murmured an affirmative, though I had no intention of doing so. Leon Makris had shown no sign of trying to find me since his release three months earlier, and I reasoned that I couldn't spend the rest of my life in the shadow of my past. I needed to move on, to trust that a change of surname and relocation to a new city would keep me safe. Plus, I felt that my chances of winning Joseph's heart would be somewhat stymied if he thought a murderous stalker might turn up at some point, or if he knew just how damaged I was.

Matt nodded and then stood to make himself some toast, launching into a tale about something inconsequential but amusing that had happened to him at work the previous day — I sat and listened, grateful for his efforts to keep me out of my own head.

My first day at work would be in a few days' time. That gave me enough time to give notice at the restaurant, fit in a few more shifts and fantasise about working in the same building as Joseph.

CHAPTER 12

September

ON THE MORNING OF MY FIRST day at Democritus's, I woke up not sure I'd been asleep. I reasoned that *of course* I must have been sleeping, since I was now waking, but I felt exhausted. I recalled a good deal of trying to get comfy, and a lot of thoughts flying round about Joseph and my new job, running through many imagined conversations I would have with him, most of which ended with a declaration of undying love and quite a bit of kissing.

I had also pulled up the website photo of Thomas Democritus and had spent time comparing his physical features to those of the man I knew so well from my dream. Looking at a photograph was completely different from looking at him in real life, though, since I couldn't perceive his aura: physically, Thomas and the man in my dream did not look alike other than that they both had that enviably ageless quality. Yet his aura had been identical — I was sure of it — and he had certainly seemed to know me, too.

How was that even possible?

I nipped into the bathroom just ahead of Matt, who grumbled loudly outside the locked door until I had availed myself of all the facilities and strolled back out. Having dressed and breakfasted, I was choosing shoes in the hall (specifically, I was trying to find two that matched) when Matt came downstairs and made himself some toast.

"I thought you were never gonna shut up last night," he complained as I wandered into the kitchen looking for my cup of tea.

I knew that I must have been talking in my sleep and I froze for a moment, wondering what on earth I could have said, particularly bearing in mind the thoughts that had occupied my mind when awake …

I decided to play it cool. "I can't help it if my intellect is not sufficiently challenged during the day and so remains active at night." This was actually a quote from a doctor I'd seen once when I was in my teens after my exasperated mother had taken me to get help for my nocturnal wanderings and ramblings.

He harrumphed quietly and got on with eating his toast, apparently not noticing that he seemed to have left more of it on the table than he had put in his mouth. I thought he'd dropped the subject but then he said, "First, there was a creature in your room, apparently, and you would not shut up whispering about it until I pretended to shoo it out. Then, at about half past two, you came into my room most insistent that you tell me about someone called Joseph, but then wouldn't actually tell me what it was you wanted to say …"

I was glad my face was turned away or he

would have seen the flush of red that seemed to spread from my feet to the top of my head. Pretending not to have heard the implied question about Joseph and fervently hoping I hadn't said anything too embarrassing, I opted for, "You should be grateful. Some people have such boring nights, just lying there asleep for eight hours. How dull."

"Yes. How dull. All that rest and recovery after a hard day at work, I couldn't think of anything worse. Half past two in the morning, Seph," he muttered darkly.

Nightmares, night terrors and sleepwalking were entirely normal for me and had been a feature of my life since I was old enough to walk. Both Matt and I were accustomed to my nightly wanderings or occasional night terrors that involved me waking Matt up in a barely coherent panic. In the early days of us living together, he would leap out of bed on full alert, looking for the source of whatever had frightened me and fully expecting to encounter an intruder. It had only taken three such nights in a row for him to relax slightly about it and eventually it had become such a normal feature of our lives together that he had worked out that if he told me he would 'sort it out in the morning', I would feel as though the threat had been acknowledged and would be dealt with, enabling me to sink back into a deep sleep (often where I stood). Matt would then guide me back to bed, or carry me if required, and would himself return to sleep soon afterwards.

Last night sounded positively tame, all things considered, and I could only assume that it was the mention of Joseph that had made Matt remark upon it at all.

I located my tea, decanted it into a travel mug and hurried into the hall, ignoring his call of, "So are you going to tell me about this Joseph or not then? I'm assuming it's that oddly intense doctor at the hospital?"

Silently cursing his amazing memory for names, I grabbed my coat and shouted through that I'd see him later, before closing the door behind me. There was no way I was getting into any kind of conversation about my crush, not with Matt.

With no other means of transport at my disposal (since we still hadn't found a car that Matt was happy with despite a weekend spent trawling used car dealerships), once again I went for the bus and once again cursed all the lazy people. On arrival at Democritus's I introduced myself properly to the receptionist, whose name was Sabina and whose smile was infectious. She phoned through to someone and told them that I had arrived. As I waited, I politely endured the obligatory small talk (about the weather and the buses in Leeds on this occasion) and managed not to turn it into 'weird talk' (which was my speciality and could have been about absolutely anything other than the mundane), before the phone rang and she excused herself to take the call. I remained standing by her desk, unsure of whether I would be kept waiting long enough to require a seat.

Soon enough, a door opened beside me and Russ Democritus put his head around the corner searching for — as it transpired — me. Seeing his dour expression, my polite smile slipped and I walked over to him feeling like I was making a big mistake. Sabina was concentrating *very* hard on her call.

Russ stood aside rather stiffly to let me walk in front of him and we headed upstairs. I spent the journey wishing he would just take the lead because I couldn't remember exactly which floor his office was on and there was an awkward pause at each landing as I dithered over whether or not we'd arrived.

Four floors was rather a lot of stairs to expect somebody to climb, I thought — especially someone wearing new and uncomfortable shoes — but we finally reached the correct floor and I tried very hard to normalise my breathing as quickly as possible. I wondered grumpily why we hadn't just used the lift — was fitness some kind of prerequisite to fitting in here or was he just scared of enclosed spaces? He seemed to have had no difficulty, but then he was built like an athlete so racing up four floors was probably normal for him.

We passed the secretaries who all returned my smile before returning to their work, and Russ ushered me ahead of him into the office we would be sharing. In honour of my arrival, a second desk had been installed so that the two faced each other with mine closest to the door. Russ gestured that I should sit and pulled my chair out for me. No one had ever pulled a chair out for me before, and it had been a long time since I'd even *seen* anyone do that, either in the real world or in a film. So perhaps unsurprisingly it caught me a bit off guard and there was a bit of a kerfuffle as I thought he was playing a joke on me and trying to make me land on my bum. But no, he was actually being a gentleman and then I felt really stupid.

He bowed his head in acquiescence at my desire to grab the chair from him and then sat in the seat behind his own desk, his back to the window. The door had shut softly behind me and we were alone. He did not seem entirely comfortable about this, nor about the fact that I was between him and the only exit. Pale yellow pulsed in his aura.

It was warm in the office and of course I had just been marched up four flights of stairs, so I slipped my suit jacket off and hung it over the back of my chair.

He drew a file towards him and said without any attempt at standard pleasantries, "So. This is a Democritus file. In it is a correspondence clip, with all the letters filed in date order with the oldest at the back. There's also a slip in each file containing billing information — either copy invoices or legal aid certificates and applications — and one containing all pleadings. Pleadings are what we call all the court applications and orders."

I smiled stiffly, thinking that I didn't know how much of this patronising behaviour I could handle: I'd been working as a trainee for two years and had had plenty of my own files; I knew what pleadings were.

Oblivious to my slightly strained expression, Russ continued, "I like my files to be neat, and the rule here is that if you touch a file it has to be kept in order and if you run a file it has to be possible for anyone else to pick it up, read and understand it without difficulty. Clear?"

I nodded, pulling the file towards me as he showed it to me. The pleadings section was in a clear plastic slip, which slid out of my grip and landed on the floor, spilling its contents. Red in the face, I scrabbled round pulling the papers back together and pushing the file back to him as quickly as I could. I saw him roll his eyes briefly before he continued to tell me about how his diary was managed. He was due in court later that morning and I would be accompanying him, and then he had clients that afternoon whom I could meet if the clients agreed. Wondering how long I would have to have my hand held like this, I forced another stiff smile.

Russ seemed to notice this time. "I appreciate entirely that you have had two years' worth of training and will no doubt have spent considerable time already trailing round after qualified solicitors. Our trainees receive an excellent grounding in several fields and particular support in the one in which they indicate they would like to specialise, or in any area in which they show particular aptitude.

"I hope that you will forgive my saying so, but I do not know that you have had the same level of training from your previous firm. I am sure that they are entirely reputable and above-board, but as they are out of area they are unknown to us here at Democritus's. For that reason — and this is not to cast any doubt on your abilities or intellect, you understand — we have decided that there will be a period of three months in which you will shadow me until I can get a measure of your strengths and any weaknesses. In short, I want to make sure that you haven't been taught that black is white for the last two years before I unleash you on any of this firm's clients. Is that acceptable to you?"

I nodded, feeling rather relieved that there would be an end to the supervision, and at the same time reassured that there would be some supervision while I was settling in.

He continued. "We have two cases in court this morning — an early financial hearing in a divorce, which should be just procedural, and a first appointment for a domestic violence injunction. We're acting for the applicant in the injunction — her husband is violent when in drink, has beaten her, locked her in the bathroom all night and done all manner of things you may choose to read about in her affidavit. However, I fully expect that when we get to court she will be not be there — in which case the court may simply reject the application or adjourn it for a few days to allow her to attend, and I will spend the rest of the morning worrying that she has been murdered overnight — or she will be there asking to withdraw the application on the basis that she loves her husband and he has agreed to seek help for his alcohol and anger issues. *Again*." He said this last part in an exasperated tone I could identify with.

I pulled across the file of the injunction client — more carefully this time — and said, "She's publicly-funded?"

"Yes, she has public funding, which I'm afraid I still call legal aid."

"Do you think she would have come for the injunction if she'd had to pay for it?" I asked.

He raised an eyebrow. "So cynical. Yet astute. No, I don't think she would. But I suppose that is why it is one of the few remaining areas of Family Law to benefit from public funding — for those few people who need and actually *want* protection against those who should love them but choose to hurt them instead. Tell me, is Family Law the field you were particularly interested in as a trainee?"

"It was my training principal's specialism: child protection in particular. Her enthusiasm rather rubbed off on me. I like that there's always a case to argue."

"Very true. I find that my clients are best served by never letting them get their expectations out of line, though. I am realistic with them from the start. That way, they're seldom disappointed and I'm seldom in front of a judge with an unrealistic case based on hysterical instructions. The hardest aspect of it is that you can become quite jaded about society, and people in general. But remember that people are not inevitably bent on revenge or filled with hatred for other human beings; there are good ones out there too."

I nodded as I scanned the file. I knew about hatred and revenge, but my Nana and Matt had taught me about goodness, too.

As though remembering who he was talking to (i.e. someone he didn't apparently *want* to talk to), Russ dropped his gaze and got to his feet, gathering his papers into his bag that looked like a pilot's case. He shrugged on his suit jacket and came around to my side of the desk. After giving the matter a moment's thought, he held the back of my chair and I stood on cue this time as he pulled it out for me, for which I mumbled my thanks. I followed him out of the door as we headed off for court, pulling on my own suit jacket as I did.

As we walked towards the stairs, I noticed with a jolt that the office next door to ours belonged to Joseph, as evidenced by the doorplate. The door was closed, though, so I couldn't see whether he was in or not. Automatically, I reached out my hand and brushed the bronzed lettering of his name as I walked past.

Russ startled me — I hadn't realised he was looking at me — when he said, "My brother is not at work today. I don't expect you will see him here very often, if at all. It is for the best." His words were quiet but firm.

With a glance behind us at the secretarial desks, he pushed through the door to the stairwell and let it drop behind him, in stark contrast to the manners he'd displayed in his office.

I caught the door before it could hit me and followed him into the stairwell. "Best for whom?" I asked stiffly, not appreciating his tone.

"Everyone," he snapped. Startling me slightly, he stopped abruptly and turned to face me. "He is not interested in you," he barked disdainfully.

I felt like I'd been slapped and stopped in my tracks, a fierce blush making my face hot with embarrassment. I saw a green tinge of guilt colour the edges of his anger and impatience.

Turning to continue down the stairs, he muttered, "And even if he *were* interested, you two couldn't be together." As we reached the foot of the stairs and I still had not found the words to respond, he added a final, "We only get involved with others like us. Whatever your history may be with my father, you are not like us."

From the corner of my eye, I saw Sabina trying to look as though she wasn't listening intently as we walked past.

A spark of indignant anger cleared its way through my overall feeling of humiliation and I asked, "What do you mean?"

He shook his head dismissively and strode through the door and onto the street.

I had to practically run to keep up with him. "No, that's not fair. What do you mean, I'm not like you?" I demanded, unsettled and more than a bit annoyed by his attitude — not to mention his apparent belief that my interest in his brother was any of his business.

He shook his head again, lip curled slightly as though in disgust. "Use your imagination."

So I did. Persistently and as irritatingly as I could over the course of the ten-minute journey to court. I was trying to cover my hurt and embarrassment — I could deal with all that later in the privacy of my own home — but part of me also wanted to make things right between us somehow. I didn't know what was wrong, why he disliked me so much, but if we were going to work together than I had to at least try to build some bridges. So I guessed at the Democrituses being everything from "Jehovah's Witnesses?" "Mafia?" "Scientologists?" "Freemasons?" to "Wizards?" "Cage Fighters?" "Drag Artists?" and "Pigeon Fanciers?"

The last few gradually broke through his icy demeanour and, despite himself, a ghost of a smile touched Russ's lips. We had reached the court and he went ahead of me to pass through security. As he did so, he tossed his keys and wallet into the tray to allow him to pass through the scanner. My eyes fell on the Bentley keyring and my heart sank.

After I had been scanned, I caught up with him by the noticeboard to which the court lists were affixed and said quietly, "You have money?"

He looked briefly at me and seemed to be weighing something up. More guilt laced his colours as he said, "Breeding."

Cold mortification swept over me at his words. I was from a council estate in Nottingham; Russ and his family were accomplished lawyers born with silver spoons in their mouths and Joseph probably had some upper-class match lined up (if, I considered with a wave of mild nausea, he wasn't already married or otherwise attached).

In case he hadn't made himself perfectly understood or perhaps to hammer home the point, Russ added, "Our family arranges matches, they do not simply happen at railway stations or hospitals with just anyone." He was trying to sound imperious, I thought, but his words were edged with an odd sort of desperation.

Shame had lodged itself in my gut and tears pricked the corners of my eyes. I blinked them away hurriedly and pretended to study the court list, though the words swam meaninglessly before me.

At his core, Russ was a kind man and perhaps it was this element of his character that made him add a quiet, "I'm sorry."

The damage was done, though. I felt utterly demeaned.

I could barely bring myself to speak to him for the rest of the morning. He had put me in my place.

CHAPTER 13

RUSS'S INJUNCTION CLIENT DID INDEED FAIL to attend, so her case was adjourned until Russ could seek instructions on whether or not she wanted to proceed. The divorce case turned out to be far from procedural, though, and more than a little weird. His client had been keen to explain to us (in graphic detail) the intimacies involved in her relationship with her soon-to-be-ex-husband, and was most insistent that we deal with what she saw as the extremely pressing issue of how they were going to divide their extensive collection of sex toys. After having been so hurt and made to feel so small by Russ earlier, I had rather enjoyed his discomfiture at having to use words such as 'Black Mamba dildo' in front of the cold-eyed judge.

We finished at court just before lunch. As soon as we got outside, Russ called his injunction client on his mobile; he was relieved and annoyed in seemingly equal measure to learn that she was still alive but had decided to give things another go with her husband.

Back at the office, I placed the file I'd been carrying on my desk without so much as looking at Russ, who took his jacket off and placed his bag on the floor as he sat down.

"I want you to dictate a note for today's hearing, and I will do the necessary letters," he said without preamble.

I assumed he wanted me to do the note so that he didn't have to mention sex toys again, but I didn't reply immediately. I had arranged to meet Matt at the café across the street because it was my first day and I'd been too nervous to face the prospect of joining colleagues for lunch in the staffroom. Under normal circumstances, I might have texted Matt to say I'd be a bit late and dictated the note before leaving the office, but after that morning's conversation with Russ, I was more in need than ever of spending time with my friend. I was looking forward to seeing Matt in the same manner as a drowning man looks forward to seeing a lifeboat. Plus, I had recovered from my feelings of shame and inadequacy and was now erring much more towards righteous anger towards my boss, for whom I now had zero respect.

"I'm meeting a friend for lunch. I'll do the note when I get back," I said stiffly and, without waiting for a response, I walked out of the office.

Matt was sitting at a table by the window of the café and gave me a wave as he saw me crossing the road. He stood up when I got to the table; I was so pleased to see him, and in such need of comfort that I hugged him tightly as tears pricked my eyes.

"What's up?" he asked, bemused.

I pulled away, wiping my eyes on the back of my hand and smiling over-brightly as I took a seat opposite him. "Nothing, just missed you."

"Since this morning? Hey, come on, have some tea," he urged, handing me the cup he'd ordered for me, which was still warm.

"Ah tea, is there no situation you cannot improve?" I sighed deeply as I took a sip. I hadn't realised quite how lonely and sad I'd been feeling until I'd seen Matt. My false smile faded quickly. I could sense that more tears were not far away and fought them with determination.

He was on his second cup of coffee. He took a sip and then reached across the table; I placed my hand in his, glad of the unspoken comfort. He knew only too well that if he said anything nice to me, or anything at all, I would get upset and he really didn't like me crying in public because (he had told me before) people would think he'd just broken up with me.

I stared blankly at the menu. I tried to get my emotions back in check and thankfully Matt gave me some time to do so.

"So how was your first morning, sunshine?" he asked after I had managed a smile to indicate that I was ready to resume being social.

I managed another wobbly-chin smile. "Completely insane. It was like an X-rated Monty Python sketch. How about you?"

Studying the menu, he shrugged and said

casually, "Same."

I laughed at his nonchalance, but I knew Matt well enough to know when he didn't want to talk about work so didn't press to see what kind of weird he'd experienced that morning. Likewise, he knew that if I were heard discussing a case outside the office, however anonymised, I wouldn't have a job the next day so thankfully he didn't ask me for details either.

Instead, he said, "So was it just a tough case this morning or is there something wrong with the place you're working?"

I didn't know where to start with that, so I opted for, "I'm sure it'll get better," and then excused myself to go to the counter to order lunch for both of us before returning to sit opposite him.

Thankfully, he chose not to question me further about what had upset me. As we watched the world go by outside, we chatted briefly about this and that: friends of his at work; stuff that was on TV; where we might go on holiday that year. Matt and I always went on holiday together every year, and every year it was an adventure; we'd covered much of Europe, although we'd never made it to Greece because the year we'd planned to go there was the year I was attacked and the associated memories had rather taken the shine off the idea.

Partway through weighing up the pros and cons of going somewhere further afield than Europe this year, I was distracted by seeing Joseph and Russ leave the office and stand talking on the pavement opposite, unaware of my presence in the café.

I stiffened and tried extra hard to focus on what Matt was saying, but it must have been apparent that

I wasn't really paying attention because he peered outside to see what was holding my interest.

"Isn't that whatshisname from the hospital?" he asked with a frown.

I sighed. It was in his nature and training to have remembered Joseph's face from the hospital and I knew that Matt would have remembered the name, too, in view of my night-time ramblings, though he was apparently not inclined to use it. "Yes. He's not a doctor; he's one of the partners. It's his dad's firm."

"Why didn't you say?" he asked with a frown. "I assumed he was a doctor — and you didn't correct me …"

I shrugged my shoulders and kept as close to the truth as I could without mentioning welly-wearing crazies or disappearing guardian angels. "We just got talking at the hospital when I was waiting to be seen, that's all. His mum was the doctor who glued my cut. I didn't know he was a solicitor, or that he worked here when I applied."

He appeared unconvinced, but didn't question it further beyond saying, "That was probably what you were trying to tell me at silly o'clock this morning." Then he asked, "And who's that with him?"

Failing to keep the sourness I felt from creeping into my voice, I replied, "That's his brother Russ, he's kind of my boss, he's head of Family Law. He's a bit of an arse, actually."

He arched his eyebrows. "How so?"

I shrugged again. I didn't know how to explain the context of what he'd said without revealing that I had a ridiculous crush on Joseph. "He's just a bit rude. Gruff. Superior. A snob. An arse."

I glanced out of the window at them but that just made my eyes swim and I had to stare at the ceiling for a moment.

"And?"

"And nothing," I said, glad that our food arrived at that moment. I hoped that it would distract him, but it didn't.

"And something. He made you cry," he said gruffly, biting into his sandwich. Between mouthfuls, he coaxed, "What did he do?"

I looked away and didn't answer. He didn't let me off, seizing on this unusual reaction in me. He put his sandwich back on his plate, started to stand and said darkly, "Listen, if you're not going to tell me then I'm going to assume the worse and I'm going to go over there and kick his arse."

Grabbing his hand and firmly holding him in place at the table I gasped, "No! It's nothing that terrible. It's just …" I sighed resignedly. "I kind of like Joseph. He was kind to me, at the hospital, you know. And Russ said—" I broke off, embarrassed.

"Russ said what?" Matt asked flatly.

"He basically said Joseph doesn't like me and even if he did then he couldn't be with me because his family only hook up with posh tarts," I said sulkily. "I may be paraphrasing," I added in response to his perplexed expression.

"So, is the problem that you're not posh, or that you're not a tart?"

That gave me a smile. "I think it's a combination of those things. They're upper crust and I'm not, obviously, and apparently that matters to the Democrituses."

"So why would you want to be with someone like that anyway?" he asked simply.

I blushed, irritated and embarrassed though I couldn't have explained why.

Seeing that I wasn't going to reply, he pressed, "Come on then, what's so special about this Joseph?"

I squirmed in my seat, red-faced and awkward. "What? He's just nice. He's … friendly. Different."

"Meaning no one else there is friendly?"

Wishing he would drop the subject, I replied somewhat petulantly, "Oh I don't know. He's just … interesting."

Matt looked me squarely in the eye and wouldn't let me avert my gaze. "Seph, I've known you all your life and I've never — - *never* — heard you describe a bloke as interesting before. And I can see how you're looking at him, too." He paused, looking over at where Joseph and his brother stood talking. They seemed to be having a disagreement.

Almost to himself, Matt repeated, "So what's so special?"

I really didn't want to discuss this, not with the morning's humiliation weighing so heavily on my shoulders so I stayed silent.

Undeterred, Matt asked, "Have you seen him much this morning?"

"No. I think he knows I like him and he's avoiding me. It's horrible. As if I'd have a chance anyway; I feel like a cub football team thinking they can take on Man United."

Matt listened to this and tipped his head back and laughed loudly enough to make people turn around and look at him. "That is the most ridiculous thing I've ever heard you say. And that includes that time you asked me whether Israel was within walking distance of Greece. Look, if you 'like' him," he put the word 'like' in inverted commas with his fingers, "that's pretty cool because it means you're getting back to normal. He's, y'know, not horrible to look at, I suppose," he said, saying it in a deeper voice than normal as though to stress his manliness. "And I reckon he does like you, whatever his brother has to say about it, because he's barely taken his eyes off you since he clocked you over here," he added.

I immediately turned to look at Joseph, who swiftly looked away from me.

Hope blossomed within my chest briefly before I stamped it out, afraid that it would hurt too much otherwise. Then I watched as Russ said something to Joseph and glanced in my direction; I had the feeling that they were discussing me and I felt a fresh wave of humiliation at the thought that they were talking about how to deal with their pathetically optimistic employee.

"He's probably just ..." I started, and then couldn't think of any reason why Joseph might be staring at me, so fell silent.

"Look, whatever, if he doesn't want to be with you then he's an idiot. I know blokes who'd give their right arm for you to think they were 'interesting'."

"Ugh, you know I hate that expression. It's ridiculous — who on earth would they give their right arm to? A genie who exchanges wishes for limbs? Like he has a collection or something?"

He smirked and then asked, "So assuming he's not clinically insane, and if he got permission from his Masonic lodge or whatever to ask you out, you'd say yes?"

My pause must have spoken volumes but I nodded slightly anyway. But then I said ruefully, "He's not going to ask me out, Matt, don't be ridiculous. Look at him."

Matt looked across the road again as Russ and Joseph walked around the corner towards the office car park. Their argument had become more animated, judging by the expansive hand gestures and aggressive body language.

"Yeah?" he asked, nonplussed.

I was feeling worse by the moment. "Well, he's gorgeous. And he's a good person. He's not going to ask me out, I'm a headcase. He's a thoroughbred and I'm just some nag headed for the knacker's yard."

Matt knew I wasn't one for false modesty, but I would never consider myself attractive, and certainly not in the same league as Joseph or any of his family. It was hard for me to like myself when I had to look at my scars every day and remember what had been done to me.

"Yep, it's the glue factory for you, I reckon," he agreed with a laugh. Seeing my glum expression, he added, "Look, you're not a 'headcase', that's a horrible thing to say about my best mate. *You're* gorgeous, and lovely. I mean that in a totally platonic way," he added quickly. "And just cos your mum's a cold-hearted, psychotic bitch—"

"Matt! Language …"

"Well, she is, and just because she didn't have a title or whatever, doesn't mean you're not every bit as good as those tossers across the road." He leant forwards a little and insisted, all trace of his new Yorkshire accent gone for a moment, "You're worth ten of them. And if whatshisname doesn't want to be with you because of some archaic, lord-of-the-manor thing, then honestly he's not worth it. You can do better. You deserve someone who thinks you're the sun and the moon, who'll look after you, bring you flowers and chocolates and know just how bloody lucky he is to have you ..." He tailed off, apparently deep in thought as he stared at his hands, picking the quick of his nail absentmindedly.

I was left speechless for a moment, deeply touched by his words and by the sincere tone of his voice. Swallowing hard to get rid of the lump in my throat, I said, "I think you're a tad biased, though."

"The blokes at the station think you're fit," he commented lightly.

My mind flashed to the enormous porter who worked on Matt's floor in the Nottingham police headquarters, whom you could hear from a mile away because of his Darth Vader breathing. And you could usually smell him before you heard him.

"And not just Fat Dave," he added, clearly attuned to my thoughts. "DC Cam, back in Nottingham, was totally in love with you. He didn't sit playing cards with you all week at court because he likes Blackjack."

DC Cam had indeed kept me company (and helped to keep me calm) during Leon Makris's trial. I'd had no family with me, since my mum had refused to attend and poor Nana was too unwell — she'd fallen ill when I'd been attacked; the shock of what had happened to me seemed to turn her frail overnight and her health never fully recovered. During the week-long court case, I'd had to spend a lot of time in a waiting room before I gave evidence; DC Cam had played cards with me and even read to me to keep my mind off what was happening outside our little room. He'd been a good friend, but I hadn't thought of him as anything more than that. I'd known him before the trial, of course: he'd been the policeman who was being beaten up when I'd intervened a year or so earlier.

"Well, I did save his life. That doesn't really count," I said dismissively.

"Of course it counts."

"He never said anything," I commented, remembering the shy man in his twenties with a shock of blond hair.

"Well, no, cos I'd have chopped his balls off, wouldn't I?"

With an exasperated eyebrow raise, I smiled despite myself. Matt and I never really spoke about this kind of thing because it had never come up before. I'd never been interested in a man before. An image of Joseph floated into my mind, his muscular torso encased in a crisp white shirt … I felt the now-familiar thrill inside me and knew that I just had never met the right man until now.

"Are Russ and Joseph both Democrituses, then?" asked Matt, too casually.

I knew immediately why he was asking. "No, please don't go digging! It's irrelevant anyway, nothing's ever going to come of it, he's not interested in me."

"Of course he is — he's not dead. And of course I'm going to check out him and his arsey brother."

We bickered for a while about this, but I knew it was pointless to argue since he'd go and do a background check on Joseph and Russ anyway and make sure they had no connection whatsoever to Leon Makris. I wasn't thrilled by the idea but I understood Matt's protectiveness, which would no doubt seem excessive to anyone who didn't know what we'd been through.

We finished eating our lunch in relative silence; the food tasted like cardboard to me because Russ's words were still causing me a lot of hurt. Too soon, it was time for me to get back to work — I dreaded to think what might be waiting for me after that morning. I gave Matt a peck on the cheek as was our custom and we parted ways outside the café.

Russ was waiting in our office when I returned. His colours were turbulent and he didn't look at me or speak to me for the rest of the day.

CHAPTER 14

THE REST OF MY FIRST WEEK at Democritus's passed fairly uneventfully. I had decided that I would rise above Russ's churlish behaviour: I would act supremely uninterested in him and his family and show him that, even without land and title, I could still act like a lady. So I was coolly polite towards Russ and made not the slightest reference to his brother, keeping any conversation strictly limited to our shared work.

During forays out of our office at lunchtime or on trips to the photocopier, I got to know the names of a few of the secretaries and associate solicitors. I also met the other Democritus partners: Russ's frankly stunning wife, Felicity (Employment Law) and Erica's rather gorgeous husband, Alex (Criminal Law).

Felicity was ridiculously glamorous. Her hair and makeup were immaculate; she was tall, beautiful, tanned and platinum blonde — every bit as flawless as the photos in Russ's office had shown her to be. She was also a pale Blue with enviably attractive trait colours. In short, she was the sort of woman I really wanted to hate because she embodied everything I wanted to be — yet it was incredibly difficult to hate someone so damned *nice*.

Alex was as dark as his wife Erica was fair, and I wouldn't have put them together in a million years — Erica was a real drama queen, from what I'd seen and heard of her round the office (though she never once so much as deigned to make eye contact with me if we happened to meet), and he was quite the opposite: taciturn and introspective and very difficult to gauge even when speaking to him. He was enormous — heavily muscled and even taller than Joseph — and, had I not been able to see that he was inherently a good person, I might have found his size combined with his aloofness more than intimidating. I could only assume that Erica's more forceful personality was the reason why Alex had taken her surname when they'd married.

Alex and Felicity had been polite (or at least not openly hostile) when we had met, and had enquired about how I was settling in and so on, but they had both taken a momentary pause during the opening pleasantries whilst their eyes had widened and their colours had flashed shock and (as I had come to expect) fear. I didn't have a clue what that shock and fear could be about, and it was so fleeting that it seemed like it would be intrusive of me to query it since they recovered themselves so quickly. Their colours told me that they were still wary of me even after they had visibly composed themselves, and (just like Erica) Alex at least had a noticeable tendency to leave the room very soon after I entered it. Felicity made more of an effort to speak to me and ask how I was whenever I saw her around the building, but her colours were always tinged with pale yellow fear.

I was beginning to get quite a complex — why were the Democrituses treating me as though I were a threat? I hadn't seen Thomas since my interview and I had to cling to the memory that he, at least, had greeted me like an old friend, not as a potential enemy. The idea that he could be avoiding me too was deeply upsetting.

I did notice that Russ began to thaw towards me slightly after I'd met Felicity. He still didn't seem pleased to have me sharing his office, but he was at least no longer looking at me like I could be a serial killer, so that was an improvement. I wondered if Felicity had told him to be nicer to me.

I realised very early on that all members of staff in the firm, from the partners to the cleaners, were Blues. I wondered if they had all been drawn to work for Democritus's because they were good people who sought good employers, or whether Democritus's HR department was just really adept at choosing staff.

***

At the end of my first week I was eating lunch at my desk so that I could finish dictating a statement (under Russ's unnervingly attentive supervision) before going to court in the afternoon, when my mobile rang. Since few people ever rang my mobile, it took me a moment to understand that the cheery little sound coming from somewhere near my feet was in fact my phone.

As it was technically my lunch break, I quickly decided to answer the call, ignoring Russ's pointedly raised eyebrows; scrabbling round in my bag, I somehow managed to accept the call before it switched over to voicemail. Glancing semi-apologetically at Russ as I did so, I registered briefly from the screen that it was my sister calling. I held the phone tightly to my ear, immediately assuming that something must be wrong for her to be calling me at all, never mind in the middle of the working day.

"Zoe? Are you okay?"

"Hi, I'm fine, how are you?" she asked.

I paused. This was unexpectedly civil.

"Um, I'm fine, thank you, how are you?"

"Fine, thanks, fine. You?"

"Fine," I repeated.

There was silence, and I wondered what the matter was: Zoe and I were always polite to each other, but we were worlds apart. She rarely called me just for a chat and indeed I hadn't heard from her since moving away from Nottingham; yet it seemed to be taking her a while to work up to her reason for calling. When it was clear she wasn't launching straight into whatever she was phoning for, I asked after her daughter and boyfriend. "Are Ella and Dan okay?"

"Fine, thanks."

"Great."

Another pause. "So you're all fine then?" I asked slowly.

"Yes. And you are too?" Her tone suggested that I'd called her, that she was waiting for me to tell her something or ask her something and I wondered what on earth I'd missed.

"Yes, I'm still fine. Um, hang on a second," I said, and pressed the mute button. Russ was looking at me quizzically, evidently having overheard our rather stilted conversation, so I asked hurriedly, "What's a polite way of asking someone what they want on the phone?"

He snorted out a surprised laugh and said, "Who is it?"

"My sister. She never calls."

He shrugged his shoulders, "I don't know, just ask her if there's anything wrong? Or if there's anything you can help with?"

Nodding, I turned my attention back to the phone and unmuted the call. "Sorry about that. So, is there something wrong?"

"No, why — should there be? Can't I just call my sister?"

Zoe sounded annoyed — I looked up sharply at Russ, who shrugged helplessly.

"Erm, no — er, yes — no, it's just that you don't often phone me," I tried placatingly.

"Well, I have a *life*, you know, and I'm always busy with Ella—" she began, her voice terse.

"Yes, I know," I interrupted quickly, anxious not to alienate myself even further. "I didn't mean anything by it. I mean, I don't phone you either. I just meant, y'know, you don't normally phone just for a chat."

"Oh. I suppose not. It's called being a mum, Persephone, it's a full-time job."

Ah, yes, there it was, the quick slap in the face. This was the Zoe I knew. I took a deep breath and bit back a retort, though I muttered, "Sephy," mutinously under my breath.

We'd never been close, perhaps because I envied her so much — she'd effortlessly garnered the love of our mother and had always been given the best of everything whilst I'd got the dregs of whatever was left. I could see that she was a nice enough person — she was a very Blue shade of Purple, and she was a good mother to my niece, Ella — but I couldn't see far past the fact that she never looked out for me, never once spoke up for her little sister.

She went on, "Anyway, I'm calling you about the wedding."

"Wedding?" I asked blankly.

"Yes. The wedding. The. Wedding."

"You're getting married?" I guessed, "To Dan?" Hearing her sigh of annoyance I hurriedly pressed on, hoping to avoid a scene and genuinely pleased for her, "That's great news! When's the big day?"

There was a silence just long enough for her to draw breath before she snapped, "*News*? For God's sake, I know you're hopeless but this is going too far!"

The conversation had taken an odd turn. "What?" I asked, nonplussed.

Clearly irritated, she said impatiently, "For crying out loud, it's only three months away and I need to know final numbers so that I can plan the seating. Are you coming or not? And if you're coming, are you bringing Matt or anyone with you, and are you having lamb or the vegetable risotto?"

"I — I don't know," I began, flicking over my

desk calendar in blind panic at being asked to commit to so many things before I'd really processed the fact that she and Dan were finally getting married. "Probably not the lamb though, Zoe, I've been a vegetarian since I was five," I murmured.

My mind was flitting back and forth as I tried very hard to remember if she'd ever told me about this before. Had I ever had an invitation? It was feasible — if I'd opened it when I was distracted, I might just have put it to one side and forgotten about it. The more I thought about it, though, the less likely this seemed — surely I'd have remembered something as potentially traumatic as a family wedding?

She let out a sigh of frustration. "Jesus Christ, Persephone, there's still so much to organise and *you're not helping*. Come on, fifteenth of December, two o'clock? Honestly, I'm having to do everything here, all Dan has to do is get his suit and one for his best man, and he'll probably get *that* wrong."

"*Sephy*," I muttered again. She knew I hated my full name. I could feel my throat getting tight with emotion. I found the date and it was clear so I told her I'd be able to come and would bring Matt, knowing I couldn't face it without him and hoping he wouldn't be too annoyed at having to go with me.

There was another pause and I could hear a pen scratching on paper at her end of the line.

To fill the silence more than to know the answer, I asked tentatively, "Did you send the invitations out a while ago?"

"Yes, '*a while ago*', I've been planning this for nearly a year!" she said in a huff.

"Oh," I said. "Well, I've had quite a busy year

myself, really, what with moving, and losing Nana and everything."

"Oh, so did you lose the invitation?" she demanded.

"No, I didn't get it," I said firmly, not liking her assumption that I was totally disorganised (though, to be fair, that was the kind of thing I might do). "When exactly did you send it? Was it before we moved?"

"What do you mean, you didn't get it? It was after you moved — Mum had to email it because you wouldn't give us your new address," she said somewhat bitterly.

"Well, I didn't get it. I think even I would have managed to text you with a reply if I had."

There was silence for a moment and I could tell she was thinking. I could hear her flicking through some papers. I tried very hard to convince myself that my invitation had been lost in the system somewhere, rather than simply never sent.

I asked quietly, wanting her to at least consider the possibility that I wasn't being deliberately difficult, "Mum definitely sent it, then?"

Her silence told me what I needed to know. I could see from the corner of my eye that Russ had stopped working on his computer and was looking at me; I avoided eye contact and tried to keep the hurt out of my voice as I swallowed the familiar ball of rejection and hurt that rose in it whenever my mum made an appearance in my life. "So who's your maid of honour?" I asked as brightly as I could.

Another pause. "Um, actually, I asked Jill, from work. I didn't think you'd mind. It's just easier with her being down here, you know, for dress fittings and things. You could be a bridesmaid, if you wanted, I suppose. Oh, but then you'd need a dress to match Ella's ... You could do a reading or something if you wanted?"

I replied automatically, "No, no, that's fine. I don't really like that kind of thing anyway. Do what's good for you, it's your day."

Russ had crossed his arms over his chest and I steadfastly kept my gaze on the calendar in front of me.

Zoe recovered remarkably quickly from being wrong-footed and was naturally unapologetic for telling me off for not replying to an invitation I had clearly never received.

With a dismissive sniff, she conceded, "Well maybe the invitation's in your spam folder or something. Whatever, I don't want it happening again. Give me your address so I can send you a paper copy as well and then there'll be no more excuses. I can send you the wedding list, though I think most of the cheaper items have already been bought."

I did not immediately reply, so she snapped, "Oh for heaven's sake, Persephone, it's not like mum or I are going to send your address to Leon bloody Makris. Even mum doesn't hate you *that* much."

"Sephy," I corrected automatically, the sound of my attacker's name bringing a sour taste to my mouth.

To avoid further argument, with a silent apology to Nana and Matt I read out my address for her to copy down; she hung up with the briefest of farewells.

I glanced at Russ, who raised an eyebrow

questioningly but I merely shook my head by way of reply. Instead, I dialled Matt's mobile, leaving a message for him to give me a ring when he had a minute. My hands were shaking a little and I didn't know if that was from anger or hurt.

I rewound the Dictaphone and listened to the last couple of paragraphs of the statement I'd been preparing, trying to focus my attention back on my work, but my traitorous thoughts kept returning to the fact that apparently my mum had tried to prevent me from attending my sister's wedding, and my sister was intent on blaming me for it. Sometimes it was very difficult to ignore the hurt I felt at their repeated rejections and deliberate attempts to distance me from the family; I had to swallow several times to rid myself of the rather painful lump that had formed in my throat.

On the periphery of my attention, I saw Russ reach into his desk drawer and pull out a bar of chocolate, which he slid silently towards me across the desk. I looked up at him, deeply touched, but his attention was focussed firmly on the file of papers in front of him again, forbidding conversation. I was rather glad of that, too.

CHAPTER 15

WHAT WITH THE CALL FROM ZOE and a fraught afternoon in court, by the time I got home from work I was shattered. Matt had called me and sounded less than thrilled by the idea of having to go to a family wedding with me — he'd never liked my mum and had detested her ever since she'd thrown me out straight after Makris's trial— but he understood that I (sort of) wanted to attend, if only to spend a bit of time with my niece. He'd agreed to accompany me, and we'd promised each other we'd on our best behaviour on the day.

He was on a late shift so wouldn't be home until after midnight; I couldn't be bothered to cook anything substantial so ate beans on toast with the plate on my lap in front of the TV. As the early evening wore on, it became harder and harder to keep my eyes open and eventually I gave in to the prospect of 'resting my eyes' for a little bit and snuggled down on the sofa with a blanket pulled over me, warm and comfortable.

I did not sleep soundly though. For one thing, my recurrent dream changed. Given that it had remained unaltered for the best part of twenty-four years, this was notable in itself. But the manner in which it changed was deeply unsettling.

I still ran through the woods, heavily pregnant; I was still pushed into the water; I still drowned and watched my baby being removed from my body. This time, though, there was something slightly off about the colours: normally the sun was blindingly bright, sparkling off the sea that would ultimately drown me; this time, it appeared to be dusk and all the colours were muted. The man I now thought of as Thomas was not there. The three Red men surrounded my body, as before, but in Thomas's place was a face I knew all too well. Leon Makris, the man who had attacked me when I was seventeen, was now holding my baby as he lifted her from my gaping body. He growled my name, my perspective shifted and I saw him as though I were the baby being held in his arms.

He bared his teeth in a menacing smile and said in the gravelly voice that would haunt me forever, "*There* you are."

I jolted awake, sweat drenching my body and dampening the blanket that had become tangled around my legs. My breathing was erratic and I drew in great heaving breaths as though I had been suffocating.

Night had fallen properly as I'd slept and the living room was in darkness as I lay panting with residual fear. I squinted at my watch and registered that it was just past ten o'clock. Matt wouldn't be home for at least a couple of hours, and without his calming presence it was sure to take me longer than usual to relax after my nightmare.

It took me a minute or two to process the fact that the TV had been turned off.

Cold fear trickled through me. Adrenaline still coursing through my veins from my nightmare, I scrambled up clumsily to turn on the lamp beside the sofa. I clicked the switch, but nothing happened. The room remained dark.

I forced myself to walk calmly to the doorway and then up the stairs to Matt's room; I was trying to assume that he had come home early whilst I'd been asleep and turned off the TV, but I needed to see him with my own eyes before I could relax in the knowledge that there was no one in the house but us.

Pushing open his door, I called softly, "Matt?" but there was no answer. I clicked on his light and, blinking against the sudden brightness, immediately saw that his room was empty, his bed still made from the morning.

The vivid quality of my dream had been beginning to fade and my heart rate had been levelling off; Matt's absence combined with the fact that the TV had been turned off, though, brought an icy chill to my blood and my fear resurfaced. Forcing myself to think rationally, I reasoned that perhaps a bulb had blown, tripping the circuit breakers and affecting the downstairs sockets. That would explain why the TV and lamp in the living room were off but Matt's light was working. Yes, that would be all it was, I told myself firmly, heading back downstairs to check the fuse box under the stairs.

I descended the stairs swiftly, my breath shallow and fast, panic not far enough away. As I passed the doorway to the living room, I caught sight of a movement in there and froze in place, eyes wide open as I tried to make out what I'd seen. All I could hear was the sound of my own breathing, and the pounding of blood in my ears; nothing moved. I forced myself to move on through the darkened hallway — and collided with someone standing right in front of me.

I yelled and staggered backwards towards my front door; the man moved slowly and deliberately towards me, his face becoming clear as he stepped out of the gloom.

Leon Makris was not in my dream: he was in my home.

I didn't want to turn my back on him but needed to get out of there — I flinched as I backed into the door and reached behind me to try to undo the various locks that were supposed to have kept me safe.

Realising that my hands were shaking too much, I remembered the alarm button beside the door and lunged for it but the movement spurred Makris into action. With lightning-fast reflexes, he grabbed my wrist and gripped it tightly, twisting it behind my back in a fluid movement and causing me to cry out in pain as much as in fear.

But Matt had not been teaching me self-defence since I was seventeen for nothing. I swept behind me with my foot and kicked the side of Makris's knee hard enough to buckle it and cause him to swear loudly; his grip slackened just enough for me to bend my elbow slightly so that I could turn and face him, relieving the searing pain in my shoulder joint.

Pulling away, using my bodyweight to tug myself out of his grip, I scratched and punched and fought hard to escape, no plan in my mind except to get away from him. By jabbing a thumb directly into one of his eyes, I managed to slide my arm free from his grip and started to run for the kitchen, my mind's eye fixed on the part of the wall where I knew there to be another alarm point.

As though I were still dreaming, Makris appeared directly in my path — he didn't run past me, he simply appeared as though out of thin air and I had to skid to a halt to avoid colliding with him. He was sneering, as if he knew I had no realistic chance of getting away, and I spun around, running in a blind panic back towards the living room and the alarm by the front door, my breathing harsh and cold terror in my belly.

He appeared in front of me once more and I skidded along the polished wooden hall floor as I attempted to change direction again. I slipped and fell to one knee as I turned, pushing myself up using the small hall table as leverage — it tipped and I fell back down, landing within easy reach of Makris's extended arm. His hand closed tightly on my arm once more and my scream rent the air as I tried again to pull out of his iron grip, kicking out with my foot, fighting to get free.

His hand squeezed tighter still and I screamed out, "Let go!"

With a snarl, he pushed me backwards and I fell against the wall, hitting my head — and then someone was hammering on the front door, startling both of us. In a split second, Makris was gone. Looking around wildly, my breath rasping and eyes wide, my blood filled with adrenaline, I couldn't see him anywhere — I appeared to be completely alone.

I felt a momentary spike of fear as the loud banging resumed, a man's voice outside loudly demanding that I open the door. Assuming that whoever was outside posed less of a threat than Makris did, and praying it was a concerned (and muscular) neighbour, I hurried towards the door.

With my hands shaking so badly, it was a struggle to undo the locks. I stopped short as I realised that Makris's abrupt and complete disappearance seemed rather unlikely — in which case, perhaps his presence in my house had actually been a nightmare rather than reality? My hands froze in front of me and I took a step back from the door. The pounding resumed, making me jump so violently that I bit my tongue. Fear snaked down my back as I realised that if Makris hadn't been inside my house, it could feasibly be him trying to break down my door with his fists right at that moment.

I took a deep breath and steeled myself to look through the security peephole, flinching every time the man on the other side banged on the heavy wood of the door. With a huge exhalation of breath I hadn't realised I'd been holding, I saw that it was Joseph on my doorstep, looking every bit as wired and terrified as I felt.

With a cry of relief, I managed to unlock the door and swung it open.

"Sephy, what's wrong? What happened?" he demanded, his own breathing erratic.

I was in his arms before I had time to draw breath.

He held me tightly and murmured, "You're

safe, I'm here," into my hair as I clutched him, shaking uncontrollably.

It had been the most realistic, most terrifying dream I had ever experienced and my mind was so focussed on reliving it and trying to reassure myself that it *had* just been a dream that it didn't immediately occur to me to ask him how he had come to be on my doorstep at such a late hour.

A few moments of being held by Joseph, breathing in his scent and feeling his firm body against mine was enough to calm my fear and I straightened out of his embrace, though his hands still held my arms as though to steady me. His shirt was very damp from the rain outside, and his hair was stuck in little snakes across his forehead, rivulets of water dripping down his face and over his stubble. I took in how tired he looked; dark shadows haunted his eyes and his colours spoke of a deep-seated sadness that hadn't been there when I'd last seen him outside the office with Russ, or at any time before then. Beneath that, though, his aura was still by far the most beautiful I'd ever seen and I was transfixed by it for a long moment.

My fear had ebbed and something altogether different was ignited. I felt both serenely calm and full of desire at the same time and my cheeks flushed as I pulled away from him, certain that my physical need for him must be written all over my face. If it was, he did not comment and I focussed very hard on trying to stay in the present and above all *not* look at his lips. I realised that he was still looking at me with fear in his eyes, though that was now coupled with a fierce protectiveness that served to make me feel safe and even more attracted to him.

"I had a bad dream," I stammered, my voice sounding weak and shaky.

"A bad *dream*?" he asked, confounded, as he took in my general state of distress and looked past me at the overturned table in the hall.

I mumbled about having very realistic dreams, night terrors and sleepwalking, mortified that he had seen me in such a vulnerable and — let's face it — unstable state of mind. Still unnerved, I kept my hand on his chest where it had been since I had clung to him and twisted round to double-check that the hall was otherwise deserted, listening intently for any sounds that might hint that Makris may actually be there.

"Are you sure you are alone?" he asked urgently, stepping round me to place himself between me and anyone who might feasibly be lurking in my home uninvited.

"I — I think so. I *think* it was a dream," I replied faintly, utterly unsure.

Without another word, he strode past me and looked in the lounge before checking the kitchen and understairs cupboard; satisfied that they were empty, he jogged upstairs and I heard him open the various doors up there before returning to my side, apparently satisfied that we were indeed alone.

Reassured that it had been a dream after all, I became more able to focus on reality. "What are you doing here?" I asked, momentarily dazed by how close we were; I took a chaste step backwards.

He glanced behind me at the door and a flash of guilt marred his colours. "I heard you scream. I — I was worried about you."

I was forcefully reminded of the time he had

shown up in A&E after I'd injured my eye at the police station. There had been no solid reason for him to have been there, either.

"But it's nearly half past ten, why were you close enough to hear me?" I asked.

His colours looked panicked for a brief moment, though his facial expression remained carefully controlled. "Oh. I was working late. My brother asked me to call round on my way home from the office as he thought you might have a file he needs to work on over the weekend."

I looked at him blankly and told him that I didn't keep files at home.

"He must have been mistaken, then," he mumbled, though he had the decency to look embarrassed. I waited for a few moments but whatever the truth of why he had come to my home so late at night he wasn't about to reveal it.

"May I come in for a bit?" he asked. "To sit with you awhile, I mean?"

Glad of his company (whatever had motivated it) I smiled, relief still predominant in my emotions. I gestured him through to the kitchen, absently rubbing my arm where Makris had grabbed me in my dream. Still unsettled by my nightmare and the memories it had unleashed, I stayed close to him as we walked through my hallway; he seemed to sense my nervousness and wordlessly took my hand.

CHAPTER 16

JOSEPH WAS IN MY HOUSE, SITTING beside me at the kitchen table. He had made me some sugary tea and settled in the chair next to mine; he seemed intent on staying for a while, at least. Under other circumstances, I would have felt giddy, excited, nervous … as it was, I was too distracted and still too shaken by my ridiculously vivid dream to really appreciate it.

For a while, he kept the conversation light and flowing, no doubt to give me time to calm down. I learnt that he was slightly older than I'd assumed at twenty-eight, a year younger than Matt, and that he lived at home with his family: I was taken aback slightly by that fact, since he was presumably wealthy enough as a solicitor to be able to afford his own place. I wondered if perhaps he had moved back home after a failed marriage — the more I thought about it, the more I realised how little I really knew about him.

Keen to keep my mind away from darker,

scarier thoughts, I asked more about his life and his past, and focussed hard on his voice and answers. I wanted — *needed* — to be distracted.

"So, do all of you live together, not just you and your parents?"

"All of us. When one of us has married, the spouse has moved in too. It sounds strange, I know, but if you could see where we live you'd understand. We each have our own space, so we have privacy, but we prefer to remain close."

"Do you … do you have a spouse, then?" I asked, using the term he had chosen.

He gave a short laugh and said with a smile I couldn't quite decipher, "No, but I remain optimistic."

"Oh, so do you have a girlfriend?" I asked, blushing deeply at the fact that the words had left my mouth — there could surely be only one reason I'd want to know the answer to that question. I was suddenly nervous about how he would answer, given his brother's insistence that his family associated only with others 'like them'.

"No, but again, I remain optimistic," he laughed softly.

I frowned slightly, unsure of how to interpret this and feeling faintly ill at the idea of his parents pairing him up with some faceless 'posh tart'. I pressed on in an effort to sound politely interested. "So there's, what, seven of you living together? Must be some house."

"It's called The Heights, and for good reason — we're up on Malham Moor in the Dales, and when I look out of my bedroom window, it feels like I'm on top of the world: I can see for miles. You should come and see it some time," he said, although he cut the very end of his sentence short as if catching himself. I saw him biting his lip, a non-verbal tic that people often engage in involuntarily when they've said too much.

To spare him discomfort, and to keep him talking about anything and everything that didn't involve psychotic lunatics from my past, I asked, "Do you really commute from the Dales every day?"

He nodded, but again there was something evasive about his colours and this time he struggled to maintain eye contact. Had this been anyone else, I might have been suspicious, but as it was Joseph I was merely intrigued. Wanting him to keep talking and hoping he would eventually trust me with the truth, I asked, "Have you always lived in Yorkshire? You don't have much of an accent."

He chuckled. "I'll 'ave you know, I'm Yorkshire born and bred," he said with a broad Yorkshire accent that was nothing like his usual cut-glass, received pronunciation.

"That was good! Matt's been working on his accent; says he wants to blend in 'wit locals'. I can't understand him half the time anymore."

"You don't have much of an accent either. Yet my father tells me that you lived in Nottingham before you came here?"

I wasn't sure how I felt about him and his father discussing me — was it a good thing, or had they been talking about me in the context of my silly crush? I nodded a brief affirmative, not wanting to discuss my childhood if at all possible — I wanted Joseph to like me, after all, even if that seemed unlikely.

When he waited for me to go on, I kept my reply within safe boundaries. "I suppose it's because Matt doesn't have an accent, really. His family all went to university, so maybe they lost their accents there and Matt never picked one up. He was the person I spoke to most, growing up, so I suppose I just copied how he sounded. Plus, Nana was pretty hard of hearing, so I was quite conscious of speaking clearly to her so she could understand me."

He nodded sadly, "I was sorry to hear that she died. It must have been a difficult year for you, moving to a new house and losing a mother-figure at the same time."

I couldn't get any words out of my suddenly tight throat, so nodded instead.

Her death had been very sudden, and I still hadn't properly grieved for her or accepted that she was truly gone. I didn't even go to her funeral: before we'd left Nottingham, she had begged me not to return to the area in case Makris found me. Perhaps it was this lack of closure that made me struggle so much with the concept of never seeing her again. I didn't believe in an afterlife, yet I also couldn't believe that she was gone forever.

Sparing me from having to speak, Joseph said gently, "I'm glad you had someone who was good to you."

A comfortable silence fell and I took the time to recover my equilibrium.

At length, I decided that the time had come to tackle the elephant in the room. "I'm sorry about tonight. It's pretty embarrassing to be found by my boss screaming at nothing."

He shook his head dismissively, "It did not

look like nothing. You were genuinely afraid, I could feel— I mean, I could practically feel your fear when you opened the door."

I shrugged, trying not to dwell on it. "I do that quite a lot. Have night terrors, I mean. It's never quite like that, though, it felt …" I tailed off. It had felt very real. I rubbed again at the area of my arm where Makris had grabbed it, trying to rid myself of the feel of his touch. I shrugged again, unsure of how to continue.

Joseph asked gently, "What was it about?"

It was my turn to be unable to make decent eye contact. I didn't want to lie, but I didn't want to tell him about Makris and how badly he had affected my life, physically and emotionally. I opted to repeat the half-truth I had given his dad at my interview. "A man who mugged me a few years ago. He was … it was a scary dream."

He frowned unhappily. "My father told me about that, too. I imagine an experience like that will stay with you for a long time."

I felt uneasy. I didn't want to reveal any more about that horrible period than I already had; I still clung vainly to the hope that one day Joseph might get over whatever issue his family had with me and might then want to get to know me better. That slim hope would surely be dashed if he knew the truth.

I shrugged, aiming for 'nonchalant'. "It wasn't a big deal, it was only a random mugging, back when I was seventeen, but I didn't handle it very well at the time and it took me a long time to get back on my feet."

Joseph was quiet. I risked a glance at him; his eyes were downcast and his colours were an odd mixture — I could see sympathy, but I could also see anger, though I didn't know what he was angry about and I worried that I was keeping him from doing something more important.

"You don't need to stay, you know, it's been kind of you but I'm sure Matt will be home soon," I told him, hoping that he would ignore me.

He remained silent and seemed not to be listening, so I waited. Gradually he seemed to refocus and absorb what I had said. He lifted his gaze to my face and said, "There is nowhere I would rather be. I would like to stay if you will allow it."

I smiled and Joseph didn't speak, but silently reached across the table and held my hand steady in his.

"What prompted you to move from Nottingham when you did?"

This seemed safe enough to answer, so I replied, "We moved the week before the mugger was released from prison. Nana wanted to know I was somewhere safe."

Nana was horrified at the thought that Makris might hurt me again and had been adamant that Matt and I should move away; she'd badgered us constantly and had practically yelled at Matt when he'd tried to insist that we stay in Nottingham to be near her. Ultimately, Nana got her way; we moved a week before Makris was released.

"Why Leeds?"

I shrugged. "Nana. I still don't know why, but she was adamant and honestly there was just no arguing with her when she'd made her mind up about something … So we came here. I thought that maybe we'd be able to visit her, when things calmed down a bit, but …" I left my sentence unfinished; Nana had died ten days later, and I felt another swell of guilt at the fact that I hadn't been there.

"Quite an upheaval for you," he commented.

I nodded. "It was hard leaving Nana. But in terms of timing it worked well because my Training Contract had finished anyway so it wasn't like I was having to leave a job, and Matt applied for a transfer and was given one very quickly. He sorted me out with the local police in Leeds, getting me CCTV and alarms and things fitted," I gestured vaguely towards the sensors in the corners of the room and towards the hallway and the alarm pad I had tried to reach earlier (very relieved I hadn't actually set it off, as I'd have had to explain to a carload of policemen why I was screaming at nothing …), "and he's got people in Nottingham Probation Service keeping tabs on my attacker so we'd know if he upped sticks and came looking for me."

He frowned. "If it was random, why would he come looking for you? Do you think that he would seek revenge for his incarceration?"

I flushed, feeling caught out by my lie and wishing I'd just kept to the basics. I sighed, feeling suddenly tired and world-weary. I had spent so much time in therapy, fought so hard to put my attack in my past, and now I'd had a horrible night terror, the aftermath of which had been witnessed by the only man I'd ever fancied, and said more than I should have.

"I don't know. Probably not," I murmured, frantically trying to think of a way to change the topic of conversation.

He frowned deeper and sat back in his seat

slightly. "He spent, what, seven years in custody for a *mugging*?"

Very glad that he could not see the lie in my aura, I managed to stammer, "He was wanted for a lot of other offences."

He nodded slowly. Gazing intensely into my eyes, he asked, "Do you feel safe here?"

I hesitated. No, I did not. My nerves had calmed somewhat, but already I knew that after such a vivid dream I would once again be looking over my shoulder and I wondered if I would ever feel safe. It was then that it dawned on me, though, that in fact I *had* felt safe ever since Joseph had taken me into his arms. Hc was still awaiting my response so, with a glance at his hand which held mine so securely, I said truthfully, "I feel safe now."

Joseph seemed miles away for a moment, anxiety creasing his brow. "The seven years since you were attacked is no time at all, a heartbeat. No wonder you are still on edge occasionally. You've had to move away from your family; you must have been very afraid of him," he said, and I could see his colours morphing away from anger and toward concern and something indefinable. For a moment I was too distracted by the beauty radiating from him that I forgot to answer and, noticing my hesitation, he raised his head and held my gaze properly for the first time since we'd begun the discussion.

I was taken aback by the intensity in his eyes, and for a moment it was as though there was only the two of us in the whole world: the background sounds had gone; the traffic outside … rain against the windows … all disappeared, and in their place — only him.

I forced myself to look aside. He continued to wait for me to reply, which I did with uncharacteristic frankness that surprised me. "I think about it every time it's dark, or every time it rains. Certain smells — cigarettes, peppermint chewing gum — remind me of what happened to me. I sleep with the light on even though I know Matt's in the next room …"

I broke off, unsure of whether to go on. I risked a glance at his colours and was relieved to see no change.

His silence and the feel of his hand on mine made me go on, my words stumbling over themselves in their hurry to be out and done. "You're right, I was very frightened of him. I had to see a psychotherapist. I told her I felt like I'd been in a bad car accident and the doctors at A&E had patched me up and got me back on my feet, but that I still had a big piece of glass stuck in me and it hurt every time something brushed against it." I'd been quietly pleased with this analogy. "She diagnosed Post-Traumatic Stress Disorder and depression; I had a lot of talking therapy, and I was on tablets for a long time for the depression. But I'm still frightened of him." Not daring to look at him, I added, "And that dream was so hard to differentiate from reality, I'm also frightened that I'm going mad again."

What had made me be so open about something I was desperately ashamed of, I had no idea. Yet I was also annoyed at myself for feeling ashamed in the first place: I always battled with myself over this; if I'd had cancer and needed treatment, I wouldn't feel this way about telling people, so why was I so ashamed of having treatment for this? But it didn't change the fact that I did, and my cheeks burned.

"Mad is a horrible word," Joseph said dismissively. "If you had walked away from an attack at such a young age without any emotional side effects, you wouldn't be — well, you wouldn't be human."

His words struck so deep into the centre of my thoughts and feelings about it that an errant tear spilled out over my cheek. I dipped my head, embarrassed to let him see me cry. He reached up and stroked it away with his thumb before drawing his chair closer to mine and bringing me against his chest — a swimmy, floaty feeling overcame me and I was immediately not just at ease but utterly content, the hug doing more to reassure me than even his kind words.

When I was sure I had myself back under control, I pulled away to sit straight and said quietly, "Thank you," which seemed inadequate. My hands were still in his and I was happy for them to remain there.

He shook his head slightly in dismissal of my thanks.

After a pause, he said, "My brother told me today that you had a call from your sister — could it be that you were reminded of that time in your life by her call? Perhaps that is what brought about your night terror?"

I thought about this. It was true that the last time I'd had any kind of relationship with my sister had been shortly before my attack. And I had given her my address today — that was no doubt what had triggered this episode; some underlying sense of guilt about giving out such sensitive information against Matt's and Nana's express wishes. That understanding, an explanation of why it had been so vivid and *different,* made me feel a little calmer. Joseph's words brought back those of his brother, though, and I felt a sour taste in my mouth as I wondered why he was being so nice to me. Was I a 'bit of rough' for him to take advantage of? Was that why he had come round so late?

I moved back in my chair slightly, releasing my hands from his and turning away from him a little to give myself some distance — it really was very difficult to remain detached and cynical when I was looking at Joseph because my body did not seem to share my brain's opinion that I should keep away from him.

"Maybe," I murmured in answer. More firmly, I added, "You should get going, I think. I'm not sure your family would be very happy that you're here with me at this hour."

Understanding dawned on his face and he reached across the table as though to grasp my hand in his once more — but it was so swift and unexpected that I flinched at the sudden movement. He checked himself and looked crushed that he had inadvertently startled me. Quietly, he said, "You need never fear me, Sephy."

I realised that I already knew that. Yet I remained still, fearful of rejection and hurt further down the road if I were just a plaything for him, or a way of rebelling against his family.

Looking fervently into my eyes, he went on, "My brother has told you something that is not true. There is no class barrier between us, nothing like that. I do not consider you beneath me and nor does my family. I am angry with my brother for misleading you that way. His intentions were good, but badly misplaced."

He was telling the truth, according to his colours, which gave me pause. "Then why does Russ think that I shouldn't have anything to do with you? Why have you been avoiding me at work?"

He dropped his head forward, his eyes closed for a moment. He sounded so wretched when he spoke that it threatened to bring fresh tears to my eyes. "Because I like you. More than I should."

I didn't speak, didn't want to break the spell. In silent answer, I reached to close the distance between our hands and felt myself relax at the warmth of his touch. I knew, though, from the swell of unhappy colours, that there was going to be a 'but'.

"But," he said (and I rolled my eyes inwardly), "even if you were to feel the same way about me, I would not be permitted to be with you."

Gently withdrawing my hands from his once more, I sat straighter and cursed myself for allowing my hopes to be raised and then dashed. "Why not?"

He let out a frustrated sigh. "I can't even tell you, that's part of it."

"Well, that's hardly fair," I complained.

He raised his hands briefly in acknowledgement. "I know," he sighed, equally exasperated.

Whatever the reason was, I was fairly sure that he was telling the truth as far as he could and that he seemed as annoyed as I was about it all. That was oddly cheering, and my traitorous heart kept leaping every time I replayed his words. He *liked* me —

probably not as much as I liked him but still, that was a step in the right direction.

A car engine on the road outside caught my attention and I recognised the slow rumble of Matt's Subaru. I stood reluctantly, knowing that our time alone together was nearly at an end and Joseph mirrored me with a glance towards the front door.

He suddenly looked nervous and on edge; taking a deep breath, he said, "It is important that I tell you something — I *must* tell you, but I'm afraid you'll ..." He broke off, clearly agitated and looking about as though the right words would magically appear before him. His usual self-assurance was gone and his words became barely coherent as he went on hurriedly, "My name ... if ever you need to call me, if ever you need me, if you're scared or hurt, or *anything*. My *name*—" He paused again and this time he didn't seem able to continue.

I waited for him to go on but instead he reached tentatively forwards and drew me into what could have been a polite, friendly hug but which felt to me far more intimate. One of his hands wound its way into the hair at the nape of my neck and I relaxed into his chest. A warm flame of hope reignited inside me as I allowed my mind to wander and dwell on the idea that he might want me as much as I wanted him ...

Then I heard him whisper into my hair, "My name is Zephyrus. Please don't use it unless ... unless you need me. Just please remember: Zephyrus."

CHAPTER 17

I PULLED OUT OF HIS ARMS and looked searchingly at him. It was rather sweet that he'd trusted me with his real name — I assumed he preferred Joseph because it was more mainstream and less likely to get him tormented at school, in the same way that I preferred Sephy to *Persephone*. I didn't quite understand, though, why he seemed so stressed at having done so.

I was prevented from asking further about it by the sound of footsteps running up the path to the front door.

"*Seph!*" Matt roared as he reached the door, pushing it aside as he charged through into the hall, looking at once terrified and furious.

I hurried into the hallway to meet him, wondering what was so urgent, and realised immediately what the problem was — in my hurry to escort Joseph into the house, I had entirely forgotten to close the door behind us. It was so out of character for me that it was no wonder Matt had panicked at the sight of the open door when he'd arrived home.

Gesturing behind himself, he shouted, "*Door,*

Seph, *door*! Close it, lock it! What's the bloody point having an alarm straight through to the police if you leave the door wide open?"

I hurriedly apologised and explained that I'd had a bad dream and that Joseph had interrupted an episode of sleepwalking by knocking on the door. At that point I became aware of Joseph standing behind me because Matt was staring daggers at him. Addressing Matt, Joseph introduced himself briefly, unnecessarily reminding Matt that they had met briefly at the hospital and assuring him that nobody else had entered the house.

Matt didn't speak immediately. He looked from Joseph towards where we had been standing together in the kitchen, then back at me. Perhaps he had seen our embrace, perhaps he could sense something in the air between us. Speaking to me, he said, "What time was this?"

"About quarter past, half past ten?" I replied, wondering why that was relevant.

"This is one of the tossers who made you cry, Seph. What's he doing on our doorstep that late?"

Cheeks burning with embarrassment I murmured, "Matt, don't be like that. It's fine, he was here looking for a file Russ thought I had. He heard me scream and he was worried about me."

From beside me, Joseph said plaintively and quietly, "I made you cry?"

My attention snapped to him and saw that he looked utterly forlorn.

"Yes," Matt growled at the same time as I said, "No!"

Joseph looked between us and I clarified, "Technically, your brother did. But that's all cleared up now. Well, sort of."

"Hang on," Matt said suddenly, interrupting whatever Joseph had been about to say, "He heard you screaming?"

"What?" I asked, distracted still by Joseph's pall of unhappy colours.

"You said he heard you scream. You never scream, Seph, that's how I know you're dreaming whenever it happens when I'm here — you're either dead silent or you whisper. It's creepy."

This brought me up short and I went cold. He was right — he'd told me before that I was eerily quiet whenever I sleepwalked.

Doubt re-entered my mind and I glanced down at my arm where Makris had grabbed it, turning it slightly so that the light caught it at different angles. Was that a bruise, starting to appear? My adrenal glands kicked things up a notch and I looked between Joseph and Matt, fear doubtless written all across my face.

With a tense nod, Matt said, "Stay here, I'll check," and set off at a run up the stairs.

I started to say that Joseph had already checked, but he interrupted me, calling back to Joseph, "Watch her, don't move."

I heard Matt stride from room to room above us, opening doors and cupboards before running back down the stairs and searching the downstairs rooms just as thoroughly. Joseph had moved closer to me and stood protectively in front of me, alert. My mind was racing. Had Makris actually been here? Had he simply left when he'd heard Joseph arrive at the door? Or was I going mad and confusing dreams with reality? I shivered, not knowing which explanation scared me more.

"All clear," Matt muttered as he came back into the hallway. "Must have been some dream, love. I'll get Nottingham to check he's safely tucked up in bed anyway," he said, and the forced air of unconcern did little to relax me. Pulling his phone out of his pocket and dialling, he casually righted the hall table on his way to the kitchen.

I was suddenly keen to get Joseph out of the house. He did not need to see this side of my life or know any more about my background, not when he'd been so cagey about his own.

"Thank you for coming, Joseph, shall I see you out?" I asked loudly to drown out Matt's voice — my desire to keep him in the dark about Makris outweighed even the idea of keeping him in my home for longer, even though the latter carried the chance of more physical contact.

He hesitated, concern furrowing his brow, so I added, "I'm fine now, Matt's here. Thank you for staying with me until I felt better, that was kind of you. You can go home now, though, I'm sure your family's wondering where you've got to. Sorry about the file, I don't know where it will be if Russ doesn't know."

I tried to lead him to the door as I spoke but he stood firm, looking through to the kitchen, where Matt was foraging for food as he spoke to someone on the phone. "I would prefer to wait until I know that the man who attacked you is nowhere near here," he insisted.

I sighed, biting back impatience and anxiety. We stood together, silently waiting for Matt to give the all-clear, which he did a few minutes later by giving me a thumbs up sign through the doorway.

With a frown and a brief nod of acknowledgement, Joseph turned to leave. At the door, he paused and said, "You have my name, but may I give you my phone number?" He took in the uncertain look on my face and clarified, "I tried ringing you earlier — before I came here. I would like to save my number to your phone — so that you can reach me if ever you need me." He must have seen the reservation I felt (remembering only too clearly that he had not called me after we'd met at the hospital) because he went on, "Even if I am not permitted to call you, I hope you will be willing to phone me if you ever need to. Or want to ..."

When I frowned slightly, trying to work out if he was playing games, he pressed, "Please."

I dug in my pocket, unlocked my phone and saw that I had indeed received a missed call. I looked at him steadily and said, "You called me when I was still asleep."

He swallowed hard and said, "Yes. I — I was still outside; I could hear you and you weren't answering the door ..." His voice was hoarse and strained. He was lying again, but I was too tired to know how to find out the truth. Instead, I started to save the number under a new contact for him.

"Do I save this under Joseph or Zeph—" I began, but he cut me off.

"—Joseph. Please. Only use the other if you really have to."

I shrugged lightly and did as he asked and he nodded to himself, guilt once more clouding his features but not as greatly as it had done previously: it was rather outshone by his relief.

"I wish it had been under other circumstances, but I have enjoyed being with you tonight, Sephy," he said as he turned to leave.

He walked down my drive and glanced back over his shoulder as he reached the pavement; giving me a little wave he walked on — I presumed he must have parked further down the street. I closed the door softly and walked slowly to the kitchen to talk to Matt.

"So what was this dream about, then?" he asked as I entered, barely glancing up as he checked emails on his phone. "I'm assuming it *was* the Bastard?"

'The Bastard' was the rather unimaginative name Matt and I often used when referring to Makris so as not to humanise him with the use of his actual name. It was petty, but we both preferred it.

I muttered an affirmative and picked up the empty cups from the table and stacked them in the dishwasher for want of something to do with my hands. Matt looked up; he knew me well enough to know that all was not well and he waited for me to speak.

With a sigh, I said, "It was so blooming real, Matt. I could *smell* him."

I rubbed my arm: if the shadow there were indeed a bruise, it could have come from falling on the table rather than from being grabbed, I reasoned. I was trying very hard to rationalise everything and convince myself that it had all been in my mind. If Makris had actually been in the house, he would not have been able to appear in front of me every time I'd turned around, and he would not simply have vanished in front of my eyes when Joseph had

133

arrived at the door. He may have *acted* demonically in the past, but he was only human.

Matt walked over to where I stood and put a reassuring arm around my shoulder. "Mate, it's alright. The therapist said these things might happen now and again, didn't she? It's how you manage them that's important. And you seem pretty calm and collected — you're not crying or asking me to search the house again, you know it wasn't real."

I nodded, though I felt a little hollow inside as I was fighting the urge to ask Matt to do exactly that. Matt, though, had moved on and was taking a bowl of cereal and a cup of coffee through to the sitting room; I followed close behind, and that's why I noticed the slight tensing of his shoulders, the moment's pause on the threshold. I looked closely at him; there was something off about his colours.

"What's wrong?" I asked, with enough urgency in my voice that he knew I was responding to whatever it was he'd picked up on.

"Nothing," he said, then added quietly, "it just smells a bit funny in here … I can see why you thought it was him."

I tensed and he quickly reassured me, "Power of suggestion, that's all. It probably drifted in through the bloody open door, Seph. Cam went to the halfway house and got eyes on him himself, and the logbook shows he's been in his room since curfew at six, you're alright."

He balanced his cereal bowl on the arm of the sofa and reached over to turn on the lamp; it failed to illuminate and after flicking the switch on and off a couple of times and checking that it was turned on at the wall, Matt reached over the top of the lampshade to remove the bulb. At his touch, the light came on; gingerly but quickly he twisted the bulb half a turn to put it in its socket more securely and sat back down.

Someone had unscrewed the bulb.

Matt was unaware of the wave of fear that had swept over me as I'd watched his casual fix-it job. He patted the seat beside him to indicate that I should join him. I did so, my body on autopilot whilst my brain was telling me very firmly that I was being ridiculous, that bulbs sometimes worked themselves loose.

Matt flicked on the TV and put his feet on the coffee table, tucking into his cereal as though perfectly at ease. "Cam asked after you — he was asking when he could come up and see us, but I don't think he was that bothered about seeing *me*," he said in a teasing voice and I remembered what he'd said about Cam liking me; I blushed slightly and swatted playfully at his arm.

He started flicking through the channels, evidently relaxed and settling down for the night yet his colours showed me only too clearly that he was still troubled, tense. When he spoke it was apparent that he was thinking of how to keep me safe when I was not physically with him — in Matt's eyes, the only safe pair of hands were his own. "Is whatshisface going to keep a lookout for you at work?"

Ignoring his rather discourteous reference to Joseph, my gaze slipped to the side and I wondered how to change the subject.

Seeing my shifty expression, he said firmly, "You have told him, right?"

I still hadn't told *anyone* at Democritus's about

Makris. I quailed, feeling stupid and reckless and utterly unable to explain why I had acted that way; I certainly didn't want to tell him that I was ridiculously optimistic that Joseph might one day be interested in me, but only if I were not perceived as a 'victim'. I decided to lie, which I found difficult, yet it was easier than admitting the truth.

"Sure." Then, partly to distract him from asking more probing questions, but mainly because I wanted to know the answer, I asked quietly, "Do you think I'm going mad again?"

He scooted closer to me and put his arm around my shoulder. "Seph, you're not going mad, and you were never mad in the first place. Most lasses your age think they're bloody immortal or something and the only difference between you and them is you've got enough experience to know that bad things can actually happen when you're alone and vulnerable. You had a horrible experience and it's stayed with you — PTSD's a bastard. But I've stayed with you too and I promise you, I'll always protect you. I will not let him anywhere near you; I'd sooner kill him before I let him hurt you again." He spoke with such vehemence that I felt warmed and reassured in equal measure.

I sighed shakily. It had been a dream. On the one hand, that was massively reassuring. On the other ... I glanced at my arm again, and thought about the smell of peppermint and cigarette smoke that apparently Matt had smelled just as I had: its vividness and the lasting effects on my nerves might mean I was losing my mind regardless of Matt's reassurances to the contrary.

CHAPTER 18

ON THE MONDAY OF MY SECOND week at work, my first day back after my nightmare, Russ was waiting for me in our office when I arrived. He exuded impatience and irritation, and stood rather than sat, rubbing the dark stubble on his chin in clear agitation.

Without waiting for me to so much as say hello, he sighed deeply and said, "Right. New rules. I have made sure that Lu knows to schedule all court appointments for you in a way that allows someone from the firm to accompany you there and back. If you are ever at court and your case finishes early, you *must* call the office and an escort will be arranged."

I hastily demurred, feeling embarrassed by the fact that Joseph had clearly told his brother about what had happened the previous Friday. Russ cut across my protests, confirming my suspicions in a heartbeat.

"My brother is most insistent. Furthermore, as from today, I will see any and all new clients, and I will only pass them on to you once I have ascertained that they pose no threat of any harm to you. I am most adept at spotting trouble, I assure you, but tell me the name of the man who attacked you, in case he takes it upon himself to make an appointment and is somehow able to disguise his murderous intentions from me."

I hesitated to answer. If I gave him Makris's full name, he might search for the details of my case online. I didn't want him to know the sordid details of what had happened; he would surely tell Joseph.

"I'd rather not say," I said quietly. "But I've changed my name, and moved away, and the police in Nottingham are pretty good about keeping an eye on him for me. He won't be a threat. It was just a nightmare I had the other night — he's in my past."

Russ frowned slightly, and repeated, "Tell me his name," more firmly.

This was awkward. I didn't want to disobey my boss, and refusing to answer any direct question was rather rude, but I wanted to keep that part of my life secret more than I cared about any stupid social rules. I shook my head.

The effect of this on Russ was rather remarkable. If I'd expected annoyance or irritation at being denied, I was mistaken. Instead, I saw shock and, following swiftly on its heels, fear. The fear that he had shown initially when we had first met at my interview had been acute, but it had definitely faded in the short time we'd shared an office — and it had mellowed significantly after overhearing my call from Zoe. The return of this unaccountably intense fear that I had triggered in him was far from welcome.

He inhaled deeply. "Very well. On your head be it."

His tone forbade any further disagreement and without further comment he walked to the door. Apparently the matter was not open for discussion.

***

If I'd hoped that Joseph might make more of an effort to spend time with me after the care he'd shown towards me after my nightmare, I was badly mistaken. I saw absolutely nothing of him in the office for the next three weeks. Whilst Joseph was not anywhere to be seen at work, though, I did occasionally catch glimpses of him elsewhere. He was always too far away for me to be sure that he'd seen me too, or to call over to him, and although it appeared as though he were looking in my direction he showed no sign of even seeing me, let alone recognising me. In fact, I realised that he was never looking directly at me: rather, he was looking at everyone else, as though searching for someone.

I saw him on the other side of the street when I walked to or from the bus stop; I saw him at the end of an aisle at my local supermarket; I saw him on a park bench on the other side of the lake at Roundhay Park when I went for a walk with Matt one Saturday. It did cross my mind that I was imagining him, too, especially since Matt never mentioned seeing him around and would surely have done so if he had (if only to point out that Joseph appeared to be stalking me). I kept it to myself, but I found myself thinking about him often, and worried about why he always seemed so despondent whenever I caught sight of him.

I was growing increasingly lonely at work. I still hadn't seen Thomas, and now it seemed that even Felicity was giving me a wide berth. Meanwhile, Russ had returned to being on full alert whenever I was near him. After a few days, I grew accustomed to being regarded as though I were an unexploded bomb and by the end of the month I barely noticed.

CHAPTER 19

October

AT THE START OF MY SECOND month at Democritus's, I was preparing a statement on one of Russ's files when his secretary, Lu, came hurrying into our office.

"So sorry to disturb you, Sephy, all the partners are in a meeting and I don't know what else to do! I've got a client on the phone, Mr Pickard, the one with the Occupation Order, and he says he's got a bad back so he's emailed a doctor's note over to Russ to excuse him from court tomorrow."

I frowned. Mr Pickard was one of Russ's more troublesome clients; I knew that the following day would be the final hearing in his case and that it was very likely that the judge would order him to leave the family home. Having a bad back on the eve of his day in court seemed rather suspicious; I assumed he wouldn't want it to go ahead in his absence.

"Is he wanting to vacate the final hearing, then?"

She nodded and then glanced at Russ's computer. "Do you think you could log onto Russ's email and find it? Mr Pickard says that his doctor sent it direct to Russ, but it'll need sending on to court asap."

I looked at her blankly.

"I think his password is in his desk drawer," she said. "I don't know when this partners' meeting will finish, and you're the next senior person I could ask. Can you get it and then sign the application to vacate?"

Faintly shaken by the idea that I was a person with authority (since, inside, I still felt like I was about fourteen years old) I nodded and walked quickly round to Russ's side of the desk. A quick rummage in his drawer turned up a Post-it Note with what looked very much like a password. I typed it in and his computer sprang to life, opening up his emails and diary without further hurdles to jump. Trying to sound casual, I asked, "Is Joseph in the partners' meeting?"

I glanced at her and saw a small smile curled in the corner of her mouth. "Yes ..." she said in a tone that asked more questions than it answered.

I blushed, looking back at the screen whilst the inbox loaded.

"I just haven't seen him much lately, that's all," I commented lightly.

"No? Well that's strange, he's in every day. He's been working in his dad's office since you came. I don't know why — it's as though someone doesn't want you two anywhere near each other," she replied, her tone equally light but a glint of intrigue twinkled in her eyes that made it quite apparent she was hoping for gossip. When none was forthcoming, she continued, sounding more concerned, "Mind you, Marta — that's Thomas's secretary — said she came in and found him fast asleep, slumped on his dad's desk the other day. Maybe he's got other issues going on. He looks shocking these days."

I felt distinctly on edge at the thought that there was something wrong with Joseph. Perhaps he hadn't been ignoring me after all — it had, on reflection, been rather egocentric of me to think that I could be the source of his recent behaviour. I hadn't tried to ring his number because he'd given it to me as a means of contacting him if I'd needed him, not to use to tap him up or to ask if *he* needed *me*; besides, he had my number too and hadn't used it ... then again, I probably wouldn't be the first person he'd think of to call if he did need someone to talk to. He might be the focus of a lot of my thoughts, but I doubted he thought of me quite so often.

"I hope he's okay," I managed, seeing that Lu was waiting for a response.

She nodded and went on, her tone quieter and more serious still, "These partners' meetings are a bit troubling, though. I keep hearing them shouting from upstairs. Do you think there's money trouble? I don't want to lose my job ..."

I told her I hadn't heard any rumours about money problems and that Russ hadn't said anything but privately I was wondering what on earth they could be shouting about.

Lapsing into silence as, at last, the inbox loaded, we scanned the emails together and quickly found Mr Pickard's note — it was from a suspiciously unofficial-sounding email address that ended in yahoo.co.uk and a glance at the attached letter suggested that Mr Pickard might have simply written it himself and made up a doctor's name for the electronic signature. It wasn't even on headed paper. I sighed inwardly at the idea of presenting it as evidence to the judge that Russ's client couldn't possibly attend and asking for a new court date amongst an always-busy court schedule. I told Lu she could leave it with me and set about printing off the application to vacate.

As a matter of courtesy, I called the court office and spoke to a lady called Val, who was always really helpful and knew me well enough to know that I wasn't trying to pull a fast one. She agreed to put my application in front of the judge with my sincere apologies and I scanned and emailed the signed paperwork across.

Job done, I was about to exit the email system altogether and close it down when an email heading caught my eye. It was an email from Felicity to Russ and it was headed, "Joseph and Sephy". It had been sent earlier that morning.

I hesitated, sure that if I opened the email then Russ would find out or perhaps walk in whilst I was reading it, but also desperately intrigued to know why Felicity should be emailing her husband about me. I clicked it before I had time to think it through any further.

To: rdemocritus@democritus.co.uk
From: fdemocritus@democritus.co.uk
Re: Joseph and Sephy

Darling,

Please support me at the meeting today. I know that it will be difficult facing down your sister, but this business about keeping Joseph away from Sephy really does have to end. For all that is troubling about Sephy, I am terribly concerned about your brother.

You cannot have failed to notice that he has not been sleeping or eating well over recent weeks, especially since that terrible night when he struggled to locate Sephy despite knowing that she was afraid. You saw for yourself — he was simply beside himself. It's no wonder he's no longer content for us to play bodyguard, but he's exhausted from trying to Shadow her himself whenever she's not at work.

That issue aside, he is being forced to be apart from the person to whom he is tied and it must be physically and emotionally unbearable. His instinct — his <u>need</u> — is to be with her. By obeying arbitrary and questionable rules set down by the High Council, we are being unbearably cruel in denying him a relationship with her.

I share the same concerns as everyone else here — Sephy is *unique* and her very existence is concerning on a number of levels, but if your sister were to carry out her threat to report the matter to the High Council we know full well what would happen to Sephy — and what *that* would do to Joseph.

I know that you share many of my views, but perhaps I feel all of this more keenly because I can see the tie for myself, whereas to you it is more ethereal, less tangible. Erica doesn't seem to believe that there even *is* a tie (no matter how many times your father and I tell her we can see it plain as day) and as long as she is in denial about this she poses a significant risk to Joseph and Sephy alike. I have said all I can to that woman — please do what you can to change her mind.

I doubt that Joseph will allow things to carry on as they are for much longer anyway. His resolve to stay away from her seems to weaken every time he sees her.

I hope that you will stand by me and be more vocally supportive today. As always, you are my only love and I am yours,

F xx

I read the email twice and it still didn't make complete sense — there were things she'd written about that meant nothing to me and that seemed like utter fantasy. But it seemed that the gist of it was that Joseph was for some reason pining for me and

'Shadowing' me (which I thought must mean following me round) because he was worried about me but couldn't be with me because of some High Council — the same High Council that would do something ominous-sounding if they found out that I existed. My brain kept skipping over the details, not processing the words. Felicity surely meant what she said, but she sounded — well, she sounded insane. Kind, and concerned for us both, but insane.

I clicked out of the email and searched for any reply Russ might have made but there was none. I searched for any other emails that might bear my name but again there were none. I looked for any emails from Joseph but there were only a handful, all connected to cases the brothers shared and contained nothing personal, judging by the titles. Next, I searched for emails from other family members, starting with Thomas.

I had to scroll back quite a way, to the end of August, before I found what I'd been looking for. There, dated the day after my interview with Thomas, was an email entitled 'New Staff Member — Agreements.'

With a guilty glance towards the door, I clicked on the email and read.

To: rdemocritus@democritus.co.uk; jdemocritus@democritus.co.uk; edemocritus@democritus.co.uk; fdemocritus@democritus.co.uk; ademocritus@democritus.co.uk; hdemocritus@lgi.nhs.uk

Re: New Staff Member — Agreements

Dear all,

Further to our frankly exhausting meeting last night, I wanted to formalise what was agreed vis a vis Sephy. Forgive my formality, I am merely keen for there to be no misunderstandings or pleading of ignorance at any later date.

Joseph has bravely agreed to maintain a strict distance from Sephy, on the understanding that if he were to pursue a relationship with her it would place the rest of us at risk of repercussions from the High Council. As long as they keep apart, the rest of us will have deniability of their connection, at least, if Sephy's existence is ever discovered.

Even so, nobody is to report Sephy to the High Council. I cannot stress this highly enough. To do so would destroy Joseph and place all of us at risk of Obliteration if the High Council were to disbelieve our ignorance.

All but one of you has agreed to Shadow Sephy, to keep her physically safe and to keep an eye out for anyone who might report her. Any sightings of Damneds or others like us should be reported to me immediately so that I may neutralise any danger.

We shall keep this under review and meet regularly to discuss developments. Felicity has concerns that Joseph's health will be impacted by being kept apart from Sephy and this will be closely monitored. Any sign of illness in Sephy must also be reported to me or Hester so that investigations can be made to ensure that she remains in good health.

You have my thanks for your discretion and support. I know that this is a difficult set of circumstances, but we shall face them successfully if we remain united.

Thomas/Dad

This was all too weird. I clicked 'print' and held my breath for the anxious few moments it took for the printer beside me to whirr into action and spew out a copy of the email; opening Felicity's email again I repeated the process. I hurriedly folded the papers and pushed them deep into my handbag under my desk before quickly closing down Russ's email and computer.

Though I read them several times that night and over the following few days, the emails made no more sense than I had originally taken from them. I wanted to talk to Thomas or Felicity about it, or even to Russ, but to do so I would have to admit to snooping in his inbox and I didn't want to do so — I valued my job and the idea of doing anything to jeopardise working at Democritus's was unacceptable.

Instead, I kept my eye out for any sign of Joseph and continued to spot him here and there. I stared more blatantly at him, hoping that he would come over to me or wave or acknowledge me in any way so that I could speak to him. I still had his number in my phone and looked at it many, many times, but he had said that I should call if I needed him — I did need him, very much, but probably not in the way that he had intended when he had given me a way to contact him.

After numerous re-reads, I had deduced the following (although I had no clue as to the veracity of what Felicity or Thomas had said):

Firstly, Joseph liked me. His family was keeping him apart from me for some reason other than a class barrier — something called the High Council would "Obliterate" us all if Joseph and I had a relationship and they found out about me.

Secondly, Joseph was worried about me. He thought I was in danger; as a result, all but one of his family members (presumably Erica was the one to dip out of this particular duty) were striving to keep an eye on me. They were apparently doing this to reassure Joseph that I was physically safe even if he couldn't be with me. Since my nightmare, though, it seemed that Joseph, like Matt, was not prepared to trust my safety to anyone else — presumably that was why I had seen him so often.

Finally, Joseph was suffering — he looked thoroughly miserable whenever I saw him and had lost a noticeable amount of weight in the short time I had known him. His family described a 'tie' between us, which I took to be some kind of romantic connection, and which made my heart skip a beat every time I thought of it. The idea that Joseph felt something even close to what I felt for him was hugely thrilling, but the idea that he was suffering because he felt unable to act on his feelings was greatly upsetting.

I'd always been single, technically alone in that respect, but I had never before felt *lonely* because I'd always had Matt. Now, though, there was a gap caused by (and lamentably not filled by) Joseph, a gap forged the moment I'd seen him at the railway station. By not allowing our 'tie' to come to fruition, Joseph was in torment — and I knew just how that felt.

***

At home a few nights after I had resigned myself to the fact that I had wrung every piece of decipherable information from the emails possible, I watched Matt as he made me a cup of tea. Feeling frustrated, I rather wished I could love him instead of fawning after the unattainable Joseph. Why *couldn't* I fall for someone like Matt? Or even just fall for Matt? He was kind, reliable, funny, protective, not bad looking; he even had a steady job. He had a lot going for him. He was certainly a lot less complicated than Joseph and much more accessible. But he was my friend. My brother. There was just no spark, no stomach-flipping warmth when I looked at him. Never had I pictured so much as kissing him and never had I thought that he was interested in me that way, either. I tried imagining kissing him now and was rather grossed out by the incestuous vibe I felt from the very idea.

No, throughout my whole life, the only man who had ever sparked an interest for me was Joseph, who apparently felt the same way, even though he couldn't act on it. I felt increasingly annoyed — why couldn't he defy his family or this High Council and be with me, if he wanted me so much?

He was the only man I'd ever had any feelings for; I couldn't even name how I felt about him because 'love' seemed wholly inadequate. I'd put it down to limerence, but now wondered if, in our case, that strength and depth of romantic, obsessive attraction might last a lifetime if we could only grab the chance to be together.

CHAPTER 20

THE EARLY PART OF THE MONTH dragged. I'd developed an established feeling of ennui and it seemed likely to continue. A large part of my overall sense of dissatisfaction was due to the fact that Joseph was still conspicuous by his absence from his office. I had resigned myself to the fact that my heart would jump a little if his car was in the car park; this was clearly something I had no control over and so I could only wait until whatever part of my brain was in charge of 'infatuation' got news from my frontal lobes that this was stupid. However strongly Joseph may or may not feel according to Felicity, clearly he had no intention of defying his family to allow those feelings to come to fruition.

As well as being constantly reminded of my unrequited love every time I walked past his office to mine, I had been hit by the realisation that this was my life from now on — that whatever intrigue and mysteries the emails hinted at, they were behind a firmly locked door and on my side of that door was routine and drudgery.

Throughout school, university and beyond, all of my time had been broken down into finite segments: GCSEs (two years); A-Levels (two years); bachelor's degree (three years); a post-graduate diploma (one year) and Training Contract (two years). Now, apparently, there was just: work, punctuated only by occasional holidays and Christmas (possibly forty-five years); retirement (fifteen years if I was lucky) and then death (infinite). This was quite a shock that was bound to take some getting used to.

On the plus side, at least my feelings of unease had gradually faded as more time had passed without Leon Makris making an appearance in any more dreams in the four week interval since the last: I had gradually accepted that it *had* been just a dream (albeit a particularly vivid one).

Also, Russ had begun to thaw towards me once more. This did not appear to be a conscious decision — he just seemed to be forgetting to be wary of me, the longer we spent in each other's company. The pale-yellow fear was more diminished, and there had even been times when I'd made him laugh. So deprived of company was I at work, and so desperate to be liked again (or at least not made out to be some kind of pariah), that this improved relationship made me greatly happy. This was probably a huge testament to my damaged childhood; any normal person would surely have been looking for another job.

Meanwhile, Matt had finally found a car for me that he was satisfied with and after some haggling we bought it on the first weekend of October. I liked the colour — blue, of course. I think it was a Honda? It had an automatic gearbox, which was all that really mattered to me.

Looking back, that was probably the last normal weekend I ever had.

***

On the Friday after I'd bought my car, I used it to get to Bradford County Court for a directions appointment on one of my cases. Russ had arranged a meeting in the town centre so that he could escort me, and so improved was our working relationship that he didn't even seem to mind very much.

He saw me to the door of the building before leaving me alone. I was the only one who was due to attend my case, since my client's ex-partner had made it clear he would not be attending, and (as it was a procedural matter intended to timetable the statements and evidence needed before the final hearing) my client hadn't been required to attend in person. The usher told me that it would be about an hour before my case would be heard, since several matters had been listed at the same time and mine was alphabetically quite low in the list, so I decided to take myself up to the canteen for a cup of tea and to dictate some notes on the file while I waited.

Once seated with my drink and a packet of biscuits, I began to flick through my paperwork and write a draft order for the judge to consider, hoping to save us both some time in her chambers. I was interrupted, though, by someone standing close to my table, politely waiting to gain my attention. Looking up from my file it took me a moment to register that I was looking at DC Cam.

"Thought it was you. Alright Seph?" he asked with a huge smile that matched the one that spread across my face.

"Oh my god! Cam!" I cried.

Delighted to see my old friend, I stood and wrapped my arms around his neck and we hugged for a moment before releasing each other and standing holding each other's arms affectionately.

"What are you doing here?" I asked, happy to see him but my mind starting to race.

I'd had no contact with anyone from Nottingham since Matt and I had left. Cam was a dear friend, and we had a lot of history together — I'd saved his life; he'd saved my sanity during Makris's trial — but Matt had been very clear about cutting all ties with our old life to reduce the chance that Makris would find me again.

Oblivious to the anxiety behind my question, he said, "I'm here on a criminal trial upstairs; a county lines thing. Bunch of forces involved, and I've got landed with giving evidence today. I can't believe you're here! I mean, I knew you'd moved to Yorkshire, but what are the chances of us both being here in this canteen today?"

"Yeah, I know — it must be fate," I smiled. Feeling bad about even having to ask, I went on, "I'm really sorry, but I'm a bit worried — you've not seen anything of Makris lately have you?"

His eyes widened in understanding and he hastened to reassure me. "Don't worry, Seph, it's fine, last I saw of him was in that grotty bedsit after Matt asked me to check up on him. What was that about — Matt said you'd had a nightmare?"

I scoffed, blushing at the memory of my hysteria. "It was stupid, it was just a dream. You know what I'm like with my sleepwalking and things, though — it felt very real. So, he couldn't have followed you here or anything?"

He frowned. "Well, no. Why would he? I'm just one of many coppers who worked on your case, and he doesn't know where you moved to or where I've come today. It's fine, mate, don't worry about it."

I allowed myself to relax and forced myself to concentrate on the fact that he was there. It had been a long time since I'd seen him. In the weeks since my nightmare, Cam had called Matt a few times asking when he could come up and see us both in Leeds: nothing had been arranged, mainly because Matt didn't want anyone having our new address in case it fell into the wrong hands. Looking at Cam now, I felt rather guilty that I hadn't made more effort to stay in touch with him — he'd been a good friend to me, whatever additional feelings he might or might not hold, according to Matt.

"How are you, anyway?" he asked.

I smiled back, replied that I was fine, and invited him to sit with me. Apparently his case was recessed for a few hours because some other witness hadn't turned up, so Cam was at a loose end for a while.

We chatted amiably for some time, catching up with each other's news; I told him about my job and he updated me with gossip about mutual friends. I found myself warming to him, remembering how fond I'd been of him when we'd socialised in Nottingham with Matt and the others from their department.

I shared my biscuits with him and he went and bought me another drink and one for himself; we were getting along quite well.

But then he said, "Listen, I know Matt's a bit protective and everything, and I know you don't want anyone knowing where you live … but I've missed you, and, well, I always liked you, you know." He paused, bright red as his bravado failed him momentarily, and then went on, "So, would you be interested in coming out with me sometime? Just for a drink, or we could get something to eat, or whatever you fancied, really? Maybe … maybe tonight, since I'm up here?"

I tensed, genuinely unsure of how to respond. His colours were all over the place and difficult for me to gauge, and I really hadn't expected him to ask me on a date.

In the back of my mind, I was longing for Joseph. He was the one I wanted to be with. But he had repeatedly blown hot and cold and I hadn't even spoken to him since the night of my nightmare some four weeks earlier. Whatever Felicity may have put in her email about Joseph wanting to be with me, there didn't seem to be any tangible evidence that he would do anything to make that happen.

Meanwhile, I was talking to a handsome young man who had a good soul and a decent job, who came from a nice family and who had already proven himself to be reliable and caring in the past. He was clearly very much interested in me and, crucially, he had actually asked me out. True, when I looked at him, I didn't have any of those same feelings I felt for Joseph — there was no sense of 'completeness' or satisfaction at being close to him, no thrill or desire. But perhaps those were the sorts of feelings that would normally grow, over time? Maybe I needed to give someone like Cam a chance if I ever wanted to be with someone who actually wanted me in return … maybe friendship could grow into more if I gave it the opportunity to do so. How Matt would feel about it was a different matter, but I could cross that bridge when I came to it.

Before I could reply, though, Cam and I both looked up because suddenly there was Joseph, standing beside our table. He had an easy smile on his face, but his colours were as dark as I'd ever seen them. He still looked as though he hadn't been sleeping well — the dark shadows under his eyes were quite pronounced, his beard was not trimmed as closely as usual and he had definitely lost some weight. I was immediately concerned, and I felt a chill pass through me as I wondered if he was seriously ill.

"Joseph," I said, my voice barely a whisper as I spoke with a release of breath I hadn't realised I'd been holding.

I'd begun to think that I may never talk to him again, sure that he'd take every step possible to avoid me altogethcr in future. Yet my palpable relief at seeing him beside me again was tempered by concern. I scanned his colours to see if I could see any hint of illness or worse, but he seemed to be in good physical health. I realised he was watching me look at him so intently and I blushed, feeling as though I'd been caught prying into what was, after all, rather private.

I cleared my throat, attempting to put some

strength back into my voice. "Are you okay?"

He nodded courteously, with a smile that didn't quite leach the sadness from eyes. Softly, he said, "Hello Sephy," before turning his attention to Cam, who stood as though unsure of whether to greet Joseph or run away from him. If I had been in Cam's shoes, I might have chosen the latter since the look Joseph was giving him was murderously angry for some reason.

"Joseph Democritus," he said by way of introduction, his voice cool and far from friendly but not reflecting the hostility he clearly felt.

I did a double take at Joseph's colours. They were a murky mess of negative emotions over his usual Blue but there, at the heart of them, was puce — a colour that he had helped me to identify when I'd seen it in Lockheart back at the hospital. Joseph was envious, I was sure of it, though of what I didn't know: surely he hadn't heard Cam ask me out, and if he had — well, he'd had plenty of opportunities to do so himself, so he could hardly envy someone for something he could have had at any time.

Cam gave an uncertain smile in response, glancing nervously between the two of us. Perhaps he was wondering if he'd just asked me out within earshot of my boyfriend — that would certainly explain his anxiety.

"DC Cam, Nottinghamshire Police. I'm an old friend of Seph's."

"Cam worked with Matt in Nottingham," I expanded, trying to fill the awkward silence that had descended. To Cam, I was carefully neutral with my wording as I said, "Joseph's one of the partners at my work."

160

Cam seemed to relax a little, and I had time to wonder if he had been relieved that Joseph was nothing more than a work colleague.

"Sorry to interrupt," Joseph said to both of us, though he did not seem to mean it. "Sephy, I was just wondering if you could give me a lift back to the office after court please? I came by train today but as you're here it would be more expedient if I returned in your car. Russ's meeting concluded earlier than anticipated and he has taken a taxi back to the office; there will be no need to wait for him."

It would take about half an hour to drive from Bradford to Leeds. Half an hour in an enclosed space with Joseph. "Of course, no problem," I said, though my voice was very soft because I couldn't seem to get enough air into my lungs.

I was lost in his eyes. I gave myself a little mental shake as I reminded myself that this was a stupid crush, nothing more, and that I should stop fantasising about what would never be mine. Crossly, I told myself that by the time I'd finished in court he would probably have disappeared anyway.

My voice flat, I went on, "I'll be done in about half an hour, but I can hang on if you need to stay longer?"

"I've done what I came for, I'll be ready when you are," he replied before he excused himself and went to the counter to order a drink, seeming to pay us no further attention.

I turned back to look at Cam, but he had paled into insignificance beside Joseph. In direct comparison, there was no competition. How could I even consider dating Cam with some vague notion of growing to want him over time, when I had such a palpable reaction towards Joseph? My feelings for the two men were night and day; I knew instantly that I could never be happy with Cam knowing how strongly I needed to be with Joseph.

"So," he said, sitting back down. "About that drink?"

"Oh … well, you know, I'm flattered, I really am, and I like you too, but you're a friend and I'd hate something to spoil that."

He scoffed lightly, "Uh oh, the dreaded friend-zone."

I was about to respond when I realised that his colours were not what I might have expected to see. There was no embarrassment (salmon pink), or disappointment (slate grey). But the colours that were there were indecipherable to me. I wasn't adept at interpreting body language, but if I'd had to guess I'd have said he looked nervous. Perhaps he was worried about what Matt would do if he found out Cam had asked me out.

I was saved from further awkwardness by the Tannoy, which announced my case. I quickly gathered my file and papers, hurriedly thanked Cam for asking me anyway and apologising for not having accepted. He was quiet but said that he understood, and we wished each other well before we parted. It left a bad taste in my mouth, though — I wished he hadn't asked; it had been nice to see him, but a line had been crossed and it would be difficult to resurrect a genuine friendship even if Matt did manage to arrange for us all to meet up in the future when things had settled down.

As I left the canteen, I also felt a little regret, wondering if I should have just said yes to Cam —

after all, how likely was it that Joseph would actually want to be with me and act on that desire? But whilst there was still a chance of being with Joseph, however slight, I felt compelled to take it and hope that something would come of it.

On my way out, I gave a little wave to Joseph but then felt stupid because he wasn't even looking in my direction.

CHAPTER 21

THE JUDGE HAD CLEARLY HAD ENOUGH for the day already by the time I went before her and was more than happy to sign off on my suggested directions, which suited me because against my better judgement all I wanted to do was get back to Joseph. I felt certain that if I didn't hurry then by the time I came out of court he would have made other arrangements and disappeared, a thought that left me fretful and anxious.

As I emerged from the judge's chambers and back out into the bear garden (the name given to the court waiting area), I was surprised — and more than a little relieved — to see Joseph waiting there for me. He reached out automatically to take my files from my arms, which I relinquished with a grateful smile. Feminism be damned on such occasions — those files were heavy.

My car was parked across the road in a multi-storey car park and aside from exchanging pleasantries we set off to walk there in silence.

Stealing a glance at him in the morning sunshine, I wondered how on earth Felicity could think that he could be interested in me — he was glorious, even if he was under the weather for now, and far out of my league.

"Are you sure you're alright?" I asked tentatively as we walked towards the main road, still worried about his appearance despite there being no obvious physical pain or illness in evidence.

His brow was furrowed as he turned towards me to answer; as he looked at me, he visibly relaxed as though pulling himself out of deep and dark thoughts and his smile lifted his features considerably. "I am fine now."

"You — you look like you haven't been sleeping well. Have you been ill?" I asked, more on edge about what could be wrong than I would have been about anyone else in the same circumstances. I realised that his health mattered to me a great deal.

He looked away from me to watch the traffic as we crossed the main road together. "No, I haven't been ill. I'm fine; you're right, I just haven't been sleeping very well."

"You've lost weight," I pressed.

"Food has rather lost its appeal recently," he said flatly.

Without consciously planning to do so, I reached across the gap between us and placed my hand on his arm. He looked down at it and it was as though I had just given him a gift; his face lit up and he held his elbow out slightly, making it the most natural thing in the world for me to slip my arm through his. We continued to walk together; I was so focussed on how good it felt to be close to him that I barely noticed where we were going and was rather surprised when I realised that we had somehow managed to arrive at my car.

"New car," he commented.

I reluctantly removed my arm from around his in order to fumble the keys from the bottom of my bag and unlock the car. These were the first words he'd spoken since we had joined arms and I was glad of the chance to make light conversation whilst I recovered my equilibrium somewhat.

"Yes. Well, it's new to me. It's second-hand, I mean. It's already been in the garage; I've only had it since Saturday. The horn broke."

"Oh." He paused then asked, "How did you find out?"

"I pressed it and it didn't work," I shrugged.

"Do you think it was broken when you bought it?"

I frowned, nonplussed. "Well, no, I've had it since Saturday." I saw from his face that more was required. "I think I use the horn rather more than most people do, and this one's not very hardy. The man at the garage actually asked me if I had it on all the time …"

Perhaps wondering if it had been wise to ask me for a lift, he nodded slowly and walked round to the passenger side, depositing the files on the back seat before straightening to stand beside the front door.

I paused before I opened my own door and our eyes met over the roof of the car. I forced myself to look away and gave myself a firm, silent talking-to about capricious men and ridiculous romantic fantasies before climbing behind the wheel.

Joseph sat beside me and closed his door with a soft *thunk*.

Suddenly tired of whatever game it was I was supposed to be playing, I asked, "Why haven't I seen you at work? Since you left my house, I mean."

He dropped his gaze and looked embarrassed but declined to answer. I resigned myself to the fact that he was never going to be honest with me; that he was never actually going to allow me to get close to him. I should have accepted Cam's invitation. With a small, annoyed shake of my head, I put the key in the ignition and started the car.

Staying my hand before I could engage the gear or release the handbrake, he turned in his seat to face me. His voice was quiet but firm, conviction in every word as he held my gaze with an intensity that was difficult to look away from.

"Sephy, I am truly sorry. After I left your house, I had anticipated that things might be different, that I might be able to make my case to my family, that they would see how important—" He broke off with an exasperated sigh before continuing, "Forgive me. I must seem ridiculously fickle to you, telling you that I— that I care about you one minute and then apparently doing all I can to avoid you the next. Please know that this is not of my choosing and nor has it been in my power to do anything differently."

Surprised that he had grasped the nettle so firmly, yet still aware of the fact that he hadn't given me any straight answers for why he had behaved as he had, I hesitated to respond, unsure of what I wanted to say. For want of something to do, I pushed the car into reverse, manoeuvred out of the space and drove towards the car park exit.

"Who *does* have the power to decide whom you should be with?" I asked at last. My tone was harder than I had expected it to be, but I was tired of tiptoeing around. "And why would they not want you to be with me, if that's really what you want?"

He paused. "It is a question of my family's safety. Beyond that, I cannot tell you."

I raised my hands up off the steering wheel briefly in irritation. "What a surprise," I muttered.

With a groan of frustration he said, "I have no say over this! It has been incredibly difficult to make myself avoid you. My family will not be happy that I have chosen to speak with you today and I fear that further such opportunities will be exceptionally rare. Please, allow me to enjoy this little time with you, without pressing to know more than I can explain ..."

I shook my head, still unwilling to look at him. I didn't believe him, and I didn't want to get dragged along with yet another change of heart.

"For someone who was avoiding me, you've certainly seemed to be in a lot of the same places as me over the last few weeks."

Out of the corner of my eye I saw him go very still. "Like where?" he asked, his voice deceptively calm.

Keeping my own voice casual, I replied, "All over. At the library, in the car park, outside the café, the supermarket. In fact, I've seen you all over the place since my nightmare, just not at work — even though your office is right next door to mine. Lu said you've been working in your dad's office; I've been trying very hard not to take that personally."

He was silent for a moment, but I could see that

his colours were all over the place as he digested what I'd said. He cleared his throat and asked quietly, "If you could see me, why didn't you talk to me?"

Taken aback, I said, "Well, why didn't you talk to *me*?"

We approached traffic lights that were turning red and I could feel his eyes on me.

"I didn't realise you could see me. Felicity said, but I didn't—" he broke off, biting his lip as though to stop himself saying any more.

I sped up to get through the light. He noticed and put his hand instinctively on the dashboard as if to brace himself as we sailed through on red to the sound of a car horn blaring beside us.

"Sorry," I muttered. "If I'd stopped at that one, I'd have had to stop at all of them."

Momentarily distracted from our original line of discussion, he replied, "You — you didn't want to set a precedent?"

I smiled despite myself. "No, of course not. It's just that the lights on this road are every hundred yards and they're timed badly — if you get stopped at one, they'll all be red when you reach them. And they only let through four cars on green. Well, four and me."

He shook his head slightly as if to clear his thoughts. "Anyway — I'm sorry if you thought I was ignoring you whenever it was you saw me. I didn't see you," he muttered, though he really was poor at lying.

"I don't see how," I replied with a petulant shrug.

He held his hands up briefly in a gesture of surrender but seemed lost for words for a moment. I gave him time and at last he said, "So you've seen me everywhere you've been, not talking to you, just staring at you, and you haven't thought to mention that to someone?"

"Well, no, why would I?"

His frown deepened. "Because I could be some crazed stalker, for all you know."

That made me smile, incredulous at the idea. "Don't be silly. You're good. You couldn't harm me if you tried—" I stopped myself from saying more, realising too late that what made sense to me would sound rather odd to him.

Far from seeming confused, I detected a pique in his curiosity when he asked, "What do you mean?"

"I mean, you're good. You wouldn't do anything to hurt me."

"Good?" he asked with a disconcerted frown. "How on earth could you know I'm good?"

"From looking at you," I said simply, with a slight shrug.

It's always better to stick as close to the truth as possible, I've found, yet this particular truth was obviously a bit difficult to explain in full. We sailed through the rest of the lights on green and headed towards the motorway.

He gestured down at himself and pressed, "So, what, because I don't have a hunch and a widow's peak or, I don't know, *fangs* or something, then I can't be evil?"

He mugged what he clearly considered to be an evil person's visage with twisted features and a scowl, bending slightly at the hips to emphasise his point — all of which made me have to stifle another smile. I quickly turned my full attention back to the road again, already cross with myself for getting involved in the conversation.

"No, I don't mean that. It's … well, it's complicated."

"Try me," he said, straightening up again, his features back to their original, gorgeous positions. "Tell me how you can know from looking at me that I'm not a deranged lunatic."

Slightly aggrieved by his flippant reference to such things, I replied, "I happen to have met one of those and he wasn't anything like you."

He sighed softly and rubbed the back of his neck in apparent angst. "Sephy, I'm sorry, that was a poor choice of words …"

We were silent for a few moments before I decided to spare him any more discomfort; in the absence of any other ideas of what to say, I chose the truth, ignoring the little voice inside me that was begging me to shut up. "I cannot believe I'm telling you this. There's something about you that makes me tell you whatever you ask, even things I've never spoken about with anyone else … it's very disconcerting."

Out of the corner of my eye I saw him give a small smile as I continued (against my better judgement), my words issuing forth with the same speed I might employ when swallowing a foul-tasting medicine to get it over with. "I know you're not bad because I see colours when I look at people that tell me what they're like, inside. Red means bad, Blue means good, Purple's somewhere in between. Then there are these other colours that float round the edges that tell me what a person's traits are, and what mood they're in."

He was silent and I began to fear for my employment prospects.

To fill the building silence, I added, "For example, Cam back there was Blue, with colours that told me he's kind and honest, but he was feeling nervous when you turned up. You are Blue, a very beautiful Blue actually. You're good, like I said. And … and I think your colours meant you were a bit envious when I was talking to Cam."

After a very long and uncomfortable pause, I expected him to say something condescending or even just placating. In fact, he said the very last thing I could have anticipated.

"Envy is puce."

I looked at him sharply, questioningly.

He nodded forwards as though encouraging me to keep my eyes on the road and for a moment there was a heavy silence in the car.

"I see auras, too," he confirmed.

CHAPTER 22

I ABANDONED ALL PRETENCE OF PAYING attention to my driving and nearly drove off the road. After a few seconds, Joseph let go of the steering wheel, which he had grabbed automatically, apparently now confident that we would remain on the correct side of the road and off the pavement.

In the silence that followed, I wondered if I'd misheard him. "You... you see colours? Auras?"

He nodded, though he looked very unhappy about the fact that he had said so.

I considered this for a moment in silence. The idea that someone else perceived the world in the same way I did was just too unlikely. "No way," I said.

"No way?" he echoed, his face a picture of shock.

"Nope."

"It's true. We all can, in my family," he replied, miffed. "We see souls. Good and bad, like you said."

"Pfft."

His voice was tinged with indignation as he sought to prove his point. "No 'pfft'. Browny-yellow is illness; deep green is pain; black is death or grief. White is anger; pale yellow is fear. Cherry red is hope; midnight blue is love; hot pink is desire. Do you need me to go on?"

I had known the first few but the latter three were news to me. I thought about it and realised that I had seen hot pink an awful lot over the years and if it were true that it represented desire then it was at once shocking, creepy, unnerving and thrilling in equal measure depending on in whose soul I remembered seeing the colour. I glanced sideways at him and my heart flew into my mouth as I pictured all too clearly the hot pink that so often seemed to surround him when I'd seen him.

Just like that, I accepted the alien and rather exciting idea that I was not alone in my ability to perceive souls. It was a wonderful feeling — as though for the first time in my life I was not alone. I'd always had Matt, but I'd always felt set apart, too. Different. The idea of there being someone who was different right alongside me was at once comforting and elating.

My mind was immediately concerned with sorting out a few questions I'd always wanted the answers to. First and foremost, given the person I was speaking to, was, "What does dusky, pinky gold mean?"

He frowned. "I don't know. That's not one I've seen. Do you have any idea from the context?"

"No. It's the main colour I see when I look at you, so goodness knows — you're very difficult to work out."

Understanding seemed to cross his features, though he didn't share whatever enlightenment he'd uncovered. "Blue, puce and this dusky, pinky gold — are they the only colours you see when you look at me?" he asked.

I paused. *In for a penny, in for a pound,* I thought, and replied with slightly flushed cheeks, "I've seen hot pink quite a lot, too."

He blushed crimson and muttered, "I'm sorry — I would have made more of an effort to disguise my feelings if I'd thought for a moment that you could see …"

I smiled shyly, my cheeks hot. "It's okay, you've probably seen hot pink from me a fair bit, too."

I risked a glance over at him and was gratified to see colours that equated to joy floating over his usual colours, but there was anxiety there too.

"You do … feel something for me, then?" he asked quietly.

I kept my eyes on the road, embarrassed and unsure of how to reply. I settled for a quiet, "Duh."

Yes, I'd seen hot pink desire in his colours plenty of times without realising its meaning, but there had never been any midnight blue. My feelings for him ran far deeper than simple lust, but it appeared that his did not.

The silence in the car lasted for some minutes as we drove along the M62. He seemed to be waiting for me to speak.

"Sorry," I said at last, embarrassed at how openly I'd spoken and inwardly cringing at how desperate I must have seemed. "I know it's entirely inappropriate, considering you're my boss and everything, and I know it's stupid because the way I feel about you isn't exactly mutual. I don't know whether that's because you're just not that into me, or because of whatever rules there are that apparently forbid you from being with me, but it doesn't really matter: it is what it is."

He let out an exasperated sigh. "Sephy ..."

I shook my head slightly and went on, "No, it's okay, just ... please don't play games with me anymore. I mean, don't act like you're into me and then drop me like a stone the next day. It really hurts."

I could feel tears pricking at the corner of my eyes and I blinked them away, choosing to feel anger rather than upset. Without giving him chance to reply, I pressed on, "The stupid thing is, I cling to this faint hope that one day you might want to be with me; I get butterflies just walking past your office, hoping I might see you. Cam asked me out today, but every other man I meet is utterly unappealing because I compare them to you. I'll end up single forever at this rate because the only man I've ever wanted to be with is *you!*"

My voice had risen with the strength of my feelings and the silence that followed was deeply uncomfortable. Even over the engine and the sound of the traffic around us, I could hear my racing heart. I had laid myself utterly bare and left myself completely vulnerable to his next change of heart and I was furious with myself for doing so. For all I knew, I was just sport for Joseph, and once he'd had what he wanted from me, he'd be gone.

With that in mind, trying to protect my heart against the inevitable fallout from such a strong declaration of feelings that were so obviously not reciprocated, I said sourly, "This is the part where you tell me you want to be with me too but then disappear for several weeks, I believe."

He remained silent and I remained mortified. We pulled off the motorway and I wound round the infernal one-way system of central Leeds, at last pulling into the car park behind the office. By that time, the silence had become unbearable and my seatbelt was off, the door opening, even as I pulled on the handbrake and turned off the engine.

"No. Please, wait," he called.

I paused, one leg out of the car, my back to him, unwilling to face him.

I felt his hand touch my arm. "Please, stay here with me, just for a moment. I want to explain."

"There's no need. I won't make things awkward at work," I said stiffly.

"No, I mean … No." His voice changed, morphing from apologetic and angst-ridden to firm and unyielding. "*No*, I'm not going to do this anymore. It hurts me, too. It has been the most trying experience of my life, and I'm sorry that you've been hurt in the process. I had no idea you felt this too." Now that his silence had broken, he spoke fervently, "I know how inconsistent my behaviour has seemed to you. I've behaved terribly, but I hope you'll understand that I would never intentionally upset or hurt you. There is just far more at stake than you could possibly imagine." With a groan of frustration through clenched teeth, he added, "I wish I could explain everything!"

I didn't know how to respond. Ever the optimist, I hoped this meant he might finally choose to go against whatever was preventing him from being with me, but that little voice inside (that sounded suspiciously like my mother) told me that I couldn't be that lucky.

Nevertheless, I wanted him to continue talking so that I might have some chance of understanding what he was thinking, so I slid my leg back into the car and closed the door. I faced forwards rather than look at him directly, still embarrassed by how open I'd been, and waited for him to speak, not trusting myself to say anything else.

After a moment, he went on, "I *was* envious of Cam today. You two have history, and he asked you out so easily ..."

I frowned, not sure if I understood him correctly. "Were you envious that Cam could choose whomever he wanted to date, whereas you're restricted by your family's rules?"

He scoffed and shook his head. "I was envious of how easily he could be with you if you wanted him. That's why I came over; I couldn't stand the idea that he might win your heart when I couldn't even put my name in the hat."

I waited, sensing that he had more to say and reluctant to interrupt his train of thought now that he'd finally started to open up.

With a sad sigh, he went on, "As difficult as all of this must have been for you, I can assure you that it has been harder for me, having to keep away from you when I would much sooner be beside you. I have waited so, so long for you, and you will only be here once. The fact of the matter is, I cannot bear the thought of going through this lifetime waiting for you to be someone else's girlfriend, someone else's wife, the mother of someone else's children. I realise I have no right to be so but I am wildly jealous of the very idea of you being with anyone other than me."

My heart was beating wildly and I forced myself to take some slow breaths.

He went on, "Contrary to your assertion, you would not be 'single forever' — there will always be men such as PC Lockheart, or Cam, or Matt, who would wed you and bed you if given the opportunity."

I turned sharply to face him, affronted. "Right, let's get something clear. *Matt* does not want to 'bed' me — or 'wed' me, for that matter."

With a sardonic tone, Joseph said, "I beg to differ. Midnight blue flushed with hot pink? He loves you, and not as a brother."

I was so shocked — and so focussed on trying to wrap my mind around this staggering truth — that I barely heard the rest of what he was saying and had to ask him to repeat himself.

"I said, Matt would be good for you. You and he would suit each other, I think — I fear. I would like to be magnanimous and say that you should be with him, as he will take care of you and treat you well, but I just can't do it. I *can't*. Because I don't want you to be with him; I want you to be with me."

I had a funny, rubbery feeling in my legs. I felt like I was on the brink of something major and the atmosphere in the car was charged — I'd never understood that expression before now. I could hear his breathing accelerate, matching my own, and my heart felt like it was beating far too fast.

He rubbed a hand over his face, clearly in some anguish. Quietly, he said, "I am forced to choose between my family and you. The fact that you want me too makes that choice simple. I choose you. Please be mine, Sephy."

It was my turn to be silent. I stared at him openly, watching for any sign that he was going to change his mind, tell me he was joking … But all I saw was sincerity and anticipation.

"I already am," I replied simply, my voice barely a whisper.

He smiled broadly and affectionately, his features and soul relaxed and truly happy for the first time since I'd known him.

My heart soared, I matched his smile and felt my breath catch in my throat as he leant forward as though to kiss me.

And then he disappeared.

CHAPTER 23

LIKE THE FOOL THAT I WAS, I sat in the car for a few minutes after Joseph had gone, wondering if I had hallucinated the whole thing. I could still smell his familiar scent in my car, and since he had never otherwise been in there I had to conclude that I had actually given him a lift, at least. Had he also really said that he wanted me? My heart was hammering in my chest from a combination of excitement and sheer bliss at the thought that he had, but my thoughts were clouded with utter confoundedness at his disappearance. Vanishing like that was ... well, 'odd' didn't really cover it. Yet something deep within me accepted it as normal; he'd disappeared after I'd first seen him at the train station, after all, and had appeared just as suddenly at my door the night of my nightmare. I was damned if I could explain it, but right then it didn't seem important.

Funnily enough, I was more preoccupied with the idea that Joseph actually wanted me — *me* — and had decided that I was worth whatever problems that would cause with his family, than I was with his sudden departure. I dared to hope that it was all true, and that his disappearance was not because he had changed his mind about what he wanted. Again.

A bang at the window next to me startled me and I spun round. Alex was standing beside my car door, his hand still raised from knocking. Hastily, I fumbled with the car door and he stepped back to allow me to exit.

"You have a client in reception, Sephy," he said in the steady, deep voice I had only heard on a handful of occasions before now.

Confused, I checked my watch and said, "Do I? Who is it?"

"It is one of Russ's clients. He wishes you to see him whilst he takes care of some family business upstairs."

Something about his tone made me feel anxious. Was the 'family business' he spoke of to do with Joseph and I, or was I being paranoid? He thrust a file at me and I took it wordlessly. I retrieved my own files from the back seat, which Alex took from me, informing me that he would put them in my office. Entirely ignoring my tentative enquiry as to whether he had seen Joseph anywhere, he escorted me back into the building and left me in reception to meet my client whilst he went upstairs without further comment.

I resolved to deal with Russ's client as swiftly as possible and then resume the more pressing business of finding Joseph.

The client had a tricky set of circumstances involving two separate wives, one of whom he'd thought he'd already divorced when he'd married the second one, so he needed a divorce (for the first) and an annulment (for the second) so that he could legally marry the latest woman in his life. He made my love life — such as it was — seem positively straightforward. It took far longer than I would have liked to take his instructions and I cynically assumed that had been Alex's or Russ's intention when he had passed the client to me.

***

An hour and a half later, I walked my client out to reception. To my surprise, Alex was leaning against Sabina's reception desk, his thumbs flying over his phone screen in a way that could only mean he was playing a game. He briefly held up a finger in a gesture intended to make me wait and I stood at the foot of the stairs, impatient for him to finish so that he could tell me why he seemed intent on taking up my time.

A moment later, he clicked his phone off and pushed himself away from the desk to stand upright. "Nailed it," he muttered, waggling his phone with a small smile at the corner of his mouth.

I gave a stiff smile in reply.

"After you," he said, gesturing towards the stairs.

Biting back my frustration and irritation, I walked up the stairs ahead of him intending to put the new file on my desk and then search the building for Joseph, office-by-office if necessary.

When we reached my office, however, Alex followed me inside and closed the door behind us. Walking round to Russ's desk and clicking onto

Russ's diary, he said, "Right, let's see what else I can get you doing this afternoon ..."

Forcing myself to be polite, I interjected, "Actually, I have to find Joseph. Have you seen him?"

He acted as though I hadn't spoken. "Ah, yes, there's another of Russ's clients in ten minutes, you can see her. Should take an hour or so, looks like a juicy domestic violence issue. If we're lucky, she'll want an injunction and that'll get you out of my hair for the rest of the afternoon."

I leant forwards, resting my hands on my desk and doing my best to look intimidating. All he would have to do to negate this would be to stand, since he was almost as tall sitting as I was standing, but I was annoyed by his dismissal and his blatant attempt to manipulate my life. "Alex, talk to me. Give me some answers, for heaven's sake. Where is Joseph?"

A glimmer of nervousness passed over him, though he swiftly masked it. "He is upstairs in a meeting with his family."

"You're family, why are you here?"

"I am family only by marriage and as I am taking neutral ground in their debate I am surplus to requirements. Furthermore, Joseph was most anxious to ensure that you are kept safe. I am here to keep you out of trouble and to keep Joseph at least half sane."

I raised my eyebrows, "Holy hell, I think I just got a straight answer out of a Democritus ..."

He looked amused. "As I said, I am a Democritus by marriage. Personally, I believe that people are more amenable if they are given facts. My wife disagrees, hence her rather candidly-phrased

184

suggestion that I leave the meeting and come to spend some time with you."

"That doesn't sound very neutral of you," I commented.

"No, perhaps not. But as it is not entirely supportive of Erica's stance it is still considered necessary for me to take a step back."

"Why does she hate me?" I asked, stung.

He spread his hands. "I don't think there will ever be enough time to answer that question. If you have any others, I will do my best to give you the facts."

I stood straight again, deciding that perhaps my fight was not with Alex after all. "Right. Facts. Good. Joseph just disappeared in front of me. Literally, not figuratively. What the hell is going on?" I asked.

"Why do *you* think he disappeared?" he asked steadily.

I shrugged expansively, thinking wildly of possible explanations just to bat the question back to him. "I don't know — he's a wizard?"

"No."

"A time traveller?"

"No."

"Was he cursed by a witch?"

He smothered a smile that was threatening his otherwise neutral visage. "Again, no."

"Then I have no answer and I am slightly disappointed about the wizard thing."

He suppressed a chuckle and gestured for me to sit down, which I was doing anyway, and looked steadily at me over his steepled fingers. "Joseph was called away to meet with his family. He was taken from the car against his wishes and without warning by my wife; normally that type of action would warrant sanctions and punishment. However, since she was acting in response to the fact that Joseph has made a decision that puts us all in jeopardy, I doubt that Erica will face any repercussions."

"What? Erica took him from my car without me seeing her? So is *she* a wizard, then? Is there such a thing as a female wizard or is that just a witch? Is Erica a *witch*? And what decision — his decision to be with me? Why is that such a problem for you lot?"

"That was a lot of questions."

"Answer them."

He sighed, counting his answers off on his fingers. "Yes. No. I don't know. No. Yes."

There was a pause whilst I matched his answers to my questions. I was slightly relieved that Erica wasn't a witch; I didn't want to wake up as a toad or something. "You didn't answer the last one. Why is it such a problem for you lot if Joseph does want to be with me?"

"Because of what you are," he said steadily.

The phone on my desk rang; I ignored it.

"And what am I? Some council estate chav?" I asked, my hackles rising.

He gazed at me, head tilted to one side, considering. "No. That part of your heritage is unimportant. What matters is that, to our kind, you are a nightmare made flesh."

He said this so matter-of-factly that it took me a moment to process.

Indignant, I replied, "Bit rude."

This made him bark out a laugh but his reply was hardly illuminating. "Russ was quite right. You are a funny one."

Lu, Russ's secretary, pushed open the door as she tapped on it to announce her arrival; she looked harried. "Sephy, I'm really sorry to interrupt, but I've been trying to put a call through. It's a DS Bishop for you, can you pick up?"

Matt.

"Sorry, can you tell him I'll call him back—"

"—I told him you were in a meeting but he says it's extremely urgent, a matter of life and death," she interrupted with an apologetic shrug.

I snatched up the still-ringing phone without further hesitation. "Matt?" I answered without further preamble, my blood running cold as I thought how unlikely it was that he would call using his formal title and interrupt me in a meeting.

I heard the relief in his voice. "Seph. Thank god you're there. Makris has gone off radar."

CHAPTER 24

ALEX MUST HAVE SEEN THE COLOUR drain from my face as he was at my side of the desk in an instant, holding me steady as my legs turned to water and I sat heavily in my chair. I felt the colour rush back to my cheeks as I registered Alex's concerned expression.

I heard Matt say, "Seph?" and I raised the phone back to my ear from where it had slid to my chest.

"I'm here," I managed to say, my voice as weak as my knees. My mind was oddly blank as some kind of protective amnesia overcame me. I did not want to think about this, so I would not.

Matt's voice filtered through the nothingness. "He disappeared from the waiting room before his probation appointment, coppers have gone round to his flat and the Bastard knows where you work; there are photos, apparently. Is whatshisname there to keep an eye on you till I can get there?"

I wasn't in such shock that I didn't feel a flicker

of annoyance at his tone. "If you mean Joseph then no, he's in a meeting."

"Great timing," he said, his voice thick with suppressed anger and ... fear? "Look, I've been out in the back of bloody beyond on another case but I'm literally on my way now. I can be with you in a half an hour."

"Are you calling hands free?" I murmured, barely aware of what I was saying but clearly still mindful of my friend's wellbeing.

He sounded mildly exasperated by my question. "Hardly the priority now, Seph, but yes. Sit tight, find the biggest bloke there and stay with him. Stay away from the windows, keep out of sight, I'll be there soon."

I nodded, then realised he couldn't see that over the phone so made a positive sound in acknowledgement. Alex easily qualified as the biggest bloke in the firm, so that was one less thing for me to have to sort out.

Alex reached over me and took the phone from my loose grasp, waving a concerned-looking Lu back out of the room. "Hello?" he said into the receiver.

I couldn't focus on what was being said. I was in that barely-there state that was a blessing, really. All thoughts about what Alex and I had been talking about and anything else had fled. My body was on autopilot, though, and I was having a distinctly physiological reaction to Matt's news. My lips started tingling as my breathing became too shallow to oxygenate my blood properly and I vaguely wondered how long it would be before I passed out. Remembering what Matt had said about keeping out of sight, I glanced anxiously at the large window beyond Russ's desk and slid off my chair to crouch on the floor, tugging at Alex's sleeve to get him to do likewise.

Concentrating on whatever Matt was telling him, Alex knelt beside me automatically. At length, he spoke into the phone, "Right. Let me give you a postcode, you can meet her there instead. It will be safer than staying at the office if he knows where she works, and it is easier to defend."

Alex rattled off a postcode and then he hung up. I could feel sweat trickling down my back between my shoulders; I felt sick and I was shaking badly.

"Take my hand," Alex said, reaching for me. "I will take you somewhere safe, and Joseph can meet you there. Matt will be able to get there in about an hour from where he is."

I looked down dumbly at his outstretched hand. "What?"

"I will take you somewhere safe—" he started to repeat.

"—No, no, I heard, I just ..." Part of me just didn't trust him.

Alex didn't let me dither any longer. He grabbed my hand and I had a split second to realise that we were no longer in my office but in a large living room decorated with bold colours, prints and patterns. Immediately after that, I felt as though I had been punched in my stomach: I couldn't breathe; I felt as though I were being ripped apart, the pain starting in and radiating from a point just below my sternum; every bone in my body was on fire. I couldn't even scream. In that moment, I just wanted to die — anything to end the pain and feeling of suffocation.

As black flowers bloomed in my vision and I felt that surely death was on its way, I was suddenly able to draw breath, pulling it noisily into my lungs and coughing it back out, my shoulders heaving and back arching. I became aware that I was on the floor, my hands clawing into the thick pile of the carpet beneath me.

"Alex, what the fuck?" I gasped, rolling onto my back to find him standing over me, his arms crossed over his chest, apparently waiting patiently for me to get over whatever it was that had happened to me.

"I apologise," he said simply.

He did not respond any further to my rather vague (yet pressing) question; instead, he focussed on what he set about doing next. His first task was to locate and flick on the light switches even though there was plenty of daylight entering through the windows to my left and right. He then made a couple of calls on his mobile, leaving short messages for, I guessed, Joseph, telling him where we were and that he should come as soon as he got the message.

Putting his phone into his breast pocket, he walked over to where I still sat on the floor and offered his hand; I snatched mine back as far away from him as I could and looked at him fearfully — the last time I'd held his hand I'd felt like I'd been turned inside out. I wasn't going to make that mistake again in a hurry.

He sighed. "I am sorry. It was the swiftest and most discreet way to get you here." He paused thoughtfully and added, "On the plus side, it might just have brought things to a head for the rest of my family. Erica may not be thrilled, but it seemed judicious to get you here in a manner in which we could not be followed. Right now, I am offering you my hand simply to help you to your feet: I shall not take you anywhere again without your express consent, I assure you."

Dumbfounded, I grabbed his still-outstretched hand and he hauled me to my feet causing me to feel dizzy as my blood pressure struggled to cope with whatever else had happened in the last few minutes and I staggered slightly against him. He steadied me, pulled out one of the chairs that was placed around a large glass dining table and gestured for me to sit down. I did so gratefully and sat with my head in my hands for a moment. He left the room and a moment later metal shutters started to slide down over the windows in the wall to my left, the noise and sudden movement making me jump in alarm. The light from the windows to my right dimmed next — I bent over to see through them and saw that they looked out onto a square atrium that was easily as large as half a football pitch. Above, a metal shutter was sliding shut over a pyramidal glass roof that enclosed the atrium, shutting out the last of the natural light.

The house in which I sat stretched the entire length of one side of the atrium. Around the other sides were three other, equally large, marble-fronted houses that met at right angles at each corner. Within the atrium, there was an abundance of olive trees in large pots, a large marble fountain and a central seating area filled with sofas and easy chairs.

I watched at a detached distance as Alex exited 'our' house via a door into the atrium; he moved from house to house, stepping inside and emerging from each shortly afterwards. He soon returned, looking slightly more comfortable, dusting his hands together after closing the atrium door behind him. He joined me at the table.

"The entire perimeter is now secured with reinforced metal shutters. Nobody but my family will be able to get in. You are perfectly safe. Welcome to The Heights."

I couldn't find my voice, even to thank him politely.

We sat in silence for a minute or so. I didn't want to speak because I thought that if I did, I would probably swear again. I knew I ought to explain why Matt had clearly felt the need for me to vanish for a while and why I was grateful that Alex had taken the task upon himself so effectively, but I didn't feel capable of rational speech, what with trying to understand what had just happened at the same time as coping with the news that Leon Makris had apparently found me again. How on earth had I been in my office once moment and in someone's pimped-up monstrosity of a dining room the next? (There really was an unnecessary amount of leopard print.) But I didn't want to ask where I was or how long it would be before Matt would get there, or any of the other, practical questions I had — I just wanted to be quiet, to *not* think.

Alex cleared his throat. "I don't imagine Joseph will be long. He will have felt your distress and is probably already searching for you; hopefully it will soon occur to him to check his blasted phone."

"What do you mean, he'll have felt it?" I asked.

He shrugged indifferently, "I'm sure he'll explain it all later, it's not for you to be concerned about right now."

"This is your house? In the Dales? How did I get here?"

Alex was texting again and rather distracted as he answered, "Yes. This is my wing of our home and you are safe. Joseph's wing is the one you can see directly across the atrium from here. Russ and Felicity reside in the one to our left, Thomas and Hester in the one to our right."

Under other circumstances, I might have been more interested in this. But I was focussed on the more immediate problem, which was not simply going to go away on its own however much I might want it to. Leon Makris was out there looking for me and I didn't know where Matt was or if he was safe. I was so scared by this that my knees were actually shaking. I felt a slight pressure as Alex, perhaps picking up on my anxiety, tentatively put a reassuring hand on my shoulder.

My thoughts were bouncing around like a ball on a roulette wheel. How had Makris found me? Would he find me here? Why was he still obsessed after all this time? Was Matt safe? My niece?

Makris, the man who had attacked me, the man who had wrecked my life for years, who had given me nightmares and stolen my future, had found me again and this time it definitely wasn't a dream. Inside my head, all the horror of his attack flooded back and I wished fervently that Matt were with me already. Then a small voice inside me said that actually it was Joseph I wanted, even if that meant telling him the truth.

My breath puffed out of me in dread at the thought of having to tell anyone — least of all Joseph

— far more about my past than I had ever wanted to reveal. But if Joseph was coming to find me in the middle of all of this then I didn't see how I could avoid telling him …

I turned to stare across the atrium at his house, lost in my thoughts. It took a second to realise that Joseph had appeared in the centre of the atrium, his eyes wide and searching as he spun round.

"*Sephy?!*" he roared, evidently not aware that I was in Alex's house.

Desperate to be with him regardless of the unpleasant task ahead of me, I didn't even question how Joseph had apparently arrived in the atrium out of nowhere — at that moment, all I wanted was to be in his arms. I stood; his attention was drawn by my movement and, spotting me, he vanished, reappearing directly in front of me a fraction of a second later. I didn't care how he'd done that; all that mattered was that I was in his arms, relief flooding through me.

"Who the hell is Leon Makris?" he asked angrily, pulling me away from his chest so that he could look me in the eyes, his hands gripping my upper arms and his expression furious.

His outrage startled me and for a moment I couldn't speak.

Not waiting for my reply, Joseph barked at Alex, "What happened?"

"Sephy's policeman friend said that it was a matter of life and death that I keep her safe. I inferred that he meant *my* death if I failed. I felt that a little protection was in order, hence the shutters," he replied drily.

"I don't understand — what are you supposed

to be keeping her safe from? What *happened*?" Joseph demanded, his voice increasingly frustrated and angry.

"I did leave a message on your voicemail. Did you not receive it?" Alex seemed rather calmer than his brother-in-law.

"No, I've been in that bloody stupid meeting — held against my will by your *wife*, I should add — and my phone was switched off, I just heard Sephy and I've been looking bloody everywhere for her — *again!*"

I still couldn't bring myself to speak.

Joseph was still holding my upper arms but he was looking at Alex, who explained calmly, "I am sorry about Erica, though she is your sister as much as she is my wife, you know, and I am no more to blame for her actions than you are. As to what happened, all I know is that Matt phoned Sephy. He told her — and me — that a man by the name of Leon Makris has not turned up for an appointment with his probation worker and enquiries have revealed that his home address is full to the brim of photographs of her and her place of work. It is feared that he may be on his way to find Sephy with a view to causing her harm. I felt it prudent to bring her somewhere safe."

Joseph pressed me protectively into his chest; I felt him nod. In a voice of forced calm, he replied, "Well, good, then. Thank you." Turning his attention back to me, he asked, "Is that the man who mugged you? Where's Matt now, what's he doing about it?" I felt his breath in my hair as he spoke, heard the barely suppressed anger in his voice.

I felt sick again. I didn't know how Joseph had

196

found me, or how he had known that I was in trouble. Alex's brief mention that Joseph could 'feel' that I was in distress had made little sense at the time and still did not; nor did Joseph's assertion that he had 'heard' me. I also didn't understand how he knew Makris's name; I could only pray that he didn't know the details of what had been done to me. A feeling of complete dread spread through my body. I fervently wished that I had told Joseph all about myself and my history concerning Makris when he'd been at my house, after my dream. Perhaps if I had, he would have decided not to approach me at court, or to go against his family's wishes and tell me that he wanted to be with me. He would then have been able to make an *informed* choice as to whether or not to begin a relationship with me.

Perhaps mistaking my silence for fear that Makris would find me, Alex's deep voice rumbled, "This is our home, Sephy. We're miles away from where he might think to look for you, and the houses are locked up completely, nobody will be able to enter. You'll be safe here."

"Joseph found me; Joseph got in," I mumbled, barely coherent.

"Well, nobody but us, then," he amended, though his words hardly registered.

I closed my eyes and kept them shut: just as I used to do when I was a child, I tried to believe that if I kept them closed long enough I would disappear. I did not want to do this; did not want to bring my past into my present. I tried to hold on to the sensation of love and safety I felt in Joseph's arms for all it was worth, believing that it wouldn't be long before all that would be taken from me.

"Don't be afraid, you're with me now. Whatever it is, it will be okay, I will protect you," he murmured, adding a soft kiss to the top of my head.

Keeping my eyes tightly shut I managed a short nod in acknowledgement, trying very hard to block out all feeling, good or bad. Joseph let go of me with one hand to reach into his pocket for his mobile, which was buzzing. A moment later he said, "Yes? Yes, put him through." There was a pause and then he said, "Matt, just what the hell is going on?"

The sound of my friend's name made me open my eyes again. I couldn't hear Matt's reply, but Joseph said next, "What does he look like? Is he acting alone?"

I cringed, hating the fact that I was too cowardly to tell him all this myself and wishing time would just stop before it all got much worse.

He hung up and said coldly to Alex, "Forty-year-old male, six foot three, slight build, brown hair. Nothing I can't handle even if he does know where we are. Thank you for bringing her here, I can take it from here."

Alex nodded reluctantly. "I can stay if you'd prefer?"

Joseph shook his head. "It's fine. I'm sure Erica would appreciate it if you would return. You may have some work ahead of you to restore harmony, I'm afraid, but I appreciate the support you gave me today."

I wondered vaguely what was wrong with Erica, but she was far from my most pressing concern so I remained where I was, held close to Joseph's chest and clinging to his shirt like a life raft in a storm.

Alex sighed heavily. To Joseph, he said, "Very well. Wish me luck. Try not to kill anybody, it would rather negate our efforts to remain under the radar." Turning to me, he said, "You don't need to be afraid. Joseph will keep you safe. I hope for this Makris's sake that your friend Matt finds him before Joseph gets his hands on him."

I managed a nod and murmured a thanks: though I had no clear idea of *how* he'd actually helped me, I knew that he had sought to keep me safe.

Joseph turned his attention back to me. "You're safe. I promise," he said softly.

I shook my head. "I'm scared."

"He can't hurt you. I promise."

"No. I'm scared you'll hate me," I whispered.

He laughed softly, "Don't be ridiculous. Why would I hate you? Some lunatic has apparently gone AWOL and may be intent on finding you — why would I leave you to face that alone?"

I squeezed my eyes tight shut once more, not brave enough to tell him the truth.

CHAPTER 25

WHEN I DID MANAGE TO OPEN my eyes, it was to allow Joseph to escort me to a large, soft sofa, where I sat with my legs curled up beside him and my head on his chest. His arm was wrapped around my shoulders and mercifully he seemed content to sit in silence. There was no sign of Alex and I surmised that he must have left.

A moment or two later, Russ strode through the atrium door. I supposed there must be another entrance to the atrium, presumably via one of the other houses, and that Russ had been able to open the shutters Alex had mentioned.

Marching to where we sat, he stood in front of me and scowled. "Alex told me what happened — why on earth didn't you tell me this man's name when I asked? We could have found him and dealt with him before he became a problem. What a ridiculous risk. And for what? Well?"

I flinched back at his ire and Joseph sat forward, hand held out as though to restrain his brother. "Now is absolutely *not* the time, Russ," he growled.

Ignoring him, Russ demanded of me, "Do you know what it would have done to my brother if you had been hurt — or *killed*?"

"Russ, that's *enough*," Joseph said.

Russ's words had made me look up at him, though, making eye contact for the first time since he had entered. His aura was a blend of anger, fear and worry and it mirrored almost exactly that of his brother. I absolutely hated the fact that I'd caused them to feel like that and I shut my eyes again, unable to cope with feeling any worse than I already did.

Wholly inadequate though it felt, I said softly, "Sorry."

Joseph sat back beside me and wrapped me in his arms once more. I closed my eyes again; I heard Russ sigh heavily and murmur to Joseph, "Give me a ring when they've got him, will you? I'm going to give Alex some backup; Erica's doing her nut. But call me if you need me here, alright?"

I felt Joseph nod in response. A moment later, I sensed that we were alone again.

I can best describe my state at that point as close to catatonic. I was trying my best to just block out anything and everything, to empty my thoughts and delay the inevitable. Matt was on his way and I knew that when he arrived I was going to have to tell Joseph about what Makris had done, knowing that I should have done so sooner.

My mum had never been warm towards me, but after I was attacked she became positively hateful: she'd called me every name under the sun, told me that she hated me and wished I'd never been born, and ultimately she'd thrown me out of her house … With that memory of rejection firmly in mind, I was really scared that Joseph might not want to have anything else to do with me. That thought was unbearable, because even though there was technically nothing between Joseph and me yet, my heart was his.

At last, Matt arrived with a loud crunch of tyres on gravel, a car door slam and a hefty thump on the doors. Joseph went to let him in, unbolting the heavy wooden front door.

Matt gave Joseph a brief glance and pushed past him, scanning the room for me. When he saw me, he moved instinctively towards me and I scrambled off the sofa to close the distance between us. Seeing that I was safe, though, Matt seemed to reconsider and halted a little way in front of me. Something about his body language made me hesitate, too.

"Good," he said. "I'm glad you're safe. Now, I'm not going to be nice to you, Seph, because it'll make you cry and *I'm* no good to anyone when you cry, so let's keep this professional, okay?" He nodded behind him and I saw that he hadn't come alone. "DC Cam happened to be up this way. Good job, because I want someone to have my back who knows what we're up against."

"Hi, Cam," I said softly. I didn't have the energy or inclination to tell Matt that I'd seen Cam at court earlier.

Cam nodded back at me, "Alright, Seph?" Agitation and discomfort flooded his colours; he had closed the door with a hefty push and now stood with his back to it, alert.

Matt said, "Right. We'll be staying here until I get the official word on where we can put you until we've found Makris. Shouldn't be long."

His voice was gruff, professional, cold, and despite his earlier assertion I knew that this was more to protect his own feelings than mine. I knew from the few times he'd been willing to discuss his feelings about the attack on me that it had been easier for him to deal with it all as a policeman than as a friend — his role had given him a shield, a barrier around the hurt he'd felt so acutely. I surmised he was doing the same thing here, protecting himself from feeling the fear and anxiety I knew he otherwise would, but that didn't mean I had to like it.

"What do you mean, 'put me'?"

Matt raised his eyebrows and, in a tone that suggested this was obvious, said, "You'll need somewhere safe to stay."

"I'm safe here," I said, not liking the way this conversation was going.

However much I didn't want to talk about this in front of Joseph, it was nothing compared to how much I needed to stay with him.

"No, you're not. *He* doesn't even know what the problem is," Matt said, gesturing with a nod towards Joseph, who looked at me for clarification whilst I avoided his gaze.

I scowled. Matt knew full well that I hadn't spoken about it: he could probably tell that from the fact Joseph was still with me. I folded my arms, mirroring his posture. "I'm safe here," I repeated, more firmly. "This place is a fortress. And I am not leaving."

"Yes you bloody well are," Matt insisted,

growing increasingly agitated.

I dug my heels in. "No I bloody well am not."

"Okay then. Fine. Let's wait for the Bastard here, he can kill all of us," Matt said conversationally as he sat down in the nearest chair.

I knew he was goading me, that this had little to do with my safety. He could, I imagined, easily arrange for police to keep watch over me here if he wanted to, rather than send me to a safe house.

"Good. Then stay. We're *all* safe here," I said, a little louder. No matter how he might come to feel about me after learning the whole sordid tale, I knew that Joseph would protect me and Matt alike — though how I could believe this with such certainty I couldn't have said.

We had reached an impasse. We both stared at each other, arms folded, dark expressions on our faces. If I hadn't been so upset I might have laughed at the tableau.

Matt broke the stand-off to answer his mobile. He answered with his surname and then said 'yes' and 'no' a couple of times, then told whomever was on the other end of the line to text him the address and postcode, before he hung up and stood once more to face me. "Right, enough now, this is getting daft. There's a hotel sorted; you'll have round-the-clock protection from two officers till they find him. Cam's volunteered to take first shift with me. I can send someone to our house to get some things together for you if you want. Clothes and stuff, I mean."

None of what he was saying felt real at all. I didn't like the momentum of this, felt like I had absolutely no control, no say in the matter at all.

Joseph moved silently to stand beside me, one

arm protectively round my back. He had remained worryingly silent throughout and I daren't meet his eyes, dreading how this would all turn out. Quietly but firmly, he said, "She is safest here, with me. She is not leaving my side."

I saw the resolve on Matt's face falter, a line of uncertainty creasing his brow. He shook his head slightly, frowning in determination once again and pointing a finger at Joseph as though to emphasise the strength of his conviction. "Not true. You don't know what you're up against. You don't know what he's capable of. Seph, you're coming with me or you're sitting here and telling him everything. If you tell him, I'll ... I'll leave you be, if that's what you want."

Joseph turned to face me and said firmly, "I know you're scared to tell me what this is all about, but your safety is what matters. You will be safe with me, I promise, but I think you should tell me whatever it is, for Matt's peace of mind and so that I can be prepared. The truth will not change how I feel about you. Trust me."

"Please don't send me away," I whispered.

CHAPTER 26

MATT AND JOSEPH WERE SEATED AT opposite ends of the long sofa, as far apart from each other as possible. I sat alone, on the armchair I'd claimed for my own, my knees tucked up under my chin and my arms wrapped around my shins.

Cam remained resolutely by the front door, occasionally checking his mobile whenever it buzzed. Even in my distracted state, I noticed that there was something distinctly off about Cam's colours, though I didn't understand exactly what it was that kept drawing my attention. He wouldn't make eye contact with me and his brow was slick with sweat. I was forced to conclude that poor Cam was even more afraid of Makris than I was; he knew exactly what Makris was capable of and was no doubt worried about what would happen if he turned up.

When I could delay no longer, I began. I spoke quietly, but the room was otherwise so silent that it was not difficult for them to hear me. I tried to pretend I was delivering a speech, acting a part in a play, talking about something that had happened in a dream or dark fantasy.

"I'd gone to a club in town with some friends. I didn't tend to go out much, but my mum was in a foul mood and I really didn't want to be in the house, so I decided I'd go this time. I don't like drinking as a rule, but I was finding it hard to relax after arguing with my mum, so I let one of my friends buy me a vodka and Coke. Feeling a bit woozy helped, and I thought the evening might be more enjoyable if I just let go for once, so I had another. And another. By the time I realised I couldn't see colours— see *properly, I mean* — I was too drunk to care."

I glanced warily at Matt, but he seemed preoccupied with checking his phone and didn't appear to have noticed my reference to the fact that I couldn't see auras when I was inebriated. Joseph merely nodded an acknowledgement and waited for me to go on. I averted my gaze once more, staring at a patch of the floor rather than watch his reactions.

"I was such a lightweight I could hardly walk with three vodkas swimming around in my system, so I just sat at the bar and chatted with whichever friends weren't dancing at the time. A bit later, Matt and some of his mates from rugby turned up and we were suddenly a much larger group; none of us knew everyone there but we all got on well.

"Leon Makris was there and acted like he was part of the group — buying drinks, telling stories and laughing at jokes; no one knew him but, at the time, we all assumed someone else did. I couldn't see what he was, y'know, *like*." This was difficult — I hadn't been able to see Makris's colours (or anyone's) but that wasn't something I'd ever explained to Matt, who was still listening to all of this. I hoped that

Joseph would understand what I meant. "Normally, that would have made me anxious, but the alcohol made me feel like I couldn't care less — and anyway, he seemed harmless. He kept asking me about my family, where I grew up, that kind of thing, nothing that made me feel uncomfortable; it felt quite good to have someone take an interest in me … A couple of my friends quite fancied him, but it was me he was interested in and I was, well, I was flattered, I suppose. And anyway, Matt was there, I thought I was safe."

Out of the corner of my eye, I saw my friend shifting uncomfortably, his colours reflecting agitation. I immediately felt the need to reassure him that I didn't blame him in any way, even though he'd always blamed himself.

"Matt was uneasy, kept suggesting we go home. Makris told him to chill, told him we were only talking, and I seemed relaxed enough that Matt didn't push it. But Matt didn't go further than about three feet away from me for the rest of the evening and kept prompting me to keep my hand over my glass — he told me later that he was sure Makris was going to slip something in my drink.

"Eventually we all went home — Matt took me home in a taxi and saw me in before he walked next door to his house. Apparently Makris followed us home.

"The house I lived in with my mum and sister was a mid-terrace in a row of eight. No one thought much of it when the end terrace three doors down got broken into that night; we all just made extra sure that our own doors and windows were locked tight. No one thought to check the lofts: if we had, we'd have realised that there were holes in the walls that would normally separate the loft spaces between the houses. That's how he got into the space above my bedroom.

"He stayed up there for two nights, waiting all that time for me to be alone." I shivered, remembering the little nest he'd made for himself up there, complete with tiny spy holes he'd made in my ceiling so that he could watch me. "Then my sister went out for the night and that left only me and my mum in the house. I was asleep, and then ... then he was there. I fought him, I promise I did, but he was much stronger than I was and I'd been lying down in bed, I couldn't stop him ..."

Images of his face, the anger that flowed off him in waves, threatened to overwhelm me for a moment and I fought hard to stay in the present. I gripped my hands, feeling the pinch and scratch of my nails against my palms; I breathed deeply through my nose, drinking in the faint scents in the air — the washing powder smell from Joseph's shirt, Matt's aftershave, some flowers on the windowsill nearby. It all helped to remind me of where I was and reassure me of where I was *not*.

When I was able, I continued. "He gagged me, and he hit me hard; I was winded, I couldn't even scream. I blacked out. I woke up lying on a wooden floor all alone; my head was killing me and I had no idea where I was; all I could hear was rain on the windows, and taps running in the bath upstairs. There was blood in my mouth; I'd lost a couple of teeth — some of these are implants," I mentioned, touching my mouth self-consciously. "I started to stand up, and then he was there, next to me. He pulled me up by my hair and dragged me upstairs. I tried to grab the balustrades but he pulled my fingers free, broke three of them. He told me it would hurt more if I fought him but I still tried to get free, so he broke my jaw, too.

"He threw me into the bathroom; I fell on the floor and he climbed on top of me … and I was so scared and so broken that I just couldn't find the strength to stop him."

I was shaking as I remembered the feeling of helplessness; I prayed that Joseph wouldn't mistake my lack of power for a lack of resistance as my mum had done. I hated myself enough as it was. I couldn't bear to look at Joseph or Matt, couldn't stand to see my own disgust and horror reflected back at me in their faces.

I fought to regulate my breathing, determined to get the whole thing out now that I'd come so far. "Then, after he — after he finished, I felt him punch me, in my lower abdomen, over and over. It took a few seconds for the pain to kick in, for me to realise that it wasn't water on the floor but blood: he hadn't punched me, he'd stabbed me."

Steeling myself, I pressed on, my arms clamped firmly round my upper body as I tried to give myself the hug I so badly needed but did not deserve. "He carried me over to the bath, and I hurt so much that I couldn't even try to get out of his arms. I started thinking about Matt and my Nana and how they'd feel when they found out I'd died; but then I started feeling really tired, and dying didn't even feel like a bad thing anymore, it was as if I could just drift off to sleep. Then he … then he … the bath … the bath was full …"

I drifted off, lost in memory. All I could think

of was the look in Makris's eyes, the rough skin on his hands, the smell of his breath, the sound and colour of his anger and disgust filling my vision, the pain, the water …

Distantly, I was aware that Matt's hands were clasped round my upper arms, that he was shaking me as he said loudly, "*Seph, Seph, you're alright, you're here with me and whatshisface … Oh, shit! Cam — give us a hand ...*" But I heard his voice only distantly, as if I were at the bottom of a well. I hadn't had a flashback in a long time and Matt had clearly recognised that one was upon me, but by then it was too late.

I was no longer in Alex's living room: I was in a grey bathroom with cork tiles on the floor and a buzzing light fixture. The bath was turquoise plastic with filthy taps and a plug with no chain. The water was stone cold, a fact that would ironically help me survive by narrowing my blood vessels and preventing me from bleeding to death, but which was also nearly enough to end my life when I was submerged in it. My mouth was bleeding heavily and the pain in my abdomen was indescribable.

Matt, Joseph, Cam — all were gone, and in their place a tall, athletic man with scraggly black hair and three days' chin stubble was picking me up, dropping me into the bath and holding my head down, my arms flailing helplessly as I tried to claw my way back to the surface, my legs kicking against nothing. Makris's teeth were bared in a snarl, pure hatred in his eyes; lights were firing randomly in my vision that was otherwise growing darker by the second. I was dying.

Endless time later, I was free — my head was

released and I pushed myself up out of the water and gasped, drawing breath into lungs that burned as I tried to pull myself out of the bath. I fell on the floor; in front of me, Matt was fighting with Makris. Matt's abdomen was torn and bleeding as heavily as mine was, yet he'd bested Makris and was straddling him, punching him even as his ripped t-shirt turned crimson. The floor was sticky against my face as it became saturated with our combined warm blood and my eyes began to close.

They opened again and I was sitting with my back pressed against the base of the sofa, soft black carpet beneath me, my shirt damp with sweat, not water … My arms and legs were braced against the floor, stiff and determined to keep me as far away as possible from the bath that still filled my mind's eye.

I gradually became aware of my breathing, which was rasping in and out as though my throat were constricted. My heart was beating so hard I was sure it would be visible externally but the fight-or-flight bit of my brain was doing its job and keeping my eyes focussed on the room around me, sure that Makris could be there, ignoring the Blue auras and searching intently for any sign of Red. My eyes were watering, not through tears but through an absence of blinking.

I was aware of a voice but there was just no capacity for communication, only survival. As I became more aware of my actual surroundings and less immersed in my memories, I fought my way back into the present by compulsively counting the individual tufts of carpet pile I could feel beneath my fingers, using this distraction to slow down my breathing and begin to allow my frontal lobes to regain function. At last, I was able to tear my gaze away from the room and instead looked at the floor, counting tufts by sight rather than by touch now, still carefully modulating my breathing. My body began to try to get rid of the now-redundant adrenaline — I was shaking badly and my jaw was clenched.

Finally, I became aware of Joseph, who was kneeling beside me, a shallow but bloody scratch running down his cheek and his colours a perfect balance of fear, shock and anger. I still couldn't process what he was saying, but I had enough control over my body now to force myself to stand. I registered that Matt was sitting back on the sofa, his head buried in his hands and sorrow flooding his aura. There was a door a few feet away and I got to my feet and walked to it on legs that felt like wood, a pressing need to escape overwhelming me.

I was in a kitchen; I felt the heated tiles beneath my feet; I counted the small mosaic tiles that made up the splashback above the sink; I forced myself to listen to Joseph who was once again beside me, my name falling from his lips in a mantra, "You are safe, Sephy. You are safe, Sephy. You are safe, Sephy." I smelt the familiar scent of washing powder combined with subtler notes of lavender, coconut, mint and cotton. Gradually, my heart rate returned to somewhere close to normal, my range of vision widened again and I was figuratively back in the room. I was safe indeed.

Perhaps sensing my recovery, Joseph wrapped me in his arms, still repeating his mantra as he held me to his chest and let me cling to him. I would have time to be embarrassed later — at that moment, I just needed comfort, and I took it from him.

CHAPTER 27

I DON'T KNOW HOW LONG WE stood that way. I had gradually calmed down to the extent that I could think rationally and clearly, and my first thought was that I'd gone from catatonic to full-on Bedlam exhibit, all in front of the man I wanted to be my boyfriend. I'd also somehow managed to claw him.

I pulled out of his arms and examined his scratched cheek in horror, looking at the welt I'd made. "I'm sorry, I'm sorry," I repeated several times, guilt-ridden by the sight of his blood, blood that I had drawn. I might have caught him when I was scrambling across the room, but I might also have lashed out at him deliberately, my brain swapping him for someone to be fought. "We need to get that cleaned up; I have some antiseptic in my bag …" I murmured, looking round vainly for my handbag, before realising it must still be at the office.

Joseph shook his head dismissively and fell silent. He turned his head away from me, not meeting my gaze. I was frightened again, this time not of the ghosts of my past but of the very real possibility that I had succeeded in pushing this man away. My mouth went dry and my adrenal glands were evidently putting in some overtime because my shaking had worsened. I moved myself out of his arms and walked over to a seat at the breakfast bar, where I perched, wrapping my suit jacket tightly round myself for warmth as much as a sense of security, my heart still hammering wildly. He did not move to follow me, and his colours told me that he was no longer afraid or worried — he was incandescent with white rage.

I swiftly turned my attention to my nails, which were always kept short but I could see that the one on my ring finger was slightly rough at one edge and had a trace of dried blood beneath it. Guilt-ridden, I tried to smooth the imperfection with my other nails, picking at the sharp edge. I knew, though, that it had been my lack of control that had been the true cause of Joseph's injury and, though it had only left him with a scratch, it was a scratch that should not have happened. I had lied to him about what had happened, and then I had hurt him. Silent tears filled my eyes, taking with them copious amounts of cortisol as they dripped onto my trembling fingers that were still industriously working on the offending nail.

Joseph spoke at last, and I glanced up, seeing that he was staring out of the picture window to our left. His voice was low and heavy with barely controlled anger. "You told me you were *mugged*. That it was nothing serious."

I stayed quiet, not knowing what I could possibly say to put things right. I simply nodded sadly.

"That explanation was bad enough," he growled. "It brought your mortality into stark relief; it forced me to imagine what could happen to you." Shaking with suppressed rage, he pointed towards the door we had just come through, and I knew that he was referring to my flashback. "The truth was far, far worse. By not telling me, you risked both our lives."

I shook harder in response, guilt too heavy in my belly for me to absorb the full meaning of his words. I could see him trembling, his jaw clenched tight and the muscles in his arms bunched as though ready for a fight but he was not looking at me. If I had been unable to see the Blue beneath his anger, I might have been afraid that he was about to lash out at me; I might have been scared of him.

Before I could react or say anything to try to diffuse the situation, he turned towards me and his voice quickly rose from quietly murderous to a roar that I felt as much as heard: "There is a man out there who raped you. He tried to kill you, and *he nearly fucking succeeded*!"

My head snapped up, my eyes wide, my mouth open slightly in shock: I couldn't recall having heard him say so much as a single, mild swear word, so the f-bomb had come as a bit of a surprise. He was panting, his eyes wild, and he looked for all the world like he could kill someone. The door burst open and Matt was there, pushing Joseph to the side and standing between us, his arms spread wide to keep me safe.

"Don't you fucking shout at her!" Matt yelled, veins prominent in his neck, his face flushed red with anger of his own.

Joseph barely registered Matt's presence. He was looking at me with such fury that I quailed, suddenly glad that Matt was there.

"I have waited *centuries* for you and now I discover that you've been *this* close to having some deranged lunatic slaughter you in your bed — if I'd known that, I wouldn't have given a damn about the High Council, I'd have been with you every minute of every day! No — I'd have found Leon Makris and torn his fucking head off! I have been sitting here waiting for a mugger to turn up so that I could ensure he was arrested. I *should* have been out there hunting a killer, who should not have been permitted to draw another breath after he hurt you!"

This last remark seemed to be directed at Matt, who responded with, "Don't you fucking dare, mate. Don't you fucking dare. You have no idea what we went through last time, what I would have done to that bastard if—"

"—If what?" Joseph demanded, his voice full of scorn.

"If I'd thought Sephy could have survived without me if I'd ended up in jail!" Matt yelled, his voice a mixture of anger and anguish that broke my heart.

I had no idea how to respond to it all. I wanted to run away from them both and be on my own; I wanted to hug them both and never leave their sides.

Cam joined us a split second later, assessed the situation and stepped deftly in front of Joseph to separate him from Matt and me. Facing away from me and bracing his shoulder against Joseph's chest as though trying to move him out of the kitchen, Cam murmured calming-sounding words. Joseph, though, stood his ground, still full of rage.

In a shaky voice I barely recognised as my own, I said, "I'm sorry. I know I lied, I know, I just didn't want you to know all the details, I didn't think you'd want me if you knew how badly he'd hurt me, what he'd done ..." My words tumbled over themselves as they fell from my mouth, desperate to stop him from leaving.

"That bastard could have found you and taken you from me at any time! I could have Obliterated his soul a thousand times over in the time since I first met you if I had known what he had done, but now he's gone missing and I have to sit and wait for him to turn up and hope I kill him before he kills you?!"

I felt bad about the scratch, bad about having such a vivid flashback, bad about having lied, bad, bad, *bad*.

Matt remained silent, seemingly content to let Joseph rage and I wondered if he was giving him enough rope to hang himself with.

Cam spoke softly again to Joseph, but I caught every word. "You're frightening Seph."

Immediately, it was as though a switch had been flicked; Joseph's features softened, his colours flooded with horror and regret. "Sephy ... I would *never* hurt you, there is no need to be afraid of me," he said softly, anguish written all over his face as his arms fell to his sides and he took a small step away from us all to emphasise that he was not a threat. "Please, forgive me. I just ... seeing that, seeing what he did to you ..." He reached up and ran his hands through his hair in distress, unable to articulate his anguish.

Matt scoffed and half-turned to look at me; I could see scepticism written all over his face. I could understand his reaction: Joseph had shouted and sworn at me and was now apologising profusely and begging for forgiveness; Matt and I both had enough professional experience of precisely that kind of domestic scenario to know that this was the point when the woman would normally weep with joy and throw her arms round him, immediately forgiving him, only to be truly shocked the next time it happened — or indeed when it escalated to physical violence at a later date. I would normally be making a face with Matt, but I could see Joseph's colours — there was no faking that. He had been very, very angry, but then very, very remorseful at how he had scared me. His intention had not been to frighten me; his anger had not been directed at me.

When I didn't immediately indicate that I wanted to leave with Matt, or tell Joseph to leave me alone, Matt looked at me more closely and frowned at the lack of fear and mistrust that should by rights have been written all over my face. "Seph, you can't seriously be thinking of staying here with this dickhead?" he asked bitterly. When I didn't reply, he turned on Joseph and grunted disgustedly, "You don't deserve her."

Joseph flared up and bit back angrily, "You should have told me about Makris! Where is he now? Why haven't you found him yet?"

Rolling his eyes a bit, Cam moved away from Joseph and stood next to me, evidently deciding that if the two of them were going to fight there wouldn't be an awful lot he could do to stop them. In a last-ditch attempt to prevent an outbreak of the violence that was clearly brewing, he called, "You two need to take a minute and calm down. Seph needs you two on the ball, not fighting each other." Turning to me, he took my arm and said, "Let's get you somewhere a bit quieter while these two sort themselves out."

"No!" Joseph barked. "She doesn't leave my sight."

"Oh, and he's controlling as well; what a fucking surprise," Matt muttered, turning Joseph's attention back to him.

As the last of my adrenaline levelled off, I found it was too much, coping with my own feelings and memories without having to cope with theirs, too. I really needed some space. "Matt, back off …" I said wearily. "Joseph, it's fine, I do need a minute. Is there a bathroom I could use? I'll still be in the house and it's all locked up …" I wiped at my face with the back of my hand, conscious that I must look a tear-stained mess.

Joseph seemed very reluctant but was no doubt aware of the fact that he'd just gone Hulk on me and was also probably mindful of Matt's accusation that he was being controlling. He gave a single nod and pointed to a door behind me. "Just through there."

On legs that felt tired and heavy after my adrenaline dump, I let Cam guide me to the WC. Cam called back to Joseph and Matt, "I'll just check it's all clear."

Poking his head through the door ahead of us, Cam verified that the WC was empty and gestured for me to enter.

Behind us, I heard Matt say in a voice full of suppressed anger, "Right, mate, you and I need a word."

If they hadn't been so distracted, they might have been more alert to the fact that Cam followed me into the WC and closed the door gently behind us.

Turning to him in mild confusion, I said, "It's okay, I can manage from here..."

I tailed off. His colours were all over the place and I wondered for a moment if he were seriously ill. His face had turned bright red, almost purple, and a large vein stood out on his forehead.

"Jesus, Cam, what's wrong?" I asked.

Through the door, I could hear raised voices. Odd words were clearly audible whilst others were a mere angry rumble that I tried hard to block out. "You don't know how lucky you are, mate," I heard Matt say; "Why didn't you kill that monster when you had the chance? You had him right there!" Joseph yelled back.

Inside the bathroom, though, the only words I heard were Cam's.

As though he were fighting some inner turmoil, he pulled at his hair and bent double. I reached out to touch his back, but as I drew breath to call out for Matt to come and help, he straightened and looked at me, his eyes wild. His voice was strangled as he spat the words out: "Seph, I'm sorry …"

Then his face went slack and he said very clearly, yet incomprehensibly, "Lupercus!"

CHAPTER 28

BEFORE I COULD SO MUCH AS open my mouth to ask what on earth he meant, Leon Makris appeared in the small space between me and Cam. I had no time to move, scream or even think before his hand touched my shoulder and, just as when Alex had brought me to his house, I was once more in unfamiliar surroundings with no idea of how I had got there. This time, I registered that I was on the floor of a forest: tall trees shaded me from the sun; old leaves and sandy soil covered the ground beneath me.

A split second later, for the second time in as many hours, I felt as though I'd been torn in half, consumed with a burning pain all over my body and a complete inability to draw breath. This time, though, the burning pain was dwarfed by the sharp, stabbing pain between my navel and sternum, though my skin remained unbroken and I could see no physical explanation for the agony I was in.

Just as I neared the point of blacking out from

the pain and lack of oxygen, I was finally able to draw breath. I cried out, my voice raw and full of agony. I began panting to reoxygenate my body. Once sure that I could breathe properly, my fear of suffocation was swiftly replaced by my fear of Makris. I couldn't see him, but over the foist of the leaves beneath me, I could definitely smell him; he was close. Dread filled my heart.

I scrambled to my knees and spun round, heart thumping wildly in my chest as I tried to raise myself to stand on uncoordinated legs. The hairs on the back of my neck and arms tickled as they stood erect, sensing the invisible threat I knew to be there. The pain in my abdomen was still intense but I forced myself to ignore it and instead focussed on my surroundings, eyes wide as I looked around frantically for Makris.

Five feet to my right was Cam. He was lying on his back, his eyes blank and unseeing. His aura was conspicuous in its absence. I stared at his body in horror for several uncomprehending seconds before I could process what I was seeing.

"Fuck!" I spluttered, staggering towards him on legs that wouldn't obey. I tripped over my own feet and fell to my knees; hastily, I covered the remaining distance on my hands and knees and fumbled to see if I could detect a pulse but there were no signs of life — physical or metaphysical. Even though I had known from a glance that his body was devoid of spirit, I still felt compelled to act and I began performing CPR, pressing hard on his chest, pinching his nose and blowing into his slack mouth.

"Oh, he's clearly dead, Fragment. Don't bother wasting your time — not when you have so little of it left," came a mocking voice from behind me.

He was close enough that I could almost feel his foul breath on the back of my neck, and I scrambled away, taking the shortest possible route. Hating myself for the fact that I had just crawled over Cam's corpse, I nevertheless managed to get to my feet and stumbled away. Still dizzy from whatever had happened to make me appear in the middle of a forest, I staggered into a tree and spun round. I had to cling to the trunk to hold myself aloft, eyes wide and staring at the figure now before me.

I blinked several times, desperately trying to prove to myself that I was dreaming by waking up. I sought some physical sensation, hoping to confirm that I was in some institution with padding on the wall rather than in a forest with Makris. I scraped at the floor with my feet, feeling the crunch of long-dead leaves; I gripped the smooth trunk of the tree behind me and pulled at a piece of bark that peeled away in a long strip. I registered that I was uncomfortably hot; the temperature in the forest was far higher than it would have been anywhere in Yorkshire at this time of year.

This was real. However Alex had taken me from Leeds to his house, Makris must have taken me here in the same manner — wherever 'here' was. Whatever had come before, however I had got here, I did not know — but I was here and so was Makris.

I was facing a fight for my life.

His eyes were almost entirely black, as though comprised of two enormous pupils; his skin was pocked and scarred; his teeth were yellowing and decayed — his years in prison had aged him terribly. I was utterly unable to find my voice or even try to run away — it was as though my body had accepted that I would never be fast enough, never be able to outrun or outmanoeuvre him. I silently cursed this 'freeze' response that had done me absolutely no favours, ever.

Standing perhaps three or four feet in front of me, he tipped his head slightly to one side as though regarding me with interest. "You would not believe how difficult it has been for me to arrange this time alone with you, Fragment. Ever since I found your new home, you have been utterly plagued by Democrituses and I couldn't get anywhere near, so I had to try another approach ..." Nodding towards Cam's corpse, he continued, "It seems I rather overestimated the speed with which this handsome young man could persuade you to be on your own with him. Still, at least he managed it eventually."

I had enough about me to feel the sting of betrayal. I'd thought Cam was my friend, yet he had allowed Makris to gain access to me ... But how? And if Cam had been complicit in Makris's plans, why was he now dead? I pushed away all thought of what had come before — friend or foe, Cam was dead and if I didn't keep my wits about me, I would end up the same way.

Right now, I had to face the enemy before me. Certain that he was insane and that I was in terrible danger, I experienced a second wind, and found the energy to run. I darted sideways, my feet slipping on the leaves; I was strongly reminded of my recurrent dream and had a horrible thought that perhaps my dream hadn't been a memory, after all — perhaps it had been a warning, some kind of imperfect precognition of how I would die.

Just as had happened in my house during my nightmare, Makris appeared in front of me. Crying out in shock, I changed directions and he appeared directly in my path again. I turned on my heel and tried to backtrack, but he was there once more; this time he grabbed my throat and squeezed, lifting me from the ground. My feet scrambled mid-air, trying to find purchase, either to kick Makris or to take my own weight so that I could breathe again; there was a ringing sensation in my ears and my lips started to tingle. Just when I thought he was going to choke me to death, he let go and threw me to the floor.

Dragging air back through my bruised throat into my burning lungs, I was filled with cold horror as Makris's face loomed above me; he sat astride me and effortlessly resisted my every attempt to try to buck his weight from me. He took hold of my wrists and lazily pinned them by my sides beneath his knees.

I struggled still, trying to find some weak spot in his grip, trying to shake him loose. He let me wear myself out for a few minutes until, gasping and sweating, I went limp from fear and exhaustion, taking stock of my situation and trying to think of a way out.

"That was fun!" Makris laughed, though his voice was hard and humourless.

My mouth was dry and my voice was barely a whisper, but I managed, "Why are you doing this? Why me? What have I ever done to you?"

He was calmer than I had expected. He seemed to reflect carefully on his answer before giving it in a measured pace and tone that made me more fearful for his sanity than if he'd been ranting. "Oh, I have nothing against you personally. This is purely business, just as it was when we met seven years ago. I have been employed to do a job and this time I intend to see it through."

This made no sense. Makris was unbalanced: a dangerous man, certainly, but not a hired killer.

Regardless of the madness behind his words, though, I knew that as long as he was talking to me, he was not doing anything worse, so I forced myself to try to engage him in what passed for conversation in these circumstances. "What do you mean, business? Who employed you? I don't understand — who wants me *dead*?" Even as I asked the question, though, I knew only one person who hated me that much. "My — my *mum*?" I asked, numb with horror.

He snorted with laughter. "Your mother? Lord, no. I mean, yes, she hates you, has done ever since she was told not to get attached to you after you were conceived, but she couldn't tell someone like me what to do even if she wanted to. No, no. I'm here on your *father's* orders."

CHAPTER 29

IN MY MORE OPTIMISTIC MOMENTS as a child I would daydream that my father was a kind, rich man who would come and rescue me from my mum's cruelty if only he knew about me; by the time I'd hit my teens, I knew that in reality he was probably just some random man she'd met in a pub one night when her husband was away. Whoever he was, though, it made no sense that he would go to the trouble and expense of having me killed.

Mystified, I said plainly, "My *father* wants you to kill me? But I don't even know who he is!"

He chuckled lightly. "That you don't know his identity is actually rather comforting because it means you don't know what you are: I had feared that the Democrituses might have told you, when I realised that you had joined their ranks. But I'm afraid I'm not at liberty to tell you who your father is. Suffice it to say, he has sought your death for years, but you have always been too well protected. You were *still* too well protected last time I tried to kill you, of course, but unfortunately your father was most insistent that I try anyway because you had chosen to book a holiday to Greece, of all places."

I gaped, utterly baffled and unable to reply at first. He was apparently prepared to give me time to gather my thoughts as he waited patiently, looking at me expectantly. When I was seventeen, before I was attacked, Matt and I had indeed planned a holiday to Greece. I had no idea how Makris had known that or indeed why it was apparently relevant to my attempted murder. Rather than engage in conversation with him about my holiday plans, I managed, "Protected by whom?"

"Hmm?" he asked, his tone politely inquiring.

"You said I'd been protected. Who protected me? Matt?"

Makris's scornful laugh made me flush with anger as it sparked a feeling of defensiveness towards Matt.

"Hah! Of *course* not," he sneered. "I mean, granted, he was the one who physically intervened last time, but he's only human; hardly a threat to someone like me or your father."

"Then who?"

The only person I knew besides Matt who had taken an interest in my wellbeing was my Nana, and given that she'd been in her seventies when I was born, it seemed unlikely that she'd managed to stave off someone who wanted me dead.

"That hardly matters now," he shrugged dismissively, extremely disinterested. "The point is, there is nobody left to protect you, Fragment, and nobody to stop me from succeeding this time."

Delusional or not, he quite clearly intended to

kill me and his much greater strength combined with his tactical advantage of sitting directly on top of me made it very unlikely that I would be able to fight him off. My only course of action was to try to keep him talking in the hope that help would arrive before he caused me any serious harm.

"What are you going to do to me?" I asked. His weight was uncomfortable to bear, and it was becoming harder and harder to draw a complete breath; my voice had come out rather faintly.

He regarded me carefully, considering his answer. "It's funny you should ask, because I have just been wondering that myself. I mean, there are a few things I intend to do to you come what may: you are, after all, responsible for the seven years I spent in prison. Ultimately, though, I *had* intended to kill you and take your body to your father, as instructed, and claim the reward he promised me. But I have just discovered that you are not just *known* to the Democrituses but are actually *tied* to one of them, and that rather opens up my options. Your father promised me that he would absolve me from my Damnation in exchange for my services, but the High Council would do so and reward me beyond measure if I brought them watertight proof of the Democrituses' deviance ..."

He tailed off, gazing round us at the deserted forest, lost in his thoughts for a minute or two.

I wondered if I was having a stroke — none of his words made sense. Tied to a Democritus? The High Council? Felicity had said something about those things in her emails; Joseph had mentioned the High Council, too, but I still didn't know what any of it meant.

I realised I was shaking, my teeth chattering, as adrenaline pumped impotently through my system.

With a small shake of his head as though clearing any indecision, he said briskly, "I don't know why I'm even thinking about it. Obviously, I'm going to take you to the High Council. The good news for *you* is that I'll need to keep you alive, to provide them with evidence of that perverted tie of yours."

His gaze raked my body and my stomach roiled at the sight of hot pink that began to suffuse his soul. With a visible effort, he refocused his attention on my face and, mercifully, the hot pink faded, leaving only white anger in its place.

Somewhat bitterly, he said, "Regrettably, there cannot be a repeat of my ... *indiscretion* this time. The High Council would understand that I needed to subdue you before bringing you in, but they would take rather a dim view of my copulating with a Fragment, I suspect." Then his voice dropped to a chilling growl as he added, "But you'd be surprised what the human body can cope with and still live, and I am owed significant retribution for my imprisonment."

Icy fear filled my heart at what was to come. Desperately, I spat out, "Matt caught you last time! You hurt him, but he stopped you, and he will stop you again!"

For the first time, he seemed less than composed. He scowled and slapped my face, hard. I braced myself for more, silently berating myself for baiting him. I opened my eyes a fraction when more blows were not forthcoming, wondering what was coming next.

He had straightened up and was removing his shirt. Seeing my dread, he spat derisively, "I have told you — I have no intention of befouling myself again. Last time was a moment of weakness and it will not be repeated."

He shrugged out of his shirt and my breath caught in my throat. His torso was covered in deep, ugly scars and cigarette burns. A large scald mark stretched from his armpit to the belt of his trousers. When I had last seen him, he had been very much in good physical shape: a very small part of me was appalled at what he must have endured in prison.

Correctly interpreting my horror, he gave a half-smile. His voice was calm and quiet once more as he said, "I am glad you are shocked. I wanted you to see what I suffered during my incarceration. I was an easy target. The other prisoners took issue with the fact that I had deflowered a teenage girl; the guards were happy to turn a blind eye to all that was done to me because I had hurt a policeman."

Pointing to his chest, his arm and then his face he listed: "Countless soft tissue injuries. One broken collarbone, three broken ribs, one broken radius and a broken nose. I shall inflict each of those injuries on you, the person who caused me to suffer them. Only then, when I have had my vengeance, shall I take you to the High Council."

I started to cry, utterly helpless to prevent what I knew was coming; I didn't know what the High Council was, but I knew what pain was and it looked as though I was going to experience a lot of it.

Ignoring my tears, he paused, scratching his head a little as though lost in thought as he gazed into the middle distance. He squared his shoulders, as though coming to another decision. "I think I will start with the broken bones and work my way out. This may take hours — days, even. But we have plenty of time alone, there's no need for me to hurry."

Panicking in earnest, I realised that, despite my best efforts, I would be unlikely to survive this time, let alone escape. "Matt!" I cried out with a gasping, barely-there voice that was constricted as much with terror as with Makris's weight. The word had passed my lips without completely understanding why — I was completely alone, and I knew that Matt was nowhere near enough to hear me or save me this time.

Makris seemed to think it was funny. He was perfectly at ease, confident that he had all the time in the world to do whatever he wanted with me undisturbed. "Matt is many miles from here. He is unlikely even to know that you are missing. Nobody will bring him to you this time."

I was sobbing in earnest now and his words barely registered.

He began patting his pockets as though trying to find something. He pulled out a lighter and gave it an experimental click to check that it was working; the flame licked up into the air and he brought it threateningly close to my face and I desperatcly pulled away from the heat. He laughed heartily and put the lighter on the floor beside me. "I'm just messing with you!" His smile seemed so genuine that for a split second I thought he might really be joking, that he wasn't going to hurt me, that it was all some colossal practical joke and I even found my lips curling in a sycophantic smile of my own … But then he added in a voice as dark as night, "Bones first, remember?"

Panic gripped me and I renewed my fruitless struggle to escape. "Matt! Joseph!" I sobbed, the words barely coherent and only spoken to give myself the comfort of hearing the names of the men I loved.

His gaze snapped to my eyes and a coldness entered his voice. "There is no point in calling for the Democritus boy either, Fragment. That is not his true name; he will not answer. The High Council will know it, though, and he and his family will all be called to account soon enough."

A tiny voice at the back of my head was telling me that there was something I was forgetting. True name …

"Enough talk now, aberration," he said softly.

The underlying whiteness of the anger that had suffused his aura throughout became more intense and I felt sick to my stomach, all thought beyond survival pushed from my brain. He lightly traced my collarbone through my shirt with a dirty fingernail. Knowing that there was no way out, no prospect of escape or reprieve, I began to fight in earnest. I spat, tried to use my head to hurt him, tried with every ounce of strength I possessed to throw him off me. I fought, I truly fought — I wanted to remember that, if I survived, because otherwise I would forever question whether I could have done more.

Ignoring my ferocious yet woefully ineffective attempts to fight him off, he began to squeeze my collarbone. He slowly increased the pressure, pushing slowly and inexorably downwards with his fingers whilst his thumb dug into the flesh beneath the bone.

The pain was excruciating. I could tell that he was enjoying hurting me, that he could easily snap my collarbone if he wanted to do so quickly but he was inflicting the maximum amount of pain possible. I wondered how much more I could endure and remain conscious. I realised that I was screaming.

A series of images passed through my mind's eye of an earlier time in similar circumstances — a bath full of cold water; Matt, torn open and bleeding; doctors telling me I'd never be able to have children because of the damage I'd sustained …

Mercifully, my mind also fed me images of those who made me feel safe, giving me sanctuary from what was happening to my body as Makris continued to press down, exerting fractionally greater pressure every second.

Matt: strong, kind, protective. Matt, sitting up with me night after night to stave off nightmares; Matt, selling his car and walking to work so that he could pay privately for me to see a psychotherapist when it became clear that I would not survive long enough to reach the top of the NHS waiting list.

Nana: the little old lady who smelt of Lily of the Valley and gave me biscuits and made up in part for the maternal neglect I'd endured at home.

Joseph—

I heard a sickening crack from beneath his fingers; the pain was so intense that spots appeared in front of my eyes. It hurt too much to breathe, let alone scream, and silent, hot tears ran over my cheeks to my ears where I lay. Dusting his hands together as if he were getting through a list of chores, he sat up straight once more and started to run his fingers over my right arm, the next target of his assault. I closed my eyes, trying hard to get back to that state of numbness, to shut my mind down so that I didn't have to deal with what I was facing.

I thought of Joseph: standing between me and a man wearing a Hello Kitty t-shirt on a cold railway platform; Joseph, catching me in his arms as I fell into them at my door, scared by a dream; Joseph, telling me he wanted me, asking me if I would be his; Joseph, just Joseph.

No — not Joseph.

Zephyrus.

Something changed in the air around me.

CHAPTER 30

MAKRIS FROZE, HIS ATTENTION SOMEWHERE in the middle distance above my head — the shift in his attention forced my focus back to reality. I strained to look in the direction he was staring, trying to see what he was looking at, praying for someone to have found us. The prospect of rescue roused me from my stupor as swiftly as if I had been doused in cold water.

"Help!" I screamed, earning a sharp slap and a rough hand clamped over my mouth.

Suddenly, Makris's weight was gone from my body, torn away from me. I was too scared to feel relief, too unsure of what was happening to dare to hope that I might escape. It was difficult to get up because every movement hurt my broken bone, but terror gave me strength and I managed to rise to my knees, trying to lift myself up from the ground. My eyes found Makris, though he was not where I would have expected him to be.

I couldn't quite believe what I was seeing — I

had assumed that by some miracle somebody had pulled him away from me, but he was being yanked through the air above me like a puppet on a string. Nothing was holding him up: he was literally flying away from me, ten feet in the air, arms and legs flailing as he fought whatever was carrying him aloft until he slammed backwards into a tree a few metres away.

It was only then that I noticed the enormous roar that continually rent the air. It was the noise of a gale the likes of which I had never experienced before; it was a hurricane, bending and uprooting the trees around me and sending debris flying everywhere. I crouched instinctively, my good arm thrown protectively over my head — it hurt too much to raise the arm on the same side as my broken bone. Stupefied, it took me a moment to realise that although the sound of the wind was so loud and all around me trees were being ripped from the ground together with huge sods of earth at their roots, *I* could not feel so much as a gentle breeze — the air immediately surrounding me was utterly still and calm. I was in a bubble, safe and untouched, in the eye of the most terrifying storm I could have imagined.

Knowing that I was somehow safe from the tempest, I raised my head, instinctively looking over to the remaining threat — Makris — to ensure that he was not coming back. His broken and battered form was held against the tree, buffeted this way and that by the forceful wind and then, incredibly, Joseph was there too, attacking him with a ferocity that frightened me. Joseph, like me, appeared to be unaffected by the storm and stood steadily as he rained blow after blow down upon Makris's prone form, white hot anger bleaching out every other colour in his soul as he did so.

As I watched, frozen in confusion and terror, Joseph grabbed Makris by the throat, gripping so tightly that his fingers drew blood and Makris's face turned purple from the pressure. Even over the noise of the storm, I could hear Joseph's roar of animalistic fury. It dawned on me that Joseph was not merely beating or trying to subdue Makris — he was going to kill him.

I had seen souls marred by murder when I had encountered them in courts over the years. The aura of a killer is an ugly sight, deeply flawed and forever tainted. I did not want Joseph's soul so marked. Rightly or wrongly, I loved that man with all my heart and I hoped that we could be together — but I could not live with a murderer.

"Stop! Don't kill him!" I yelled, as firmly and as loudly as I could, struggling to hear my own voice above the sound of the wind.

As quickly as it had started, the wind dropped completely and all was still around me — the only sound was that of branches creaking and crashing back into position and flying debris falling noisily to the ground.

Joseph looked over his shoulder at me, frustration added to the anger flowing from him. His eyes found mine and he seemed to regain control over himself once more. Then something new crossed his face — puzzlement, as he took in our surroundings, and then a flare of fear.

"We are not in England," I heard him say, his voice hollow.

I couldn't reply; I had no idea where we were or how we'd got there, but he didn't seem to be focussed on me anymore. His attention was on the forest around us — his eyes scanned the area as though searching for a threat other than the one presented by Makris.

Through swollen lips and broken teeth, Makris managed a sneer and spat blood on the floor. "We're in Greece," he told Joseph.

The effect on Joseph of those words was dramatic. The colour drained from his face and pale-yellow fear flooded his aura. "Sephy, come here." His voice was steady but I felt the urgency behind them.

Trying to stand was difficult because every movement sent a flash of shooting pain down my arm from my collar.

Seeing that I was struggling, he said, "Wait."

Then he was next to me, still holding Makris, who looked as though he had been kicked afresh in the stomach; he was clutching his middle and clearly finding it difficult to draw breath. They had moved from the tree to my side, a distance of about twenty meters, in less time than it had taken me to blink.

I didn't have time to question this, and Joseph appeared to be in too much of a hurry to explain himself. Now that I was within arm's reach, he pulled me towards him with his free hand and held me to his chest, his attention still fixed on our surroundings.

"I am sorry if this hurts," he said quietly.

A split-second later, we were no longer in the forest. We were under a pier on a beach, ankle-deep in wet sand, and it was very dark — the beach was lit only by a crescent moon and a smattering of stars.

The tide was coming in and the noise from the waves was considerable as it echoed off the wooden boards ten feet above our heads.

Joseph asked urgently, "Are you okay? Can you breathe?"

I managed to nod but was so confounded by what had just happened that I couldn't find any words to respond or to ask any questions of my own.

Without waiting for any further response from me, Joseph turned his attention back to Makris, who had succumbed to unconsciousness. He patted Makris's clothing, searching his pockets but coming up blank.

I heard him cursing under his breath before straightening and running an agitated hand through his hair as though considering his next move. After a pause, he roared, "*Corus!*"

At the time, I thought that perhaps this was just a rather odd alternative to an expletive, but I was distracted from questioning it because just then Russ appeared next to me from out of nowhere. He was wearing a suit and holding a pen.

I was so startled that I fell sideways and splashed into the sodden sand with a cry of shock and pain. Russ seemed just as surprised as I was that he was there and he automatically reached a hand out to help me up, the bemusement clear on his face. Remembering only too clearly what had happened to me when Alex had held out a hand for me, I hesitated to accept the help ostensibly on offer.

Joseph thrust Makris at his brother (who stopped reaching for me and instead obediently took hold of the scruff of Makris's collar) and then stepped to my side, cradling me as he helped me to my feet but his attention was largely on Makris, as though he was still a threat in spite of his extensive injuries. Satisfied that I was physically safe and able to support my own weight, Joseph resumed his grip on Makris's shirt.

Relieved of the need to restrain an unconscious and battered man, concern swiftly replaced the confusion on Russ's face as he took in my bruised and battered form. Looking between me, Joseph and Makris, I could see the moment the penny dropped.

"Is this the man who attacked you when you were younger? The one who has been searching for you?" he asked, gesturing towards Makris.

I gave a tiny nod.

Of Joseph, he asked, "Where are we?"

"New Zealand."

"Oh," I commented lightly. "So *that's* why it's dark." A slightly hysterical giggle bubbled in my throat, but it was so quiet that it was lost in the sound of the crashing waves.

"What happened?" Russ demanded.

Through gritted teeth, Joseph spat, "He *took* her. She — she called me. I found her in Greece."

"*Greece?*" he asked, and for a lovely moment I thought that maybe I wasn't alone in wondering just what the heck was happening. But then he added, "He's one of us?" which returned me to feeling as though I must have had a stroke.

Joseph simply nodded.

"Is he with the High Council?" Russ asked, tension pouring from every syllable.

Joseph shrugged expansively. "Why else would he have taken her to Greece?"

"Was he alone?"

When Joseph confirmed that he was, Russ shook his head decisively and said, "Then no, he can't be with the High Council. If they'd known about her, they would not have sent a single agent to retrieve her. There would have been a battalion there. She would already be dead."

Joseph looked sick to his stomach but nodded an agreement.

"Joseph—" I began.

"Bounty hunter, perhaps?" Russ interrupted, speaking to his brother as if I wasn't even there.

Joseph shrugged again, and lifted Makris up as though he could see his intentions just by looking at his unconscious body. As though a thought had just occurred to him, he swiftly turned Makris over and tugged down the back of his shirt collar and his lip curled up in distaste at whatever he saw.

Russ leant across to have a look and said, "Ah, a Damned. Bounty hunting would make sense, then. The question is, has he told the High Council about her already, or was he just going to turn up with her unannounced?"

"Russ—" I tried.

"We'd better hope it was the latter. He tried to kill her some years ago and failed. If he had told the High Council about her earlier, then she would not have survived this long …" Joseph left his sentence hanging heavily in the air.

I had, by now, sufficiently regained my equilibrium to begin to assert myself. In the last twenty minutes, it seemed I had been transported to Greece by the man who had viciously attacked me when I was seventeen; I had seen an old friend killed and had to scramble over his body to try to escape;

I'd been badly hurt; the man I was obsessed with had magically appeared in the middle of a hurricane and rescued me before (apparently) taking me immediately to New Zealand, where his brother had popped into being without so much as a by-your-leave. Now Joseph and Russ were talking about the High Council — presumably the same High Council that Makris had referenced — and about how Makris was damned, which Makris had also alluded to, and how likely it was that I would or should be dead soon.

My voice was louder than I had anticipated as recent events came to a head. "One of you needs to tell me what the *hell* is going on, right now!"

The brothers wore matching expressions of surprise as their heads snapped up to look at me. It was as though they had forgotten that I was there.

Joseph was the first to answer. "This man is very dangerous, Sephy. We are afraid that he has informed the High Council about you — if he has, then we have very little time left."

I shook my head slightly in annoyance at still not understanding what was happening. "No, I meant — I was in the office, then I was in North Yorkshire, then I was in Greece and now I'm here. In New Zealand. I don't know how any of that happened. I don't know what the High Council is or why Makris is damned and what that means, and I don't know why you're both so scared. So *spell it out for me!*" My voice rose again as I battled with hysteria as feelings of powerlessness and residual fear raged inside me.

Russ answered this time. "The High Council governs our kind. Makris bears the mark of the Damned, which means that he is mortal now. In you, he has a way of reinstating his immortal status by taking you to the High Council. We are scared because if Makris has already told them about you, if they are expecting you and Makris does not turn up with you, they will track you down and kill you. And us."

There was a pause. I waited in case Russ was going to elaborate, but apparently he thought he already had.

"*What*?!" I exclaimed, frustration adding an edge to my tone.

"I would explain in more detail, my love, but I'm afraid we don't have the luxury of time," Joseph said, the calm tone of his voice belying the panic in his colours. He glanced down at Makris and then back at his brother. "We need to wake him up, ask him what he's done."

Russ grimaced and threw his hands up. "As if he's going to tell us! If he refuses to answer, we can hardly go running to the High Council to report him!"

"What else can we do?" Joseph complained bitterly.

It was as though I had disappeared again for all the attention they spared me. Russ stepped forwards and slapped Makris on the face, seemingly trying to rouse him. Makris mumbled something and Russ slapped him again and Makris grumbled louder, pulling his face away and attempting to bat Joseph's hand away from his collar.

"Damned, listen to me," Russ commanded. "Who knows about her? Have you told the High Council about her?"

Makris opened his eyes slightly and then

closed one of them as though he was struggling to focus on Russ. A sneering smile crept over his face. "You're all going to be in deep shit when they find her and they see that tie." Makris nodded from Joseph to me and back again and earned a punch in the mouth from Russ.

Joseph and Russ looked at each other, apparently at a loss as to how to proceed. Makris's eye closed again and his head drooped forward onto his chest as he lost consciousness once more.

"Did he say anything to you about his plans?" Russ asked me sharply.

I sighed heavily, rather envious of Makris's lack of awareness. I wanted to go to sleep, to forget everything that had happened and slip into blissful nothingness. As that didn't seem to be an option, I chose to answer and hoped that doing so would expedite the events that lay between me and my bed.

"He was going to kill me," I said flatly. "But then he changed his mind and said he was just going to hurt me and then take me to the High Council." I added pointedly, "*Whatever* that is."

"Did he say why?" Joseph asked, tension making his voice gruff.

I bit my tongue to stop myself screaming in frustration. I hated being in the dark; I was scared and tired and in serious pain, my clothes were wet with seawater and I was cold. I was fast approaching the limit of what I could cope with without losing my mind. "He said my dad wanted me dead and that if Makris killed me he'd be "absolved from his damnation". Which I'm sure makes sense to *you* if not to *me*. But then he said the High Council would reward him more than my dad could. So he decided to take me to them instead. But then you turned up. Magically. Out of nowhere. In a hurricane. And beat him half to death."

"Your dad? Do you know who that is?" Russ asked sharply.

I gave a pointedly exasperated sigh and said, "I don't know *anything*!"

Apparently my snarkiness was lost on the brothers and they turned back to their own conversation.

"Whoever he is, her dad must be on the High Council if he could absolve damnation," Joseph said, his tone sharp and panicked.

Russ put a placating hand on his brother's shoulder. "If he's fathered a Fragment he won't want the rest of the High Council to know about it. And he wouldn't have hired a Damned to deal with it if he'd had the option of using the might available through official channels."

Joseph, though, was beyond reassurance. His adrenaline and anger from the fight was dissipating and leaving more fear in its place. With a distinct tremble in his voice he told his brother, "I can't lose her. Please, help me."

Russ nodded an acknowledgement and turned back to me. "Had Makris told the High Council about you already? Think — this is really important."

I was distracted by Joseph's distress; I walked over to him on unsteady legs, giving Makris as wide a berth as I could, and stepped into his waiting embrace. He held me as tightly as my injuries would allow, as though afraid to let me go.

Russ pressed, "Sephy. You can help him by answering my question."

As hard as it was to think about it in such detail, I forced myself to remember. When I was certain of my answer, I reluctantly pulled out of Joseph's arms so that I could speak clearly. "No, he hadn't told the High Council about me yet. He said he'd found out that I was tied to a Democritus and the High Council would reward him if he brought them proof of, erm, your deviance, so he needed to keep me alive. He'd only just decided on going to them rather than my dad when he started hurting me, just before you turned up."

Russ and Joseph shared a guardedly (and surprisingly) optimistic look.

"So if he hasn't told them already, we just need to stop him telling them in the future. He's just a Damned …" Russ began.

"Yes — and he is *mortal*," Joseph said through gritted teeth as though impatient with his brother.

"Well for fuck's sake — just kill him!" Russ exclaimed as though this were an entirely normal and natural thing to do.

With a pointed glance in my direction, Joseph said, "I *cannot*."

After a short pause, Russ's eyes widened in comprehension. Without further ado, he darted forwards and grabbed Makris's head. Fortunately for Makris, I realised what he was going to do in time and I shouted at Russ, "No! Don't you dare! Neither of you two is killing anyone unless I say so — that's final. Makris is going to prison and he can rot there for all I care but I'm not having either of you two murdering him!"

His jaw clenched in anger and frustration, Joseph growled, "He must not live, Sephy! He is

Damned and therefore cannot reincarnate. If he is parted from his body now he will not return and will never be able to harm you again. You will be *safe*."

I must have looked as dumbfounded as I felt. After a moment of stunned silence, I replied, "Yes, Joseph, I know — if you kill him, he'll be *dead*, I get it — I just don't want either of you to do it! He's not worth damaging your souls."

Russ shook his head in agitation. "We cannot let him live. He will hurt you — if not now, then in the future. He will inform the High Council and we will all be doomed." His hands were still clamped on either side of Makris's head, a small movement away from snapping his neck.

At a loss for what to do but knowing that I could not let Joseph or Russ kill anyone, I cried, "Then we'll call Matt! He'll arrest him and he'll go back to prison."

Joseph scoffed, "For what, a handful of years? You will still be young when he is freed again, you will be in danger for the rest of your days because you are valuable to him. He can trade you for his freedom from Damnation, for the ability to reincarnate after this lifetime is over. If he even bothers to wait until the end of his jail term, I will have to kill him when he is freed anyway — there is no benefit to delaying."

Incredulous, I threw my arms to the side and cried, "Killing him is not inevitable here! This is not *normal*! I haven't a clue what you're talking about, but *I'll* be damned if I'm letting you spoil your soul over that monster." I shook my head, exasperated. "Russ, let go of him!"

Apparently in response to my tone of voice as

much to my words, Russ pushed away from Makris's head, wiping his hands on his trousers in distaste as though they were unclean from the act of touching him. Joseph kept a restraining hand on Makris's arm as though to stop him from moving if he were to suddenly rouse.

"Please, just call Matt. I don't have my mobile." I gestured vaguely at my person and saw a look of sorrow and aching sadness bleed through Joseph's colours as he took in what must have been a pitiful sight. I was wet and sandy; my shirt gaped, my jacket and skirt were torn and I must have been badly bruised; I wiped the back of my hand over my lip in response to a tickling sensation and my hand came away bloody.

Joseph's aura was a picture of compassion mingled with fury, fear and sadness. Moments before, he had been capable of such violence it had frightened me, yet he reached for me and stroked my hair with such gentle tenderness that I felt tears welling of their own accord. I had been in battle mode — frightened, yes, but fighting. Now a gamut of other emotions was surfacing and, at his kindness and care, I felt my reserves of strength leave me.

I wanted to be held and comforted, to be made safe — right then, knowing why or how we were all there was not a priority. The shock began to wear off and I screwed my eyes up tight, the pain more acute and the residual fear more tangible now that the threat had been neutralised. My face stung and my broken collarbone felt like a fresh stab wound with every breath. My bottom lip began to quiver; tears were not far off.

I pressed myself into Joseph's chest but

flinched and stifled a cry as I jarred my broken bone. His anguish was palpable, and he moved slightly so that he could hold me without touching my injured shoulder. My head nestled under his chin and I wet his shirt with the threatened shocked and silent tears, my body shaking uncontrollably as the adrenaline worked its way out of my system now that I was safe.

Gruff with emotion, Joseph said into my hair, "Sephy. You are safe. I am here."

"We need to get Matt," I repeated.

He let out a frustrated groan and said insistently, "Let us deal with this, Sephy. You do not understand what this creature is."

"No!" I cried, more sharply than I had intended. "No. Don't do anything else to him. He's — he's been hurt, too. Let Matt sort it out."

Russ exhaled sharply in annoyance. Both men were looking at me with identical expressions of frustration, anger and fear. Since Makris was clearly incapacitated I didn't see what they could be afraid of, but it seemed that they felt he was still a threat.

Russ turned to his brother and said, "If he lives, we will all die."

"Do you think I don't know that?" Joseph snapped. Running an agitated hand through his hair, he appeared to be deep in thought. At length, he said, "There may be a way to prevent him from talking without killing him, but I don't know how successful it will be. If we are to try it, Sephy will need to be told everything afterwards. There would be no going back."

I sighed, now resigned to being largely excluded from whatever secrets they were keeping and being kept on the periphery of a rather important conversation.

Russ looked mystified too for a moment, but when Joseph tipped his head slightly in my direction comprehension dawned. Agitated, Russ chewed on his thumb nail, evidently weighing something up. "She can deliver orders that bind him ..." he mused, deep in thought.

"According to legend, yes," Joseph replied, "and given that we have evidently been compelled to let him live, I would suggest that that legend is based on truth."

Russ held up his hands briefly in submission. "It's worth a shot. If the orders are given clearly enough ... they need to be watertight, though, do you think you can manage that?"

Joseph pulled a face. "I am a solicitor. I think I can manage it."

Russ rubbed his forehead in agitation and Joseph seemed to be waiting for his approval before doing whatever it was they had decided upon.

"Alright, fine. As long as we both promise that Erica will never find out that it was us who taught a Fragment how to give orders."

Joseph's eyes crinkled a little in amusement. "Agreed."

And on that mystifying and rather ominous note, both men turned to face me.

CHAPTER 31

JOSEPH LOOKED AT ME INTENTLY and I was engulfed by the dusky-pink-gold colour that I had only ever seen in his soul. For a moment, it was all I could see; the fear and anger that were so prominent in Joseph's aura were muted and his eyes softened as he looked at me. Russ cleared his throat discreetly and Joseph seemed to gather himself.

Speaking softly, he said, "Please trust me. Makris is still a threat, even in his current state. If he gets the chance, he will go straight to the High Council and tell them about you, and that will be the end for all of us. But if you are certain that I cannot kill him—" he paused, but when I didn't contradict him he continued with an unhappy sigh, "There may be another way to keep us all safe. I will need your help, though, and I only ask for it in the knowledge that after tonight, my family can surely not deny our bond and will permit me to be with you. And then I need never leave your side again unless you tell me to do so; you need never use the power I am about to acquaint you with."

I flushed at his words, not understanding their context but appreciating that it meant that he wasn't going to kill Makris and that he still wanted to be with me, even after all that had happened.

Makris stirred on the floor next to us and Joseph shook him more violently than seemed necessary in order to get his full and undivided attention. Bending down to his level, Joseph held him by his collar and stared aggressively into his eyes. "Do you understand, Damned? She is sparing your life. You owe her your miserable existence. You are indebted to her. I will respect her wishes and allow you to live."

Makris managed a sneer and through broken teeth he spat, "You couldn't disobey that monster if you tried."

Joseph's hand bunched into a fist, but Russ moved swiftly to put a restraining hand against his arm.

With great effort, Joseph turned away from Makris and told me, "You have to tell him what to do. You must copy my words exactly, so that he cannot exploit any flaws in your commands, and you have to speak firmly — deliver the words as an order, not as a request. Tell, don't ask. Do you understand?"

I looked at him, a cynical eyebrow raised, nonplussed. "You want me to tell him what to do," I repeated doubtfully.

With a glance at Russ, he said steadily, "You have incredible power, Sephy. I do not tell you this lightly; it may prove too much for some of my family to bear if they know that you are aware of the extent of that power, but if you forbid me to kill this creature then I have no choice but to help you use it." He paused for a beat, and added, "Though I'd be grateful if you didn't mention any of this to my sister."

I must have looked suitably unimpressed because he sighed, dropped his head to his chest momentarily and then said, "Please, just do as I ask."

I shrugged an acquiescence and he cleared his throat, deep in concentration.

"Leon Makris. Answer all my questions truthfully. Does the High Council know about me?" Joseph began and then looked at me encouragingly.

"Leon Makris, answer all of my questions truthfully, does the High Council know about me?" I repeated, somewhat self-consciously.

Makris spat in derision by way of response.

"No, like you mean it," Joseph insisted.

I tried again. "Leon Makris. Answer all my questions *truthfully*. Does the High Council know about me?" My voice was firmer this time and even I could hear the command behind it.

Makris looked as though he was going to be sick, I was gratified to see. "No, only your father knows about you," he muttered.

Russ and Joseph shared another optimistic look.

Seemingly satisfied, Joseph told me, "Good. Just like that. Repeat everything I say."

Russ interjected, "Wait, ask him this next: does my father, the High Council or anyone else know that the Democrituses have any involvement with a Fragment?"

The question made little sense to me, but I repeated it anyway, trying to keep the tone of command in my voice.

"Not that I know of," said Makris sulkily.

Russ looked distinctly relieved and both men seemed more hopeful.

Accepting cues from Joseph, I continued, "Who is my father?"

"I do not know his true name. He is a serving member of the High Council."

"Will he tell the High Council about me?"

"That would be suicide," Makris scoffed.

"Will he come for me himself?"

With a pointed look at the two men beside him, Makris replied, "*That* would be suicide."

"Will he send another Damned after me?"

Makris replied simply, "Perhaps."

Troubled, but seemingly satisfied with the answers he'd received, Joseph moved on to some more direct orders.

Echoing him, I told Makris, "You will plead guilty to any charges the police lay against you. You will not put me through the torment of giving evidence against you. When your sentence is complete you will not seek to find me or to harm me in any way. You will never come near me again."

As though ticking through a mental checklist, Joseph gave a nod and then thought quietly for a moment before continuing.

Parroting his words, I went on, "You will never report me or the Democrituses to the High Council and you will not tell my father or anyone else *anything* about my existence, my whereabouts or my associates. You will never speak to anyone of the Democritus family's involvement with me. You will report directly to the Democritus family immediately upon your release and await further instructions."

Throughout, I kept expecting Makris to become abusive, resist or try to escape, but to my surprise he was merely submissive. Joseph, holding tightly to Makris's arm, did have the physical edge and I supposed that with a six-foot-five man as physically powerful as Joseph leaning over him, a prisoner was bound to be compliant. I did not think for a moment that my 'orders' would be binding on Makris but it seemed to make Joseph happier and less inclined to murder him.

Apparently content that the threat had been neutralised, Joseph stood straight again. He was agitated but his colours were no longer filled with anger or frustration; his fear had subsided considerably, too. But in the place of those emotions was intense sorrow as he looked at me. Wrapping one fist in Makris's shirt collar, Joseph wordlessly and carefully drew me back into an embrace I needed more than air. When at last I felt able to release my grip from round his broad back and still stay upright, Joseph looked at me and said earnestly, "Thank you. You were perfect."

Russ remained quiet, watching me carefully. It reminded me of the way he used to look at me, back when I had first joined his family's firm: he was afraid of me again, though not as much as he had been back then. I didn't have the strength or energy to reassure him or to find out what exactly he thought I was capable of.

Joseph continued, "Sephy, I will take you back to Matt, and bring the monster with us. Taking you there might be uncomfortable. I am very sorry, but I think it is the safest way."

"What about Cam?" I asked faintly.

Cam had befriended me and earned my trust when I was a teenager. I kept flitting from feeling betrayed and angry, to confused and upset depending on whether or not I believed that Cam had deliberately brought Makris to me. None of what had happened to me that day made sense, that least of all. I clung to the idea that perhaps none of it had really happened — perhaps I had suffered a breakdown, and this was all just a side effect of the antipsychotic drugs they were giving me at the hospital.

Joseph frowned in confusion, and I told him that Cam was lying dead in the forest in Greece. He looked at Russ, who gave a small nod and said, "I'll get him. Meet you back at the house to put something together we can explain to the policeman."

Then Russ disappeared as abruptly and completely as he had arrived. My legs finally gave out and Joseph had to grip me tighter to hold me upright. The pain in my collarbone became more than I could bear. I closed my eyes and welcomed the blackness that swept over me.

CHAPTER 32

"LIE STILL, LIE STILL," WERE THE FIRST words I heard on opening my eyes.

Groggily, I tried to lift my head from the ground beneath me and instantly regretted the movement — a sharp spike of intense pain shot from my collarbone into my shoulder and my stomach rolled.

Matt came into my line of sight as he leant over me, looking as confused and afraid as I had been, though relief was the predominant colour in his aura. "God, you never listen to me. I said *lie still*. You're alright, you're alright," he insisted, apparently for his own benefit as much as mine.

Joseph appeared in my field of vision, his eyes fixed on mine. He was drenched in sweat and his chest was heaving as he caught his breath. "*Are* you alright?" he asked urgently, his face a picture of concern and tension.

I did a quick assessment. I was in acute pain. It was difficult to swallow; my throat throbbed from when Makris had grabbed me. My hands were bruised and swollen; my nails were torn and bloody from defending myself; my wrists hurt from where Makris had knelt on them. My face was inflamed and very sore from where he had hit me. My collarbone was definitely broken. At least the searing pain I'd felt below my sternum had vanished.

Telling him all of that would have taken more energy than I had, though, and shaking my head would only make him worry. So instead, I gave him a small and careful nod.

"Where am I?" I managed. I could feel soft grass beneath my head but I didn't even try to look around.

"You are in the front garden of my brother's house. It looks as though Makris brought you out here through the bathroom window," Joseph said with a slightly strained expression and a subtle nod in Matt's direction.

I sighed, too tired and confused and in too much pain to do anything else. However I'd got here, whatever had happened before, I was safe now.

I had survived.

I wondered if I'd been unconscious for long. I also wondered what type of mental illness could have caused such realistic and detailed hallucinations as the ones I'd experienced. The idea that Makris had taken me to Greece, that Joseph had conjured a storm and then taken me to New Zealand (where it had been night time, of course), that Russ had appeared out of nowhere — it was clearly insane, but the fact that my brain had accounted for the time difference between continents was really quite impressive. Someone would probably want to write a paper about me for a medical journal.

A very, very small part of me clung to the idea that I had somehow hallucinated it *all* — perhaps I'd been in a car accident, or fallen off the roof? But no, as much as I wanted to believe that, I knew that Makris had attacked me: even if Joseph hadn't just mentioned his name, I could smell him on my skin, feel his hands on my throat and hear the echo of his words clear as day. No wonder my brain had tried to take a break from reality when faced with all that.

I became aware that Matt was fussing round me, trying to make me more comfortable by pushing his jacket behind my neck. I wanted to reassure him, to soothe his frightened soul, but speech was beyond me for the time being. Instead, I reached for his hand and held it tightly, grimacing against the pain in my fingers but needing the contact; we both took comfort from the familiar touch.

"Jesus, Seph," he breathed softly.

From the corner of my eye, I saw Joseph move away slightly as though to give us some privacy. At his movement, though, I heard a groan that I recognised as emanating from Makris, who was far closer than I'd realised. With a start, I scrambled backwards, pushing myself upright slightly as I looked around wildly to see exactly where he was. The pain of doing so was overridden by my desire and instinct to put as much distance between me and Makris as possible.

Joseph was holding him by the scruff of his neck, though it was clear that Makris was going nowhere in his condition — he was barely conscious. They were both just a few feet away from where I lay.

"I am sorry," Joseph said hurriedly, "I would have taken him further from you, but I didn't want to leave you."

Meanwhile, alarmed by my movement, Matt had put his hand out to settle me and followed my gaze. He looked at Makris, evidently noticing his presence for the first time.

In an instant, white hot anger flew from him as he leapt to his feet, running straight towards Makris.

"Joseph, stop him!" I shouted.

Joseph caught Matt before he reached Makris. Keeping one large hand on Makris's collar to keep him in place, he used his other to restrain Matt, though neither he nor Matt seemed happy that he did so. Matt fought to get nearer, kicking and reaching towards Makris as though he would tear him apart with his bare hands: Joseph was bigger and more powerfully built, but Matt's rage was lending him greater strength, and gradually he began to gain ground.

"Matt, stop!" I yelled, managing to sit up properly despite the pain. Shouting hurt my shoulder even more and I cried out; perhaps it was that more than my words that brought Matt to his senses.

With a roar of frustration and a volley of curses directed at Makris, Matt stomped away from him, pacing between Joseph and me in a state of utter fury.

Very slowly, he managed to compose himself and started to marshal the first of the many questions I knew I'd face in the coming days. Gesturing to my dishevelled clothing, he seethed, "Did he — did he *touch* you?"

He broke off, his voice failing him, turning to stare daggers at Makris.

"No, no, nothing like that. I'm just bruised, and my collarbone is broken. Joseph got him before he could do anything worse," I hurriedly reassured him. "I'll be fine, Matt."

Matt gave a nod of acknowledgement and ran a shaky hand over his face. "Where the hell's Cam?" he muttered, peering around briefly before reaching into his pocket and checking his phone as though expecting Cam to have rung him, or perhaps to call Cam to tell him that I had been found.

With a wave of nausea, I pictured our friend, lifeless; I remembered pressing his chest, remembered Makris telling me that my efforts to revive him were a waste of the little time I had left … But I didn't want to tell Matt that I thought Cam was dead; I didn't want to believe that myself. I cleaved desperately to the idea that his death, at least, was a figment of my imagination.

I looked at Joseph. "Is Cam …?" I managed, fervently hoping that Joseph would be confused, or just look at me blankly in response to my deliberately vague, largely unspoken question.

By way of reply, though, Joseph nodded sombrely towards the corner of the house. There, in a raised flower bed at the foot of the wall, lay Cam's body. As focussed as I was on Cam, I still noticed Matt stiffen beside me, shock registering in his body language and throughout his aura.

My eyes travelled over the scene: the shrubs had been trampled, the metal shutters on the window immediately above Cam had been forced open from the inside. The tableau might have suggested that Cam had fallen badly from the window, presumably in pursuit of Makris, but I looked at Joseph and took in his muddied shoes and sweat-soaked shirt; he swallowed guiltily and I knew better than to believe the story that had been staged.

I could feel my own shock setting in and I began to shiver.

Wordlessly, Matt walked over to Cam's body. He had seen enough death in his career to know it well — there was no sense of doubt or uncertainty in how he approached Cam's body. A wave of black suffused his colours as he reached Cam, but he gave no other external sign of grief, or of any emotion at all. I watched as he knelt and checked for a pulse, but he must have known the futility of any attempted resuscitation as he made no efforts in that regard. Had he not been a police officer mindful of forensic preservation, he might have covered his friend's body with a jacket, or at least closed his eyes, but he denied himself even that small comfort.

With obvious effort, Matt stood and squared his shoulders. He kept his face turned away from me, looking up at the house, taking a moment to compose himself whilst simultaneously piecing together the story of what must have happened. At last, he walked back towards us. I wondered if he would quiz Joseph, perhaps accuse him of being involved in some way.

Instead, he told him quietly, "Thank you."

Joseph wordlessly patted Matt's shoulder in a gesture of comfort and solidarity.

The confirmation of Cam's death combined with this display of bonding between the two men I cared most about in the world was what finally broke me. I started crying — loud, gasping cries full of pain and anger — and they both turned sharply towards me, identical expressions of concern on their faces.

My break in emotions was enough to make a chink in the wall that Matt had constructed around his own. "Don't, mate, don't," he murmured, his voice gruff with suppressed tears of his own as he walked over and crouched beside me, hugging me carefully round my good shoulder. "Backup's on its way and I need to call for an ambulance too, pet, I need to get you to a hospital. Then you'll be alright, we'll get you sorted."

I managed a noise of agreement and made an effort to get my tears back under control; I really loathed crying and fought hard to stop.

Matt was looking over at Cam again. With a troubled sigh, he said, "I'm damned if I know how I'm going to explain all of this. I mean—" he gestured vaguely towards the flowerbed, "—it looks like the poor bugger fell badly coming out of the window, but how did I not hear any of that? I was right outside the bloody door ..." Becoming agitated, he carried on, "I don't understand *any* of this. How did Makris get in there in the first place? Cam *checked* — it was empty. How did he get past us, get through Cam and get you out here? I know Cam — he wouldn't have let Makris take you without a fight; at the very least, he'd have called out for help ..."

I didn't even try to answer him.

He looked at me as though seeing other details for the first time. He lifted a strand of my hair from where it lay limp on my shoulder, running it through his fingers. "And why the hell are you wet? Where's this sand from? ..." he tailed off, lost for words for a moment.

The sand and the wetness were things I didn't want to think about. They strayed too close to madness. Instead, I focussed on his questions about Cam. I didn't know what role Cam had played in what(ever) had happened, and I didn't want to besmirch his good name by suggesting that he had colluded with a criminal. Moreover, though, I didn't want to put doubt into Matt's mind about what kind of person he'd befriended and trusted to look after me.

When I didn't answer, Matt said, "Jesus, they'll think I'm mad if I tell them what I *think* I saw." Gesturing to Joseph, he said incredulously, "He — he vanished. Like, actually *vanished*, right in front of me."

My mouth went dry. Reality was slipping away from me and insanity loomed.

Matt went on, "He grabbed his stomach, like he'd been shot or something. I thought he was dying — then he chuffing *vanished*. You were locked in that WC and I had to break the door down, but when I got in there it was empty—" Suddenly, he stood up, frowning at the window, thinking hard. "Hang on. No. No way. When I went in there, that metal shutter was down and in one piece. Makris couldn't have got you out that way and Cam couldn't have climbed out after you, I'd have seen—"

Joseph interrupted him, his voice loud and commanding. "Matt Bishop, listen to me. I did not vanish; you are simply in shock and your memory has been adversely affected."

Matt was looking at him in stunned silence. I was, too. I listened closely in the desperate hope that he could explain everything to both of us; that there was a rational explanation for all that had happened.

Focussing on Matt, Joseph pressed on, "Tell

your superiors this: Leon Makris was hiding in the WC. He attacked Sephy soon after she entered. DC Cam was overcome and despite Cam's best efforts to prevent it, Makris was able to carry Sephy outside after forcing open the shutters — in your panic to find her you did not immediately notice the broken shutters when you entered the WC. It has been raining here recently and Sephy is wet from the ground. We ... we have very sandy soil here." His voice had faltered slightly on that last point as though even he found it a bit far-fetched.

Matt was still staring at Joseph, listening to him as closely as if his life depended on it.

Joseph cleared his throat and continued, "DC Cam gallantly tried to pursue Makris out of the window to intervene but Makris pulled him, causing him to fall awkwardly — killing him instantly. Makris proceeded to assault Sephy and caused her significant harm, intending to kill her. Fortunately, she was able to call for help; I heard her and came to her aid. You were out of earshot initially but arrived soon afterwards upon hearing my call for assistance."

Matt nodded once to acknowledge this; his face was oddly neutral.

Joseph went on, "This is what you must do now: in respect of Sephy, charge Leon Makris with breach of his probation, assault occasioning grievous bodily harm and attempted murder. In respect of DC Cam, charge him with murder. He will plead guilty to all charges. Call that ambulance for Sephy and arrange for one to collect Cam's body." A groan from Makris made him glance down and add, "I suppose you should ask for one for this creature, too."

Matt made a brief call on his mobile,

apparently on autopilot because he didn't question any of what Joseph had said. "They'll be here in twenty," he said distractedly.

It appeared to me that Joseph was deliberately avoiding my eye when he addressed Matt again, the authority that rang in his voice belying the tiredness and misery I could see all too clearly in his colours. "While you are waiting for your colleagues to arrive … if there is anything you wish to do to Makris, now is the time to do it. I will gladly give a statement that you were acting in defence of Sephy. You will face no consequences."

Matt glanced at Makris, understanding dawning and a dark desire crossing his colours. I realised a second later that Joseph was attempting to circumnavigate the clear instructions I'd given to him and Russ about not killing Makris.

"No! Matt, don't touch him. Let the court deal with him. I need you here, not in jail," I said loudly, outraged.

Joseph reached his hands out in supplication. "Please, Sephy …"

It was so tempting, so difficult to resist … Yet I shook my head. It was the hardest thing I'd ever done.

Matt looked a picture of anguish. A very visible internal struggle crossed his features until at last he sat back on his haunches, and then sat on the floor, his chin dropped to his chest, and for the first time in many years I saw my best friend cry.

When the police backup arrived, Joseph was still holding Makris by the scruff of his neck; I was holding Matt.

CHAPTER 33

I NEED MAKRIS LOCKED UP. I need a shower. Then I will ask all the questions I've got and try to work out how crazy I am. I kept repeating that mantra silently to myself over and over, partly to calm myself and partly to reassert control over my life once more.

With a glance at Makris's unconscious state and my battered and bruised form, one of the police officers said that the ambulances weren't far behind. Another prised Makris from Joseph's grip and placed him in the recovery position; Joseph allowed this reluctantly and probably only because Makris was by then completely senseless. Noticing Joseph's foul demeanour, bloodied hands and clothing, the officer seemed to be considering arresting him: Joseph spoke to her dismissively, murmuring something too quiet for me to catch; she nodded and evidently abandoned the idea.

Shortly thereafter, the ambulances arrived amidst a shriek of sirens and crunch of gravel as they halted on the large turning circle beyond the garden. Their arrival drew my attention to my wider surroundings: we were in the middle of nowhere, with miles of heather-covered moorland surrounding the house in all directions. Behind me, Alex's marble-fronted house stood three-storeys tall; I remembered that Joseph had once told me that from his bedroom (which lay around the corner from where I now lay) it felt as though he was on top of the world, and I could believe it: The Heights was aptly named. It was all really rather beautiful and I wished that I were there under different circumstances so that I could actually enjoy it and explore.

Relieved of the need to restrain Makris, Joseph had come to my side and was unintentionally making it difficult for a paramedic to lay me on a gurney and apply a neck brace. Joseph made it clear that I would not be going anywhere without him, and so rode with me in the ambulance to the LGI. Matt rode in the second ambulance with Makris, and would find me at the hospital as soon as he was satisfied that Makris was properly secured.

Throughout the journey, Joseph was quiet and I might have assumed that he was tired, or perhaps still annoyed with me for not allowing him to kill Makris, but I could see that his predominant emotion was one of lingering fear. He was on full alert; I wondered if he was afraid that he would be charged with assault or worse, given Makris's fragile state of health.

Wanting to reassure him, I said, "I'll talk to Matt, I'm sure you won't be charged with anything. You were protecting me."

The uniformed police officer sitting beside us gave me a highly sceptical look. Joseph didn't reply, he merely continued to hold my hand and stare into the middle distance as though listening for something.

***

The nearest hospital with the forensic facilities I would need was the Leeds General Infirmary. Arriving there under very different circumstances from the last occasion, I was seen quickly and had my physical injuries assessed by a team of doctors and nurses. I had extensive bruising to my throat and my collarbone was indeed broken, but the break was clean and I would only need a sling to help keep my arm steady, plus paracetamol and ibuprofen for the pain; I declined the offered co-codamol because it has the same effect on me as alcohol and I needed my wits about me.

I was soon declared physically fit enough to go to the specialist suite where I would be examined by the police doctor for forensic evidence to be gathered.

The world had taken on a surreal, dream-like quality as exhaustion had overcome me and the remnants of my adrenaline had dissipated. Tired to the bone, I sat obediently in the wheelchair I was offered and allowed a porter to transport me to the far side of the hospital, Joseph steadfastly by my side: since leaving his house, he had not spoken unless directly addressed; he had also barely looked me in the eye. His eyes were continually roving all over, and I realised that he was monitoring the doors and windows as though expecting someone to enter — from the fear that laced his aura, I judged that he did not expect that 'someone' to be friendly.

Matt entered the waiting room at a brisk pace and assured me that Makris was under the careful watch of two armed guards. He had donned his detective's persona once more: steely, professional and determined to secure the evidence needed to put Makris away for a long time. He indicated the side room in which I would be examined and wheeled me over to it.

Joseph held the door open and Matt pushed me inside but stopped Joseph at the threshold, and said, "No, mate, sorry. She needs to make a statement and it needs to be watertight. I can't have Makris's solicitors saying you were an undue influence or that she lied to protect you or anything."

He had spoken quite apologetically, though it appeared that this was merely through courtesy rather than genuine regret because when Joseph showed no sign of allowing the door to be closed between us, Matt said more assertively, "You can't come in. I've got evidence to collect."

"And I have to protect her," Joseph replied through gritted teeth.

Taken aback, Matt said, "What the chuff do you think *I'm* doing? I need this evidence watertight so that I can charge him with everything I can throw at him when he wakes up. *That* is what's going to protect Seph, not some stuck-up solicitor who thinks he's God's gift to women!"

Joseph didn't rise to the bait but said firmly, "You are not taking her out of my protection whilst that monster lives. You have no idea what he really is or what else is out there. She doesn't leave my sight. *Let me in.*"

For a brief moment, Matt looked as though he was going to step aside and let Joseph through in spite of his firm words — then he gathered himself and straightened his back. "No," he growled.

Joseph looked genuinely surprised to have been denied. He looked at me and I shrugged. I didn't have the energy to get involved in an argument.

"Can we just go in there instead?" I asked Matt, gesturing behind Matt to a side room with a glass door, "Then Joseph can still see me, and you can still say I gave you my statement on my own."

Neither man looked terribly happy but I was in no mood to have to take sides, and perhaps that was evident from my voice because they acquiesced.

Wheeling me into the other room and closing the door behind us, Matt turned to face me, putting his hand on the top of my good arm as if to keep my attention and stop me running (or wheeling) off. "Right. For the minute, you don't have to say anything — just nod your head for yes, shake for no, and keep smiling. Do you want me to get rid of whatshisname?"

I knew that *Matt* wanted to get rid of him, though I was struggling to understand why he was being so aggressive. Perhaps it was because of their earlier argument. Whatever the reason for his question, I knew that above all else I needed to be near Joseph.

I replied firmly, "No."

He looked frustrated. "Are you sure? We don't have to tell him anything, I can just tell him it's procedure."

"I'm sure. Why would I want Joseph to leave?"

He frowned. "Well, are you sure he didn't have anything to do with what happened to you? Makris was in his sister's house, after all. Yes or no is fine for now."

I sighed. "I knew you'd do this sooner or later. No, he didn't have anything to do with it. He saved my life."

Matt seemed disappointed that he couldn't send Joseph away, but he was evidently satisfied that Joseph wasn't a physical threat, at least. "He seems a bit … wired," he commented, with a nod through the window to where Joseph stood, arms folded, eyes firmly on me.

I gave Joseph a small smile and I saw him swallow hard, his jaw clenched. I felt a rush of warmth, a need to reach out and comfort him — he looked as though he'd been to hell and back and I realised just how frightening the experience must have been for him, too. Joseph and Matt, both traumatised because of Leon Makris — because of me.

Turning back to Matt I saw that he held a pad of carbon-backed paper and a pen. Pulling a chair up next to me, he was close enough so that I could rest my head against his shoulder for a minute as I drew comfort from his sheer normality and familiarity. Aware that his shoulder was very hard and tense, I raised my head and looked closely at him. "Are *you* alright?" I asked gently.

I'd caught him off-guard with my question and he struggled to respond for a moment before saying quietly, "I think I'm losing my mind."

I forced a laugh, "I know how that feels."

He shook his head in irritation, "No, Seph. I'm not being flippant, I really mean it … I think I must be going mad, because I can't explain what I saw today. I know what whatshisname told me happened, but that *isn't* what happened. I *know* I saw him crumple over, clutching his stomach like he'd been shot. I *know* I saw him literally disappear; one second there in a heap, next second completely gone. I *don't* know how Makris got inside that WC — that house was like Fort Knox. I *don't* know how he got to you past me *and* whatshisname *and* Cam through a locked door and then got you outside because I *do* know that those shutters were not broken like that when I got in, whatever whatshisname says.

"So no, I'm not alright. I'm far from it. But right now I need to get your statement and let the doctors do their stuff so I can start the process of getting the Bastard locked up for good. I really hope you can tell a good story, Seph, cos that's what I need right now. I can worry about the truth later."

I swallowed hard at the thought of having to dissect what had happened anyway, let alone having to create a tangible, believable narrative that would pass muster in court and then having to talk to Matt candidly when this was all over …

I knew that this was the first step in a long and truly horrible journey, yet right then it was Matt who caused me greatest concern. I wasn't used to seeing him vulnerable, unsure of himself.

Gently, I squeezed his hand, "That's not quite what I meant when I asked if you're alright, though. Please promise me that you won't keep all this bottled up this time. Talk to me, let me help. I know we don't really say these things to each other, but I love you — you're my best friend, and I don't want you to be hurt."

He pursed his lips slightly and nodded briefly, though I wondered if he'd live up to his promise. "Same," he murmured. With a visible effort, he resumed his air of professional toughness. His voice slightly louder and more assertive once more, he said, "Right. I don't like this any more than you do, babe, but I need to take a statement from you while it's still fresh, and before the physical evidence is taken."

I sighed, resigned to having to give Matt time to open up. "Let's just get it done," I said resolutely. If I was going to have to lie, it was better that I did it now than risk forgetting it later.

Unable to meet Matt's eye, I recounted a highly edited version of what had happened, drawn from what Joseph had told him. Naturally, I made no mention of a Greek forest or a beach in New Zealand, and I omitted about ninety percent of what Makris had said. By fabricating what had happened in this way, I could at least keep my emotions in check. My tale concluded with Joseph's timely arrival and intervention.

"Did he do anything to Makris?" Matt asked, his voice brisk and business-like.

I hesitated, not wanting to allow Joseph to suffer any legal repercussions for beating Makris so severely but unsure of how that could be avoided.

Matt pressed, "Seph, the guy's half dead. They can't even take him down to surgery yet, he's not stable enough — he keeps fitting. He's in a bad way."

"Will he live?" I asked, and I really didn't know what answer I wanted to hear.

"They think so," Matt said flatly.

"Shit," I muttered darkly, realising that this was not the answer I'd wanted after all.

"Shit, indeed," he agreed grimly.

After a moment, I reached out and gently removed the pen from Matt's hand. "I don't want Joseph to get in trouble," I told him. "He found the Bastard on top of me; he was … well, he was much like you were the first time it happened: angry, and full of adrenaline. I think he would have killed Makris if I hadn't told him to stop. But I don't want him to be charged with anything. How can I keep him safe? Tell me what to say so that Joseph doesn't get charged with anything and I'll say it."

Matt looked pensive and I judged that he was torn between feeling aggrieved at being usurped as my hero and feeling grateful that Joseph had actually stopped Makris from doing major harm. With a sigh, he said resignedly, "Is it possible … Is it possible that the Bastard appeared to have been rather badly beaten up when you first saw him in the bathroom, which was before whatshisname intervened?" He raised both eyebrows encouragingly and I seized on the excuse.

I handed back the pen and he added notes to the statement in the relevant part as I spoke. "Makris was bruised and bloodied when I saw him in the WC for the first time. I thought he'd been in a car crash."

Satisfied that I had given a coherent statement, Matt handed me the pen and the sheets of paper for me to add my signature to each page. "We'd better hope the Bastard doesn't remember what really happened, and we'd better hope the forensics match up," he muttered. "Tell whatshisname to keep his

277

hands out of sight if he doesn't want to have to explain how they got knackered. And tell him to get rid of his shoes and clothes," he added.

As much as he clearly disliked Joseph, it appeared that he was protecting him and I was touched. I leant forwards to kiss his cheek but he dodged out of the way.

"No, no, not before the physical," he warned.

I knew that experience was fast approaching and I wasn't looking forward to it, but rather than standing and leading me to the door as I'd expected, Matt remained seated and looked decidedly uncomfortable about something.

He opened his mouth to ask me something two or three times before finally managing, "Are you and whatshisname …"

"Matt, please call him Joseph," I sighed.

"Ugh, fine. Are you and *Joseph* … I mean, have you two been … intimate?" he asked, red in the face and his colours a swirl of agitation, worry and — *puce* — jealousy, really? "I'm only asking because when they do the physical they'll find DNA …" he added hurriedly.

I blushed right back at him. "No! No, Matt. Nothing like that. Oh, but I scratched him, when I had that flashback. That'll show up, won't it, when they scrape my fingernails?"

Straightening in his seat, he sighed deeply. "Don't worry about that, we can explain that. I'm sorry. I had to ask about the other stuff. They'll be taking samples off him as well to eliminate his DNA from the samples they get off you and I had to be sure nothing would show up we couldn't explain."

Understanding dawned. "Wait, they don't need

to do an intimate examination, do they? Makris didn't rape me, he didn't even touch me like that. He just beat me up. I don't even think he would have killed me—"

Matt looked at me sharply and interrupted crossly. "—Seph, I *never* want to hear those words from your mouth again! I want the Bastard for attempted murder and for that I need to show he intended to kill you. Alright?"

I nodded my head, wincing slightly at the pain. "But he didn't do anything sexually."

Matt looked at me apologetically. Gently, he said, "You were unconscious when I found you. If you weren't conscious throughout the whole thing, we've got to assume the worst."

I knew I hadn't blacked out until after I was safe, with Joseph, but that wouldn't fit my statement. So I tried, "Well, surely I'd know if he'd, y'know, *done stuff.*"

He leaned back slightly in his chair and spoke softly. "Not necessarily. I've known lasses raped on date rape drugs who didn't feel a thing afterwards and only found out when the pregnancy started to show."

With a glance back at the door to reassure myself that it was still closed and that Joseph was still on the other side of it, I lowered my voice and said, "It's not like that could happen to me, though."

Matt shook his head dismissively. "What if he did something and you need treatment for some STI or something?"

I was prepared to accept that I had imagined much of what had happened as some kind of elaborate coping mechanism, but I was ninety-nine percent sure that I'd have *known* if I'd been molested. But without explaining all the details (even the ones I knew) I could see that Matt would not be dissuaded — and ninety-nine percent probably wasn't really sufficient in this situation. I sighed and murmured my consent.

He took a deep breath and stood. "Well, let's get this over with then, my love."

CHAPTER 34

As Joseph and I sat silently in the waiting room together once more — Matt had gone to find the doctor — my eyes started to close; fatigue was rapidly setting in. Joseph remained on high alert, but I craved sleep, not only because I was so weary but also because I wanted to escape reality for a while. I knew what was coming — I'd had to go through an intimate examination once before — and I did not relish the prospect. As I began to drift off into merciful oblivion, I thought sadly of Nana and wished she were with me. I took great comfort from Joseph's presence, but there were times in my life when I really needed a mum, and this was definitely one of them.

Joseph's voice startled me awake, though he wasn't addressing me. "What are you doing here?"

To his side stood Russ and Russ's wife Felicity. Immediately self-conscious, given my dishevelled appearance (which looked even worse in direct comparison with Felicity's perfection) and emotional fragility, I sat straighter and smoothed my hospital gown. I gave up almost immediately when a flash of pain radiated from my collarbone down my arm.

Seeing that I was awake, Russ said, "Alright?"

I raised my eyebrows, wondering whether this was a greeting or a question — if it were the latter, it was a pretty stupid question. I was spared the need to reply by Felicity, who moved towards me and crouched so that she was level with where I sat in the wheelchair.

"Sorry to wake you. They're nearly ready for you and I wondered if you'd like me to accompany you?" she asked, her voice kind but her colours reflecting fear and anxiety.

Did I want a work colleague, who was clearly scared of me, to accompany me into a room where doctors were going to scrape and probe and photograph me from all angles?

"Not really, no. But thank you for offering," I said, as politely as I could.

Felicity seemed surprised. "It's just that Hester and I thought you'd like a woman with you."

I did, and it was kind of her and Joseph's mother to think of me, but I wanted my Nana, and that wasn't going to happen — a raw fact that made her death feel real for the first time since she had passed. Tears welled up and I turned my head away, embarrassed to let Felicity see me cry.

Russ stepped forward and put a plastic carrier bag on my lap. "Well, *I* said you'd need *this*," he said gruffly.

I glanced down at the bag, which was full of bars of chocolate. Sniffing back more tears, I asked with a small laugh, "You thought I'd need diabetes?"

Russ's colours were still notably marked by pale yellow fear and he did not look entirely comfortable with how close his wife was to me, but at my words a smile curled at the corner of his mouth. "Have a salad tomorrow, it'll balance it out."

In a way, his evident fear made his gift and attempts at making me feel better all the more touching and I extracted a Twix from the bag with a warm smile of thanks.

As I fiddled with the wrapper, Felicity stood up straight. With a resigned sigh, she said, "Okay, I'll be straight with you. Joseph won't be allowed to be with you when you're in that examination suite, and nor will Matt. Thomas needs to talk to Joseph, but he's stuck for the moment keeping an eye on Makris. Until he can give Joseph some reassurance that you're perfectly safe, I doubt that Joseph is going to let you out of his sight. Am I right?"

Joseph nodded once, his face set.

"Well then, we did feel you would benefit from a female presence, but I'm mainly here to prevent a very large man from becoming a very large problem. Would you allow me to do so, please?"

I looked at Joseph, who seemed to be considering this.

Russ told his brother, "Might as well get used to one of us looking after her. You'll have to sleep at some point and you really need to sort yourself out — you look like crap."

Joseph scoffed and slid a hand self-consciously through his rather messy hair, with an embarrassed glance in my direction. I busied myself with the Twix wrapper; either it was made of some specially reinforced material or my coordination was suffering from the residual shock and lingering adrenaline in my system. Probably the latter.

Felicity added, "We're *here*, Joseph. Your mum is on hand to make sure the forensics match up and your dad will be here as soon as he can. Whatever else happens, we are on your side."

The pall of worry and sadness that had sat round Joseph's aura for the last few weeks seemed to lessen and his fear began to dissipate somewhat. He smiled briefly, but then an edge crept into his voice as he asked, "What of Erica?"

Felicity and Russ shared an uncomfortable glance. "Alex is working on that," Russ said apologetically.

"So, would you consent for me to come in with you?" Felicity asked me gently.

As much as I disliked the thought of being so vulnerable in her presence, I had to admit that Joseph seemed much more relaxed at the prospect of Felicity accompanying me.

Before I could respond, though, Matt arrived with the doctor. She was wearing a white coat, a Purple aura and an austere manner. She did not smile, and she plucked my notes from Matt's arms without so much as a glance in my direction. Perhaps she was just busy, or tired, or had had a bad day — but I needed warmth and kindness, not detachment and formality.

Felicity reached over and unwrapped the Twix for me; hearing the rustle, the doctor spared me a glance and frowned — she strode across to me and plucked the bar of chocolate out of my fingers and confiscated it.

"Nothing to eat or drink until we've finished," she snapped. "I have to take mouth swabs and I don't think anyone at the lab will want to pick through toffee to get to any usable DNA, do you?"

Wordlessly, I reached out and slipped my hand into Felicity's. She gave it a gentle squeeze of acknowledgement and put her other hand on my good shoulder to reassure me that she wasn't going anywhere. Her lips were pursed; she didn't speak, she simply stood beside me in a show of feminine solidarity that was exactly what I needed.

Joseph reached over and held my other hand.

Matt had noticed that Felicity and Russ had joined us. Pointedly ignoring Russ (against whom he clearly bore a grudge for once upsetting me) and looking anywhere except at Joseph and our joined hands, he introduced himself formally to Felicity. He looked expectantly at her after she had returned his greeting and introduced herself, waiting for her to explain what she was doing there.

Felicity was polite but her tone brooked no argument, and she repeated her assertion that I needed a woman with me. "Ideally, she should have her mum or her sister, but I gather those particular women leave a lot to be desired, so I will stand in their stead."

Matt looked at me enquiringly and I shrugged a passive agreement, beyond tired but rather relieved that I wouldn't have to be on my own with the intimidating doctor. Joseph looked far less agitated than he had so far and I thought that his sister-in-law must have judged his mood accurately.

The doctor finished reading my paperwork and turned to me at last. "Right, let's get you into the examination room, shall we?" she said briskly.

To my intense relief, Felicity didn't leave my side; she took charge of the wheelchair and pushed me into the room. Joseph reluctantly released my hand and he and Russ shared a grim look as they both took up positions outside my room, alert and on guard for — my dad? Makris? Another 'Damned'? Or whatever other foe they apparently thought was going to appear. Matt leant against the wall opposite the door and tipped me a reassuring wink as the door closed between us.

Once my gown had been removed, Felicity helped me to arrange a modesty sheet that the doctor provided. The examination was as clinical and as invasive as I'd remembered the last one to be. I drifted away, my mind blank, a self-preservation technique I had mastered long ago that had always served me well in times of trauma.

When it was over, the doctor pulled off her gloves with a snap that brought me back from my self-induced torpor. She rechecked my notes and, in a display of epic insensitivity, said brightly, "Well, at least there's no chance you could be pregnant, not with no womb. No need for emergency contraception, at least."

I flushed, bruised by her harsh words. When I'd been stabbed, I'd been so badly damaged that they'd had to remove my womb, though my ovaries remained intact so at least I had been spared an early menopause. My psychotherapist had wanted to address my sudden lack of fertility, but I hadn't given it much thought at the time because it was just so abstract … I was very young at the time, and I didn't have a boyfriend or any intention of finding one, so the idea of not having a family of my own was not a pressing concern. Since meeting Joseph, though, my thoughts on my inability to bear children were already becoming more troublesome, and I felt the sting of hurt and worry at the doctor's words.

Felicity, meanwhile, had taken a sharp intake of breath. She looked at me and a swell of an unfamiliar colour came to the fore in her aura. Her eyes were full of compassion and I felt a connection with her that hadn't been there before. A moment later, she turned her attention to the doctor, her face hard and radiating anger. "Excuse me," she murmured to me as she strode to where the doctor stood finalising her notes.

I watched as she leant over to whisper something in the doctor's ear. Whatever she said, the doctor's face became drip white and she hurriedly left the room without a backwards glance, taking with her the bags of evidence.

I looked inquiringly at Felicity, wondering what on earth she'd said, but she didn't volunteer to enlighten me and I was in no mood to press for details. She looked furious, though, and I reflected that as lovely as she had been to me, I wouldn't want to spill her proverbial pint.

I gingerly sat up and Felicity helped me into a fresh gown that had been left for me. I'd also been given an attractive pair of paper knickers, which I struggled into with as much dignity as I could under the circumstances. I avoided Felicity's gaze but could sense that her anger had morphed into concern from the gentle way she held my arm to steady me and from the sadness in her voice.

"Does Joseph know?" she asked softly.

I shook my head.

"Well, I won't say anything: that's up to you, when you're ready. But I wouldn't worry — he'll love you no matter what, you know."

She was not lying, so she believed it to be true, at least, and that made me smile a little, grateful for her kind words and support.

"Thank you for looking after me," I said, my voice hoarse from suppressed emotion and tiredness.

She gave me a small smile and waved away my thanks as unnecessary. At last, my second ordeal of the night was over, and a nurse came to take me back to a private room to recuperate for the night; Felicity, Russ and Joseph accompanied me whilst Matt spoke to the doctor about statements and reports. The empty corridors echoed with our footsteps. It was just after four o'clock in the morning, though so much had happened that I could not quite fathom that it had only been hours ago that I had been chatting with Cam in the canteen or driving home from court with Joseph.

My room had a shower and I marvelled at the strings that must have been pulled by Matt or possibly Joseph's mother, Hester, for me to have such luxurious surroundings in an NHS hospital. Shooing Joseph and Russ outside again to wait for us, Felicity helped me to remove my sling and gown so that I could shower.

I spent ten minutes relishing the feeling of hot water on my skin, doing my best to wash with only one usable arm. Turning the water off at last, I found Felicity waiting with a large towel for me and she helped me to slide back into my sling whilst I did my best to conceal my imperfect body from her. She was kind enough not to comment on the scars that criss-crossed my abdomen and I could almost pretend that she hadn't seen them.

Instead, she focussed on my small outline tattoo on my shoulder blade.

"Oh, that's pretty," she commented, running a manicured fingernail over it.

"Thanks," I murmured. "Matt chose it. I had it done when I finished my therapy, sort of a reminder of getting through it all."

"A phoenix. How apt," she commented lightly, though there was a note of curiosity behind her words.

I gave a small smile; it was a bitter-sweet memory. "I chose one for him, too — a shield. I wanted him to remember that he'd protected me, even though he's always felt like he didn't."

"He's a good friend," she replied. "He's also *very* organised," she added with a smile, and she handed me a bag containing a nightie, change of clothes and my toothbrush.

She seemed to be on the cusp of commenting further — something was troubling her — but in the end she shook her head slightly as though to dispel unwelcome thoughts and didn't care to share them. I didn't feel that I knew her well enough to ask her what was worrying her, so after brushing my teeth perfunctorily I simply allowed her to help me change into my nightie before she fussed with the sheets so that I could climb into bed. I noticed with a smile that Russ's bag of chocolate had been placed on the bedside table, though I had no appetite to speak of yet.

I was feeling very sore — every part of my

body seemed bruised and uncomfortable and the bed was not nearly soft enough. Joseph re-entered the room, looking stressed and exhausted, and his eyes never left mine; seated beside my bed, he took my hand in his the moment I was settled.

"Matt is checking on Makris," he told me, "and he has a few pieces of evidence to procure, but he asked me to tell you that he will be back as soon as he can to check on you."

Felicity gave my arm a gentle squeeze before she walked to the door and switched off the light. Before the door closed, I saw that Russ was standing outside, his posture ramrod straight as though on full alert.

Joseph lifted my hand and kissed the back of my fingers. At his touch, I felt the wall I'd built around my emotions begin to crumble and a sob escaped my lips before I could shore it up again. I'd always been told that crying was a weakness, that tears would elicit no care, no sympathy, no love, and I fought them hard. But Joseph moved to sit on the bed beside me, lifting me gently into a sitting position so that he could take me in his arms and hold me; the tears came unrelenting and I cried like a child into his chest. I felt a mixture of relief that it was all over, shame about not having been open with Joseph all along, and shock at all that had happened that day.

"Sleep, Sephy. It will help you to heal," Joseph murmured after the worst of my tears had subsided.

Tiredness swept over me in a wave at his suggestion and I felt my eyes begin to droop.

"Please stay with me," I mumbled, already halfway to sleep.

I shuffled over a little, and he lay on the bed

beside me. He slipped his arm around my shoulders; I rested my head on his chest and fell asleep listening to the steady thrum of his heartbeat.

CHAPTER 35

I WOKE AS SUDDENLY AS IF someone had thrown a bucket of water over me. Jerking upright with a gasp, I was wrenched from a horrible dream — my brain had conjured a perfect replay of the attack and combined it with scenes in which Joseph and Matt had both been murdered for good measure. I was trembling with residual fear and it took a few seconds to work out where I was.

Joseph sat up beside me, alert; judging by the dark shadows beneath his eyes, it appeared that he had not slept. Impulsively, relieved that he was distinctly not-murdered, I leant towards him and hugged him fiercely with my good arm. His body stiffened momentarily, no doubt taken by surprise by my sudden movement, but he then relaxed into the hug and held me tightly against his chest. Gradually, I calmed and my breathing became steadier.

"It's okay, it was a dream," he murmured.

Still clinging to him, I asked anxiously, "Where's Makris?"

In a clearly discontented tone, he replied, "He is downstairs in ICU — still alive." He added, a touch optimistically, "I could still remedy that."

"No! No, I don't want you to do anything to him. Let the police sort him out. Is he still unconscious?"

I felt him nod. "They are unsure of when, or even *if* he will wake. He is under the watch of two armed officers at all times; there is another armed officer and my brother outside your door. Leon Makris is not going to get near you via conventional means even if he experiences a miraculous recovery."

I glanced towards the frosted glass of my door, through which I could see the outline of my very own armed police officer. I couldn't see Russ, but the thought of his presence was somehow more reassuring than that of the armed officer: more comforting still was the fact that I had Joseph next to me.

As though reading my thoughts, Joseph added, "Moreover, I have not left your side. Nor will I until that monster — or any other — is no longer a threat."

Though I was comforted by Joseph's reassurances and his very presence, I could not relax. So much had happened, so much I didn't understand. My aching body told me that I had definitely been attacked. Since Makris was in hospital, I could at least be sure that it was he who had hurt me, and since Joseph was sitting beside me threatening to kill him I could be sure that it was he who had saved me. The rest — the impromptu and rather sudden trips to the Yorkshire Dales, Greece and New Zealand, the hurricane, Makris flying round a forest, talk of High

Councils and Damnation and my father — they were clearly all products of a traumatised mind.

I looked at the man beside me. He was strong, and gorgeous, and his colours told me how kind and decent he was. In comparison, I was battered and bruised, essentially flawed, mentally unstable and not even close to being good enough for him. He deserved better.

"You don't have to stay, you know, I'll be okay now."

His eyes widened slightly in surprise before narrowing in a concerned frown. "Do you — do you want me to leave?" he asked.

I dropped my gaze, staring at my hands so that I didn't have to look at him. "No, but I don't want you to feel like you have to stay. I have way more baggage than you signed up for yesterday, and I want you to know that I wouldn't blame you for leaving things here."

He sighed deeply and reached up to run a hand gently through my hair. "I hate what he did to you. I wish you had told me more, so that I could have been better prepared to protect you, but I don't blame you. You felt that his actions were a reflection on your strength and you didn't want me to perceive you as a victim. I do not: I know full well how strong you are, even if you don't."

Unsatisfied with what I saw as empty reassurances, I pressed, "Still, you don't have to be with me. You could choose anyone. There are a lot of women out there who would kill to be in my shoes — well, maybe not right now, with the broken collarbone and everything, but in general, with you. You could have your pick."

Without missing a beat, he replied, "And I pick you. I cannot bear to be without you and I hope never to have to be again. Please don't ask me to leave, because all I want is to be with you."

His colours betrayed no lies. I revelled in the feeling of relief that his words brought and leant carefully into his chest; I felt him relax alongside me and we spent a long moment locked in each other's arms.

Content that he wasn't about to leave, I sighed, suddenly weighed down by the thought of all that would come next. When I was seventeen, the trial had been almost as traumatic as the attack itself. "I don't know if I can do all this again," I said, gesturing vaguely, my voice cracking slightly as I fought tears.

"Do what again?" he asked.

"The reports, the statements, the questions, the waiting, the trial, the cross-examination ..." I listed, each word weighing heavier around my shoulders than the last.

I dreaded the whole process. I didn't even know how much of what had happened the previous night had been real and how much I had imagined or hallucinated: how on earth would I fare as a witness at Makris's trial, assuming he survived? The defence would tear me apart.

"Ah. No," he said firmly. "If and when Leon Makris regains consciousness, he will plead guilty and be remanded until trial in the Crown Court. You won't need to give evidence, there will be no trial as such — only a plea and sentencing hearing. I promise you; he will not get anywhere near you ever again."

I shook my head sadly, wanting very much to believe him but not sharing his optimism that Makris would be so cooperative. He had chosen to represent himself at his last trial and seemed to take great delight in cross-examining me and giving long, ranting speeches to the jury and judge about how he couldn't be convicted of attempted murder because I wasn't human and therefore could not be 'murdered'. The trial had had to be halted whilst psychiatric reports had been prepared, but the experts who examined him had all agreed that he was fit to stand trial … Weariness at the very thought of going through it all again washed over me.

I thought of Matt and hoped he was coping.

"Where's Matt?" I asked anxiously.

Joseph smiled stiffly. "He has been at the police station all night, but he has texted me to enquire as to your wellbeing roughly every fifteen minutes since he left the hospital. He is presently collating the evidence gathered last night. He is … fiercely efficient."

I smiled to myself at that description but then frowned, concerned about Joseph. "You must be shattered …"

He shook his head dismissively and tucked an errant strand of my hair behind my ear.

"Can I borrow your phone please?" I asked, thinking I'd forestall Matt's next text.

He readily agreed and passed me his phone; I texted Matt asking if he was alright and telling him I was awake and okay. Almost immediately, he texted back with a brusque, 'I'm fine. Glad you're awake. Will text with update when available. Don't leave hospital without police. Eat something. Xx'

Feeling more composed, I returned the phone to Joseph. After a bit of a struggle, I sat upright, making a vain attempt to restore order to my hair and make myself a little more presentable. Almost immediately though, over and above the physical discomfort, I experienced an almost palpable wrench at moving myself away from Joseph's warmth and the comfort I was drawing from being in his arms. As though he felt the same, he gently drew me back towards him; I nestled there against his chest once more, content.

Every time an image of what I thought I'd seen the night before popped up in my memory I pushed it firmly away, focussing on something in the real world, something I could verify as true.

"What time is it?" I asked.

"It is a little after ten o'clock. The nurse brought you some toast earlier ..." he glanced distastefully at the plate on the cabinet beside me, on which rested two very soggy and sad looking slices of white, buttered toast. "But if you're hungry I can arrange to get you something more appetising. And there's always the bag of diabetes from Russ ..."

I smiled briefly but said, "No thanks, maybe later." I had absolutely zero appetite; that was probably exactly why Matt had told me to eat something, but I just couldn't face it.

I shifted position slightly but jostled my shoulder in doing so; the sharp pain from my broken bone joined and amplified the aches and severe discomfort from practically every other part of my body. I stifled a cry; Joseph tensed, and anxiety flashed through his colours. He reached for a glass of water and two paracetamols from the bedside table and held me steady so that I could take them.

I thanked him and sighed with relief as I settled

back against his chest. "Lord, why does everything hurt *more* today?" I groaned quietly.

We were quiet for a moment or two and I peered down at what I could see of my body. I dreaded to think what my face must look like: my left cheek was swollen enough that I could see it, and my lips felt puffy.

Even so, I managed to find a positive in it all. "You know, it's weird," I began, and I knew he was listening closely. "I spent years torturing myself, blaming myself and hating myself for the fact that I couldn't stop Makris back when I was seventeen. But Matt's been giving me self-defence lessons practically every week ever since and keeping me fit and things. I'm stronger than I've ever been, and I *still* couldn't stop him." Gesturing towards my injuries, I concluded, "I *know* how hard I fought. I couldn't have done anything more and I still couldn't stop him. That's ... strangely comforting. Liberating."

He nodded and replied softly, "Yet, as I said, you are stronger than you know."

Needing to see his face and his colours to start to understand how he was feeling about everything that had happened, I straightened more willingly this time. I looked at him carefully. Sadness. Worry. Pain. Fear, though less than there had been. "What's wrong?"

He scoffed lightly. "Aside from the fact that you were abducted, injured and nearly killed a few hours ago?"

At his words, a thousand images came flooding back and I forced them away just as quickly, neither ready nor willing to think about them just then.

Besides, that was definitely not all that was wrong. "Well, yes. Are you okay?"

He seemed lost for words and ran a hand across his unshaven chin before settling for, "You are safe now: so yes, I am okay."

His hand tentatively and slowly moved towards the uninjured side of my face and gently cupped my cheek in his large, warm palm, his thumb delicately tracing the contour of my cheekbone. A frown and pulse of sadness were in evidence as he tipped my head slightly and examined my face and throat. Despite my agitation, fear and confusion, I felt an amazing sense of calm when he held me and my breathing became more regular. A resurgence of all that I had felt for Joseph made me dizzy and it were as though there was nothing else in the world aside from the two of us. I was surrounded by the unique dusky pink/gold colour I would forever associate with him and I felt utterly at peace.

Yet he looked indescribably despairing. I sensed that he needed my comfort as much as I needed his; it felt entirely natural to reach up to run my fingers gently through his hair, down his neck and round his back, pulling him close to me. He hugged me close in response and I felt as much as heard his sigh of contentment. At that moment, I felt detached from what had happened — what actually mattered was we had each other.

After several minutes, Joseph gently pulled away from me, though he took both of my hands in his. My attention was caught by his hands, which appeared to be the source of his physical pain. He was hurt because he had defended me, a fact that caused me great anguish, and I moaned softly, "Your poor hands …"

He shook his head dismissively, "It is nothing."

The knuckles were badly bruised and swollen. I understood what Matt had said about needing to keep them hidden to avoid anyone asking questions as to how they got that way — there could be no doubt that they'd been injured in a fight. I was filled with fresh anxiety about whether Joseph would face legal repercussions for the force he had used. Wishing I could take away the pain, I said, "These are really swollen. Did you put ice on them?"

He gave a small laugh and shook his head in amusement. "Of all the things I'm worried about right now, my hands are the least of them. You really don't need to concern yourself with—"

He broke off when, without stopping to think whether it was appropriate or not, I raised each of hands in turn and softly pressed my lips to the back of his fingers.

His colours were far lighter and more positive almost immediately. In response, he moved one of his hands to lightly brush my bruised cheek; he moved forward and placed a tender, feather-light kiss there that made my heart float and did more to help me feel better than any words could have.

He looked as nervous as I felt about being in such close proximity to him and yet not knowing what we were to each other. Did his kiss confirm that he really did still feel something for me?

When we had been together before and during the attack (images of a forest and a pier flashed up and were firmly shoved aside), and later in the rape suite, it had been all about survival. He had saved me from a dreadful fate and yet I had not thought to thank him until now. I whispered fervently, "Thank you for saving my life yesterday. You were amazing."

He tensed, making me look up again and I saw that his colours were suffused with fresh guilt, anger and frustration. Through clenched teeth he said quietly, "I should not have *had* to save you. If I had not been removed from your car against my wishes and forced to hold myself to account for much of the afternoon, I would have never left your side. If I had not allowed myself to be drawn into an argument with Matt and distracted, I would have seen that DC Cam was not in control of himself and I would never have let you out of my sight!" He sighed heavily and his voice softened and much of the anger left him as he went on, "You should have been in my arms, safe. I am truly sorry. I failed you when you needed me most."

His words sparked a jumble of memories, images and questions that fought each other for my attention. *How* had he disappeared so completely from my car? What did he mean, he'd been removed from my car against his wishes? Alex had said it was Erica who'd taken him, but how could she — or anyone — have removed a man of Joseph's size at all, let alone without being seen? He had literally disappeared in front of me ... Then Alex had taken me from the office to his house in a split second ... Makris had taken me to *Greece* in the blink of an eye ... then Joseph had been there too, and there'd been a huge storm that had lifted Makris into the air but not so much as messed up my hair ... and then I'd been in New Zealand, and there had been talk of

Damneds and orders, the High Council and my father and ...

I let out a sharp sigh and muttered shakily, "Oh god, I think I've finally lost my mind ..."

"What do you mean?" he asked, concern in his voice.

I gave a half-hearted, self-conscious laugh. "I keep imagining things. Things that didn't happen — that *couldn't* have happened. But I can't remember what really *did* happen."

He shook his head briefly, looking sourly through the window to our left.

After a moment, he said quietly, "You are not imagining things."

I shook my head and tried to speak through a voice that was cracking with pent up, confused emotions. "I am. I keep remembering things that didn't really happen. Like — like I was in Alex's house yesterday, but I didn't drive there, I was just suddenly there. And Makris appeared out of thin air in the bathroom, and took me — ha! — took me to a forest in Greece. And you conjured a tornado or something to stop him, and then took us to a beach on the other side of the world where it was night ..." I hung my head, too worried for my own sanity than to think of anything else.

I had expected silence, but Joseph spoke without hesitation, his voice steady and low. "You did not imagine any of that. My brother-in-law did not use conventional means to transport you to his house from the office yesterday. Leon Makris did indeed take you to Greece, and after I had incapacitated him I was afraid that his choice of location meant that we would be ambushed, so I took you somewhere safer. We were in New Zealand, a random destination not connected to me or my family in any way, where we were unlikely to be discovered by chance." He frowned slightly and went on, "I'm afraid I misjudged the timing of the tide somewhat, but it could have been worse, I suppose. Anyway, I returned you safely and instantaneously to your home after you had been able to ascertain that the High Council did not pose an immediate threat and ensured that Makris will not be able to report back to them in the future."

Seeing my highly perturbed expression, he said insistently, "You imagined none of it; your mind is perfectly sound, but it has experienced many things that it had not previously thought possible."

I was beginning to feel a little lightheaded as reality and fantasy began to blur and I wondered if I might end the day in a psychiatric unit, assuming that I wasn't already there and hallucinating everything else.

Decisively, he said, "Come what may, today I am going to explain everything. It looks as though most of my family will support me in that, which makes things easier for me, but right now *you* are my only concern. You have been incredibly patient with me and I know how lucky I am in that regard; I hope my luck will hold and you will still countenance a future with me, for however long we may have. Please be patient for just a little while longer, until my father arrives — I have promised him I will wait until he is here to begin explaining it all."

I shivered a little as a thrill ran down my spine at his words: the idea of a future with Joseph made me feel like I'd won the lottery. But I frowned at the idea of Thomas coming back to the hospital; I really didn't want any more fuss and fawning whilst I was in such a wretched state.

Before I could protest, he scrolled through his phone and began composing a brief text to his dad. He paused, though, and said, "You should eat, even if you're not hungry; I will ask him to bring you something."

As though having second thoughts about sending his text, he paused again, lowered his phone and sat quietly for a moment. He swallowed several times, as though finding speech difficult, before managing quietly, "I am not what you think I am."

"Alex said you're not a wizard. Bit disappointed, if I'm honest," I said.

He looked up, amusement wrinkling his eyes. His smile was gone too soon, though, and his tone was flat when he said, "When you hear … when you understand what I am, what we are … you will have a choice to make. If you choose not to see me again, then I will accept that decision." His voice was achingly sad, and he couldn't meet my eyes.

I thought about that for a long moment. Whatever it was, this family secret of his was clearly a big deal. But looking at Joseph, feeling that new, unfamiliar and yet intense connection with him — I couldn't imagine any circumstances in which I wouldn't want to be with him.

"I don't care what you are. I know *who* you are," I began, before echoing his words from the previous morning: "And I want you to be with me."

Something indefinable changed in the way he looked at me. I studied him for a moment to try to work out what was different and then understood that all trace of uncertainty — together with the little frown I was so familiar with — had vanished and in its place was a look of resolve. He sent his text.

"Let's do this," he said with a nod, his voice steady and assured.

CHAPTER 36

A MOMENT LATER, THE POLICE OFFICER at the door shifted her position to talk to someone who had approached her. I stiffened, sure that at any moment Makris was going to push past her and burst into the room. Joseph stood, acting as a barrier between me and the door, but immediately relaxed and sat back down again as the door opened and his dad, Thomas, walked in carrying a paper bag containing what smelled like fresh croissants.

It was the first time I had seen Thomas since my interview and I was taken aback once more by the familiarity of his soul, which I found comforting and more welcome than I had anticipated.

Whilst his features were calm and reassuring, Thomas's colours told me that he was distinctly on edge, though I couldn't guess why he should be. Joseph's fear had abated somewhat overnight, but was still there at the edges and I could feel myself tense at the thought that the danger had not truly passed.

I pulled the bedsheet up a little and sat up as straight as I could to greet him; noticing my movement, Joseph moved to arrange the pillows and adjust the mechanical bed to assist me.

Thomas greeted me warmly and enquired as to how I was feeling; I told him I was rather sore but otherwise fine. Polite formalities concluded, he then said, "Please excuse me for a moment; I must set my son's mind at rest about a few things that you may not fully understand. I know that it will be rather impolite of me to do so but I'm sure you can see how worried he is, and I must do what I can to reassure him."

I gave a brief nod and looked back at Joseph — the worry was indeed written all over his face and aura. If Thomas could say anything that could alleviate that then I was all for it.

To Joseph, Thomas said, "The others have all agreed that she should be told. Some more reluctantly than others, of course."

Joseph merely nodded in reply and I noticed that his tension eased a little as though he had been preparing himself for an argument. He slipped his hand into mine and I revelled in the sense of comfort brought by that casual gesture.

Thomas went on, "Russ is with Makris; he has fully briefed me on the information obtained last night, and on the orders given. I am satisfied that Makris no longer poses a threat, even if he regains consciousness, and that the High Council remains oblivious."

"Her orders to Makris will be binding?" Joseph asked, still tense.

"Utterly."

"And they were worded with sufficient clarity?"

Thomas nodded. "You did well, son."

Not quite satisfied, Joseph pressed, "What of her father? Makris thinks that another Damned could still be sent."

Thomas tilted his head, considering this. "Theoretically, that is possible. Indeed, it is probably the only option open to her father. But so long as one of us is around her or she is in the presence of another human, such as Matt, none would dare to act. The reward would not be worth the risks."

Joseph visibly relaxed at last; I felt the muscles in his arm soften slightly and his colours were drained of the last remnants of fear.

Turning to me at last, Thomas said, "Thank you for your patience, Sephy. We have been so worried about you." His face was sombre as he pulled a chair from the corner of the room and sat beside my bed. "Oh, here, I hope these will suffice?"

He handed me the bag of what were indeed croissants. I took them with grateful thanks and offered the bag to Joseph, knowing that he hadn't eaten any more recently than I had. He declined, but I took a doughy pinch of pastry between my fingers and pulled, popping it in my mouth and savouring the warm sweetness. The taste ignited a fierce hunger and before I knew it I had consumed two of the buttery, flaky pastries.

Feeling instantly better for the sugar and fat, I felt myself relax a little; I then became aware of the rather expectant silence building around me. I looked at Thomas, who seemed to have been waiting for me to be ready to hear what he had to say.

Seeing that he had my full attention, he began. "I know that you have been through a terrible experience. I also know that it has undoubtedly been made worse by not understanding much of what happened to you."

I didn't trust myself to speak in case I derailed whatever truth I was finally about to hear, so just nodded an agreement.

Thomas looked at me apologetically. "I am sorry. Much of this secrecy has been down to our laws, but I could have been more flexible about how strictly those laws were adhered to in this case. It has been a difficult time for my family, and I have been trying to balance a lot of interests and find the safest path for all concerned ..." He smiled ruefully as he caught sight of the impatience that must have been written all over my face. "And I realise I am still not giving you any answers. Again, I am sorry. It is hard to know where to begin."

"Dad, just tell her," Joseph said wearily.

He was tense again, and I thought that perhaps he was worried about how I would react and whether I would still want to be with him. In silent answer, I carefully scooted over in bed to sit even closer to him and affectionately squeezed his arm. His colours lightened instantly, though Thomas's were stressed and full of turmoil.

Thomas breathed out heavily. "You are not going mad, that is the first thing you need to know. I do not expect you to believe me when I tell you the truth, though, and if you need time to digest it then take as much as you need; I will always be here to talk to you about it whenever you are ready. I think, though — and most of my family agrees — that if you and Joseph are to stand a chance of being together and surviving, then you need to know what we are."

"Go for it," I replied, sounding far calmer than I felt inside.

He nodded. A sheen of sweat broke out across his brow as he formulated his next words.

"Sephy, I — we — the Democrituses … We are gods. Immortals."

I stared at Thomas for a moment longer than was strictly polite.

Hurriedly, he added, "I know how that sounds. Please just trust that I am telling you the truth, even if that truth seems utterly unbelievable."

I glanced at Joseph and he looked back at me steadily, his colours reflecting only nervous anticipation. Flummoxed, I returned my attention to Thomas and I waited in expectant silence for him to continue.

Thomas was apparently seized by an idea and he leant forwards in his seat. "Do you — do you believe in a god of any kind?"

I didn't immediately respond, unsure of how to answer without giving offence. In the end, I opted for honesty. "No."

Slightly crestfallen, he replied, "Ah. Well, that may make this harder for you to believe, then." He sat back again and bit his lip in a gesture of uncertainty. It took a moment for him to try again. "Well, I'm sure you'll agree that mankind *as a whole* has always believed in gods — higher beings who can be called upon in times of crisis or turned to for comfort. The Mayans, the Egyptians, the Greeks, the Romans and countless other tribes, communities and civilisations: all have believed in and prayed to many gods over many millennia. Faith is a powerful construct, and when enough people have faith in a god, that god comes to exist."

I paused for a moment before replying, trying very hard to keep my tone measured and free from incredulity. "Gods ... gods actually exist — because people made them up and believed in them?" I asked. In my mind, I was thinking about other things, like the tooth fairy or Father Christmas, and wondering if Thomas thought the same was true about them. I decided not to ask as it seemed a tad disrespectful if not downright blasphemous.

Thomas did not, apparently, detect any note of doubt in my comment and must have assumed that I was reasserting his statement rather than gently challenging it because he merely corrected, "Well, no, not quite. *Faith* creates gods, not *belief* — there's a difference. If everything humans *believed* in popped into existence, then we'd be surrounded by vampires and yetis and ghosts and all sorts of things."

"Father Christmas and the tooth fairy," I murmured.

"Exactly! No god created mankind, as far as we know, but mankind frequently creates gods through their faith. Even after their faith wanes, the gods they have created remain — they are created as immortal, after all."

This was going to be one of those times when I'd have to look as though I were listening politely whilst privately thinking of how to extricate myself from the situation without seeming rude. As Thomas began to speak again, I only half listened whilst I weighed up my options.

As a confirmed atheist, I had little time for devout spoutings, and Thomas's words sounded like they'd come from The Great Big Book of Cult Beliefs. But if I turned my back on Thomas, on the Democrituses, I would lose my job and, on a practical note, newly-qualified posts were as rare as hen's teeth; I really needed the work and I didn't want to have to rewrite my blasted C.V. again.

More importantly, if I chose not to believe Thomas's lunacy, it seemed highly likely that I would lose Joseph …

On balance, I decided that I wanted to be with Joseph more than I wanted to put distance between me and a bunch of deluded fanatics. And if Thomas was going to offer an explanation, however implausible, for how I'd been teleported from one side of the world to the other and back, then the least I could do was hear him out. I took a deep breath and forced a look of polite interest on my face. I tuned back in to what Thomas was saying.

He paused, doubtless aware that I was looking at him with what must have been a highly guarded expression, and I made an effort to relax my features to make me look interested instead of worried for his sanity.

"Do you have any questions, so far?"

"I'm following, thanks." I didn't trust myself to say anything else on the subject. "I might need a cup of tea, though?" I peered round the room to see if there was a kettle and then remembered that I was in an NHS hospital, not a hotel.

Thomas stood quickly, almost as though he were glad of an excuse to take a break from talking about what was clearly a difficult subject. "Oh, let me," he said distractedly and then vanished.

I remained sitting in bed, staring at the space he had occupied a split second earlier. I bent over a little to see if he had somehow fallen to the floor but he was utterly gone. "Is that the sort of thing he's going to explain to me soon, Joseph?" I asked, keeping my voice as steady as I could.

He smiled awkwardly. "I sincerely hope so."

I nodded hesitantly.

A few minutes later, Thomas popped back into existence beside me and leant across the bed to hand me a cup of tea in a mug that bore the legend, 'Fish are friends, not food'. The fact that I managed to take it from him and have a sip without spilling any was testament to all the years I had spent suppressing external signs of distress (which would have been like throwing petrol onto a fire at my mum's house).

In his other hand, he held two large carrier bags and passed one to Joseph, saying as discreetly as he could in such close confines, "Your mother sent these. She thought you'd like to change your clothes and get washed, son."

Joseph appeared to become properly aware of his appearance for the first time; he glanced down and grimaced at his wrinkled, blood-stained clothing and nodded his thanks. "You'll stay with her?" he asked and, accepting Thomas's assurance that he would, excused himself to the en suite.

A moment later, I heard the shower turning on and had to work hard not to picture Joseph naked in there; not while his dad was standing beside me.

To me, Thomas passed another bag and said awkwardly, "Hester's been shopping. She thought you might be cold."

I peered into the bag and found a fluffy dressing gown and a pair of matching slippers. "Is *she* a god?" I asked faintly.

Thomas replied, "We all are, yes."

"A god went shopping and got me a dressing gown and slippers," I commented numbly.

Thomas rubbed his hands together anxiously. "She's goddess of the home and family. Shopping is kind of her thing. That and baking. She — she made you a cake, too."

I dug deeper into the bag and found the cake, a lemon drizzle, nestled in wax paper. It smelt amazing.

"She made me a cake," I repeated. "Why … why is that making me cry?"

I took a tissue from Thomas and began to compose myself just as Joseph returned to the room. Seeing my silent tears, he hastened to my side. "What? What did you say?" he demanded of his father.

"Nothing, nothing," Thomas insisted.

I quickly added to his reassurances, "Your mum … your mum got me a dressing gown and she made me a cake. It — it was just a really nice thing for her to do."

I swallowed hard to get rid of the fresh lump that had formed in my throat. I was just so touched that she had treated me like a member of her family and so unused to being treated kindly by a mother figure that my emotions didn't really know how to cope.

A look of understanding passed over his features and he sat back down on the bed beside me, giving my hand a gentle squeeze. "She worries.

You'll get used to it," he said with a barely perceptible roll of his eyes.

He was freshly washed and wearing soft trousers and a comfortably snug t-shirt that, even in my rather delicate state, I could appreciate hugged his muscular torso rather beautifully. Aware that his dad was still in the room, I made a concerted effort to keep my eyes on them or on Joseph's face, and my hands firmly clasped on my lap.

When I felt more in control, I scooped the dressing gown out and removed the label, wrapping myself in the soft material and drawing more than physical warmth from it.

To fully rein in my emotions, I fell back on the British staples of drinking tea and being polite. "Sorry, Thomas. Thank you for the tea, and please tell Hester thank you for my lovely gifts." I took a much-needed sip. My mind was surprisingly blank. I knew that by rights I ought to be filled with turmoil, questions, concerns, but I was just a bit numb. Good old tea.

Thomas seemed slightly perturbed by my apparent nonchalance and said, "Shall I go on? I know that you must feel highly sceptical, and I am frankly rather surprised that you are simply sitting and drinking tea …"

I shifted uncomfortably, realising that I was not acting as a normal person would. "Would … you prefer it if I started screaming?" I asked uncertainly.

He laughed heartily and said, "No, no, on second thoughts your way makes it much easier to be heard."

I waved my hand for him to go on.

"Well, as I said, we, the Democrituses, are

315

gods. Our souls have existed for many millennia, reincarnated many times. We have all the powers bestowed upon us when we were originally created. We can create life and we can end it. We are not quite omnipresent, but we can teleport to any point on the globe at any time. Some of us have control over certain elements or areas of human life, depending on the qualities our followers gave us through their faith. For instance some, like Hester and Joseph, have the ability to heal — though, regrettably, they appear unable to heal *you*," he paused, gesturing vaguely towards my many injuries.

There was a pregnant pause and Thomas looked at me expectantly. I couldn't think of a single thing to say in reply, though. Dreams and reality had blurred once more and I did not know what was real and what was madness. Joseph felt real beneath my fingers and looked very much real sitting beside me, but everything else was surreal. *So this is what a complete breakdown feels like,* I thought wildly. I swallowed back my anxiety at the thought of how fragile my mental health must be, and fought the urge to give in to the swell of tiredness at the thought of all the therapy I'd need to deal with it.

Seeming a little disquieted (either by my complete lack of verbal response or by the still highly guarded expression on my face), Thomas went on, "Perhaps I am being too abstract to be believable. To use some concrete examples: yesterday, you were transported across a county, a continent and the globe in the blink of an eye. You have witnessed both of my sons and me appear and disappear before your eyes. You have therefore had direct experience of our ability to teleport — you imagined none of it."

I nodded an acknowledgement but didn't trust myself to speak.

Thomas went on, "We also have the power to command humans to do whatever we may want them to; usually, that power is used with great restraint. I can offer you proof of this in the form of poor DC Cam. I would bet my soul that you witnessed DC Cam call out a name immediately before Makris arrived, am I correct?"

I didn't want to think about it but reluctantly I agreed. "He shouted something I didn't understand. It was in another language, I think, but not one I recognised. Then Makris appeared between us and touched my shoulder: the next thing I knew, I was on the floor, in a forest, feeling like I'd been turned inside out."

Joseph winced as though feeling that pain himself, but Thomas asked insistently, "Can you remember what the word sounded like?"

Tentatively, I guessed, "Looby Loo or something. It had three syllables and it started with an 'L'. It wasn't a word I knew. Sorry ... I'm normally pretty good with remembering things; I think I was in shock."

Thomas frowned, whispering the nonsense sounds to himself and looking intently at Joseph, who looked similarly displeased at not being able to decipher what had been said.

With an aggrieved shake of his head, Thomas continued, "Knowing Makris's true name might have made things easier, but it is of no real consequence. The point is, Makris is also a god. He ordered that young policeman to call him to you yesterday as soon as you were alone. DC Cam would have had no say over the matter, so please do not think badly of him."

Over and above any surprise I felt at the thought that Makris was a god, I felt a pang of sadness as I thought of Cam, lying on a slab in the mortuary by now. I'd tried to give him the benefit of the doubt anyway — his actions had been so strange, so completely out of character — but I cleaved to the explanation given, which helped me to let go of the idea that he might have betrayed me deliberately.

Turning to face me, Joseph looked me squarely in the eyes and said, "What my father has told you is true. We are gods, Sephy. Even if you are not yet ready to believe that, please understand that it means that there is no force on earth that can harm you whilst you are with me."

Although Joseph sounded utterly sincere (and his colours indicated that he was telling the truth), it all sounded beyond incredible; had anyone else been telling me all of this I would have assumed they were insane, made no sudden movements and carefully extracted myself from their presence.

… But I had seen Thomas every night since I was a baby, in my dream. Joseph, Russ and Thomas *had* appeared and disappeared out of thin air right in front of me. Joseph knew about colours and perceived them like I could (though that raised more questions than it answered). Cam had looked exactly like someone who was fighting with every ounce of his soul against a command that was forcing him to act against his will …

"You can heal people?" I asked Joseph quietly. He nodded, and so with a nod towards his injured hands I asked, "Can you heal yourself?"

He looked taken aback for a moment then

huffed out a laugh, "After all that has happened, after all that you have been told, you are concerned about some bruising to my hands?"

I shrugged and nodded again towards his hands. "Consider it a test, then. Show me that you can make your hands better."

"Excellent idea," Thomas enthused.

Acquiescing with good grace, he said, "Very well, if it is important to you." He moved his right hand a centimetre or two above the swollen knuckles of his left. I watched as the dark green and dark yellow colours swirled and faded until, at last, his hand was entirely healed. He repeated the same process for his right hand.

I held his hands up to examine them closer, turning them this way and that. "Awesome," I commented numbly, trying to absorb the enormity of the truth behind that miraculous act.

Joseph laughed, "You're handling this remarkably calmly …"

"You healing your hands is probably the least weird thing I've seen in the last few hours," I replied. "And that's not the first time I've been told I don't react in the way people usually expect. It's a talent. Or a curse, I don't know."

Perhaps I hadn't imagined it all — perhaps Alex had transported me across the county in a heartbeat; perhaps I had been taken to Greece and New Zealand and back within seconds. The explanation I had been offered suddenly didn't seem all that far-fetched under the circumstances. Somehow, Thomas and Joseph had achieved the effect they had been seeking: I began to realise that this was not all a figment of their imagination or a product of my insanity.

The room was silent for several minutes while I processed what I'd been told and shown. I let this new understanding and belief flow over me for a moment, turning and examining it from every angle in my mind. At last, I turned to look at Joseph and the unwavering certainty I saw in his eyes — the sense of utter truth reflected in his aura — made me fully accept that none of what had happened to me had been fantasy. It had all been real.

Maybe I'd bought into some form of mass hysteria, or maybe they were telling the truth: either way, I believed them.

"You're gods," I repeated, my voice barely a whisper.

CHAPTER 37

THE DEMOCRITUSES WERE GODS: gods who could teleport, command humans, create and end life. And so was Makris.

"Makris is a god, too," I intoned slowly, my mind fastening onto a horrifying truth. "And gods can *teleport*."

Correctly inferring the worry that lay behind my statement, Joseph gave me a reassuring squeeze. "Yes, but even gods cannot teleport when they are unconscious. He is not a threat right now." His voice dropped a notch and he added through gritted teeth and clenched jaw, "And if he regains consciousness, if he is stupid enough to try to take you from me again, I will deal with him. I am more powerful than that Damned monster."

"You keep calling him that — Damned," I said with a confused frown. "Russ said that means he's mortal — so is he a god or not?"

Thomas looked grim. "He is a god who has been Damned by the High Council — our

321

government — for breaching one of our laws. There are not many things we are prevented from doing, but those laws that exist are enforced with enthusiasm. As a Damned, Makris cannot reincarnate like we can, and there are certain other restrictions on his freedom and autonomy."

Joseph added sourly, "Taking you to your father or to the High Council, with or without us, would have seen his Damned status removed and his immortality restored." He added with a scowl, "He will *not* get that opportunity again."

I tried to relax a little in the knowledge that Makris was unconscious and that Joseph was going to stay with me and keep me safe, but the idea of a teleporting Makris was still rather disconcerting.

A thought occurred to me and I frowned. "Why the heck did he spend all those years in prison if he could just teleport out? They really hurt him in there."

Joseph made a sound in his throat that told me that he didn't give a damn about how much Makris had been hurt.

Thomas, meanwhile, shook his head slightly and replied, "If a god breaches a *human* law, they can choose whether to be dealt with by the human justice system or by the High Council. Under the human system — at least in this country — the worst that can happen is that they spend some of their last life on earth behind bars. Naturally, Leon Makris would rather have spent a few short years in a human jail for attacking you than risk immediate Obliteration by the High Council for conspiring with your father on some highly illegal escapade whilst Damned."

"Obliteration?" I asked numbly. I kept

picturing Makris's injuries — he had suffered greatly, yet all that he had endured in prison was apparently not as bad as whatever the High Council would have done to him. I was beginning to get a clearer picture of why Joseph, Russ and Thomas had all shown fear when talking about their government.

Thomas answered, quite matter-of-factly, "If he were Obliterated, his soul and life force would be immediately extinguished. He is already Damned, for reasons I do not know, so that would be the only possible outcome if the High Council had dealt with the matter."

By agreeing to kill me, Makris had risked everything for the chance of regaining his immortality. I could understand *his* motives, but not his employer's.

"Why did my dad want me dead, though? Who is he? He must be a god, right? And why did he get Makris to try to kill me, why not just kill me himself?"

Thomas and Joseph looked uncomfortable.

"That's a lot of questions," Thomas said. "The easiest to answer is why he instructed Makris to carry out the attacks. Your father cannot let you live, because you are proof that he has committed a very serious crime. Yet he could not harm you in person — if he ever met you, a parental tie would form and he would be unable to tolerate your death. He needs to kill you without ever meeting you."

"A parental *tie*?" I asked, remembering the word used by Makris, and in Felicity's emails.

"A bond; a connection. A physical and emotional link between a god's soul and another's. There are different types, the strongest two being the bonding tie between a couple, and the parental tie to a child."

I filed away the notion of a bonding tie between a couple for later consideration, and asked, "So he is a god, then?"

They both nodded and I could feel the tension in the room grow until it was almost palpable.

"So does that make *me* a god?" I asked slowly. I could see colours, like Joseph, but surely I couldn't be a god? If I'd lived before, had been reincarnated, surely I'd have remembered some of those lives? My dream popped into my head — my dream, in which I had transitioned smoothly from being a mother to being a baby. I had known Thomas when he'd had a different body, but his soul had been the same. We had known each other in a past life … I definitely couldn't teleport, though, and I clung to that idea as the last vestigial proof that I was human.

Thomas grimaced slightly. "You are not a god, no. But you are not entirely human, either."

CHAPTER 38

THERE HAD BEEN A NUMBER of questions I'd wanted to ask leading on from my discovery that the Democrituses and Makris were honest-to-goodness *gods* but Thomas's last statement rather pushed them to the back of my mind.

"I'm not *human*?"

Joseph shifted in his seat and slid his arm from around my shoulders; he sat forward slightly and ran his hands through his hair before resting his face in them. I was instantly on edge, wondering what more I was about to be told. I tentatively put a hand on Joseph's back, half expecting him to stand and walk away — or just vanish. Instead, he seemed to collect himself and straightened, putting a reassuring hand on my knee and giving a good approximation of a reassuring smile.

Thomas sighed softly and it seemed to take him a while to formulate his answer.

"Not entirely, no. If you were a god, your relationship with Joseph would not be an issue, your father would not feel the need to expunge you from existence and the High Council would not be remotely interested in you if you came to their attention. No, your father may well be a god, but your mother is undoubtedly a human — there can be no other explanation for how you present. And therein lies the problem. Your unique parentage makes you a demigod: in our society, you are known as a Fragment."

It had been a bad moment to take a sip of tea. I coughed and spluttered, startled by the word — a word that Makris had used on numerous occasions to describe me. I had never paid it any heed because it had meant nothing to me and I had taken it to be a term of derision, given the context in which it was always used. Apparently, though, he was being astute rather than merely abusive.

"Makris called me that," I said once I'd regained my composure. "He always said it like it's a bad thing: but it's just a name for someone with a god and a human as parents? What's wrong with that? Why does that make my father want to, um, *expunge* me or the High Council do ... whatever the High Council would do?"

Thomas dropped his gaze. "You are — for want of a better word — illegal. As far as I know, you are unique, because the rest of your kind have long since been made extinct."

The painkillers were beginning to wear off again, and on top of the discomfort from my injuries I was developing a headache as I tried to make sense of what I was hearing.

Rubbing my forehead to get rid of the knot of pain that had established itself there, I asked, "Why are Fragments illegal? And what happened to the rest of them?"

Thomas glanced nervously at Joseph, who gave a slight nod of encouragement. He replied, "Well, to make a Fragment is strictly against our laws; the Fragment Law carries an automatic Obliteration as punishment if breached. Furthermore, it is deemed highly unpalatable, socially speaking, for a god to procreate with a human. It would appear that your father — whoever he is — chose to ignore our laws and conventions. He and your mother produced you; hence, your father would face Obliteration if it were ever discovered that you exist, and you … you would be punished for the crime of existing. The rest of your kind was wiped out by the High Council for the same reason."

"Did … did my mother have any say in any of that, do you think?" I asked. The idea that I was a product of rape (celestial or otherwise) would make her rejection of me understandable, if not acceptable.

Thomas shrugged slightly, "Normally, a tie is required for a god to, erm, engage in a physical relationship with another. So perhaps they were tied — I would be able to tell if I were to see her in person, since I can perceive ties and would know a bonding tie from a mile away. In that case, your conception would have been entirely consensual. Or perhaps not — perhaps he is a rapist as well as a potential murderer. Either way, I'm afraid, the High Council would regard the situation in the same way — you exist, and therefore you are illegal."

That seemed a tad unfair. "What, so they'd punish me just because I was born to a god? It's not as if I had any choice in the matter!"

There was an uncomfortable pause and I saw a significant look pass between the men. They had gone very quiet and would not meet my eye.

"What? What am I missing *now*?" I pressed.

Thomas squared his shoulders and forced himself to look me in the eye. "I have not made myself terribly clear. The truth is, Fragments are not illegal because they are the product of an illegal act between a god and a human. That's rather putting the cart before the horse. It is illegal to conceive a Fragment because Fragments are widely believed to be highly dangerous."

I blinked. 'Dangerous' was not a word I'd ever had applied to me. "Go on," I insisted.

He sighed heavily. "Well, as I mentioned, gods can command humans. We can control what they do, think and feel. We have no such control over other gods — or, indeed. over Fragments."

"So, because you can't control what Fragments do or feel or think, the High Council wiped them out?" I asked, squinting my eyes against the building headache.

Thomas licked his lips nervously. "Well, yes, but compounding that fact is the worrisome truth that Fragments — you — can command gods as well as humans. As far as the High Council is concerned, Fragments pose too great a threat to their authority and to our kind's very existence, and so they have been trying to eradicate your species for millennia. Until you found me, I thought that they had succeeded."

I frowned at this, trying to marry that concept with *me*. Unable to keep the incredulity from my voice, I exclaimed, "But *I* can't make people do what

I tell them: I can't even get Matt to put his kit in the wash after rugby training!" I thought of all the times in my life when it would have been genuinely handy to be able to command or control others. Quietly, I added, "And I certainly can't control gods. Makris nearly killed Matt, and *me* for that matter, and I couldn't stop him."

Joseph adjusted his position so that he was turned more completely towards me and placed his hands on the top of my arms, forcing me to look at him. This had the merciful effect of sparing me from surrendering to a flashback to darker times and I focussed hard on his eyes, getting lost in their beautiful shade of blue. "You could not stop Makris because you did not know how to. You fought fiercely yesterday, but you were utterly outmatched in terms of strength and size. And when you were seventeen, you were badly injured and barely conscious when he sought to drown you: you could not have issued any commands in your state, and you did not know that your words would have any effect anyway. There was *nothing* you could have done in those circumstances to stop him."

Hearing those words spoken with such certainty struck deep into my long-held, damning certainty that I had somehow allowed Makris to hurt me, and the effect on my psyche was immeasurable. I felt as though I could begin to forgive myself.

I was worried by their slavish belief that I had some kind of power over the gods, though. The idea that a Fragment could control any human or god just by telling them what to do sounded like an urban legend; I wondered why Thomas and Joseph were so convinced by it. The fact that their government was of the same view was even more concerning: it was for that reason they had wiped out others like me in the past and would do the same to me if they knew I existed. I was beginning to understand why Joseph and Russ had been so keen to kill Makris rather than risk him reporting me to the High Council.

"If Makris wakes up, how will we stop him from telling the High Council about me?" I asked.

Thomas replied, "You already have. You ordered him not to do so."

I looked at Thomas doubtfully. "Well, I told Makris what Joseph and Russ told me to tell him. He could just ignore me; I don't think you should rely on that …"

Joseph gave a wry smile. "My love, you are a Fragment, and your words of command *will* bind him."

I didn't know how to respond to that level of delusion. Instead, I thought out loud, trying to understand why they were still so worried. "So, if Makris and my father are the only ones aside from you guys who know that I'm a Fragment … and my dad won't tell them about me because he'd be Obliterated for making me in the first place, and Makris won't tell them because I've ordered him not to … how would the High Council find out about me? Aren't we safe now?"

Thomas tensed as though bracing himself for delivering bad news. "It is possible that you will be seen by chance by another god and reported. By rights, my family and I should have reported you to the High Council ourselves the moment we first saw you. However, my son saw you first and I have known you for longer than you might realise, so reporting you was never really an option, not when you mean so much to us."

Even though I was not clear on the details of what he'd said, the obvious care and affection with which he spoke them was clear and I felt oddly warmed inside.

"But how would anyone know what I am, just from looking? How did *you* know?" I asked.

Apologetically, Thomas said, "To our kind, I'm afraid you stand out like a sore thumb."

Self-conscious, I felt my cheeks colour, wondering what on earth he meant and privately thinking that I was going to need a lot of therapy to cope with even lower self-esteem on top of everything I'd experienced over the last twenty-four hours.

No doubt seeing my discomfort, Thomas hurried on, "We cannot see your aura, and we have no way to manipulate it, either. We think that's why Joseph and Hester cannot heal you. If another god outside our family ever happened to see you, they would know in an instant what you are ..." He left the threat unspoken but I felt a chill run down my spine.

I gave him a look of consternation. "I don't have any colours?"

Thomas shook his head and I became fretful. Did that mean I didn't have a soul? The only person I'd ever seen without any colours had been Cam, after he'd been killed. I bit my lip, hoping I wasn't secretly dead. I'd thought I couldn't see my own soul because I had to be looking directly at a person (not in a mirror or a photograph) to perceive their colours and thus it was impossible for me to see my own, but perhaps I just couldn't see it because I didn't have one …

A few things clicked into place. "So is that what freaked you all out when you first saw me? Well, not you two, I suppose. But Russ, and the rest?"

"You are very scary for our kind to behold, Sephy," Thomas said, before adding quickly, "No offence. It's a little like I imagine you might feel if you saw someone who looked normal but didn't cast a shadow or a reflection — you would know that there was something terribly wrong and that they were someone to be feared, perhaps."

I stiffened, trying very, very hard not to be offended. To them, I was like a vampire, or the undead? Well, no wonder Russ hadn't liked sharing an office with me … I felt a small surge of affection for him, since he had apparently endured having a soulless creature sitting across a desk from him for weeks so that his brother could know that I was at least safe. He'd even given me chocolate.

Joseph added, "You frightened me, too, when I first saw you at the railway station."

My eyebrows raised fractionally. I did remember that when he had first turned towards me, he'd looked very afraid — but I had assumed that he'd been scared of the man in the Hello Kitty t-shirt who had tried to attack me.

Joseph went on haltingly, "The man who sought to do you harm that night was a Damned, fortunately: I was therefore able to issue him with commands; making them subservient to law-abiding gods is another way of punishing Damneds. After I had sent him away, I turned to face you and … and suddenly you were my only care. Since then, your lack of a visible soul has 'freaked me out' not because I think you are something to be feared but because I cannot see whether death overshadows you or whether you are unwell, and I cannot heal you. I cannot tell you how much angst those two factors combined have caused and continue to cause me — I cannot foresee harm and if it were to occur, I could do nothing to prevent or resolve it."

He shuddered slightly. I squeezed his arm gently, unsure of how else to respond but wanting to give him some measure of comfort.

"Why did you send the Hello Kitty guy away if you were so frightened of me?" I asked.

The question helped him to regain some composure. "I have never agreed with the High Council's treatment of the Fragments," he said grimly, then nodded towards his father and went on, "It is a matter on which we have always been in agreement. Thomas and I may be a father and son in this lifetime, but we have known each other as friends for millennia, and we have always fought on the same side of that issue."

Thomas nodded sombrely.

"Knowing that you were a Fragment, my instinct was to protect you until I could liaise with my father on what steps to take next. But by the time I'd looked into your eyes, your status as a Fragment was irrelevant. You were suddenly the only person I cared about, and I would have laid down my life to protect you ..." He tailed off, looking at me with an intensity that matched his words. "Alas, when I returned to the railway station with Thomas, you had boarded a train and were lost to me. By fate or fortune, I happened to see you walk past our offices on your way to the police station, and from there I was able to follow you to the hospital." He smiled with apparent relief at the memory of reconnecting with me, and I felt a swell of happiness at feeling so wanted.

"Your connection with Joseph is one more reason why we must keep you hidden from the High Council," Thomas said emphatically. "We can protect you from rogue individuals, but there would be nothing any of us could do to protect you from the might of the High Council if they were to discover your existence." An unexpected swirl of black grief flushed through his aura briefly and he added softly, "It has been tried."

He didn't elaborate, and I became worried that he was going to clam up and say no more, so I asked, "They'd kill me, right?"

With a tone of apology, Thomas replied, "Undoubtedly."

My mouth had gone a little dry, so I took a sip of tea. They seemed to be waiting for my response, but all I could manage was, "Bit harsh."

My attempt at flippancy fell flat. They looked like I'd already been tried and sentenced, their pallor telling me as much as their auras that the looming prospect of discovery by the High Council really worried them.

"How many other gods are there? How likely is it I'll be seen?"

Joseph shrugged lightly, "Not many in England; the weather doesn't suit us. We are mainly found in warmer climates — many are based in Greece, the seat of the High Council — but our numbers are relatively few anywhere. Perhaps one in two million souls are gods."

Those didn't seem like bad odds. That the High Council was based in Greece would explain Joseph's panic at finding me there with Makris. It also shed light on why my father had sent Makris to kill me the first time, even knowing that I was 'protected' by whomever had helped to save me — I would have travelled to Greece on holiday that year, and it must have seemed too risky to allow me to do so in case I was spotted. I wondered briefly how I'd find out who my guardian was — who had brought Matt to me in that bathroom seven years ago? I needed time to think about that more before sharing; it felt oddly personal and I found that the more I tried to formulate my thoughts into a question or statement the harder it was to hold onto them.

Instead, my attention turned to the Damnation that Makris had apparently been slapped with for breaching the gods' laws and wondered if Thomas and Joseph were worried that they would suffer the same fate as he had.

"What would the High Council do to *you*, if I was caught? Is knowing a Fragment illegal?" I asked.

When neither of them answered or indeed made eye contact with me, I shook Joseph's leg a little in agitation and said, "Tell me!"

Joseph replied in a low murmur, "Failing to report the existence of a Fragment is a crime of the highest magnitude. To protect me, my family has not reported you. They *might* be Damned for that: my father was once a member of the High Council, and his former colleagues may be lenient. If not, my family will be Obliterated there and then."

Numbly, I asked Joseph, "And what about *you*?" He seemed reluctant to answer, so I urged, "Just tell me straight."

"I have not reported you, either, but more importantly our encounter at the railway station created a tie between us: as a result, I would undoubtedly be Obliterated. But if the High Council killed you first, I would not live long enough for them to carry out my sentence. Ours is a bonding tie: we cannot live without each other."

I had thought I had known fear and anxiety: I had experienced more than my share of frightening situations in the past, after all. Perhaps the worst had been seeing Matt injured, hurting, struggling to regain his strength for months after my last attack — that had been horrendous, far worse than coping with my own pain and psychological issues. I loved Matt deeply, but somehow the idea of Joseph being at risk because of me was even more unbearable.

I fought a swell of panic and lost.

CHAPTER 39

WATCHING THE COLOUR DRAIN from my face, Thomas looked at his son with dismay. "Did you have to be quite so blunt?" he scolded.

In response, Joseph said flatly, "She *told* me to tell her straight. I had no choice."

"Ah," Thomas said apprehensively, watching me with trepidation.

I barely registered their words and I couldn't find any of my own. Instead, I swung my legs off the bed and tried to stand, with the vague intention of running out of the door.

Both men quickly put paid to that idea and gently but firmly helped me back onto the bed.

"You need to stay here, with us. We will keep you safe," Joseph soothed.

I shook my head. Even if Joseph and his family could protect me from Makris and my father, it was clear that they could do nothing against the High Council, either to protect me or to save themselves.

My words came in a flood as I looked around,

expecting to see the High Council swooping down upon us. "You *can't*. If the High Council finds me, I'm going to get you all killed! I can't be near you — any of you …"

The horror and sheer unfairness of my new reality descended upon me in fierce waves. Joseph wanted me as much as I wanted him; Makris was going to be locked up … and yet I was doomed to have that happiness taken from me.

The two of them were silent, concern etching their brows and anxiety flowing from them in waves of pale grey.

Muffled slightly as Joseph drew me into his chest once more, I pleaded with him. "Joseph — this can't happen. This is too much to risk. You can't hide me; you can't even *know* me. You'll have to leave me, or I'll have to leave you. I'll move away again …"

Joseph hugged me as tightly as he could without hurting me. Speaking into my hair, his voice plaintive, he tried reasoning with me. "My love, they are very unlikely to find you if you allow us to conceal you. But away from our protection you are more likely to be found, and you and I are tied: they won't need to find me; if they kill you, I am lost. Please, don't leave me. Don't make me spend the rest of my life without you."

This brought me up short. I should have known that the sense of completeness, of happiness, of *wholeness* that I'd felt whenever I'd been permitted to be with Joseph could not last — nothing that good possibly could. Though it made me physically ache with pain and sadness to even think of it, it seemed logical that if our tie placed him at risk — if there had to be a choice between being with Joseph and keeping him safe — the tie would have to go.

"Well then, we have to break the tie," I said firmly.

He looked physically ill, his face blanching and his smooth visage creased with pain. "No," was all he could say, his voice barely a whisper.

Thomas touched my shoulder placatingly. "Sephy, you do not understand. A bonding tie *cannot* be broken. If it were, it would kill both of you anyway. There is no way out of this — all we can do is protect you. You must allow us to."

I scoffed, "A complete stranger might spot my lack of soul from across the street and report me to the High Council. Makris or some other Damned could just magically appear, snatch me and take me to them, or just slit my throat before Joseph could even draw breath! How can you possibly protect me from that?"

There was silence for a moment. Then Thomas said quietly, "We don't have to. As I have repeatedly assured my family, you have the power to protect all of us."

I made a dismissive sound. "Yes, and if I had wings I could fly," I replied acerbically. "I *don't* have that kind of power, that's some kind of folklore or fairy-tale."

Thomas shook his head. "It is true. As I said, Fragments have the power of command over gods and humans alike and can end lives as easily as we can create them. You could destroy anyone who sought to do you harm or stop them before they reported you to the High Council. We could teach you how to spot such a threat and deal with it effectively."

I shook my head, irritated by his slavish belief in powers I simply did not possess. "I am clearly not what you think I am. I don't know if Fragments were *ever* that powerful, but even if they were, *I'm not.* I hate that you're relying on some magical ability you think I must have when by rights you should be getting as far away from me as possible. Or if it's really only a matter of time before the High Council finds me, you should be making the most of what time you have left."

"You *can* protect us, Sephy," Joseph insisted. "You have the power to command Makris, your father and any other Damneds he cares to send your way. You could control the entire High Council. Nobody need ever hurt you again. You saw Makris's submission for yourself."

Highly perturbed by their apparent reliance on this, I angrily demurred, "Well, I wish I shared your confidence. You're very strong, Joseph, and you had your hands round Makris's neck: he wasn't obeying me, he'd have agreed to anything to stop you from killing him."

"But what exactly *did* stop me from killing him?" he pressed.

The words caught in my throat as I replayed the memory of what had happened.

Joseph responded for me: "You. You stopped me from killing him. Believe me, I wanted to — so, so badly — and was more than prepared to end his life, not only in revenge for all that he had done to hurt you, but also to ensure that he could never report back to your father or the High Council. Yet you commanded me to let him live."

As attractive as it was to believe that I had some mythical ability to compel the gods to do as I told them, I still didn't believe it. Perhaps Joseph had obeyed me because he knew that killing was wrong, deep down, and his psyche had given him a reason not to do it — blaming my 'commands' rather than his conscience.

Shaking my head slightly, I responded quietly, "I don't have the power you think I have. I just don't. I can't protect you — I'm going to get you *killed*." I heaved a sigh, tears not far away as despair and tiredness swept over me. I pulled out of Joseph's arms and turned my head away, full of sorrow and utter hopelessness.

After a long pause, Joseph's next words were to his dad. "I need to prove it to her if we are to rely on her protection." Thomas must have nodded in agreement, because then Joseph asked, "Can you make sure the hospital staff don't interrupt us in Makris's room please?"

I looked up sharply. "Makris's room?" I asked anxiously, thinking of the armed police who would be in there, not to mention the fact that I'd hoped never to lay eyes on that monster again.

"Please trust me, Sephy. You will be safe with me, and I assure you, this will help you to feel less afraid. Makris is still unconscious, he will not be able to so much as look at you. Please be brave one more time and allow me to show you what you are capable of."

I did not relish the idea of seeing Makris again, but I found I trusted Joseph implicitly. I slid from the bed and began to walk towards the door but halted when I realised that Joseph was not following me.

He reached out his hand for me to take. "It will be better if I teleport you. You were fine when I brought you home from Greece: our tie evidently means I will be able to teleport you again without the pain or discomfort you experienced when Alex and Makris did so."

Throwing caution to the wind, I closed my eyes and reached to take his hand.

CHAPTER 40

"STOP! DO NOT MOVE OR MAKE A SOUND!"

My eyes sprang open again at the sound of Joseph's voice, which was loud and authoritative. I found myself staring at two very surprised-looking police officers who were armed to the teeth and presently pointing their rather serious weaponry directly at Joseph and me.

They neither moved nor made a sound, but then again nor did I. I stayed as still as I could, but moved my eyes to look at Joseph, who turned to me and gave what I'm sure he intended to be a reassuring wink. I was frozen to the spot, yet he seemed perfectly at ease.

To the police officers, he said in that same, commanding tone, "Unless you are given a direct order by either of us, you will neither hear nor see us in this room and you will forget that you ever did. You may resume your positions."

The police officers turned to look at each other and I waited for them to either open fire or at the very least call for backup. Neither did — indeed, they were looking rather nonplussed. One of them, a short, beefy man with curly brown hair peeking out from under his hat, shrugged and said, "Thought I heard something, did you?"

They both eyed Makris's bed suspiciously.

The other officer, a taller, slender man walked to Makris's side; Joseph deftly sidestepped out of the way and we watched in silence as the officer peered intently at Makris's face and the machines surrounding his bed. Frightened by the proximity in which I found myself to Makris, I was unable to look at him for long and kept my attention on the policeman at his side.

"Seems to be no change," he murmured, evidently satisfied that Makris was still unconscious.

Both officers returned to the foot of the bed, taking up positions from which they could observe Makris, the door and the window for any sign of movement. Neither so much as glanced at Joseph or me.

Seeing my rather bemused expression, Joseph said brightly, "So far, so good."

His voice was so loud in the otherwise silent room that I flinched and turned instinctively towards the police, certain that they would spin round and start blasting away, but they remained impassive and oblivious to our presence.

"You can do that, too," Joseph told me. "Go ahead — give them an order. They'll hear it, and they'll obey you."

I scoffed and immediately clamped my hand over my mouth at the sound, but they gave no sign that they had heard me, either.

"Go ahead," Joseph pressed. "I want you to see what you can do. It's important."

I looked at the officers, highly doubtful that I could tell them to do anything, but the fact that they were acting as though I were completely invisible gave me enough confidence to at least try.

"Do I need to know their names?" I whispered, still extremely conscious of the guns that were less than five feet from us.

He shook his head. "You merely have to deliver your words as a command, not a request. Just like you repeated my instructions to Makris in the forest. Tell, don't ask, and you will be obeyed."

Still doubtful, I cleared my throat, keeping a careful eye out for any sign that they heard the sound and, when they remained unaware of my presence, I addressed the shorter man, who was standing closer. "Stand on one leg."

He did so, drawing a puzzled look from his colleague. My eyebrows shot up and I let out a shout of amazement, which neither officer heard.

With a nod of encouragement from Joseph, to the second officer, I said, "Stick your tongue out."

He did. Both police officers were now looking at each other with utter incredulity and were clearly baffled by their own behaviours.

Feeling a bit giddy, I told them both, "Make a noise like a chicken."

They did, and neither seemed happy about it.

"Stop!" I said hastily, worried that the noise would draw attention from outside. They both stopped everything immediately.

Unless these two officers were in the employ of Joseph and were extremely good actors, I had just successfully taken command of two armed policemen. To dispel any remaining doubt I held, I told them both, "Give me your guns."

Immediately, they walked towards me and held out their weapons.

"Take them back," I said hastily, not wanting to touch them.

Instantly, they obeyed and returned to their original positions, both looking at each other with great uncertainty.

"Are you satisfied, or would you like to see them do more?" Joseph asked me calmly.

I shook my head, shaken by what I'd just witnessed.

"Forget all that has happened in the last two minutes," Joseph told them.

They resumed their natural positions of alertness at the foot of Makris's bed.

I took a moment to absorb what had just happened, what I had witnessed with my own eyes. Joseph was looking at me patiently.

Eyes wide at the possibilities open to me, I whispered, "Pretty cool."

He cracked a smile in response, but we both sobered as I turned towards Makris. Even so vulnerable, lying in a bed unconscious and covered in wires and tubes, he was frightening to look at and I tensed. Joseph gave my hand a gentle squeeze and I reached to cling to his arm with my free hand, needing the comfort of knowing that he wasn't just going to disappear and leave me there with Makris.

I sensed Joseph looking at me, but I couldn't take my eyes off Makris now that I'd been brave enough to look at him properly.

Speaking softly, Joseph said, "You and I can both order humans to do whatever we command. I have no power over Makris, though; a Damned may choose to obey a god rather than face further punishment from the High Council, but they are not physically compelled to do so. You, however, have the same level of command over him as you had over those policemen: he would not be able to resist you."

"But he's not conscious," I murmured, instinctively keeping my voice low despite knowing that nobody else in that room would hear me.

"He is alive. He will obey you."

I glanced at Joseph, a sceptical frown on my brow. With a small shrug, I leant a little closer to Makris — still careful to keep out of arm's reach — and said clearly, "Open your eyes."

His eyes sprang open and I stumbled backwards, bumping into a machine that monitored his heart rate. Joseph steadied me; the policemen spun round but before they could do any more than that, he told them, "Forget that happened."

I watched as they resumed their natural, watchful states, completely undisturbed. Makris was now staring at the ceiling.

"Wow, that's creepy," I breathed. "Can he see? Is he awake?"

"No. His eyes are open, just as you instructed. He is still unconscious." To prove this, Joseph reached over and waved his hand across Makris's eyes. With a sudden frown, he drew his fingers back into his palm and slowly withdrew his hand. Seeing my questioning gaze, he said, "I was very tempted to poke him in the eye. I am not sure I'd have the strength to stop at that, if I started down that route."

347

I gave a surprised laugh. It was all too surreal.

Nodding back to Makris, Joseph said, "You have given him very clear orders to plead guilty to whatever he is charged with, and to not report you or any of us to the High Council. He *will* obey you. If there is any other order you wish to give him, you may do so."

I stared at the man in the bed. Leon Makris had kidnapped me, beaten and raped me, stabbed me, half-drowned me and deprived me of the ability to bear children. Because of him, I had been afraid for seven years; I had slept with the light on every night; I'd had alarms installed and still checked under the bed and in my wardrobe every night before lying down to sleep. Looking at him, even as vulnerable as he was, I was afraid of him and I was tense, half expecting him to leap out of bed and attack me.

As the minutes passed, though, a different set of thoughts began to emerge, and with them a different set of feelings altogether.

He had stabbed Matt and nearly killed him; he had made my best friend cry more than once. His impending release from prison had made my Nana so scared for me that she had insisted we move away from the area so that he would not find me; I had not been at her side when she died, I had not been able to go to her funeral. Yesterday, in nearly killing me, he had nearly killed Joseph by virtue of our tie; if he had succeeded in taking me to the High Council, he would have killed me, Joseph and his family. He *had* killed Cam.

The harm he had done to me was something I might have been able to forgive, if I had felt he was just doing what he'd been contracted to do in order to save himself from Damnation. But the harm he had inflicted on those I loved — *that* made me angry.

The police officers and even Joseph faded from my range of attention. There was only Makris. Matt; Nana; Cam; Joseph; Matt; Nana; Cam; Joseph: the names consumed my thoughts as I stared at the man responsible for hurting them all.

Steadily and clearly, in a voice I barely recognised as my own, I spoke.

"Stop breathing."

CHAPTER 41

I WATCHED WITH COLD DETACHMENT as Makris's chest stopped rising and falling. The monitors around him began to beep and one of the policemen came over to look.

"Ignore it," I intoned, barely registering that I was casually giving orders to armed police.

I judged by the lack of a response from any medics that Thomas had intervened to ensure that we were not interrupted. In passing, I wondered if that had been Joseph's intention all along.

Makris's skin gradually turned very white, then palest blue; I watched him with nothing but a sense of peaceful resolution over the course of the next two or three minutes.

Joseph put a hand on my shoulder, reminding me that he was there — I had felt quite alone for a time, just standing and watching a man die slowly in front of me.

His voice was calm and quiet as he spoke. "Sephy, I have proven to you *what* you are. You have the power to keep yourself and my family and me perfectly safe." With evident difficulty, he added, "I would be doing you a grave disservice if I did not ask you now to remember *who* you are."

It was as though I'd been in a bubble that was burst by his words. I stepped back, hit hard by the reality of what I had been doing. I would have killed Makris just because I could.

Makris was a very unhealthy hue.

"Breathe," I commanded.

He took several heaving breaths that sounded very loud even against the noise of the monitor alarms. The monitors registered that he was breathing again and fell silent. The colour began to return to his cheeks and lips.

Shocked by my own callousness, I turned to Joseph and couldn't find the words to express how horrified I felt. Where was that spark of morality that should have pulled me out of my murderous intentions even without Joseph's timely prompt? How could this man ever trust me, when I could order him and his family to drop dead if I felt like it? Thomas was right — I was not human. I was a monster.

As though he had read my thoughts, he said quietly, "You are not a monster. That man has caused your loved ones a great deal of pain. The anger you felt was righteous, not selfish, and perfectly understandable. The fact that you stopped is most telling of your true nature."

Far from reassured and still wretched about how quickly I had allowed such power to affect my value system, I turned back to face Makris again.

"Close your eyes," I muttered, and he did so.

He looked as though he were sleeping.

Satisfied that he was still alive, I asked Joseph, "Is that how he killed Cam? He just told him to die?"

Joseph replied, "More than likely. My mother informs me that DC Cam seems to have no visible external injuries. Makris may have told his heart to stop beating, or his brain to bleed; we won't know for certain until the post-mortem."

With a great effort, I forced down the anger I felt and thought about what I wanted to happen next. The orders I had given him in the forest had been clear, and I now believed that they would be binding. For all I knew, though, he could die of his injuries — or indeed of the asphyxiation I had just put him through — and never face trial or further time in prison. I wanted him punished; I didn't want him dead.

In a surprisingly calm tone, I spoke to Makris's unconscious form again. "Heal. When you wake up, plead guilty to everything you're charged with. Apologise to DC Cam's family. Pay them whatever compensation they might gain through the civil courts. Stay in jail for a very, very long time." My tone dropped as anger coloured my final words to him: "Tell me who my father is, and *never* hurt me, or anyone I love, again."

I was pleased with my restraint but still worried about how Joseph and his family would feel about me after I had confirmed everything they had been taught to fear about the Fragments. No wonder Russ had seemed on edge after he had helped Joseph to teach me how to deliver orders to Makris back on the beach — he had helped to give me the power that could destroy all of his kind. The thought that he was afraid of me (and for good reason) made me feel sick.

Careful to form it as a question rather than an order, I said to Joseph, "I'm finished here. Can we go back now please?"

With a nod, Joseph touched my hand and a moment later we were back in my hospital room.

CHAPTER 42

THOMAS HAD BEEN SEATED AT THE EDGE of my bed but stood immediately as Joseph and I returned, looking at us both expectantly. From the corner of my eye, I saw Joseph give a miniscule shake of his head. I wondered if that was to confirm that I had not killed Makris or that I had not been able to control myself — either way, it made me wonder about the conversations that must surely have taken place between Joseph and his father about what would, could or should happen today.

I could barely bring myself to look either of them in the eye.

Thomas broke the building silence. "Whatever happened in there, I'm sure it was nothing more or less than anyone else in your position would have done if given the opportunity. You have nothing to be ashamed about," he said firmly.

I gave a nod of acknowledgement but kept my eyes cast downwards, still worried about how Joseph and his family would perceive me now that I had shown my true colours and demonstrated just how capable I was of misusing my very dangerous power.

Joseph led me back to my bed; Thomas resumed his seat in the chair beside me whilst Joseph sat close on the bed next to me and slid his arm round my waist.

Thomas placed another cup of tea in my hands and the three of us sat quietly, each with our own thoughts.

As the initial shock I'd felt at what I was capable of (physically and emotionally) wore off, I was left feeling conflicted. I was simultaneously horrified by the notion that I had abused such power — and quietly elated by the idea that I could use that power to keep Joseph and his family safe.

I began to believe that I could keep Joseph, be part of his lovely family and have nothing to fear from the High Council, or indeed from anyone — I could protect myself and the Democrituses far more than they could protect me. If anyone grabbed me, or came for Joseph and the others, I could kill them with a single word: my father and anyone else who posed a threat to my safety or that of those I cared about could be exterminated instantly. I squeezed Joseph's arm protectively, wanting to keep him near me, and wished that Matt were there so that I could keep him safe, too.

I became lost in thought, the idea of having such extraordinary capability taking root inside me and growing. A cold little ball of fury, of power, burned brightly. Looking at Thomas and Joseph, I realised how unnerved they must feel at the notion that they had sowed a seed capable of growing into something so destructive. I resolved there and then to keep that knowledge deep within me, to draw upon it if I needed the comfort of knowing that I could shield my loved ones from harm. All the same, the idea of being able to turn someone to dust if they hurt me, Matt, Joseph or anyone I cared about was darkly intoxicating.

There remained one element of doubt, however.

Trying to sound as though I were simply interested rather than testing my limits, I queried, "You said that the Fragments had been practically eradicated — but if they were so powerful, why am I the only one left?"

They seemed unsure of how to answer, so I pressed on with my point. "I mean, if we were able to order the gods around, you'd think at least a few of us would have said, '*Don't kill us!*' at some point?"

Thomas shook his head sadly. "They weren't able to. The gods who killed them would Shadow the Fragments — follow them without their knowledge — until they were asleep or otherwise vulnerable. Then they would teleport them deep within a body of water so that they could not issue any orders. Usually death happened almost instantaneously, because the Fragment would fight to draw breath after being winded by being teleported and pull in enough water to cause catastrophic injury. Their brains were so full of thoughts of dying that they were unable to think of defending themselves, let alone articulate the same in any meaningful way."

Joseph frowned, deeply aggrieved, "I should have realised what Makris was when I learnt what he did to you when you were seventeen. There are easier ways to kill a human than drowning, but it is the only known sure-fire way to kill a Fragment."

I frowned, suddenly fearful again. "Right, so how can you or I possibly keep us safe from them if they can appear out of nowhere and drag me off to the middle of the North Sea?" I asked, bitterly disappointed that there was such an obvious limit to the protection I could offer.

Joseph was quick to reassure me. "Gods cannot Shadow other gods: if you were with one of us, we would see anyone who sought to ambush you. Furthermore, no god — Damned or otherwise — would be willing to risk Obliteration by acting in front of a human, so you would also be safe with Matt."

"Well I can't be with you or Matt 24 hours a day …" I began, thinking privately of how awful it would be if I were snatched and taken to my doom when I was on my own — but how much worse it would be if that meant I couldn't even go to the loo on my own anymore.

Joseph's colours were tinged with guilt and he studiously avoided looking at his father as he went on, "If you were alone, or if you were taken anyway and unable to speak to issue commands …" He paused and spared his father a guilty glance. "If the worst happens, you have my true name."

I frowned. I remembered Makris, telling me that Joseph would not be able to find me because I didn't know his true name …

Thomas's eyebrows raised. "You have already given it to her?" he asked sharply, distracting me from my train of thought.

Joseph's tone was quietly defiant as he replied,

"Of course. It was how I found her in Greece. She called me to her. We would all be in rather hot water now if she had not."

I blurted out, "*Zephyrus*? Your true name is Zephyrus Democritus?"

His colours bloomed and he gave me a small smile, though he glanced uneasily at his father before he nodded.

"Zephyrus Democritus ..." I mused, almost to myself. "Nice poetic meter."

As I'd hoped, this made his smile broaden. "I am very, very glad you remembered it when you needed it," he said earnestly.

Thomas sighed heavily. "Russ appears to have forgotten to mention that part to me. Well, what's done is done." He gave a soft laugh and added, "At least we know that particular old wives' tale isn't true."

Zephyrus, perhaps relieved to be off the hook for whatever he'd done to annoy his father, allowed himself a small chuckle. "True."

In response to my enquiring expression, Thomas clarified, "In each lifetime, we take an inconspicuous name that blends with our era and country of origin, but our souls have just one true name, which we recognise and are compelled to acknowledge when used. In order for us to reincarnate, someone living must know and say our true names upon our death so that we may continue to exist for another lifetime in a new form. Over the millennia, we've all become a little superstitious about it and only give our true names to those we really trust."

"Which is why I gave mine to Sephy,"

Zephyrus muttered pointedly.

With an appeasing nod of acknowledgement, Thomas went on, "For as long as I can remember, it has been widely believed that if a Fragment knows and speaks a god's true name it will Obliterate the god's soul. I therefore forbade my family from giving you theirs. This was not entirely of my choosing, but I deemed it a necessary compromise to placate all concerned and alleviate their fear."

Zephyrus said firmly, "That fear was clearly unfounded. You don't need our true names to have power over us — you were able to command Makris and Russ without knowing their true names — and although you've used my true name, I'm still alive to tell the tale."

"I didn't call for you, though. I — I was just thinking of you. I had your name in my head, but I could hardly breathe, let alone speak …"

Zephyrus stroked my back affectionately and said, "DC Cam knew Makris's true name and used it to call him to you, but he had to speak it out loud. You and I are tied, so if you ever need me all you need to do is *think* of my true name and I will be by your side in a heartbeat."

Thomas took a deep breath and confessed with a laugh, "Well, now that we know that you won't turn me to dust by saying it, *my* true name, should you ever need it, is Thaumas. I am god of the sea."

Distractedly, I said, "I thought that was Poseidon."

There was a general shuffling and sense of discontent at my words.

Zephyrus murmured into my ear, "Sore subject."

I marvelled at the fact that I had known about the existence of gods for less than an hour and had already managed to commit some kind of divine faux pas.

Taking a calming breath, Thomas — *Thaumas* — went on as though I had not spoken, "My wife's name is Hestia. Use our true names if you ever need us and we will be by your side in an instant, just as Zephyrus was. You would need to articulate ours verbally, though, as you and I have no bonding tie and I cannot hear your thoughts."

Distracting me from asking more about being able to hear my thoughts, Thaumas went on, "Russ is still a little anxious about all of this, but he and Felicity asked me to pass on their true names if I felt it appropriate. Russ is Corus, god of the east wind; Felicity is Freyja, Norse goddess of love, sex and beauty. She's also their goddess of war, so try not to get on the wrong side of her because she has quite a temper when she gets going," he added with an affectionate chuckle.

It was not difficult to think of them with their 'new' names — the names fit better, somehow, than those I'd been using to date. I remembered Zephyrus shouting for 'Corus' when we were in New Zealand; he had called his big brother to him for help.

I didn't quite trust myself to reply to Thaumas, so kept silent.

He went on, "You have retained your true name, it appears. That is what drew you to my attention initially. You were named for a goddess, as was traditional for Fragments."

"Oh, so I'm not actually Persephone, Queen of the Underworld?"

Thaumas shook his head.

"Well, that's a relief. I am really not ready for that kind of responsibility," I said sincerely.

Thaumas smiled briefly but his eyes were troubled. "I know that I have asked you to believe the unbelievable today. Know this, though: you are safe with us, and we are safe with you."

I nodded in acknowledgement.

Externally, they could not see my colours and I was careful to conceal my emotions by maintaining a suitably neutral expression on my face. Internally, though, my thoughts were deafening and my mind was racing.

CHAPTER 43

THAUMAS STAYED WITH US FOR MUCH of the rest of the morning. I listened passively to some of his history — he had served on the High Council for a time but had been dismissed over what he called a 'difference of opinion' that he did not care to elaborate upon. Evidently his perceived disloyalty to the High Council made him particularly vulnerable to reprisals and he explained that it was probably his name that had made taking me to the High Council so attractive to Makris. The High Council would indeed pay a high price to anyone who brought them Thaumas Democritus to be legitimately and quietly disposed of.

I'd hoped he might expand upon how he had known me in the distant past, as he had alluded to earlier, but he didn't volunteer that information and I didn't press for it — it seemed oddly personal, and I had more than enough to be thinking about for the time being.

I was reassured by the fact that he had not been

swift to leave me; neither he nor Zephyrus seemed at all afraid of me. Maybe, in the absence of being able to see my colours, they were giving me the benefit of the doubt and assuming that I was Blue. I thought briefly of those colours that they could not see — were mine totally absent, or were they merely concealed? And if they were concealed, what colour would they be if they were revealed? From the small thrill of excitement I felt every time I thought of what I was capable of, I had to allow that they may not be as Blue as I had always assumed.

At length, Thaumas took my empty cup from where I must have put it on the bedside cabinet at some point. He reached over and gave my hand a gentle pat. "You two have a lot to talk about. I'll leave you in peace. Please do call me if you need me, though. And thank you for being as accepting as you have, you have made it easier than it could have been, under the circumstances. It is of great credit to your strength of character that you have taken all this in your stride."

Huh. If he *could* see my soul, he'd know it was totally weirded out. "What are you going to do next? About my dad, I mean."

"I will find out who he is; I shall make enquiries of your mother, if necessary. I wish I had Makris's true name, it might be possible to trace him to your father that way. It is important that I find him one way or another, since I doubt he will be content to let you live when you pose the greatest threat to him." Seeing the alarm in my face, he added, "I repeat, though, that nobody will harm you now that we are alert to the threat. We will protect you, Sephy, and hopefully you will have confidence that you can protect yourself — and us, too."

"What will you do, when you find out who he is?" I asked.

Thaumas paused. "I am still considering that. I will let you know if I am in need of your assistance, though."

He turned as though to leave but paused and faced me once more. He was clearly finding it difficult to find the right words; he made several attempts at beginning a sentence before catching himself each time. I waited patiently until at last, quietly, he said, "When we reincarnate, our past attachments cease to exist, except the bonding tie to a partner. We still remember those we loved as family in past lives, though. I do not know if the same is true of Fragments. I am just curious … Do you … do you remember me?"

He asked the question so plaintively that it brought me up short. Despite his attempts to sound detached, I could hear the sorrowful longing in his tone, the hope-against-expectation in his words and I wondered what I had meant to him in our shared past life.

Not having the strength to go into detail about my dream, I replied with a tired smile, "I met you a few weeks ago. But I've known you all my life."

He didn't smile back, but the lift in his colours, the change in his posture as if a great weight had been lifted, told me that I had given the answer he most wanted to hear.

I sighed and closed my eyes for a moment; when I opened them, I was alone with Zephyrus.

CHAPTER 44

ALTHOUGH I HAD MORE QUESTIONS, overall I was satisfied with what I'd been told. Although what Thaumas had told me had sounded like some colossal joke or the ramblings of a lunatic depending on which way you looked at it, I firmly believed all of it. How could I question what I'd been told when I had been teleported to Greece and New Zealand and back; when I had seen Thaumas appear out of thin air and Zephyrus heal his hands; when Zephyrus and I had wielded complete control over two armed police officers? I was a little disappointed that nobody was a wizard, but still. As to my own identity, I was convinced that I was every bit as powerful as the High Council feared I would be, and I wasn't entirely certain of how that made me feel.

Zephyrus was looking at me as though expecting me to bolt out of the room at any moment. "Are you happy for me to stay in here with you or would you rather I wait outside?" he asked quietly. "I expect you will need some time to yourself to think about all of this …"

"No, stay!" I exclaimed, alarmed at the very idea that he might leave me — not because I was afraid of being alone, but because I didn't want to be apart from him. It seemed that the longer I spent in his company the harder it was to bear the idea of being separated. Suddenly, I realised that I had given him an order and quickly amended, "I mean, please stay — you don't have to." I wanted Zephyrus to want me of his own free will, though I was still having difficulty in understanding why he would.

He nodded, instantly more relaxed, though he still looked troubled. "Are you all right?" he asked.

I had absolutely no idea how to answer. They were gods, and I was a Fragment, the product of an illegal union, something to be feared and hated; I had no visible aura. I settled for, "Well, I'm not dead."

That made him smile at least.

At last, holding my gaze and speaking unfalteringly, he said, "Allow me to introduce myself properly. I am Zephyrus, god of the west wind. If you ever need me, wherever you are, you need only think of my true name and I will be by your side in an instant. Last night, I nearly lost you — I am not prepared to risk that again."

"Zephyrus," I whispered to myself. The word still sounded alien on my tongue and yet felt deeply familiar inside me.

He smiled at the sound of his name.

I was quiet for a moment, digesting this. "God of the west wind. Is that … I thought I'd imagined a lot of what happened yesterday, with Makris. I didn't, though, did I? That storm that hurt him, that didn't so much as touch me …?"

"It is rather handy to have power over an element," he said simply, "though I might have preferred to be god of fire last night. I made do with what I had at my disposal. I wish I had been quicker to finish him before you could prevent me from doing so."

I grimaced. "Please stop talking about killing him — I really, really don't want you to do that. I've seen what murder does to a soul and yours is just so beautiful ..." I drifted off a little, my attention focussed on the colours I saw around him that made me feel so happy and at peace ...

I realised he was smiling again. At length, his eyes saddened and he swallowed as though his next words were having difficulty coming forth. "I know that you have been asked to believe and accept a great deal today. When you have had time to think about it all, if you decide that you have changed your mind about wanting to be with me, I will — I will not make it difficult for you. I will always ensure that you are safe and do my utmost to make you happy but you must have the freedom to follow whichever path you wish to pursue."

"You go very Queen's English when you're serious, did you know that?" I asked.

He smiled sadly at me but did not reply.

I regarded him carefully. He looked sick to his stomach, his colours murky and dark with upset and nervousness. I tried to see all this from his perspective and realised how hard this must be for him. He had clearly gone against his family's wishes and entire belief system to be with me and risked estranging them so that we could be together, yet he thought that I wouldn't want to be with him after what I'd been told. A rational person *might* turn and flee in my position: after all, either Zephyrus and his family were a pack of crazies, in which case I should leg it before I ended up as some sacrifice inside a burning wicker man, or they were telling the truth, in which case … Well, I wasn't sure how I felt about that yet, but I did know that the only place I wanted to be was with Zephyrus.

I shook my head firmly. "Luckily for you, I'm not a very rational person," I smiled. Then, throwing caution to the wind, I added quietly, "If you could promise me that you won't vanish next time I think I'm finally going to get to kiss you, then I'll promise you that the path I pursue will always be the one that leads to you."

He met my gaze steadily and gave me his first proper smile since we had been in the car (had that really only been the previous morning?), his eyes sparkling. His hand cupped my uninjured cheek gently, and his smile faded naturally as he dipped his head so that our lips could meet.

My breathing was shallow and fast, and I felt myself tremble with a heady mixture of nerves and excitement as I leant in towards him. This time, true to his word, he didn't vanish and as our lips met I felt a wave of warmth flow over me. My hand moved from his arm upwards over his shoulder and cradled his head, my fingers buried in his soft hair; I could feel my body responding and a brief glimpse revealed hot pink desire suffusing Zephyrus's soul.

At length, we gently parted and he said gruffly, "I have waited a long time for that."

I smiled giddily, my head spinning and lips tingling.

He opened his arms to me, an invitation for me to lean in towards him for a hug that I took up without hesitation. I rested my head on his chest and relaxed into the feeling of his arms and hands gently caressing my back. I was lost in the sensation for a long time.

Zephyrus spoke, startling me slightly — I realised that I'd been drifting to sleep.

"Would you like me to take you home?"

That was exactly what I wanted. "Yes please. But I think we'll need to speak to Matt about the police first, and probably a doctor?"

He shook his head slightly and stood, walked to the door and opened it to speak with the armed police officer outside. I didn't hear what he said, but a moment later he had returned to my side and held out his hand. "She and my brother will meet us at your house."

"Wait, what?" I asked, askance as I watched the police officer simply leave her post. My hand patted the bedsheets, automatically seeking out my phone (which I realised a moment later must still be at the office), thinking that I should really call Matt if the security he had organised had just disappeared. "I don't think she should just leave like that; Matt'll go mad, he'll have her job taken off her if something happens ..."

Zephyrus shook his head dismissively. "Nothing will happen. Matt may think that his arrangements are protecting you, but the police are utterly redundant considering that the threat against you comes from the gods. If anyone in the employ of your father had the opportunity to do so, they could command that police officer to shoot you just as easily as I commanded her to meet us at your house. Until you are confident in your ability to command, I am your protection, Sephy, not some human with a gun."

"Oh." I hesitated, feeling rather disquieted about the ease with which he had apparently compelled the police officer to obey him. "Well, I think I probably still need a doctor to discharge me before I go — I don't think I can just leave, can I?"

In reply, he held up his phone, "It would be quicker if I asked my mum to sort everything out, if you'd like?"

I nodded my consent and he used his phone to send a text. "All sorted. Let's get you home; my brother has left his car here for us to use."

Pulling myself together, I frowned at the fact that he held Russ's car keys, which seemed illogical in the extreme. "Actually, wouldn't it just be easier for you to teleport us?"

He stood stock still, apparently unsure of how to reply. He settled for, "You'd … you'd be happy with that? And you're certain you felt no ill effects last time?"

"Yes, it was fine, and it's a lot quicker than driving. No red lights, for one thing."

He grinned, "Russ — Corus — did say that under no circumstances was I to let you drive his car. I can't imagine why, of course."

I laughed happily and he drew me to his chest, whispering into my hair, "I am so glad that you still want to be with me. And I am also glad that I don't have to drive, either — it would be difficult to keep my eyes on the road with you by my side."

Before I could reply, I felt a change in the air

around us.

I looked up, pulling out of his arms slightly; we were standing in my living room. I nodded approvingly. "Teleportation is my new favourite means of transport," I said firmly, making his shoulders lose some of their tension. "I am thrilled that I will never need to get on another bus," I added, making him laugh.

"I must say, you're handling all of this better than I expected."

I shrugged lightly. "I've spent my whole life pretending to be normal. It's quite nice to know there's a reason why I'm not."

He still held me in his arms and seemed as reluctant as I was to part. He placed his fingertips underneath my chin to gently tilt my head upwards as he bent to kiss me. Warmth flooded through me, as did an intense desire to ask him to teleport me upstairs.

After several very pleasurable minutes, we parted and I reached up to stroke his freshly trimmed beard as we smiled happily at each other, secure in the knowledge that we both clearly held the same feelings for each other. Remembering my manners, I asked if he would like a drink. He accepted but insisted on making the drinks for both of us while I stood in the kitchen and pointed out where all the accoutrements were kept. After some prompting, he agreed to make himself something to eat; the first bite of toast sparked a fierce appetite and he ate as though he'd starved for weeks — which, I realised with a swell of worry, he had. I found I was rather touched that his desire to eat had returned upon being permitted to be with me. The opposite was true for me — the butterflies in my tummy at being in his presence, at being his girlfriend, left no room for food.

After he'd eaten his fill, we sat and drank tea as though the last twenty-four hours had been perfectly normal and not at all earth-shattering. With a start, I caught a glimpse of my reflection in the blank screen of the small TV on the breakfast bar and recoiled slightly. I was a mess: my face was bruised; my hair had still been damp when I'd fallen asleep and so was bushy and tangled. My wrists were black and blue from where Makris had knelt on them, and a quick glance down the neck of my crumpled nightie revealed yet more gruesome discoloration.

I knew I could either crumble — be a victim — or I could stand tall and be a survivor, like Matt had always told me I was. Bruising and a broken bone would heal soon enough. I was alive, Matt was alive; Zephyrus was safe and he wanted to be with me.

Resolutely turning away from my reflection, I looked instead at Zephyrus, who was watching me with a guarded expression. I wondered if I'd ever get used to the idea of having a boyfriend who was literally a god; how did I get so lucky?

"I'm the lucky one," he murmured.

I frowned slightly, remembering what Thaumas had said about bonding ties and being able to hear each other's thoughts. I definitely hadn't spoken out loud — could Zephyrus hear what I was thinking? Adding that to my long list of questions, I allowed him to lead me to the living room where we could sit together in more comfortable proximity.

I realised just *how* comfortable that proximity felt. With a contented sigh, I said, "That's better," as

I lay my head against his shoulder and he wrapped his arm around me once more.

He smiled his agreement. "That's our bonding tie," he commented. "The closer we are, physically, the more comfortable it is for both of us. Only a few gods can perceive them; the rest can only feel them if we're lucky enough to have formed one. Dad tells me ours looks like a thick, rose gold length of twine."

"How did we get it?" I asked.

"Well, usually a bonding tie forms between two gods, often only after significant social engineering by the two families. In our case, it appears to have occurred spontaneously the moment I first looked into your eyes at the railway station."

I warmed at the memory. "I felt something too. It was like the world just dropped away and there was only you."

His smile broadened, "That's the one."

"Then when you disappeared, I felt — *empty*."

He nodded as though he completely understood. "The effect of our tie is that we will only ever feel complete when we are together, and it will be physically uncomfortable for us to be apart. That discomfort can be mild, a general sense of disquiet and unease, or it can be acute if we are far apart. Yesterday, when Makris teleported you to the forest, what did it feel like?"

I remembered all too clearly. "Horrible, like I'd been in a car crash, and like I'd been stabbed, too. Right here," I pointed to the spot just below my sternum.

"I felt exactly the same, stabbing pain in the same place. We were too far apart, too quickly. It was how I knew there was something badly wrong. I think I probably caused Matt considerable alarm … Then I saw what that monster was doing to you — I saw what you saw, through your eyes. I was with you, even though I could not find you. It was truly horrific, and to see you hurt like that was more than I could bear." He grimaced at the memory and ran his hand distractedly through his hair. "I went half-mad trying to find you. It was bad enough when you had your nightmare and I felt your distress — I found you relatively quickly then, but yesterday was … I never *ever* want that to happen again."

He looked so anguished that I put my hand on his arm and leant into him to offer him the comfort that I could tell we both wanted and needed.

"Our tie is the reason why it has been physically very difficult for me to keep away from you since we first met," he said softly.

I thought of his weight loss and air of tiredness that had worsened during the weeks I had worked at Democritus's, when he had sought to avoid seeing me.

"And you can read my mind?" I asked, half fearing the truth. There were some things I wanted to keep private.

He tipped his head slightly. "Yes and no. I can hear and see particularly clear or 'loud' thoughts, just as I can feel your emotions; when you experienced your flashback, it was so vivid that I saw it as though it were happening in front of me. That is why I reacted as badly as I did. That trauma aside, being able to hear your thoughts should be very handy, because I can't see your aura and I have to admit that I'm not very adept at interpreting body language — I've never needed to before."

I had always struggled with that, too. "Well, if you *ask* me how I'm feeling I'll always tell you the truth. And if I'm with you, then you can bet that I'll be feeling happy."

He smiled warmly and kissed my nose affectionately, which made me laugh.

"Why can't I hear your thoughts, though?" I asked.

"You didn't know it was possible, so you haven't been listening for them. With awareness and practise over time, I'm sure you'll be able to hear me. Then I'll really have to be careful ..." With a cheeky smile, he added, "I think about you a great deal, and some of those thoughts might make you blush."

I blushed anyway at the very thought that he found me attractive enough to have such thoughts, and that made him laugh softly.

Intent on distracting myself from similar (and broadcast) thoughts, I asked, "Thaumas said you've been around for millennia, do you get tied every lifetime?" and I tried hard not to be jealous of women probably long dead.

He looked nonplussed and then seemed to remember that he was speaking to someone for whom this was all new. "Oh no, not at all. In each lifetime, we form familial ties with our parents and siblings, which last until death unless we choose to sever them. We also form parental ties with our children, which cannot be severed but do not last beyond death. A bonding tie is exclusive, and it lasts forever. I was created in Ancient Greece. and I have never had a bonding tie with another in all the time since. Once formed, it is the only kind of tie that survives death and it is there waiting once both parties are — are reincarnated ..." he tailed off, his voice suddenly hollow.

Understanding dawned. "But I certainly won't be reincarnating, and according to your folklore I don't even have a soul. What will happen to you, you know, next time round?"

"Of course you have a soul. And it's not impossible for you to reincarnate — my family and I will call for you, and we would only need for a Fragment to be conceived after your death for your soul to return in that body."

"And what are the chances of that happening?"

He grimaced. "Not good: not unless there is a sea change in policy and societal norms. But I will move the earth itself to make it so," he said firmly. His tone flattened and he added, "I honestly do not know how I will live without you in future incarnations. It has been so lonely, to be without a tie for all this time, but I think it will be far harder next time round, to have had you and lost you ..." Then his brow creased slightly in puzzlement and he looked at me sideways, "Is your most pressing concern really what I'll do in my next lifetime without you?"

I smiled and shrugged. "I don't know, it just popped into my head. There are so many questions I really, really don't know where I should start." I paused, trying to marshal my thoughts. My gaze kept focussing on his lips, though, and my body wanted to know what the hell my brain was doing by insisting on merely talking. Forcing myself to concentrate, I asked, "Why do you think you can't see my aura?"

He shifted uncomfortably and looked rather displeased at this fact. "I don't know. Some have postulated that it is a protective measure, an evolutionary trait designed to bestow the Fragments with autonomy. The fact that I can neither see nor manipulate your aura vexes me greatly and has caused me considerable distress over the last few weeks. I cannot tell you how many ways I have pictured you dying or being injured; how many ways in which I have tortured myself with thoughts of your death and being powerless to prevent it ... Then, when I discovered that there was somebody out there who had hurt you in the past and who might well seek to do so again ... After that, I couldn't stand to have you out of my sight."

He squeezed me more tightly still and I stroked his face, trying to soothe him.

I thought back to those times after my nightmare when I had seen Zephyrus everywhere except work. "I started seeing you everywhere after that night."

He nodded. "Until then, my family had taken it in turns to Shadow you, to keep watch over you so that I could sleep knowing that you were safe even though I had agreed to keep away from you. After that night, I no longer entrusted your safety to anyone else and that was when I attempted to Shadow you myself — with limited success, as it turned out, because apparently you could see me. You were in my sight every moment except when I absolutely had to sleep. And even then, I made sure you were with my brother or Matt. Makris had absolutely no way of getting to you without being seen and dealt with. Thankfully you did not think to report me to the police for stalking you — or worse, Matt."

I felt a pang of sadness at the memory of how

tired and unwell Zephyrus had seemed during that time and I was touched at how much he'd cared about my safety.

I smiled, "Yeah, Matt would have had a few things to say about that, probably …"

He rolled his eyes a little. "No doubt."

I frowned at the bitterness behind his words and felt the need to defend my friend. "Matt's protective of me, that's all. We've been through a lot."

He sighed. "I know. I am just — I am envious of him, I admit. I covet all the time he has spent with you. When he came home after you'd had that nightmare, I hated the fact that it would be he — not I — who would be there if you woke in the night, if you were afraid, or if Makris did actually make an appearance. And he is something of a curiosity … he is oddly resistant to our orders."

I waited to see if he would clarify this or further his point, but when he didn't go on, I said, "Like when he wouldn't let you in that room at the hospital, do you mean? Why do you think that is?"

He shook his head. "I do not know. Nor do I know how he managed to reach you before Makris drowned you; in your flashback he was suddenly there, but I do not understand how."

This was something that Matt and I had discussed only briefly in the past. I had broached the subject with him, but he had been extremely reluctant to talk about it and had flatly refused to answer any questions about it; all he would say was that he'd had a tip-off about where I'd been taken.

To discuss this with Zephyrus felt oddly like a betrayal of a confidence shared with Matt. Instead, I said, "I don't know either. I didn't really care — I was just glad he was there."

Zephyrus frowned sadly. "I am sorry I wasn't there for you yesterday. I'm sorry I had to leave you in your car. And I am *so* sorry I allowed myself to be distracted at Alex's house. I had been enraged at what I had seen Makris do to you in your flashback, and Matt rightly pulled me up on my behaviour. I should have calmed down, but I was antagonistic and angry — and I let my guard down. I am sorry."

I hastened to reassure him that I didn't think for a minute that he'd failed me. "*None* of it was your fault. And you'd given me your true name, you'd done everything you could to keep me safe," I said firmly, wanting to reassure him.

He nodded grudgingly. "I should have given you my name earlier. I had tried to respect my father's wishes, which were really my sister's wishes …" he scowled, before adding, "If you'd had my name before your nightmare, you could have called me to your side the moment it began. Instead, it took me precious moments to realise that the sudden sense of dread and fear I felt was not in fact mine, but yours and I came looking for you. If I had arrived sooner, I might have seen Makris, known what he was …"

I was quiet for a moment, remembering that night. "So you — you don't think it was just a nightmare? You think Makris was really there?"

He sighed sharply, his brow furrowed. "Yes. Since I saw Makris in the forest and realised what he is, I have had to accept that it is entirely feasible that he was in your house that night. The very thought makes me sick to my stomach — what if I hadn't arrived in time? You have been so very, very vulnerable."

I struggled to get any words out. I was so stung, suddenly absolutely certain of how Makris had found me, that my throat ached with suppressed anger and tears. At last, I managed, "That was the day my sister called. She asked me for my address, and I gave it to her even though Matt had told me not to give it to anyone. She or my mum must have given it to Makris. Why — why would they do that?"

Zephyrus kissed my forehead and said sadly, "I don't know. I want to say something comforting, but frankly I am at a loss. Your family is a mystery to me. We may get some answers when my father has had a chance to investigate everything, I suppose."

I nodded, though I did not relish the idea of Thaumas speaking to my mum or sister — what if they persuaded him that I was every bit of a monster that the gods' legends suggested?

We sat together quietly for a moment, each lost in our own thoughts.

Perhaps he saw my slight frown, because he asked, "What are you thinking about?"

I sighed sadly. "I'm trying to remember everything I've ever said to you."

He laughed, "Is that all?"

I didn't smile and he leant forwards, taking my hands in his, waiting for me to explain. "I'm wondering if … if, at some point, I've told you to be with me. Maybe I've said something that made this tie, or made you think there's a tie, or something. I can't quite believe you'd want me of your own free will, not when it involves so much drama and fear and danger …"

He scoffed. "Sephy, in human terms, I love

you. I have loved you since the moment I first saw you. You have said nothing since then to change that in any way and nor could you ever do so. The danger from the High Council cannot be overstated, but I would far sooner face it with you than spend another day apart."

I smiled and his eyes were drawn to my lips, which were in turn drawn to his.

CHAPTER 45

WE SPENT LUNCHTIME AND MUCH of the afternoon sitting together, alternately talking, kissing and hugging. Despite the physical pain and underlying anxiety about what would happen if and when Makris regained consciousness, I was the happiest I could ever remember.

I needed a lot of time to absorb all I'd been told, but the thought I found most intrusive was not that Zephyrus and his family were gods, but that I was more powerful than any of them. Never having had any power in the past, I wondered whether the thrill of it would wear off or grow stronger over time.

My phone buzzed and, with an apologetic glance at Zephyrus, I answered the call.

"Seph? All alright?"

Matt sounded as tired as I felt.

Glancing at the clock on my phone I noticed that it was four-thirty and it was starting to get dark outside.

"Hi Matt," I replied, mainly for Zephyrus's

EPILOGUE

THE PAST TWENTY-FOUR HOURS had been intense. A lifetime ago, I had been a slightly quirky twenty-four-year-old solicitor with a weird sense of humour and a lot of emotional baggage. Today, I was a demigod whose very existence was illegal, in the arms of a god who could teleport me anywhere in the world and would apparently love me until the day I died.

I reflected on all of this as I lay beside said god on my sofa. We had spent the rest of the evening together, alone, talking about everything from the mundane to the world-shattering, all whilst wrapped in each other's arms. I was sore and stiff from my ordeal, but he kissed me so tenderly that I felt only pleasure at his touch. Never before had I wanted a man so badly; I was finding it extremely difficult to focus on what Zephyrus was saying at times because I kept imagining him naked. I was uncomfortably aware, though, that at some point an actual god was going to see *me* naked and I wanted time to prepare myself for how self-conscious that would make me feel — I was half-human and therefore far from flawless; I was scarred physically as well as emotionally.

As the hour grew later, Zephyrus's eyes grew heavier and the fact that he was still awake by early evening was nothing short of miraculous, given the physical exertion and emotional upheaval he'd endured lately and his lack of sleep throughout the previous night. I stretched up to kiss his lips and said softly, "You should sleep. I'll still be here when you wake up," and I lay my head on his chest, feeling his arms wrap round me as he sighed deeply and contentedly. A few minutes later, his breathing grew more regular and he slept.

I took the opportunity to slip to the bathroom. Showering was out of the question with nobody to help with my sling, but I managed to have a wash and brushed my teeth. A glance in the mirror told me that my efforts had been rather like rearranging the deckchairs on the Titanic, but it did make me feel a bit better to assert some control over my body.

I stayed in the bathroom for some time, reflecting on everything Zephyrus and his father had told me.

A germ of a plan was already forming.

I would need time to recover physically, yes, but then … Maybe I could begin to right some wrongs. I would work with Thaumas and Zephyrus to hone my power, to make me an effective shield against whatever my father might send our way next. But there were other things I needed — wanted — to do.

I wanted to find out how Makris had discovered my address, for a start; if it were indeed my mother or my sister who had led him to my door and endangered Zephyrus and me, I would make sure that they could never hurt us again. I didn't yet know how I intended to achieve that, but years of injustice and hurt burnt brightly inside me.

Moreover, with or without Thaumas's efforts, I would discover my father's identity. He had tried to have me killed — twice — and my death would cause Zephyrus's, which was absolutely unacceptable. The very idea made me burn with anger and a fierce protectiveness that bled easily into a need for revenge.

I could ensure that my family could never again threaten my life or Zephyrus's, directly or indirectly through agents like Makris. I had seen what I was capable of and if I needed to Obliterate anyone to protect the man I loved then that's just what I would do.

Then there was the matter of the High Council. *They* were the real threat, not my father. Sooner or later, my existence was bound to be discovered and when that happened, Zephyrus and his family would be at risk. The system was wrong; the law was wrong. Something had to change.

Fragments had been all but exterminated for the crime of being too powerful, yet they had not been able to protect themselves, let alone realise the full potential of their power. They had lacked organisation, forewarning, meaningful protection and knowledge of their capabilities.

I suffered none of their disadvantages.

With a few carefully chosen words, I could end the threat to my family. Heck, I could reinstate my entire race. I could ensure that I could return lifetime after lifetime to be with Zephyrus …

I glanced once more at my battered and bruised

reflection in the bathroom mirror. It dawned on me, though, that these reminders of my attack, fresh and vivid though they were, did not induce me to fear the memories they evoked.

Fear had followed me, every hour of every day, since Makris first attacked me. At times, it had been acute and I'd needed a lot of therapy and coping strategies to live with that fear and force it back into manageable proportions. Mostly, it had merely lurked in the background, a feeling of unease and vulnerability — an awareness of my mortality.

I hadn't realised how much fear had featured in my life until now. I only noticed now because it was gone.

Inside, beyond all the discoloured flesh, was someone new. My old life — the one in which I'd thought I was almost normal — had ended. A new one was just beginning; one in which I knew I was distinctly abnormal. That didn't feel like a negative anymore.

For the first time in my life, I was not weak.

I was not afraid.

I was not the one who needed to be.

Finished in the bathroom, I walked quietly back downstairs and carefully returned to my position beside Zephyrus. In his sleep, he turned slightly to face me and wrapped an arm around my waist. I lay there, listening to the thrum of his heart, content to remain there until whenever Matt returned from work. I'd deal with the sleeping arrangements then.

I was happy in Zephyrus's arms.

Nobody was going to take him away from me.

GET IN TOUCH

Thank you for reading Enduring Fear, I hope you've enjoyed it. If so, I'd be really grateful if you could leave me a review on Amazon and/or Goodreads – reading your lovely review will warm my heart and may even entice others to buy it!

If you have any questions or comments, feel free to drop me a line at:

enduringfear2019@outlook.com

I'm in the process of building a website at:

www.enduringfear.com

Keep checking for progress to see more about your favourite characters and news of Book 2, coming soon...

COMING SOON...

Irresistibly powerful.

Utterly unstable.

Sephy has a lot to come to terms with — her understanding of the world and her place in it has been completely altered in the space of a few short weeks. Her boyfriend is a god; she is a demigod. Her existence is illegal; their relationship is forbidden — if discovered, both will be killed.

Of more immediate concern for Sephy is that her newfound romance doesn't seem to be progressing as she'd hoped. Her burning, physical longing for Zephyrus seems to be alarmingly unrequited.

On top of all that, she still has to help the Democrituses to identify her father and neutralise the threat he poses. After that, there's just the small matter of tackling the High Council's Fragment Law. Overhauling the gods' entire culture and belief system will require skilful diplomacy and subtlety — things that have never been among Sephy's strengths.

But Sephy is about to discover that some mothers will do anything to protect their children, and now there is no time for diplomacy or subtlety.

There is no room in her heart for anything but hate.

Grief and fury are a dangerous combination in anyone, but the High Council is about to discover that in a Fragment they are positively deadly.

...

Read on for an extract of Book 2, due for release in 2020.

SEATED AT MY KITCHEN TABLE, Thaumas looked every bit as tired as his son. Nevertheless, he rose from the chair without hesitation when we entered the room and smiled warmly in greeting. As I approached the table, he walked around it to meet me and kissed my forehead affectionately; I don't think anyone but him could have done that without me instinctively swatting at them or ducking out of the way — from him, it seemed a natural, paternal gesture and one that I found I rather welcomed.

"Did you manage to sleep at all? With the pain from your shoulder, I mean?" he asked, before handing me a box of paracetamols that he produced from his pocket. "Hestia sends these and reminds you to take them every four hours. She has sent another cake, too."

I took the box with thanks and swallowed hard to get rid of a lump that had formed in my throat from Hestia's acts of kindness. I set about taking a couple of painkillers with a glass of water; I offered Thaumas and Zephyrus refreshments including a slice of cake but they both declined: whether this was from tiredness or lack of appetite caused by stress was not clear. I helped myself to a slice of cherry cake, reasoning that there was fruit in it (so was automatically healthy), and it had been baked by a goddess so the calories probably didn't even count. It was a magic cake, I decided.

Seating myself between them with the cake on a plate in front of me, I waited for Thaumas to speak, since it was clear that he had much on his mind. As quietly as I could, I dug my fork in and began eating: it certainly tasted every bit as magical as I'd hoped.

After a moment of gathering his thoughts, he cleared his throat and began.

"As you know, I have been trying to establish your father's identity by making enquiries of your mother. I have been unsuccessful. It would appear that she has been given earlier orders — presumably by your father — not to reveal his identity or whereabouts, and since he and I are of equal status, his more timely orders have taken precedence and I cannot override them. I am sorry, Sephy."

I glanced at Zephyrus, who seemed oddly reluctant to meet my eyes. Unnerved by Thaumas's grave tone and Zephyrus's discomfort, I wondered where this was heading.

"So, do we have to wait for Makris to wake up, then?" I asked, knowing that he was the only other person who knew my father's identity. The fact that he was in a coma was unfortunate, but whilst he remained unconscious he could not alert my father to my whereabouts either.

Zephyrus answered for his father, "We do not think it is wise to wait for him to wake up — that might not happen for weeks or even months. At any time, your father is sure to learn that Makris was unsuccessful in his attempt to kill you. He may surmise that you were assisted by our kind, or that you discovered your power and used it against Makris to escape. Either way, he will redouble his efforts to eliminate the threat that you pose, probably by instructing another Damned to finish what Makris started. We need to identify your father before he can find you."

"And if you identify him, what will happen then?" I asked.

Thaumas looked uneasily at Zephyrus. "I will find him, make it clear to him that we know who he is and know that he has fathered a Fragment. Then, hopefully, we will be able to reach an agreement as to how to proceed."

I frowned, perturbed by his answer. "You'll *negotiate* with him?"

Thaumas grimaced slightly. "We will reach an understanding. A standoff, if you like. He will know that if he forces our hand, his identity will be revealed to the High Council by one of us. In return, he will be reassured that my family will not want to be reported to the High Council for the crimes of associating with you and not reporting your existence as our laws require. Both sides will have mutually assured destruction and there will be no need to escalate matters."

I sat back a little, feeling a bit more relaxed than I had. "I thought you were going to say you were going to kill him, or Obliterate him or whatever. Or maybe that you were going to ask me to do so."

Thaumas replied, "Whilst that would be my first preference, it would be impractical to say the

393

least. We do not have the power or authority to kill or Obliterate him without the High Council becoming immediately aware."

Zephyrus added, "And we couldn't ask you to do it. He's your father, however depraved he might be."

I breathed out heavily, wishing I could just enjoy having a boyfriend and do normal things together like go to the cinema or enjoy a nice meal in a restaurant. Not sit around a table and plot to outwit a god.

"So how are we going to find out who he is if my mum wouldn't tell you and Makris is still out of the picture?"

Now there was a definite change in the atmosphere and both men looked distinctly uncomfortable. It appeared that they had already discussed the matter, presumably while I was sleeping, and they were clearly of the opinion that I was not going to like what they had planned.

Thaumas shifted uneasily in his seat. "Well, I was unable to extract the information required because, as I said, your father and I are of equal status: we are both gods, both immortal and neither of us Damned. There is parity in our authority. If I were to continue to deliver orders to your mother, ultimately it would do no good and it may cause her significant harm as her brain tried to cope with two such different sets of instructions that she felt compelled to obey ... I tried a number of different lines of approach, from simply ordering her to tell me his name to telling her to explain why she named you Persephone. I thought that there may be some loophole in his orders to her that I could exploit ..."

I raised my eyebrows. "Thaumas, I know I haven't been a solicitor for as long as you have, but I know when someone isn't answering a question."

He chuckled awkwardly and apologised. He became sombre again and said steadily, "We need you to find out who your father is by ordering your mother to tell you."

"You — you want me to speak to her?" I asked quietly. My palms became clammy, my heart rate sped up and molten dread filled my stomach at the very thought. I had last spoken with my mother before Makris's trial — I had called out to her from the doorway as I'd left for court, begging her to come with me. I was seventeen and scared and I'd needed my mum; she hadn't even replied. When I'd returned home from the last day at court, after the jury had delivered a guilty verdict, I had found all my possessions bagged up and stacked in her hallway. I'd never seen Matt so angry as he'd been that day.

Any thoughts I'd privately entertained about confronting my mum now that I knew that I had the power to bend her to my will vanished. In their place was a cold ball of fear and anxiety that lodged in my heart.

I managed to find my voice. "I — I can't. Please. I can't."

Zephyrus reached out and squeezed my hand gently. "My love, we would not ask if there were any other way. As a Fragment, you alone have the authority and power behind your commands to override your father's orders and compel your mother to part with the information we seek. You can order her to forget that she has spoken with you, and there will be no comeback against you. But please, we need your help."

Thaumas added, "Your life, and that of my son, depend on finding out who your father is before he finds you."

It was the mention of the threat to Zephyrus's life that did it. I found I couldn't stop looking at him; the idea that he could be taken away from me, or that my death would lead to his, was unbearable.

However much I hated the idea, I knew there was no choice.

Searching for some way of reassuring myself, I thought about all that I had faced and survived. If I could face down Makris with Zephyrus beside me, I could certainly face my mother.

"When do we leave?" I said, my voice stronger than I felt.

Thaumas's shoulders visibly relaxed and he and Zephyrus shared a look of relief. He rubbed his face to dispel some of the tiredness that had settled there and said, "I do not want you to go anywhere near her at the moment. Your father may be watching her, anticipating this next move; I took a risk in visiting her last night, placing a lot of faith in the notion that news of Makris's defeat would not yet have reached your father's ears. But I do not want to risk a direct approach again, not without safeguards in place."

"So … when will it be safe? What safeguards do you mean?" I asked.

Once more, both men seemed ill at ease and there was an awkward pause before Zephyrus answered. "Your father will be desperate, and he will have access to any number of Damned gods who would be willing to do anything he asked of them in exchange for the chance to be immortal once more. Those Damneds would take any chance to kill you if given the opportunity to be in your presence. The only thing that we believe might give them enough pause for us to be able to step in and protect you would be if there were other humans present. Lots of them. More than any Damned could silence in a single order.

"All Damneds are acutely aware that if they seek to harm any human, the High Council would be immediately alerted and the Damned would face immediate Obliteration. Moreover, your father will be aware of that and has probably instructed them to avoid human casualties at all costs: otherwise, the High Court is likely to discover that that not only did your father sire a Fragment, but he also allowed humans to be harmed in his attempt to cover up his actions. It would be another piece of our armour, that's all, but it might be a sufficient deterrent to prevent a Damned from immediately Obliterating you."

I was still unsure of what they had in mind. Was I going to have to accost my mother in the street? In the frozen food aisle at Asda? At a party—

The penny dropped. "My sister's wedding," I said numbly.

Thaumas gave a single nod.

Of all the thoughts that were whirling through my mind, the loudest made its way out of my lips. "You've obviously never met my sister if you think she'll let me make a scene at her wedding."

ABOUT THE AUTHOR

Jessica lives in Yorkshire and collects careers. So far, she's been a solicitor, will writer, copy writer, teaching assistant and mum. The latter is by far her favourite, even though the pay is terrible and her boss often makes her work unsociable hours.

As a copy writer, Jessica has written about everything from dental implants to how to install an orangery roof. Bearing in mind that her list of careers makes no mention of dentistry or the building trade, it just goes to show you shouldn't believe anything you read on the internet, however well-written it may be.

Enduring Fear is her first novel and she hopes it will be the start of her latest (and second favourite) career.

Printed in Poland
by Amazon Fulfillment
Poland Sp. z o.o., Wrocław

49503557R00240